PRAISE FOR *THE BETRAYAL OF THOMAS TRUE*

'A rare gem of a novel. Gorgeously gritty and compellingly constructed with the pungent, evocative vernacular of the era, it's a darkly thrilling romp in eighteenth-century London that simmers with sinister menace and illicit temptation' Susan Stokes-Chapman

'A.J. West has a rare ability to bring voices from the past so vividly to life, they whisper in your ear and send shivers down your spine ... stunning and powerful – an atmospheric thriller that's both heartfelt and meticulously researched ... a romance, an adventure and a vivid insight into a secret world. You'll never forget Thomas True' Janice Hallett

'*The Betrayal of Thomas True* is quite simply divine. Genre-defying, it is historical, a thriller, comedic, fantastical and above all a love story that had me in all sorts of tears' Jennie Godfrey

'I've rarely been so transported, moved and gripped by a story from the first page ... heartbreaking, beautiful, lyrical. You won't want to put it down' Catriona Ward

'Really very, very good' Stephen Fry

'A clever mystery, a powerful love story, and chock-full of atmosphere and historical detail. One scene near the end affected me more than anything I've read in a long time. Essential reading' Gareth Brown

'Plunges readers into the dark, treacherous streets of Georgian London in this epic adventure of love in a time of danger – a must-read for lovers of gritty, thrilling, historical fiction. An absolute page-turner!' Hallie Rubenhold

'With echoes of C.J. Sansom's Shardlake series (though very different in other respects), this is an exuberant, moving story of double lives, forbidden love and personal identity. It also has great insults' Rosie Andrews

'Vivid, impressive and utterly immersive, *The Betrayal of Thomas True* is a timely tale for everyone who fights to live and love as they wish. I was weeping by the final pages. A masterful work of historical fiction' D.V. Bishop

'What a ride of mystery, murder, mayhem – and molly houses, as we follow Thomas True encountering new friends and pleasures, but also violent persecution as experienced by gay men in the days of Georgian London. A big-hearted novel. You will gasp, and smile, and cry' Essie Fox

'Fierce, funny, and fabulous; this is an important and deeply moving story. Highly recommend' Jonathan Harvey

'Both a roaring Georgian romp and a moving story of injustice and discrimination. This is an original and hugely entertaining read' Anna Mazzola

'Bursting with memorable characters and stunning imagery, this pacy novel brings alive the smells and sounds of the city and its "molly houses" – places of safety, but for how long? A thriller, a tragedy and a love story all in one, lit by humour and pathos, this novel faces the shocking persecution of the times head on' Sean Lusk

'Suspense, adventure and romance combine in a thrilling historical mystery, brilliantly researched and lavishly written. Congratulations, A.J.: your passion shines through on every page' Emma Stonex

'Writing like a modern Fielding ... A.J. West packs humour, horror and a raging sense of justice. Camp, complex and heartbreaking, don't miss this gloriously authentic romp through the molly houses and culture of eighteenth-century London' Kate Griffin

'A beautiful, dark love story set in the foetid streets of Georgian London. Somewhere between a romance and a thriller, it is unputdownable historical fiction. Perfect for fans of Philippa Gregory or Niklas Natt och Dag' Gareth Russell

'A beautifully told story that broke my heart and energised my soul in equal measure ... A cunningly plotted, twisty and twisted tale of love, betrayal, and the human spirit, *Thomas True* is a timely reminder of the heavy cost of freedom and the work still to be done. The world truly needs this book' Tracy King

'There has never been a book that made me cry ... until today. It chewed me up hard more than once, but it was also funny, colourful, decadent. Truly extraordinary' Suzie Edge

'Very droll – the wit of Wilde still lives!' Gyles Brandreth

'A gripping epic tale set in the stinking back streets of Georgian London, complete with tragedy, humour and heartbreak. The writing is visceral and the atmosphere taut. This is only the second novel from A.J. West, but it proves he's a powerful new voice in historical fiction' Gill Paul

'A.J. West gives us a picaresque gay romp through an eighteenth-century London with a dark and troubling heart. A salutary reminder of a bleak history we shouldn't forget and still seems regretfully close' Annie Garthwaite

'Decadent, gritty, deliciously seductive and absolutely beautiful' Dan Bassett

'Easily the best book I have read in a very long time. Funny, sad and beautifully written. A story that you can truly get lost in. Everyone needs to read it!' Graham Sillars

'Heartbreaking, gut-wrenching and eye-opening. A.J. West truly has created a beautiful masterpiece with the world of Thomas and Gabriel ... A winner in the historical fiction genre!' Grace McGuire

'The story is so fast-paced and immersive ... The plot twists are shocking ... so cleverly done' Cassie Steward

'There's such an immediacy to A.J.'s writing that it pulls you into the world he creates ... pulses with authenticity and a wonderful sense of time and place. loved it!' Michael J. Malone

PRAISE FOR A.J. WEST

'A fiendishly clever tale of ambition, deception, and power' Derren Brown

'Haunting, witty and deeply moving' Jodie Whittaker

'Such a deliciously creepy, unsettling read ... a melancholic gothic triumph' Jennifer Saint

'A work of true invention and drama that moves at a cracking pace from the very first page and keeps you guessing' Jeremy Vine

'Set in a historical moment where science and spiritualism meet, *The Spirit Engineer* is an ingeniously plotted debut novel' Sarah Burton

'Dark, powerful and twisting – *The Spirit Engineer* will leave you wondering what is real and what is illusion' W.C. Ryan

'A delight of a debut, an atmospheric and entirely gripping chiller that calls to mind the best of M.R. James and E.F. Benson' Billy O'Callaghan

'Based on an absolutely astonishing true story, it kept me guessing right till the end' Frances Quinn

'Is Goligher a fraud? Is Crawford himself a reliable narrator? ... West answers these questions with ingenuity and invention' *Sunday Times*

ABOUT THE AUTHOR

A.J. West's bestselling debut novel *The Spirit Engineer* won the Historical Writers' Association Debut Crown Award, gaining international praise for its telling of a long-forgotten true story.

An award-winning BBC newsreader and reporter, he has written for national newspapers and regularly appears on network television discussing his writing and the historical context of contemporary events.

A passionate historical researcher, he writes at The London Library and museum archives around the world.

To connect with A.J. and discover more about his research, visit www.ajwestauthor.com. Follow A.J. across all social media @AJWestAuthor.

The Betrayal of
Thomas True

A.J. WEST

**ORENDA
BOOKS**

Orenda Books
16 Carson Road
West Dulwich
London SE21 8HU
www.orendabooks.co.uk

First published in the United Kingdom by Orenda Books, 2024
Copyright © A.J. West, 2024
Illustrations composed by Andy Goff.

A catalogue record for this book is available from the British Library.

B-format Hardback ISBN 978-1-916788-15-2
eISBN 978-1-916788-16-9

Typeset in Garamond by typesetter.org.uk

Printed and bound by CPI Group (UK) Ltd, Croydon CR0 4YY

For sales and distribution, please contact info@orendabooks.co.uk or visit www.orendabooks.co.uk.

To the mollies of old London. Not forgotten.

LONDON

Abandoned Chapel

To Highgate

Red Lyon Street

Tyburn

Mother Clap's

Arcadia

Flint Ditch

St. Paul's

Bedlam

Sodomites Walk

Miss Muff's

The Exchange

Squink's Candles

Tower Hill

RIVER THAMES

THE MOLLIES

Mister Gabriel Griffin ~ Lotty Lump

Mister Thomas True ~ Verity True-tongue

Mister Nelson Fump ~ Nelly Fump

Mister Frank Vivian ~ Vivian Guzzle

Mister Jack Huffins ~ Sweet Jacky

Mister George Lavender ~ Lavender Long-legs

Mister Timothy Rettipence ~ The Duchess of Camomile (née Prune)

Mister Daniel Godolphin ~ Daisy Dandy-shanks

Mister Martin Lightbody ~ Martha Moggs

Old Bob Buckleburn ~ Polly Pieface

Part One

Part One

CHAPTER ONE

Thomas True sat upon the roof of the postal coach as it trundled over divots and bumps, descending the North Road to London. Piles of boxes and trunks bounced beside him, straining their lashings as the wheels screeched against the ancient track. The hills were behind them now, so too the dappled groves and leafy thickets, for the countryside was growing sparse and thin, devoured by the rapacious city.

The coach turned a gentle corner then mounted a bridge spanning a brook – and there was London rolling up on the horizon, grim and grand, the freshly budded dome of St Paul's Cathedral gleaming amidst a morass of timber and brick. Far below, the distant spires rang with happy bells, calling God's children to prayer.

My new home, thought Thomas as they descended the cleft of the valley. *My new life.*

He watched in wonder, hardly noticing as the fields folded in around them and the crops blackened. A chill was growing through him despite the sweltering weather, and he wondered whether he shouldn't turn back.

'Driver,' he said with a gulp, 'perhaps I might climb down and make my way home?'

His request was cowardly, he knew as much, yet if the coachman heard his feeble voice above the din of the ungreased axles, he gave no sign of it and whipped the horses on.

Thomas had made the decision to escape his father's rectory the night before, yet now he saw the danger of it: after a lifetime of imprisonment, might he find himself lost and lonely amongst so many people?

Surely there was no need to worry about that: his cousin Abigail was waiting for him in the candle shop on the bridge, and besides, London had to be friendly, or why should so many people choose to live there?

He held on to his hat and gripped his trunk as they dropped down a steep slope into a tunnel of trees.

'Are we nearly there?' he called to the coachman, ducking under a low-hanging branch as they burst back into the sunshine. Thomas let out a startled cry, for the magnificent city had grown three times the size. 'By the saints!' he laughed. 'Will you look at that?'

Glory, oh blessed glory to be away from home. Farewell Highgate with its grey rectory and its gloomy little taverns and paltry expectations. Goodbye sermons and sins, goodbye graveyard, goodbye dry food, farewell pretence and piety, good riddance to misery, tearfulness, and waiting. No more waiting for Thomas True, only beginning!

He was overcome with excitement, his every nerve tingling as the horses charged towards the City gates.

Ever since boyhood, he had dreamed of this. For how many hours had he stood on tiptoes with his nose on the sill of his attic window, peering down at the sinful stew? Countless thousands of hours, every day and every night for all his twenty years. Unable to contain himself, he twisted with a triumphant cheer and waved goodbye to the receding countryside.

He turned back and hunched his shoulders, realising the buildings were almost upon him, and he had a premonition that the second he passed through those gates he would somehow cease to be Thomas True at all – which perhaps was the point of his journey. Yet while he relished – yes he really *did* relish the thought of disappearing amongst so many strangers – he hardly fancied being a stranger to himself. At least he would have his smart new clothes to wear. He looked over his shoulder and gave a squeak.

'Driver,' he said, pulling on the horse's reins. 'You must take me back; I have forgotten my trunk!'

The coachman ignored him, and soon the wheels were grinding across cobbles, the unbearable noise blending with a gathering roar so furious that Thomas thought he heard his father amidst the din. He shut his eyes and covered his ears.

Instantly, he was a boy again. Cowering beneath a Bible to the incantation of a sermon. He was a foul sinner, a devil child, a demon fit for nothing but flame. His ribs contracted to the memory of a snapping belt, and with tears in his eyes he was hiding in a burrow dug into the side of a graveyard wall...

There came an almighty *bang*, jarring Thomas's bones, and when he opened his eyes he found himself surrounded by tottering homes six storeys high, and everywhere so many people of all shapes and sizes, with every style of gown and wig, a din of jostling men in tall hats, broad hats, tricorn hats, buckled frock coats and silver-topped canes, rubbing shoulders with sailors, lobstermen, cockle sellers and thieves. It was a wonder any of them could hear amidst the din, for there wasn't a moment of peace, and oh! Thomas clapped his hands across his mouth and nose. The rivers of piss that flowed down the dusty kennels and rose up in clouds of steam. He couldn't breathe.

At last, the driver was forced to steady the coach behind a clot of tumbrils and chairs. He gave his horse an impatient flick of the reins before looking over at his passenger with a dry chuckle. 'You'll grow used to the stench, young sir,' he said. 'Just have to take it in a few times, see?' He pursed his lips and sucked a deep breath as though smoking a hookah pipe. He turned a nasty shade of green until his fourth gulp, when he smacked his lips and shook his jowls, hearty as a king.

Thomas frowned at him, holding his breath with his cheeks puffed out. He could feel the acrid air pressing its fingers up his nose. He could not do it, he would have to choke, yet just as his vision went blurry the coach bounced over a loose cobblestone and tipped him to the ground with a hard thump, rolling across the road like a baker's pin.

'Wait!' he coughed, climbing to his feet, yet before he could push his way through the crowd, he was lost amidst the tumultuous racket of the packed street. 'Come back!' he said, turning in circles, clasping his face. 'Oh my saints, what shall I do? What shall I do?' He searched his coat pocket and found his purse with all his money, wiping his brow with relief as he looked about.

He bit his lip, tracing his eyes across the high stones of a building by his shoulder. It was very large indeed, with blank slits for windows. A prison, surely, and a forbidding one at that, while on the other side of the street the houses and inns were busy with so many hoardings and swinging signs he could hardly see the bricks behind them. He stopped still, catching sight of some movement at the rooftops, and craned his neck. He could hear a bell tolling, faint and ethereal. At first, he took what he saw for birds, then for black cats, yet they couldn't be, for they moved with skinny limbs and jutting knees. It was a gang of twenty soot-black children, he was sure of it, skittering over the brickwork below the eaves. He shielded his eyes for a better look, yet he found himself blinded by the sun.

'By your leave, sir!' came a bellowing voice as a pair of charging chairmen hurtled by, and with a yelp, Thomas tripped over his heels and fell face first into a narrow alleyway.

'For the sake of angels,' he said, brushing himself down. 'What a clumsy oaf you are.'

'Clumsy but handsome, I'd say.'

Thomas rolled over to see a young, attractive man leaning against the bricks. He was slender with a long nose, freckles all over his face and a twisted periwig. He had his foot cocked against the bricks, and he was smoking a pipe.

'Good day to you,' said Thomas. 'Is this your alleyway?'

The man raised his pale eyebrows, looking around. 'It's anybody's if they want it.'

'Ah,' said Thomas, nodding sagely, for London seemed to suit such things. 'I only arrived a few minutes ago and I'm already lost. I said to myself this morning: "Now Thomas, don't get lost and don't forget your trunk," and what did I do? I forgot my trunk, and here I am lost.' He looked at the man with a hopeful smile. 'Where am I exactly? It hardly matters; I'm lost no matter where I am, even in my own brain, and I forget to remember things, no matter how hard I try, and doesn't it annoy my mother and father, who don't even know I've left, and well, if they had known my plan to run away I don't doubt for a second...' He caught sight of the man's eyes glazing over and gave a nervous laugh. 'Forgive me, I do prattle; it's only that I feel sometimes, or rather I do wonder sometimes...' He shrugged. 'What use I am to anybody?'

The man pulled his pipe from his lips, revealing a jumble of wonky teeth. 'Funny, I was just thinking the same thing.' He folded his arms, the muscles stretching the faded sleeves of his patched coat. 'Where you supposed to be then, if not by Newgate?'

'Is that where we are? Newgate? Saints, that can't be near the bridge. I was on my way there when the coach took a swerve and tossed me into this alleyway...' Thomas fiddled with his coat buttons '...with you.'

'Right you are,' said the man with a quick smile. He flicked his eyes over Thomas's shoulder. 'The bridge, is it?'

'That's right, I must get there as soon as possible, or I'll be missed, you see, and then—'

The man placed a finger on his lips. 'Not such a nasty walk on a day like today. We'll cut through St Paul's Churchyard I reckon then along Watling to Budge and maybe Cannon to Eastcheap and down Fishy Street.' He stepped towards the mouth of the alleyway, turning back with his hand outstretched. 'That's if you fancy a dander?'

'I do, and I'm most grateful to you, Mister...?'

The man grinned and gave a little bow, his wig falling from his crown to reveal thick curls of red hair. 'Jack Huffins,' he said, before adding with a wink: 'Most of the time.'

CHAPTER TWO

High against the shining stones of the new cathedral, men were climbing through the scaffolding, dismantling the platforms one by one in slow and steady measures. On the loftiest of all the gantries stood Henry Sylva, watching his friend with concern. He knew that dismal look too well. He swung himself on a rope to the nearest ladder.

'Reckon we've done a morning's work, don't you, Gabe?'

'Ay.'

'My neck's roasted.'

'Looks it.'

Henry rested his heel against a standard and tugged at his breeches. 'I need a piss. Probably quicker to jump off than take the ladder.'

'Reckon so.'

Henry tutted. 'Might as well talk to the wall as you these days.'

Far below them, London spread out like one of Wren's scale models of the City, the churchyard stretching out to miniature streets of stone and old timber. Henry kicked a chip of Portland stone from the gangway and watched it skitter over the edge.

Gabriel's throat rumbled. 'You'll have us in trouble.'

'He wakes!' said Henry, throwing his hands out in mock celebration. 'Won't do any harm, we'll be out of work in a fortnight anyway, once the scaffolding's down. All them years our fathers spent building these gangways, never thought the day'd come we took 'em down.'

'We'll find new work.'

Henry pushed back from the beam, stowing his mallet in his belt. 'We'd better, or my good wife will have words. Time for a beer; should get an extra flagon in this heat.'

'I ain't thirsty.'

Henry laughed. 'Not thirsty, he says.' He rapped his knuckles on the foot of a stone apostle. 'Did you hear that? Must be the end of days at last, and just when we've finished the church.'

Gabriel huffed. 'Get away.' He rubbed his face with a shovel-sized hand, feeling the prickle of hot water rising behind his eyes. 'Leave me be.'

Henry went to speak but thought better of it. 'Ho then,' he said, passing his friend with a slap on the back. 'Enjoy the view.'

Gabriel waited for Henry to climb down before he took the locket from his neck and allowed the tears to come. High on the scaffolding surrounding the new St Paul's, he could cry for a while. Up there, far away from noise and grime, it was only him and the birds. He clicked open the locket and wiped his nose. 'Ay,' he said to himself, 'another year.'

How he hated the sound of his own voice, especially when he was sad: too soft for a man of his size, so feeble he could tear out his own tongue. He looked along the side of the cathedral, past the smooth columns of white stone, and buried his face in his arms. It had been three years to the day. He gripped the lintel, levering his nails from their beds. 'You never loved them well enough,' he said. 'Never knew what love was.'

He felt the shudder of the wooden frame far below his boots and quickly pushed the locket back into his shirt. He wiped his eyes and stood back from the ladder, accidentally knocking a hammer with his elbow, watching in horror as it toppled over the edge.

The hard crack came three seconds later, a distant paving slab spitting a puff of dust where it took the blow. Gabriel gripped his heart and caught sight of two young men staring back up at him, their hands shielding their eyes from the sun.

'Christ!' said Henry, hoisting himself into view. 'What are you doing, man, chucking hammers about?' He was slapped away. 'Ay Gabe, you'll be the one dangling at Tyburn, damned idiot. You think your wife and daughter would thank you for that?'

Gabriel threw him across the gangway, pushing him against a standard pole as the scaffolding shook. 'You mention my daughter today of all days?'

Henry kicked his feet in the air and was about to fight back, when he saw Gabriel's eyes. He let himself hang like a puppet and grinned. 'Hush now, Gabe, be calm, be calm. I could thump you into next week if I wanted to, no matter how big you are. Always could.'

Gabriel dropped him and stood back. 'Ay, and carts can pull horses.'

They worked on in awkward silence after that, sweat trickling down their shirtless backs. They made smart progress, pulling down a full storey of scaffolding and lowering the poles with ropes on pulleys to the men waiting below. In turns, Gabriel felt his temper cool. It was good to feel the weight of the timber in his arms, and though his mind was still heavy with memories, the repetition of the simple task at hand – cutting ties, loosening joints, wrenching struts, ripping up planks – felt like sweet comfort. After a few hours, he rested a while, looking down to where the hammer had landed. The two men were long gone, yet the memory of them had been following him around ever since he'd spotted them. One was Jack Huffins from Mother Clap's Molly House, but the other he didn't know. Gabriel picked splinters from his fingers, thinking about him. He'd been too far away to see clearly, yet – to Gabriel's excitement and shame – there was some unidentifiable quality in the way he was standing, some character in his distant face, that was pleasing to him.

Gabriel huffed, returning to work. Whoever Jack's friend was, he'd be one of those popular, strutting men, no doubt: effortlessly handsome with a wealth of friends and barrels of confidence. He rested his hammer and twisted his mouth. *Will Jack bring him to Clap's?* he wondered, his heart squeezing with a pang of jealousy. *And are they in love?*

CHAPTER THREE

Thomas hadn't had any friends as a child. He wasn't like the other boys in the rectory schoolroom in Highgate, though he admired them greatly for their daring and the way they threw themselves into the world without a care. He would hide himself away in a small den behind a crumbling patch of wall at the back of the graveyard and wait to be scared out like a rabbit, then he would run from the mob as fast as he could, to the front of the rectory, only to find the door locked, and there he would have his ribs dug or his skin twisted, depending on the boys' mood, the pain growing ordinary to him over the years. As a very young child he would call for his parents, yet they were agreed that it was best to leave their son alone until he stopped crying and learned to be a proper boy.

Alas, they had waited in vain for such a blessing, for in spite of his love of nature and talent for artistic pursuits, boyhood was a skill Thomas could never master. 'Stand up for yourself,' his father would shout through the locked door of his attic room. 'Fight back or I shall throw you in the stocks so everyone can see what a womanish little demon you are, and then you can cry while they pelt your face with eggs.'

It was not an empty threat, for one day, when Thomas had been caught making chains of flowers, the good rector of Highgate had dragged his son by the ankles to the green and locked him in the stocks by his neck and wrists, encouraging three local boys and girls to play at pillorying him. Reverend True and his wife found it difficult to bear this necessary kindness, but bear it they did, knowing it was to the boy's benefit.

Thomas knew his humiliation was merely another horror to suffer with patience and resignation, for he could no more escape himself than he could the stocks, and at the age of twelve, the mystery of Thomas True had finally revealed itself.

It was a dark Sunday afternoon in the depths of an unlit winter, when the village was cloaked in grey snow, and the older boys were plunging into the black ponds with hoots of delight. Thomas had moved to the attic window, curious to see what the noise was about. Might they let him play with them? It was not to be, for while he watched the naked lads cavorting, rubbing their pimpled skin in the shivering cold, he felt his own body grow hot.

That was when Thomas True first understood what he was. He had remained at the window for many hours, transfixed, long after the boys had finished collecting their clothes and gone home. Shame. Deepest shame. Impossible, burning horror. No finger moved, nor toe, not even a blink, until the snow-caked valley turned blue and the moon rose beyond the distant city. 'Demon,' Thomas had said to himself. 'Demon.' He watched his breath blow against the glass and turn to tears. 'Demon.'

He had never in all his isolation felt so lonely. The stocks winked at him between the black branches of the bare trees: a pair of manacled posts casting a long shadow across the snow.

Yes. The boys had been right to hurt him. Their violence had not saved his soul. And his father was justified in all he'd tried to do for the sake of his boy's perverted mind. He belonged in those stocks. He belonged in Hell.

'Look out!'

Thomas felt a thump on his shoulder as a missile whistled past his ear and struck the ground with an almighty smack. His skeleton nearly jumped from his skin. 'What was that?' he said.

'It's a bloody hammer, that's what it is.' Jack stood back and jabbed his finger at the scaffolding far above their heads. 'Blasted idiot, you!'

'A hammer?' Thomas wrenched it from the hole. 'Who'd throw a hammer off a cathedral?'

Jack tutted. 'The so-called molly guard, that's who. Big laugh, that is.' He cupped his hands to his mouth and bellowed, 'Lotty, you clumsy great ox!'

Thomas held up the hammer. The handle was split, the neck twisted. 'Do you think he'll want it back?'

Jack snorted, shaking his fist. 'Who knows what he wants, the great pig. Come on, let's get you to the bridge.'

Thomas allowed himself to be tugged away as Jack elbowed through the crowd. What did a forgotten trunk mean to him now? Or anything else for that matter? All those dark memories from his childhood were forgotten. So was Highgate. So was he. Nothing could hurt him, nothing shame him. He took a deep breath, sucking in the foul air like honey.

Free, he thought, as a smile ripened on his face. *Free and safe at last.*

CHAPTER FOUR

Down a tight warren of bewildering streets they went, all the noise bouncing from slab to brick.

Jack charged ahead, calling back over his shoulder. 'Why you in London then?'

'I must learn a trade since the Church won't have me.'

'The Church doesn't like sinners; can't take the competition.'

They turned up a dark passageway and onto a street lined with elm trees, jumping over stray dogs, dipping under shop signs, dancing around hurtling chairs as buckets of filth splashed around their shoes.

'Is it very far to the bridge?' said Thomas. 'My uncle and aunt are very kind people, and my cousin will be worried about me, I am sure.'

Jack spun around with a twinkling eye. 'Your cousin, eh? Tall? Pretty?'

'Abigail isn't particularly tall I shouldn't imagine,' shrugged Thomas, 'and it's been so many years since I saw her, I can't say whether she's pretty...'

Jack waved his hand impatiently. 'Oh, what do I care about Abigails?' And with that he was off again, rounding a corner past an endless scramble of taverns.

'So what trade will your uncle teach you?'

'I'm to be an apprentice candlemaker.'

'A chandler! You'll enjoy dipping a few wicks, I'm sure. Stinking trade, mind you, but there's worse I suppose. Could be a soil man.'

Thomas felt himself bridle. This new friend seemed rather too sure of himself for a frowzy-looking fellow wearing torn breeches and a rumpled shirt. He was about to speak when a hue and cry blew up at the far end of the street as a boy came pelting towards them, pursued by a gang of baying apprentices. His eyes were wide with terror as the brutes closed in.

'Christ,' hissed Jack, 'it's them.'

'Who?'

The boy drew near, his eyes streaming with tears. 'Help me!' he begged as Jack yanked Thomas to the wall.

'Don't look.'

Thomas could not help himself, for the young man looked like he'd been in a dog fight. He was wearing a pale-yellow shirt torn to the stomach, while his breeches were ripped up both legs to the crotch. He had downy blonde hair on his upper lip and his legs were thin as scantlings. He cannot have been much more than fifteen years old.

'They're going to cut my throat, Jacky,' he yelped. 'Save me!'

Jack tugged his hat low, refusing to turn from the wall. 'Don't know who you are,' he hissed. 'Get away.'

The boy stared. 'I'm Martin. We're friends from Clap's.'

'I said get away, Martha, or I'll cut you myself. Whatever mistake you made, I hope you don't have to pay for it, but I can't help you now.'

The boy caught Thomas's eye. 'Help me, please? I didn't know. I didn't think ... I had no choice ... The rat! Beware the rat!'

The mob was almost upon him, and with a look of hopeless panic, he sprinted away.

'Come here, vermin,' cried the hounds, throwing their clubs under his feet. 'Nasty little pup, we'll catch you by the tail and chuck you in the ditch!'

Jack pulled Thomas into an alleyway. 'Quickly,' he said. 'Before you're spotted.'

The high walls towered above them as they picked their way through arches and pressed sideways past piles of crates overflowing with rotten vegetables.

'Where are you taking me?' said Thomas. 'Is this the way to the bridge?'

Suddenly, he found himself yanked behind a wall and pressed up against the bricks. Jack kissed him on the mouth, and Thomas could taste sour wine on his tongue, could feel the man's fingers pressing inside his waistcoat, under his shirt.

He pushed away. 'What are you doing?'

'What do you think?'

Thomas *couldn't* think. He pulled at his breeches as a woman appeared at the far end of the alleyway carrying a screaming baby in her shawl. She passed them with suspicious eyes, before disappearing through a concealed doorway. Thomas had never been kissed by a man before, nor by anyone for that matter, not even his own mother. He covered his face as Jack's voice brushed his neck.

'You're one of us.'

'I don't know what you mean.'

'Yes you do.'

'You didn't help that poor lad.'

'Barely knew him.'

Thomas opened his eyes to see Jack leaning against the wall, his lips flushed.

'Martha's just another sod from the streets. Another careless molly.'

'They'll kill him.'

'Not if he runs quick enough.'

'Who were they?'

Jack looked back to the street, his eyelashes glowing red in a slice of light from above.

'Hounds,' he said. 'In the pay of the Society I'd wager.' He tutted, seeing Thomas's innocent frown. 'The Society for the Reformation of Manners. Don't say you never heard of 'em?'

'I haven't.'

'Count yourself lucky.' Jack laughed then glanced both ways, checking they were alone. 'It's a gang of bloodthirsty murderers by another name. Gentlemen and ladies of fine morals: a glorious institution, loved by the king himself.' He blew a raspberry as he bowed low, straightening up with his hands clenched together in prayer. 'All of them Hell-bent on hunting us sinners down. Stringing up the likes of us while they romp with whores and steal and kill and covet like the good book tells 'em to.'

'Sins,' whispered Thomas to himself, hearing the word in his father's voice.

Jack laughed, cupping Thomas between the legs. 'Ay, and here's one for a start.' He shook his head and pointed back to the street. 'Go that way for your uncle and aunt. Straight on to Fishy Street – you'll smell it before you see it – then left. And don't tell nobody a thing about your new friend Jack, you hear?'

'But where are you going?' said Thomas.

The young man was already dashing up the alleyway and around a corner. 'To Clap's,' he called back. 'Meet me there tonight.'

'Clap's?' shouted Thomas. 'What is it?'

'Everything you ever dreamed of; everything you ever feared. You'll see, you'll see. Field Lane over Fleet Ditch after dark. Look for the ivy door by the Bunch o' Grapes.'

'But I'll be alone.'

'Nah you won't, Thomas True. Together, always together. You'll see!'

CHAPTER FIVE

'Have a care you don't fall from your pediment, you bird-witted old termagant. I wouldn't want you to bump that potato face of yours against the wall. Blasted trollop, you. Blasted crow!'

So bellowed Thomas's Uncle Squink, poking his wife with a spindly finger.

'Ha!' replied Aunt Squink. 'I would hit my face against a thousand walls sooner than take a promise from you, lousy, bent-backed, bracket-faced old stoat!'

Aunt Squink stamped her boot while the folds of her neck gobbled up what ought to have been her chin. She flicked her husband's finger to his face. 'Get that filthy claw off me. I'm not one of your poisonous candles. You told me you'd have it fixed. Zoods! I shouldn't wonder you want all of us to drown in that stinking river.'

This was not how Thomas remembered his dear relatives. He moved his head to avoid a flying jug, then stood back as a candlestick travelled past his shoulder and into the passing traffic on the bridge.

'Uncle?' he said. 'Aunt?'

They turned in unison, a scowl on every feature, even their ears.

'Who are you?' demanded Aunt Squink.

'And what did you call us?' said her husband.

'Uncle and Aunt,' he said. 'I have been corresponding with Abigail; weren't you expecting me?'

'Expecting you?' said Aunt Squink, exchanging an incredulous look with her husband. 'I doubt that very much. If we were expecting you, we would have told you not to come.'

'Oh.'

Uncle Squink shushed his wife, shaking Thomas's hand most heartily. 'Forgive my disgusting wife. She only means to say that we have no nephew and we do not want you here.' He stood back quite pleased with himself, his thumbs in his buttonholes, grinning pleasantly towards the door by way of suggestion.

Thomas blinked. 'You want me to leave?'

'Would you mind? We are rather busy.' Uncle Squink swung his hands around the shop, knocking a box to the floor.

'Clumsy oaf,' cried Aunt Squink, poking a candle up her husband's left nostril. 'I should never have married you, bringing me nothing but rotten walls and nephews.'

Uncle Squink snatched the candle from his wife's claws and stabbed it into the massed curls of her yellow wig.

'I ought to set you alight, nag that you are!' He shot a pointed finger to Thomas. 'That,' he declared, 'is your nephew, not mine.'

They glared at Thomas so angrily he could imagine each of their heads popping into flame. He stepped inside, closing the door softly behind him.

'I have been writing to Abigail for weeks. She reassured me many times that I would be welcome to stay here with you on the bridge and I've been so looking forward to seeing you again.' He looked around at the shelves piled high with spindles of lumpy tallow. 'I have travelled alone to visit you and...' he steadied himself as the floor tilted below his feet '...I hope to return to Highgate a celebrated candlemaker.'

Aunt Squink scoffed, yet her husband's eyes grew large as plates.

'A celebrated candlemaker?' he whispered, soft as smoke. 'Celebrated,' he repeated, before adding: 'candlemaker.'

'Yes, a chandler, just like you. I wish to be your apprentice.'

Uncle Squink gave his wife a wholesome look, his rage extinguished. 'My darling, perhaps I was too hasty. I am this boy's mother's brother after all.' He turned to Thomas, his voice a-quiver. 'Forgive me, you are indeed my nephew, I see wax runs in your blood.'

Thomas wasn't entirely sure what that meant but he nodded anyway. His aunt glowered at him, the candle in her wig slipping to the floor with a clunk. Still, he gave her a smile.

'You must remember me,' he said. 'Your daughter and I became fast friends one summer thirteen years ago.' He reached into his pocket, fumbling in vain for his purse. 'You mustn't worry about costs; I have been saving my small allowance for years with nothing to spend it on. I can pay for my keep.'

The woman melted instantly. 'My husband is a turkey-brained doddle-head, yet I had not forgotten you, er...' She opened her arms, evidently waiting for a reminder.

'...Thomas,' said Thomas.

'Yes, Thomas! I am your father's much neglected sister. Come boy, you are our nephew twice over and double welcome you are. Now why do you stand there by the door? Will you not embrace your own family?'

Thomas stepped across the shop, feeling the floor tilt further, and with a creaking noise, so that he travelled the last distance in a slide.

'Then I can stay?'

'You can stay!' said Uncle Squink, cheering, while Aunt Squink preened and prodded Thomas's neat periwig and shallow-brimmed hat.

She shouted up the stairs, gripping Thomas by the hand: 'Abigail, Get down here at once.'

There was a brief pause before a pair of heeled shoes appeared on the highest stair, descending to reveal a petticoat and skirts of painted cotton, the material dancing with English flowers and butterflies. Thomas could hardly believe the striking woman who lowered herself into the shop. She was tall and hearty, her yellow hair tied up in a lace cap to frame a most gentle, kindly face with blushing cheeks and a pixie's nose. She seemed confused at first, looking Thomas up and down, but when he grinned, she leapt over the sloping floor with a cry of delight.

'Oh Thomas, you came! I didn't think you would.' She stood back, drinking him in. 'Forgive me, Father. I never dreamed he'd come to live with us, it's been too long. Look at him. Isn't he the handsomest man in London? Why, I'd never imagined that skinny little boy could grow so tall.'

'Look at him indeed,' said Uncle Squink, with a knowing glance at his spouse. 'A man of wax is young Thomas; I can sniff a tallowman from a mile away. My nephew, my apprentice.'

'He is most welcome,' said Aunt Squink. 'My darling nephew, our paying lodger.'

Darkness. A faint creaking. The soft thunder of water. Thomas lay on his bed fully clothed. The Squinks had fed him well enough on bread and cheese, yet he was desperately hungry. He climbed to his feet and made his way over the creaking floorboards to look out of the window. The river was sparkling silver in the moonlight, embroidered with ships in silhouette, while either side – Thomas stared out in wonder – a glittering mass of houses, piled in their many thousands like a blanket of raked embers.

His knees ached as his mind wandered. He was indeed hungry for food, yet hungrier still for adventure. What had that young man said to him in the alleyway? Field Lane, over a ditch. Something to do with an ivy door. Mother Clap's, was it?

He opened the rotten window, which squeaked and duly fell from its hinges into the river. Waiting for the splash, he leaned out and remembered his brush with the hammer, then looked up at the moon, remembering the shirtless man perched high on the scaffolding. He smiled to himself and felt in his coat pocket; but wait – it was empty! He stuffed his fingers inside and scrabbled around for his purse, yet there was nothing there. Lord, was there anything he couldn't lose? He ran back to the bed, knocking his head on the frame as he searched under it, then felt inside his waistcoat pockets again to be certain, his fingers finding something hard and metallic. He pulled out a single half-guinea coin, turning it in the gloom with a miserable sigh, then sat on the bed with his head in his hands. He was a sorry young man indeed, yet London was still calling. Perhaps he could find Jack at this Mother Clap's and ask him to buy them both a cup or two of wine?

Within a minute, he was creeping through the living quarters to the shop, unbolting the door with dextrous fingers, then onto the bridge.

Even at such a late hour, carts and carriages were rumbling between the tight buildings in a steady stream, making their way to the City. Humming to himself, Thomas stepped from the bridge onto a crossroads, staring up as a star shot over the roofs, sparkling at its tail. He watched it burn and die, rolling Jack's words on his tongue. They seemed to offer him all he had ever wished for.

'Together.' Isn't that what his new friend had said? 'Always together.'

CHAPTER SIX

Gabriel tried to keep his patience, drumming his fingers on his knees under the table. He picked his nails, chewed his lip, clicked his tongue, bounced his heel, anything to control his frustration. He needed to leave Red Lyon Street for Mother Clap's to stand guard at the door, yet Henry and Bet wouldn't let him go. Normally, they couldn't wait for him to sleep so they could have their portion of the cramped living quarters to themselves. Yet on this night, every possible thing Gabriel had to say was instantly and un-questioningly seized upon with fascination. No matter how many times he stretched his arms for a bear's yawn – thumping his chest so they could see how very tired he was – no matter how often he said 'that was a long day', no matter how many times he gave a sigh and an 'anyhow, time for bed...' they would keep him there with some idle question, delivered slowly while the pair of them invented whatever nonsense they were supposed to be asking. They had been sidling nervously around something for weeks, conversations taking place without words, the pair of them giving each other knowing looks.

Two hours had passed, and for the first time that night, Gabriel yawned and meant it.

'Best give you two peace,' he said, standing from the table. 'Take my night-time walk, then bed. Just fetch my boots.'

'Boots?' said Henry, looking down at Gabriel's feet. 'You're wearing them.'

'Right. Meant my coat.'

'It's warm still,' said Bet, shifting uncomfortably. 'Henry, don't you want to tell Gabriel ... something?'

'Not now.'

Bet pulled her table knife from a hunk of cheese and pointed it him. 'Then when?'

Gabriel was already through to his own quarters, closing the door on them both. He should have eaten at one of the taverns on his way home, but then he wouldn't have spent any time with his wife and daughter. He closed the door with an apologetic smile.

'Evening Em,' he said. 'Evening Dot.'

He crept to the partition wall and listened to a low rumbling of voices.

An argument had already started between Henry and Bet. 'I'm causing trouble again,' he murmured.

He stood back and lowered himself into a chair by the window. 'Clumsy oaf, getting in everybody's way as usual.' He took a long breath and peered across the empty floor to a pair of beds standing against the wall. He'd built them himself, one wide-framed, the other small as a crate with rails at either side. Emily stared back at him, her hair loose, bare legs covered with folds of red blankets. She seemed insensible to the rising racket from their neighbours.

Gabriel nodded at Dot in the cradle. 'Sleeping, is she?'

The baby was lost amidst a swaddle of grey cloth, only her eyes peeping out. They had been like that for three years now, mother and daughter, always apart as though some invisible wall divided them. They created no shadows, inspired no disturbance in the dusty light. They *were* the dusty light. Still, what he would have given to see his wife cradling Dot in her arms. That had never been possible, not even in life, for they had spent no more than a minute together before they'd died. How quickly the aching time had raced by, and how lonely he'd felt without them. He had loved his wife and, brief though her time had been, loved his daughter too, yet when they left they seemed to take all women with them, and Gabriel had found himself all sinfulness, no love.

'For the best,' said Gabriel, looking back through the window as old Peter stirred in the stables below. 'For the best. They took you as punishment for my sins. My fault.' He gave another sigh. There was no sound in his quarters but for the faint rustling of his whiskers on the collar of his coat.

'They want us out, Em,' he said, after an hour's gloomy pondering. 'They think I don't know, but I do. Bet's having a baby. Nice for 'em after so long trying. Hope it goes kinder for her than you.' He looked back at the ghost. 'How can God ask women to bear his children and make it so hard on 'em?' He sniffed back a tear, pretending it was a little sneeze, and hid his face. 'I ain't got a friend to go to for lodgings, see. No money for a place to stay. That goes on vittles and ... well it goes, that's all you need to know about that.'

Just then, a bright light flew across the rooftops towards the river. Gabriel watched it with a curious frown. 'Shooting star, Dot,' he said, pointing it out so his child could follow his finger. 'That you up there, is it? Telling your silly old pa to keep hopeful?'

The baby blinked.

'Ay,' said Gabriel. 'Ay, that's my Dot, that is.'

The voices had grown quiet on the other side of the wall now.

'Have to go over to my special place tonight, Em. You knew I went there when you was alive, didn't you? Can't stop it. My sickness, that's all. Potions and physics don't work.' He bowed his head. 'I am a sinner.'

He moved to the bed and sat down between his wife and daughter, and for some un-clocked time they waited together in silence like a family of owls, until a triangle of light moved across the bare floorboards and Bet appeared in the doorway.

'You sleeping, Gabe?' she said.

'Ay.'

She stepped into the room, casting her eyes around the bare space. She hated being there, he could tell, standing amidst the mouldy stink of a lonely widower. She hardened her throat, cradling her belly.

'Henry says the scaffolding's almost down.'

'It is.' Gabriel stood up, hands in his pockets. 'Two weeks, then we'll be done. More than thirty years since we started the—'

'We don't have any money.'

Gabriel stopped himself from saying what he wanted to say. That they'd have plenty if it weren't for Henry's drinking and her fancies. He noticed the smell of rose water and the lace collar at her neck. The profusion of candles on the mantel, the table, the walls, beside the bed and everywhere she could find space. He held his tongue. 'That's for Henry to manage.'

'How blessed I am. Don't you fret about money?'

'Ain't no pockets in shrouds.'

She walked over and stared earnestly into his eyes. 'You know what Henry's trying to tell you. He won't ask 'cos he's afraid he'll lose a friend. Don't tease him.' Her faint smile drifted away, and she gave a sad shake of her head. 'I don't know what we'll do.' She looked down at the empty mattress and cot. 'They won't leave you, Gabe. They'll stay with you, wherever you go.' She pressed a finger against Gabriel's heart where the locket hung. 'They live in there ... not in this room.'

'No, Bet.'

'But...'

'No.'

The light was cut as Henry appeared at the door.

'What you both gossiping about?' he said, walking sheepishly into the room and standing behind Bet, wrapping her in his arms. 'Might as well tell you tonight as any night.' He took a deep breath, struggling to hide his smile. 'I'll be a pa soon, Gabe. After so much trying.' His expression was one of great pride, then as soon as it flashed up, it was strapped with embarrassment. He kissed Bet's head and gave her a squeeze. 'A son to take my name eh, good wench?'

'Or a daughter to suffer it.'

There they stood, waiting for Gabriel to accept the inevitable. He had to. What a fool he'd been, thinking he could stay. He paused, trying to ignore the powdery eyes staring at him from the bed and cot.

'Got nowhere.'

'You have money,' said Henry. 'Money's as good as a home, no matter where you are.'

'Got none.'

'Where's it gone?'

'Where's yours?' snapped Gabriel. 'And what friends cast a man and his wife onto the streets with a new baby?'

'They're dead, Gabe.'

'Not to me.'

In a sudden fit, he lifted the chair to the ceiling, meaning to fling it through the window, but Bet and Henry managed to grip it by the legs.

'God damn it,' said Henry, 'I told Bet it was a bad day to ask, but we don't have time.'

All Gabriel wanted to hear was the smash of glass, to be given that much of his rage, just for a moment of release.

Bet stood in front of him, her hands raised. 'The baby's coming soon. A few short weeks, maybe less.' She waited for Gabriel's arm to soften, for the chair to dip from the ceiling. 'We need you to leave. I don't want my child to live with ghosts.' She took Henry's hand. 'You will always be our family, Gabe. So will Emily and Dot. But not here, not together.'

Gabriel lowered the chair to the floor. He had known this day would come. When your family dies, your essence dies too, and nobody wants to suffer it. Bet and Henry had been kinder than most, forbearing his gloom and strange habits, and it occurred to Gabriel in that moment –

looking at the sincere faces of his two friends – that it wasn't fair to impose himself on them any longer, nor anybody else for that matter, nor himself, nor the world...

Bet raised onto her tiptoes and kissed Gabriel's cheek. 'Good man. You'll find somewhere to live.'

'Ay,' said Henry, 'you will.'

Gabriel tried to smile, yet it came out like a grimace. 'Can't stand the crying anyhow,' he said.

Henry clapped his friend's shoulder. 'It'll be me doing the crying. You're good to give us space, Gabe. See?' He pulled Bet close. 'Told you he'd understand. All these weeks worrying.'

Bet closed her eyes and shook her head with a weary yawn, leading Henry back to their quarters.

Alone once more, Gabriel sat heavily in his chair. 'Would you, Em? Come with me if I left? Would ye bring Dot?'

The ghost tilted her head and gazed at him with passive eyes, her lips parted.

Gabriel sniffed. 'I won't ask you to.'

Already, Henry and Bet were snoring on the other side of the partition. He waited for the sound to deepen as the last thread of the evening turned black and the rooms of the houses opposite snuffed out their candles. As they did so, he caught sight of his sinful face, silver in the glass. There was still time to get to Mother Clap's – and what might Lotty Lump do then? More than just guard the door? Would Jack be there with his new friend?

Careful not to tread on any of the creaking floorboards, he opened the partition door, padding past Henry and Bet, then down a flight of stone stairs to the stable yard.

Hooves shuffled in one of the stalls and a long nose appeared above the stable door. 'Hello, Peter,' said Gabriel, stroking the horse with a gentle hand. 'Don't look at me like that, old friend. Get enough of them looks from Em.' He glanced up at the window to their quarters.

'Night night,' he said, stepping to the gates. 'Time to go.'

CHAPTER SEVEN

Field Lane above the Fleet Ditch couldn't be so difficult to find, could it? Besides, if London was to be his home, then Thomas had better acquaint himself with it. He stopped halfway up a cobbled rise and turned in a circle, already lost.

He scratched his head through his periwig and decided to turn left along a wide, bow-bellied street, then slowed down to admire a grand building with a soaring tower. *The Royal Exchange* declared a legend above its double doors. He passed alongside it, tracing a shallow arcade, then darted inside, expecting silence beneath the arches, yet there was an urgent rush of hot breathing and whispers, his face brushed by the swish of anonymous clothes. He stopped to gather himself against a wall, stretching his fingers into the blind darkness and touched a moving limb.

'Who goes there?' said a voice from beside his ear. Thomas saw the outline of a woman in a tall wig.

'Thomas True.'

The woman snorted. 'Sweet Thomas True, are you seeking the lips of a soft and supple virgin t'night?'

Thomas thought about that. 'What for?'

The woman drew closer, smelling sweet and sickly as boiled jam. 'Ah, the discerning fellow seeks a woman of experience to bring him to Paradise.'

Thomas moved his hands about, finding a soft shoulder. 'Are you a whore?'

The shoulder stiffened. 'I am whatever a gentleman asks me to be, pert thing.'

'Then be my guide. I seek Mother Clap's on Field Lane.'

A torch passed by, flashing the woman's face: a nose pressed flat against a cheek, one eye white as a boiled egg, her skin pocked and plastered with flour. As quick as she was there, she was gone again with a flap of her tail into the dark water.

'Lavender,' she cackled, 'this one's for you.'

Thomas felt his way through the arches, bumping his head on an unexpected wall as his way was blocked by a giant leaping frog.

'Where are you off to?' said a high, lisping voice. 'Not good enough, am I?'

The young man had the most singular expression of indifferent curiosity. Lit up by the crackling flame of a torch, Thomas could make out his flat nose and broad face with bright-pink cheeks, while his clothes were covered in ribbons from his ankles to his collar.

Thomas looked around, assuming the man was talking to someone else. 'Good enough?'

'If you're looking for a kiss and a cudgel, I ain't pricey. Who set you against me? Huffins, was it, I'll bet?'

'You know Jack Huffins?' said Thomas. 'I met him earlier today after falling off my coach, well not *my* coach, a mail coach, and forgetting my trunk. He saved me really, and showed me where to go, then told me to meet him at a place called Clap's, whatever that is, and isn't he funny the way he speaks? I could hardly keep up with him, but I'm pretty sure it was on somewhere called Field Lane by some grapes and something about ivy, though I couldn't tell you what it was, I don't know, but I only have a little money so I'm hoping to get a drink or two, not that I'm much of a drinker usually, you understand, but do you know where I'm supposed to be going?'

The man waited for him to finish with a flat stare then spoke in a wafting sigh.

'Yes, I know where it is, I am the most popular molly there.' He checked his fingernails. 'I suppose Jack told you about Lavender Long-legs?'

'Not that I remember.'

The man pursed his lips and looked Thomas up and down, wiping every inch of his clothes with his eyelashes. 'Like I thought,' he said. 'Jack wants all the fresh blades for himself, greedy bitch. Clap's place is up that way...' He was about to say more when a flying stone struck him on the temple and he folded instantly to the ground.

A dry laugh came from behind a column and Thomas caught a glimpse of a face deep within the arcade. It was pale as bone, the skin slightly translucent, as though the eyes were peering out from bloodless flesh.

'Well then,' said a man, stepping out from the arcade, wrenching a bald dog on a chain. 'What do we have here?'

Thomas crouched beside the jittering body, forcing the stricken man's jaw open and pulling out his tongue so he could breathe.

'Did you throw that rock? You've hurt him badly.'

The man wrapped the chain around his fist and gave it a sharp tug. The creature on his leash was not a dog after all, but a half-naked child, covered in black grime with lank hair, a pendant of green glass tied around its head. The man gave the chain a second, harder yank, forcing the child to cower and tremble at his feet. 'Heel, nasty pup,' he snapped, 'or the Society will have words.' He met Thomas's eye. 'Hurt him badly, did I? Poor sod. Not so bad as I could have, though, but give it time. One molly's enough for today.' He looked behind him as more young men appeared, carrying clubs.

Quickly, Thomas reached into his pocket to pass his last half-guinea to the urchin on the chain. The poor creature snarled at him, its eyes in a fury, though curious nonetheless, and quickly stowed the coin in its rags. Thomas straightened up with a friendly nod, hiding his trembling hands behind his back.

'It was you chasing that boy earlier today.'

'You mean Martin Lightbody, the little molly boy?' The man sniffed. 'Ay, that was me and my comrades.' He nodded to his friends. 'Good riddance to the little bugger; orders well met.' He shifted his arm, a club appearing at his hip. 'Thomas True.'

Thomas frowned. 'How do you know my name?'

'Word travels fast hereabouts.'

'I am not afraid of you.'

The man cocked his head. 'Should be.'

A whispering came from within the arches and, on hearing it, the man tilted his head with a curl of his lip.

'P'raps Thomas True don't need to be afraid. Depends, depends...'

'What do you mean by that?'

The gang stretched out across the road, now looping like a cat's tail around Thomas until he was encircled.

He tried to push his way through the circle but was shoved back, stumbling over the unconscious body on the ground. The gang swung their weapons into view, barbed clubs and long butcher's knives, rusted chains and mason's mallets. The circle tightened and Thomas shook his head.

'What have I done? Please.'

He knew there was nothing he could do in such situations but wait.

After a lifetime of taking his punishment, no man in London was better qualified to withstand a beating. He closed his eyes and wrapped his arms over his ribcage, bracing himself for the blows to begin. Seconds passed without pain, then a minute. Eventually, he opened one eye and peeped out to see an empty road, nothing but a stray dog blinking at him from the gutter.

'They left you alone,' came a voice from his back.

Thomas looked around to see the frog-like man climbing up from the dust, his knees and eyeballs pointing in all directions. He wiped blood from his swollen head and narrowed his eyes.

'Now why would that be?'

'I honestly don't know,' said Thomas, reaching out to help him, but his arm was slapped away.

'Get back,' said the man, 'and don't you dare follow me. Culls like you ain't welcome at Clap's.'

The young man limped off, cupping his head. If it weren't for the sight of the broken figure, Thomas might have thought the gang was a figment of his own exhausted imagination. It would hardly be a surprise after such a day. He scanned the street, and as he turned in a circle, tracing the roofs of the buildings, he caught sight of scurrying shapes moving silently over the tiles, to that familiar chiming sound. He pulled his coat tighter around him.

'I should go back to the bridge,' he said to himself, collecting his wig from the ground. He spied the young Mister Lavender already staggering from view around the corner of a far building. 'Still, there's nothing else for it. Mother Clap's, whatever you are, I am on my way.'

CHAPTER EIGHT

Thomas followed George Lavender up the wide street, the windows seeming to watch his every step. The great city was falling asleep, or so Thomas thought, yet as the light died, so the night-time creatures slipped from their burrows, shook their furry flanks, sniffed at the moon with twinkling eyes and scurried every which way, searching for mischief. It was the custom, Thomas realised then, for such nocturnal creepers to dress themselves in dark clothing so that their bodies became indistinct: shadows within shadows, mysterious, shifting shapes that burned up like carved lanterns at the passing of a torch. And then, did their faces not tell a dreadful story? The purple lips, hanging cheeks, bedraggled clothing, and the eyes ... how they glared at their own feet, bent their furtive backs to hoard their ripped gloves and empty bottles with jealous twitches. They possessed nothing, those jealous misers, not even their minds.

It was in a moment of fearful panic that Thomas lost Mister Lavender's tail and found himself greeted by the outline of a lantern-topped dome peering down at him from above the rooftops. He looked across the open churchyard – proud to have found his way to a place he recognised – and rounded the railings to the very spot where he and Jack had stood that afternoon. It seemed such a long time ago now. Why, what a naïve fool Thomas True had been then! Not a clue about London, no hope of making his way from the bridge to the cathedral without a guide – no address, no friends, never kissed, never threatened by a gang of vanishing hounds. He peered at the paving to find the spot where the hammer had fallen. The hole was still there, and Thomas winced, rubbing his head. He brushed his toe across the cracks then looked up at the cloudless sky, remembering the man who'd been clambering amongst the timber struts. He scowled, for he could have sworn the stranger was still there, standing right up at the top of the scaffolding, dark against the pale stones. Thomas rubbed his eyes and looked a second time, and yes, there he was, the shape of a tall figure with broad shoulders and a round head, just visible where the rising nave caught the last of the twilight. He stepped backwards, curious to see what arrangement was tricking his eyes: a bucket and pulley perhaps, or a discarded hat left on a nail for the following day.

It was not so, for as he moved, the figure moved with him, and in the casting light of the moon, he saw that it was indeed the very same man, his shirt flapping in the breeze like a ship's flag. His arms were crossed over his chest like a dead man, and he was leaning out, tiny against such a vast structure. Thomas felt a sudden sense of vertigo as though the world had tipped upside down and he might fall headfirst into the sky. He steadied himself, gripping his knees, and when he looked up again, the man had leaned out even further.

You'll fall, Thomas said to himself. *One slip and you'll be buried deep as your hammer.*

Thomas rushed back and waved his arms, hopping on his heels. 'Be careful!' he shouted. 'Don't jump!' He could hardly tell from so far away, yet he sensed he'd been spotted, for the man softened his legs and leaned back between the struts. Thomas waved again, and to his delight, the stranger lifted his hand in return, before disappearing into the thatch of ropes and tresses.

Relieved not to have witnessed a terrible accident, Thomas made his way out of the churchyard, passing the statue of the old queen with a tip of his hat, and made his way through the City wall. There, by Providence, he found a long, stinking ditch, which struck up from the river. As Thomas followed it, he caught sight of his new friend, George Lavender, up ahead. The young man was standing on a flat bridge, his unmistakable frog-like silhouette beside a second man; pot-bellied and apparently in a fit. Thomas crept closer to them, keeping himself in shadow. The second man was of middling years with a nose that stuck out like a round peg from his squashed head. Thomas drew along the side of a warehouse. He couldn't hear what the two were saying, only their S's reaching his ears above the bubbling ditch. He held back in a doorway, waiting to see where they went. He did not have to wait long, for they were disturbed by a passing stranger in a cloak, and they hurried away, dropping into the mouth of a dark lane.

CHAPTER NINE

Thomas True stepped onto Field Lane with a grimace. He half expected his foot to burn off at his ankle – yet finding himself complete, he shuffled along between old rookeries held apart like fighting drunks by beams at their sloping heads. It was as though a spell had been cast across the opening of the thoroughfare for, though it had seemed darker than a crypt from the outside, inside it was lit up with so many torches, Thomas jested to himself that the Great Fire of London must still be burning in that peculiar thoroughfare, for no Christian had ever dared enter to extinguish the flames.

There was no time for such fancies. George Lavender and his friend were already halfway up the path, and there was such a crowd of people criss-crossing between the taverns Thomas couldn't begin to think where Mother Clap's might be.

He turned up his collar and pressed deeper, listening to the drawl of the men and women around him in case they gave him a clue. He pushed his way into a drinking hole, only to be bowled out again by a gang of drunken sailors. He collapsed against a tavern opposite with a swinging sign:

The Bunch o' Grapes

He peered up at it, wondering if he'd remembered Jack's instructions correctly: 'Look for the ivy door by the Bunch o' Grapes.' That was most certainly the name of the board above his head, yet there was no such door to be found. He was about to walk on when he saw a pair of men in bright coats and even brighter wigs sidling up to a wall covered in ivy. With covert looks and furtive nods, they pulled back the ivy and stepped straight through the bricks like a pair of ghosts.

Thomas rubbed his eyes, thinking he must have imagined it. He moved closer to the wall, trying not to draw any attention to himself. Up close, the ivy was made of twine and paper, and when he parted it, he glimpsed a cut in the plasterwork running above his head and down through the middle of a shuttered window. It was the outline of a concealed doorway, perfectly invisible to the casual eye. Thomas stood sideways, looking around to make sure he wasn't being watched, then with a quick thump of his heel and a jump, he found himself standing inside a long passageway, lit by lanterns of every colour.

The door swung closed behind him and Thomas took courage, creeping around a tight corner to a courtyard overlooking a wasteland of ditches and half-sunken homes. The lanterns led him up a flight of stairs to a precipitous gangway, which cut a shaded path around the belly of a towering warehouse. Thomas trod carefully, for the crooked pylons below his feet quivered with every step and he gripped the rail in case he fell. He passed beside a woodshed and arrived at a platform that fanned out to a broad approach like the deck of a galleon, at the far end of which stood a door. Thomas held back, observing it from a distance. There was a sign hanging above it, no name, only a painting of a peacock with its green tail fanned out, and below the bird: a window glazed with rose-coloured glass.

There was drumming beyond the door, deep and insistent, the boards of the gangway beating up beneath Thomas's feet. He could hear the rumble of men's voices too, and their bawdy laughter. A fiddle screeched, playing some old shanty, while the men's voices joined in, assaulting the melody with improvisation and embellishment.

'Mother Clap's,' said Thomas, stepping up to the door. He pressed his hand against the glass and felt the warm glow on his face. 'I found you.'

CHAPTER TEN

Thomas had never seen anything like it before. He was standing in a cavernous hall two storeys high, ringed with a lofty balcony, its railings trimmed with candles in multi-coloured balls of glass. He stepped away from the door as a vision in blue feathers strutted past him, spinning a wheel of lanterns above her head. She swished her hips to the beat of the drum, winking at Thomas as she passed by. There were ten or more such creatures weaving their way through the crowd, their lantern wheels slapping the walls with glancing diamonds as white clouds burst green and red above their heads like enchanted cannon fire.

Deeper to the drum he went, deeper down as the dancing men dipped and spun about him, deeper past looming faces, deeper to bare chests and tangled legs, where bodies boiled, fingers brushed and pinched and tweaked, all to the riotous screech of the fiddle and boom of the beat.

Thomas pressed past a pair of men pinned against a wall, realising they were none other than George Lavender and his portly friend from the ditch. Either they didn't recognise him or they didn't care to, so he pushed his way through a clot of dancing sailors and made his way to the front of a wooden stage. Everyone was wearing gowns, apart from those wearing nothing at all, and in the heat and commotion, he fell back against a circle of topless lads who picked him up by his ankles and arms and threw him up to the stage with a cheer. He climbed to his hands and knees, a thrill rising through his body, and as soon as he stood up, a cup of wine was slapped into his hand and he was dragged back into the drumming press, pushed and elbowed from every angle, his feet slipping in pools of liquid. He trod on people's toes and fell into people's arms, but nobody seemed to care, and when a handsome, freckled fellow twirled past him in a gown cut below his nipples, Thomas grabbed him and kissed his cheek with relief. 'Jack,' he said, 'I found you!'

'By Jehovah's tits,' shouted the young man, ripping his wig off, 'the country squire made it. A very good evening to you, my man.'

Thomas laughed. 'Why, thank you, Mister Huffins, I—'

Jack waggled his finger, laughing. 'Not Mister Huffins. You may call me Sweet Jacky.' He dipped to the floor in a curtsey, his eyes staring up, black and round. Milky sweat dripped down his nose, revealing the freckles below, and he raised his hand for a kiss. 'We use our molly names here.'

'For safety?' shouted Thomas.

'For truth, darling! We are mollies and no true molly dresses so plain as men. Now take this...'

Thomas felt something drop from Jacky's outstretched fingers into his palm. He stared in disbelief.

'My purse!' he said. 'Where did you find it?'

Sweet Jacky's face pulsed to the flash of red lights as she raised herself out of the curtsey.

'In your pocket, silly bitch.'

'Well, thank you, I thought I'd lost it.'

'Makes no odds to me. It's been a good day's work on Tower Hill, like most Sundays, all them tourists thronging to see the lions and cat-a-mountains. Too busy gasping and gawping to watch their own purses.' She winked. 'Now their pockets are empty, and mine are full.' She gave a little jig as two mollies appeared, pushing their way through the dancers. One of them was plump as an apple, dressed preposterously in a glittering mantua of deep crimson, her head adorned with a wig so tall it had space for two hats, three stems of white roses and an entire stuffed magpie. She was evidently too tired to dance with her feet, though her hands were keeping a constant jig, flicking a pair of fans in all directions. Her companion was of equal age and exhaustion, though bent and bony with a face that might easily have been unkind (pinched cheeks, thin lips, low-lidded eyes) yet there was a natural warmth that shone through her old skin like a dancing flame. She too was dressed in a fine mantua, deep green with pale-blue roses stitched down the sleeves, while her wig exploded in all directions as though someone had planted a barrel of gunpowder in a crate of rabbits. Thomas could not help but laugh.

'Vivian, dear,' said the larger of the two dames, 'I think this handsome knave is mocking you.'

The second rolled her eyes. 'Nay, Nelly dearest, it is *you* he is mocking.'

'Impossible,' said the first, turning to Thomas with a flick of her fan. 'Who are you laughing at, sir, she or I?'

Thomas grimaced. 'Both of you.'

'That's better,' replied the molly, taking her companion by her bony fingers. 'We hate to be separated.'

Jack stepped between them. 'Nelly Fump and Vivian Guzzle, meet my new friend, Talbot Trowel.'

Thomas looked behind him, then realised Jacky's mistake.

'Why no, my name's Thomas True.'

Nelly Fump took his hand immediately, caressing his knuckles and rubbing his fingers. 'Thomas True? My goodness, what a splendid name, wherever did you find it?'

'My father gave it to me.'

'Is that so?' said the dame, looking directly at his breeches. 'And what else did you inherit?'

The second dame stepped in. 'Leave the boy alone, dear. Come, young blades, won't you join us in the gallery – we have a table for the show.'

They crossed to a curtain, passing up to the balconied platform above. From there, the mass of dancing mollies seemed to churn like the sea below them. Thomas leaned over, spotting George Lavender talking animatedly to his friend, and there behind them was the young lad from earlier that morning: so, he had escaped the hounds after all. He might not have bothered by the looks of him, for he seemed more scared than ever, pushing his way through the crowd as fast as he could go.

'Look, Jacky,' said Thomas, 'it's Martin, the young man from earlier.'

It was too late, for the boy seemed to have disappeared, and anyway, it was evidently time to sit, for Thomas was tugged down to a chair by the back of his breeches.

'Here we are then,' said Nelly Fump, cradling three jugs of wine. 'We have the finest seats in the house, my darlings.'

'Finest and most expensive,' said Vivian.

Fump tutted, arranging her embroidered skirts into a dazzling cushion. 'Forgive my sweetheart, dear friends. She enjoys finer things, though spending money on them is, apparently, an unhappy surprise.'

'Here, Nelly,' said Jacky, 'is there enough space for the rest of us with your arse taking up all the room?'

'Plenty,' said Fump, clearly enjoying the view of Jacky's freckled legs stretched out on the balustrade. 'My arse is most accommodating and who doesn't like a squeeze?'

Old Vivian settled herself into a chair by her companion's side. 'Don't forget, young Lavender Long-legs says she's bringing the Duchess tonight. She'll be wanting the best view.'

'The Duchess!' said Fump, fanning her face and pursing her lips. 'That goose. I'd far rather keep Sweet Jacky and her handsome new beau to ourselves.' She poked Thomas in the small of his back, forcing him to look away from the dancers. 'Picked one yet? We shall give you a molly name so you can get christened and have some fun. Come along now, sit closer – or shall I perch on your lap?'

Thomas gave a shy smile. 'You might be a little heavy.'

'The bitch!' said Nelly. 'My goodness, did your mother teach you no manners?'

'Ay,' said Jacky, 'he speaks the truth, such is his name. He is the oracle!'

Fump picked up a jug of wine with a sulky flounce. 'That may be so, but nothing offends an honest lady so much as the truth.' She peeped at Thomas from behind her fan. '*Can* you be, I wonder?'

'Can I be what?' asked Thomas.

'True.'

'I try to be.'

'What a pity,' she said, snapping her fan shut. 'I cannot trust an honest man.'

'Then you won't like me at all. I don't think I've ever told a lie, not in all my life.'

Nelly blinked furiously, trying to understand what she'd heard, then leaned out to address her companion. 'Did you hear that, Vivian dear? He only tells the truth.'

'The perfect qualification for a lonely life,' Vivian replied.

'Indeed so. Well then, Viv, as the oldest molly amongst us, you must christen our boy. What name do you choose?'

Vivian looked Thomas over with an impish eye. 'Verity, I should say. Verity True-tongue, and Heaven help the bitch.'

CHAPTER ELEVEN

A voice rang out to cheers as the fiddler screeched to a halt and the crowd below turned to face the stage. A man had appeared, with dark, shining skin, his complexion as rich as coffee. He was wearing heeled riding boots and a military suit of bright-red beads, which jangled from his lapels, and a silver periwig with long quills that seemed to sprout from his head, while his hat trailed golden ribbons to his heels. Verity True-tongue (as Thomas had just been christened) looked harder, for there was something about the man that she – yes 'she' for that was apparently the mode of the community – could not place.

'Look at you, filthy sods!' bellowed the masculine figure to whistles and applause. 'You're very kind, very kind. I do like a warm hand on my entry...'

'Who's that?' said Verity.

'Why, that's Mother Clap, of course,' said Jacky.

The man swept his coat from his shoulders and with a stretch of his chest the buttons on his shirt pinged off and a pair of plump paps popped up from his waistcoat.

'There,' laughed Jacky, seeing Verity's startled face. She leaned in close, speaking low. 'Clap's the only verified woman allowed in here. They say her mother played concubine to a Barbary pirate before the Spaniards cut the man to ribbons. She must have used her special skills on the sailors, for they kept her alive and put a baby in her belly, only to sell her in Penzance to a violent financier. She escaped soon as she could, bringing her daughter to the London stews. Poor Margaret Clap, daughter of a Limehouse wench, then an orphan and a harlot herself, till she discovered a certain kind of man who'd rather pay for her protection than her body. Now pipe down and watch.'

Mother Clap spread her hands before her with a grimace. 'Look at you beautiful lot; I've never seen such a likely bunch of outcast whores in all my days!' She stood back, shielding her eyes as she searched the hall, resting on the gallery. 'Bless my soul, if it ain't Queen Nelly Fump. Hey, Nell, I hear you went to the fayre last week and won best pig.' The crowd hooted with laughter. 'And I see Sweet Jacky's with you an' all. Such a good Christian girl, when the bishop says "turn the other cheek" she rolls over.'

'Shut yer trap,' shouted Jacky, jumping to her feet.

Mother Clap gave a hearty laugh. 'I'll shut my trap when you shut your legs.'

'I'll shut my legs, when your husband lets me.'

'I don't have a husband.'

'And I'll never shut my bloody legs!'

The crowd whooped and whistled. From her vantage point Verity could see a thousand little dramas being played out below, some happy, some titillating, some tearful. After so many years watching the Highgate boys from her attic window, she willed them all to be happy, herself included. She swallowed a gulp of wine and looked over at the entry door, noticing the frightened lad from earlier looking straight back at her, his face petrified. There was no time for Verity to wonder why the boy was so scared, for a sharp finger was jabbing her shoulder. It was George Lavender, now dressed in a lady's wig and loose lemon dress.

'Get up,' she hissed. 'These seats are for me and the Duchess.'

Verity went to move but was stopped by old Vivian Guzzle.

'Jacky and her new friend Verity are joining us in the gallery tonight, Lavender dear; find a couple of stools and sit on the end.'

Lavender was so furious her wig slipped, exposing a purple welt on her temple.

Verity looked up at her with a smile. 'I hope you're feeling better after—'

'I'm fine,' snapped Lavender, taking a stool and sitting down, her knees higher than her chin.

Her plump companion, the Duchess, gave Verity a timid nod, extending a hand. 'Pleasure to meet you; I'm Timothy Retti—' She coughed as Lavender's elbow connected with her ribs. 'That is to say, I am the Duchess of Camomile,' she blushed, pushing greasy ringlets from her round forehead. 'A silly name, I always forget it.'

'It is a grand name,' said Nelly Fump, pointing an accusatory finger. 'Befitting such a fascinating and high-born lady. Now hush and watch the show.' She gripped Thomas's leg (almost at the groin) and wiggled. 'I am approaching my favourite part.'

Mother Clap was still strutting around the stage. She pointed at a sozzled man halfway across the hall. 'Look at this one! I've seen her tonight, slugging wine like the puritans are coming back. Squeeze her nose and wine comes out. Squeeze her paps and beer comes out. Squeeze her arse and you'll get whisky. I don't know what comes out the front, but the measures are poor.'

The crowd split into peals of laughter, pointing and jeering at the wretch, who duly vomited and collapsed on her painted face.

Mother Clap stamped her boot. 'Oh gawd, get her out. Where's Lotty when I need her?'

Jacky leaned out, and shouted, 'She ain't here, Clap. Door's been unguarded all night.'

A ripple of concern spread through the crowd. Mother Clap shielded her eyes and peered over to the far door.

'Is that so? My Lotty, away from her post? Well, my sweethearts, I reckon I'd better stand there myself.' She pulled back her shoulders and flexed her arms to show off the preposterously padded muscles in her sleeves. 'After all, guarding's a man's job, ain't it?'

She gestured to either side of the stage, calling her plumed creatures to line up behind her. The spinning lamps were gone from their heads now, replaced with tall crowns of shimmering peacock feathers. They had flaccid tails too, which swept the stage as they moved their hips in a slow shimmy to the rising drum.

Mother Clap thrust her legs apart. 'Come along then, girls,' she said, raising her hands as though her outstretched fingers controlled the growing power of the beat. She wiggled her shoulders and the fiddle began a continuous high note. 'Rip your stitches, my bitches.' She gave an evil grin, flashing her eyes as the mollies began tearing their dresses from their naked shoulders. She pointed into the crowd. 'Stamp the floor, whores.' The drum beat louder and faster as every foot in the place pounded in unison. The feathered creatures moved towards the front of the stage, their tails growing erect at their backs. Clap raised her hat, shaking pink sparkles to the floor. 'Empty your cups, sweet harlots!' She reached out with lightning at her fingertips, clawing her nails through the smoky air as she boomed a battle cry:

'Pull up your skirts! Push out your paps! Show us your arses, you're at Mother Clap's!'

Wild applause swirled around the room like a tempest, her voice sailing above it all like the whistle of a hurricane. 'Whoever you love, whoever

you are, we shall always be righteous ... always be free ... and...' The room
bent inwards, and the crowd erupted, joining in one single voice:

'ALWAYS TOGETHER!'

The peacock tails fanned out behind Mother Clap in a glorious blaze
of iridescent feathers, enveloping her in green and blue fronds.

And when they parted, she was gone.

CHAPTER TWELVE

Gabriel groaned as he rushed up the lantern-lit passageway from Field Lane. It was his own fault for being so late – Mother Clap would give him a tongue-lashing, he knew, but what choice had there been? Stuck at home with Henry and Bet, then ... well, a madness had called him to the cathedral. Thank God for the young stranger who'd spotted him and waved.

He heard footsteps approaching above him and mounted the stairs just as young Martin Lightbody came running the other way with a frantic expression on his face. He was going so quickly he didn't spot Gabriel until it was too late and he crashed directly into him.

'Woah there,' said Gabriel, catching him around the middle. 'What gives, Martin?'

The lad looked back along the gangway, then gripped Gabriel around the stomach. 'Danger!' he said. 'There's a rat at Mother Clap's.'

'A rat?' said Gabriel. 'What do you mean?'

'Just saw him!' said Martin, desperately trying to wriggle free. 'In there now, I saw him! Let me go.'

But Gabriel held tight, lifting the lad off his feet. 'Saw who?' he demanded.

'I won't say. They'll cut my throat, Lotty. I warn you, there's a false molly in there tonight. A bad one. I saw him this morning, after I outran the hounds, he was talking to stewards from the Society for Reformation of Manners, right there in their own quarters.'

'A molly, talking with the Society?'

'A false molly, I said. A rat! He was talking with them, close as comrades, I tell you, and now he's in there. He saw me, I know he did. Looked at me just now with his eyes sharp enough to cut my throat. Let me go or I'll tell everyone you're a molly, Mister Griffin. And I'll tell everyone where Clap's is too if you don't let me go.'

Gabriel threw him to the gangway. 'Tell who you like about me, boy, but breathe a word about Clap's and I'll rip your arms off.'

Martin picked himself up and gave Gabriel a suspicious look. 'Call yourself the molly guard. You can't keep any of us safe. You're just a fat old sod like the rest of them. Ugly Lotty Lump, the coward. They all laugh at you, you know. They say you cry when nobody's looking.'

Gabriel caught him by the collar and carried him like a sack of wheat back along the gangway. 'Stop trembling lad, you're going to point me to this rat of yours.'

'Never! He'll have me killed, I know it.'

'Hush yer gums. Won't give him the chance; we know what to do with spies.'

After all, it wouldn't be the first time the Society had sent men into a molly house to entrap sodomites. They were always so obvious, dressing too clumsily, speaking in silly voices, wearing their mothers' wigs. They were booted out soon as they pranced in, then handed over to Mother Clap's mysterious protector who – it was said – made sure the imposters were sent away on the ships before they could go wagging their tongues. Gabriel wondered for the thousandth time who this protector might be. Surely someone important – how else could they make the Society's foot soldiers vanish without an uproar?

He lifted the struggling lad over his shoulder and stepped back inside the hall. The peacocks were already strutting the stage to the beat of a favourite song, men cheering from the balcony as the floor boiled with dancers. Gabriel kicked the door shut behind him, and dropped Martin to the floor.

'Right then, look about. Where's this rat?'

'I see him,' said Martin. 'There he is. That's the molly right there.'

Gabriel looked up, following the lad's finger across the height of the room to the far end of the gallery, where a row of mollies were enjoying the show, swinging their cups of wine. He knew most of them by sight: Old Nelly Fump and her companion, Vivian Guzzle. Sweet Jacky the harlot cutpurse, then miserable Lavender and her sweetheart, the Duchess of Camomile. There was only one molly he didn't recognise. Gabriel felt the floor drop below his feet. His head became light and his heart thumped in double-time to the drum. The young man's skin was as white as the inside of a shell, his straight nose and strong jawline carved in perfect symmetry. Every part of him was strong and slender, so nicely proportioned, so pleasantly arranged, that Gabriel thought he must be a Greek statue come to life.

'And where the Hell have you been?' came a voice, snapping him from his stupor. Mother Clap was marching through the hall, throwing drunken mollies to the floor.

'Had things to do.'

'Things to do? Things to do! Was being my guard not a *thing to do*? Was keeping us all safe not a *thing to do*? I have been up on that stage filling time with my nonsense waiting for your arse to come walking through that door. Lord, what if the night watch had discovered us without you being here, eh? I can tell you what.' She stepped up, prodding him on the chest. 'Chained up in Newgate, that's what, while half of these sweet fellows kiss their mothers goodbye at Tyburn. Oh, but never worry,' she said with a theatrical shrug, 'Lotty Griffin turns up past eleven in her daytime garb and no face because she had *things to bloody do*!'

'Three years today, Clap,' said Gabriel. 'They left me.'

Mother Clap was about to respond, her finger frozen at his face, when she turned away, rubbing her forehead. 'Today?'

'Ay, today. Forgive me.'

She scraped off her hat and wig, smoothing her black hair over her scalp. 'Darling Lotty, forgive *me*, I clean forgot. Christ, three years today. God, don't it go quick?' She stepped up to Gabriel and took his huge hand in hers, squeezing it. 'Daft thing, still worrying about them up there when you're down here in Hell with the rest of us sinners. Why, they should be worrying about you, not t'other way round. Probably are.' She shifted, catching Gabriel's eye. 'You been up on that scaffolding again, ain'tcha? I can see it in your face, ye daft bugger.' She punched him on the arm and stood back. 'Well you're here now; better late than buried. Hold the door, and I'll send some hot beers your way along with your pay for the week.'

She went to leave, but Gabriel grabbed her elbow, looking up at the six men on the gallery. 'Beer can wait.'

Clap wrestled her arm free. 'Said no molly ever.'

Gabriel chucked his thumb over his shoulder. 'Young Martin here reckons we've got a spy from the Society sniffing about.'

'Martin who?'

Gabriel looked behind his back. The young lad was gone, the door swinging open. He charged outside just in time to see the lad running around the far end of the warehouse, his shrinking figure sprinting over the crooked struts then down the steps into the passageway beyond.

'Poor lad,' muttered Gabriel. 'If there is a rat, no way you'll outrun him now.'

He tutted to himself and turned back towards the doorway, then stopped, a cold shiver running across his shoulders. He felt it before he saw it, a mere slip of something in the corner of his eye, beckoning him with its silent glare. He glanced and there it was, some hundred yards across the stretch of wasteland, standing on a far gangway. A wraith in a black cloak, which fell from its head to its feet, only its face visible: such a face as Gabriel had never seen before. White as bone, the unblinking eyes staring out, as though peeping through a sheep's skull. A vision of death itself, it was, and Gabriel sensed a blow of crisp wind as the figure raised its arm and pointed towards him without a word.

'What is this?' murmured Gabriel. 'Who are you?'

But he already knew, for the vision could not have been a more perfect rendering of Death, and the dark angel was an acquaintance he knew too well.

Part Two

CHAPTER THIRTEEN

Justices Grimp and Myre sat behind a butcher's table in a barn, false noses stuffed with herbs strapped about their heads like ravens' beaks to ward off the putrid stench.

'Calm, please,' said Justice Grimp, as a rotten egg flew over his head.

Justice Myre stirred, scanning the faces of the crowd. How dirty he felt – how utterly rancid – subjected to the odour of so many sweaty peasants and their sordid lives.

Parson's Dell was a sinful ditch, squatting in the valley of a turgid river like the crack of an unwiped arse. Precisely why the village had been built in such an incommodious location nobody knew, yet just as people tend to suffer insufferable marriages, so the community persisted in the swamp, feeling more compelled by tradition than opportunity.

There were two accused wretches: a pair of local boys who, to the horror and disgust of all Christian men, had been discovered deep in the Devil's act. The younger lad's own father had chanced upon them in the bog, their sinful bodies entangled like eels.

Grimp paused to smooth his silver hair below his peruke. He checked his notes, tapping his finger on a particular point of evidence. It was the younger lad, William Berry, who had been the recipient, thus Samson faced the full charge of sodomy, though he had already dispatched himself from an apple tree, so it didn't matter.

The judge looked up at the crowd, sucking a fortifying cloud of air though his herb-stuffed nostrils. The barn this Sunday afternoon was charged with a violent atmosphere, the midsummer heat twisting the beams above their heads, making them squeak like witches.

Master Berry was standing before the bench, staring at his mother. She had sworn upon the Bible that her darling child was no sodomite, yet his father, a squat fellow with no ears and a forehead like a shovel, gave a more compelling testimony. He had shown the court his son's torn and stained breeches, then performed a spirited impression of the scenes he had witnessed, mimicking the boys' various movements with all the gusto of a mummer. No entreaty from his wife could shut him up, and it was a relief to all when the man at last exhausted himself, turning to his friends, who patted his dripping back in admiration of his bravery.

Justice Grimp nodded to his companion and lifted his stuffed nose to take a sip of beer.

'Now then,' he sighed, setting his mind to judgement, 'such a sorry affair.' He peered down at the boy before him, whose skinny arms and legs were shackled in chains. 'Come,' he said, 'look at me, Master Berry, do not be afraid.'

The lad raised his eyes with a sniff. 'Sir?'

'You repent your grievous sins, do you not? I can see it in your eyes; you are truly sorry for what you have done? Say so.'

'I have no sin to repent, sir. We was only fighting.'

His father folded his arms and looked away with a huff.

Grimp smiled. 'Come now, lad. I was young once; it is quite normal for unchecked lusts to lead young men up the mucky path. Such ways are often sprinkled with merry blossoms and sweet scents, are they not, Justice Myre?'

'Move along,' replied the old justice, squinting at his notes.

Grimp shook his head with a happy chuckle. 'Master Berry, you are not the first young man to ride the Devil's horse.'

'I did not ride a horse, sir.'

'Liar!' snapped Justice Myre, shooting his hand across the table like a whip, stabbing the air with his quill.

Justice Grimp placed a calming hand on his colleague's arm. 'Two days and so many hours in court, yet still we search for the truth. Such a pity the Samson boy hanged himself before we arrived, or we might have spared his life.'

'Another soul lost amidst the wanton baubles of the apple tree,' intoned Myre. 'Womanish men are no less tempted by sin than Eve.'

'Indeed, good Myre,' said Grimp. 'I mean, really, good people' – he glowered at the restless crowd like a schoolmaster – 'I must say it is quite infuriating when common folk take the king's justice into their own hands. Law is not to be dandled by the peasantry. Already, one soul lost, his family banished in shame, and here...' He reached out to the lad in chains, beckoning for him to stand. 'Look at him. Is he such a demon? A bright and popular young fellow, by all accounts; his life ahead of him, trussed up like a common highwayman for petting a friend?'

'He's a molly boy, that's what he is!' came a shout from the back of the barn, where a large-bosomed woman sat atop a cow.

'Ay,' came another voice from the middle of the scrum. 'Damn the pretty fellow!'

'And what sort of damnation does he deserve, pray tell?' asked Grimp, arching his fingers.

'Pillory!' shouted the boy's father.

'Whipping!' squeaked a girl.

Justice Grimp rolled his eyes. 'Pillory and whipping. Honestly. What a cruel society we are to one of our own.'

'Please,' begged the boy's mother, crawling on her knees to her son, kissing his broken fingers. 'Spare him.'

Justice Myre rested his quill and gave an almost imperceptible nod to his associate, who nodded back, fixing his glasses above his false nose with a ceremonial flourish.

'Hush now,' said Grimp, offering a kindly smile. 'Let us find a happy resolution.' He nodded impatiently at the lad, who was shaking from head to toe. 'You are accused of a horrible crime, to wit that you did use yourself with another man to the dishonour of God and the outrage of mankind. Yet there is scant evidence.' He tapped his fingers together with a cheerful wink, always at his best when a soul was ripe for the saving. 'Really, I'm not sure why we're here at all; the lad is innocent!' He looked at the prisoner and smiled. 'Have you nothing more to say?'

The boy looked around the barn, then lost all strength and collapsed in relief, clasping his shackled hands together in gratitude. 'Only that I am sorry to my ma and pa for causing them such grief.'

The words had barely left the boy's lips when Justice Myre began spluttering.

'Ah now,' said Justice Grimp, leaning back, his eyes haunted by a sudden misery, 'an apology, is it? Well, my lad, what a pity, what a pity. That does rather change things. Let us see what we can do about that.' He closed one eye, turning to his companion. 'It ought to be *hanging*, wouldn't you say?'

'Hanging, most certainly,' said Justice Myre, and indeed he had already written as much on his papers.

The boy, who had been whispering his prayers, peered up from the floor, astonished. 'Hanging, sir?'

'Marvellous,' said Grimp, shaking out his long sleeves. 'Hanging by the neck it is, very nice. Will you make a note of that for me, Justice Myre?'

'I will, Justice Grimp.'

'Do you have the ink?'

'I do.'

The boy stuttered. 'Justices, no.'

Myre shot across the desk. 'Justices, yes! Let this be a lesson to you in your final minutes. Vice is grown to a great and lamentable pitch in this wicked age, and a man who has God in his heart might still have the Devil in his breeches. Spare us your tears, wicked demon.'

'Indeed,' said Grimp, settling his fellow justice with a gentle hand. 'My boy, you have confessed; now you must try to be brave for your mother.'

'Confessed?'

'Absolutely,' said Grimp, clicking his fingers for Myre's attention. 'Unless – am I mistaken?'

'No, you are quite correct,' said Justice Myre, holding up his notes. 'As our ears heard it, so I recorded it. "I am sorry," you said, in those words precisely, and if that is not an acknowledgment of your foul deed, then what is?'

'I was only saying sorry to my ma and pa for their distress.'

'Quite a turning point at such a late stage,' said Grimp, tutting to himself. 'Thank goodness you admitted your dirty secret in time. Why, I was about to let you off with a spell in the pillory.'

The boy let out a whimper, a puddle of water appearing at his feet. He begged to be given a moment, sinking to the straw before his mother, weeping that he was afraid to die. And then he was dragged away squealing by his friends.

Grimp applauded, calling after the sorry knave, 'William Berry, you are found guilty of the criminal act and grave sin of sodomy. You are a disgrace to your father, and an enemy to God. I have therefore sentenced you to be hanged by the neck at the earliest opportunity until you are dead. May the Lord have mercy on your soul.' And with that he stepped over the boy's mother, flinching as she screamed.

William Berry was taken directly to the edge of the village and lifted into the noose by his kicking legs. With merciful speed, he dropped and dangled with watering eyes, the gibbet creaking until, after some dreadful minutes, his father lifted his son to his shoulders. The boy gasped as the rope slackened around his throat.

'Thank you, Pa; I won't do it again, I—'

They were his last words, for his father quickly kneeled hard to the floor, wrenching the miserable sinner's neck from his skull, and with a dull crunch, all was done.

There was a hot silence as the body jerked, a final tear rolling down the lad's purple cheek, and then the birds returned to the corn, and the creatures snapped twigs in the forest, and a cart trundled along the Big Road across the way, and the vegetables grew, no doubt, and the animals fattened with meat and milk, and the broad solemnity of the sky began to patter the trees with drizzle, and wasn't it everyone's fancy that the heavens were pleased?

Later that evening, in the bedchamber of a peaceful coaching inn some six miles south of Parson's Dell, Justice Spiritus Grimp settled into his bedclothes and turned to Justice Praisegod Myre.

'Well,' he yawned, 'the Lord's day was kind to us, all in all.'

'Kind enough.'

Grimp took up his annotated sketches of the condemned lad's anatomy and peered at them in the gentle flicker of the candlelight.

'What a waste of a young life. What a terrible waste. Damn you, Satan, foul catamite.'

With a sigh, he placed the pictures to one side and yawned dreamily. 'Next stop, Craven Hill.' He studied his partner, who was making a queer squeaking sound, a letter grasped in his bony fingers. 'Do you hear me, Praisegod?' said Grimp with a frown. 'Craven Hill next, I say.'

Justice Myre turned to face him from his bed, and Grimp gasped to see such a sight, for the man's eyes were wild with excitement. In the dim light, his cheeks were like clay pressed up by invisible thumbs, so that his teeth were bared in a lusty grin.

'Correct,' replied Justice Myre, folding up the letter. 'And in Craven Hill, we shall meet a rat.'

CHAPTER FOURTEEN

Thomas woke up with the lids of one eye stuck together and his tongue rough as a dog's backside. He could hear boatmen shouting beyond the walls, birds pattering across the tiles above his head. He smacked his lips and sniffed his own putrid breath then rolled sideways to shield his burning eyes from the light. Monday morning, and the air was boiling hot, while the charging river below was goading his bladder. The building swayed as he lifted himself up and placed his feet gingerly on the floor, rubbing his face. How had he found his way home? He couldn't remember a thing. It had been well past dawn, he knew that much. He looked down at his clothes, tangled around his feet, and spoke a name he only half recognised.

'Verity True-tongue.'

Who was she? It took a few seconds before he remembered. Verity True-tongue was Thomas True, and yet ... was Thomas True Verity True-tongue? He rubbed his face and spoke it once more, thinking it a strange and awkward thing, like a pair of shoes two sizes too small. It didn't matter; he was accepted and he had made friends. Or – a vision returned of Verity dancing shirtless with peacocks, accidentally elbowing a frog-faced man in the chin – had he made friends or alienated them?

He groaned, scratching his chest, and made his way to the hole where the window used to be. Undoing his breeches, he sent a long torrent of water to the river below and stretched his arms over his head.

'Morning!'

He jumped in surprise and looked over his shoulder to see the Squinks standing together at the top of the stairs, their bright faces filled with perky sunshine. How long had they been standing there? He buttoned his breeches as quickly as he could.

'Abigail!' he said, slipping on a stocking and bumping his head on a low beam. 'Uncle, Aunt – hello there, is everything alright?'

'Wonderful,' said Uncle Squink with a confused smile, watching his nephew stuff his bare foot into the sleeve of his shirt. 'Is that how you get dressed in Highgate, dear boy? In London, we tend to wear shirts on our backs.'

'Oh,' said Thomas, swallowing acid. 'Yes, of course, silly of me.'

'I see my apprentice has much to learn besides candle craft.'

Thomas looked up to see the man waggling a long pair of beeswax candles, his eyebrows jumping up and down in a suggestive manner.

'Yes, I do have a lot to learn.' He belched and in his effort to cover his mouth, slipped on his discarded periwig and fell to his knees with a *thump*. 'Are we starting today?'

'Not until we've had a lovely hot cup of honey,' said Aunt Squink, pressing her husband's candles down with a firm hand. She held up a sheaf of paper and a quill. 'I should very much like to hear about my sister, she being too busy to visit me in spite of my ankles, and I thought we might discuss your board and lodging.' She looked around the room, her nostrils twitching. 'You will want to get all that nasty financial business out of the way so you can relax in your new quarters.'

The building creaked and tipped sideways.

'Oh,' said Thomas. 'Yes of course, I would be happy to pay for my keep a month in advance.'

'A month? Three months at least, I should think.'

'Three months seems a little much.'

She dropped her smile like a hot pan. 'Whatever suits, I suppose. I assumed you needed a room for longer.'

With a wrenching sound far below their feet, the building creaked.

'I do,' said Thomas.

'Well then, let us agree six months in advance and then we needn't worry. If you choose to leave us earlier than that, we can spare you the nastiness and give you one quarter of a month back.' She gave Uncle Squink a glare. 'Perhaps now, at last, we might employ someone to fix this house.'

Abigail tutted. 'Mother, can't all this wait? And Father, must he really start messing around with your stinking string and tallow pots today? Dear Thomas only arrived yesterday, and look at him: a full night's rest and still he's exhausted. Hardly surprising coming all that way from Highgate. I should think he'll be sleepy for a week. Besides,' she said, holding up an arrangement of cheap linen embroidered with pink flowers, 'I want Thomas to walk with me to the park so I can show everybody my new cap.'

Thomas managed to push his feet into his shoes and do up his shirt. He turned, leaning an elbow against the wall, and assured all three of his eager relatives that he would be downstairs for rent payment, honey tea, chandlery and parading in a trice, as soon as he'd attended to his morning scrub and enjoyed a little bread and cheese, if they had any.

Contented, they left him to wipe himself down and slap on his periwig, and in minutes he was licking the insides of his mouth in anticipation of sweet tea and sustenance. On the way down he stopped at Abigail's bedchamber door, opening it a crack to take a peek inside. It was impossibly tiny, with a low bed by the open window, which, just like Thomas's quarters, looked out along the river to the west of the city and up towards the cathedral. There were little scratches in the yellow paint by the sill, marking off the days. Thomas had done the same thing in his attic room at the rectory, counting down to his daring escape. *Poor Abigail*, he thought. *No need to escape now though. I'm here for you.* He looked at a table against the wall, stepping closer to inspect its contents. There were delicate flowers of every kind sprinkled over a silver tray, and woodland creatures too, all of them fashioned from wax in the most breathtaking detail. He picked up a mouse with miniature feet and wavy fur etched with a careful fingernail into its back. Thomas held it close to his eye, admiring its delicate snout and hazelnut eyes. Abigail had made its body a little too long perhaps, its face a touch too square, yet it truly was a work of a most talented sculptress. He sniffed the animal, enjoying the scent of the beeswax, then placed it gently back on the table.

He paused. What else had taken place the previous night at Clap's? He could remember right up to the thrilling moment the peacocks had spread their tails and then ... then the huge man down by the entry with his stern brow and muscular torso had appeared and...

It was no use. He pressed the heels of his hands into his eye sockets to quell the thumping in his head. There was an indistinct face, and a voice asking him intrusive questions. Carnal questions, he was sure, though the specific words eluded him. It was less a memory, more an uncomfortable feeling. Yes, one of his new friends had made him unhappy ... Oh, what did it matter? Thomas had left before the dancing was over, stumbling back along the gangway to Field Lane, where ... he blinked, doubting his memory ... where he'd been followed as he descended alongside that stinking ditch, tripping over his own feet. He'd looked up from the ground to see a cloaked figure passing above him, the sight of a hideous, distorted face. There was nothing he could remember after that, other than a few brief flashes of his stumble home to the tolling of bells.

He stretched his neck and lowered himself carefully down the steep staircase of the candle shop, willing himself to endure what promised to be an arduous day.

CHAPTER FIFTEEN

Gabriel passed into the heart of London, yawning as old Peter the horse clopped down the hill. It had been a sleepless night, for Gabriel had been thinking endlessly of Martin Lightbody, fearing the worst for the daft lad. Who was this 'rat' he was on about? Martin had implied the Society's spy wasn't the usual imposter; this devil was a molly himself. What sort of a man would betray his friends, his own kind, knowing they would likely hang? For the hundredth time, he went over the six men Martin had gestured towards. Fump and Vivian? He shook his head. They were too ancient, too silly, too good-hearted. Sweet Jacky then? Yes indeed, she was a knave, no doubt about that, but as Jack Huffins, he never stole from mollies: that was his own rule, and as far as Gabriel knew, it was a principle he stuck to steadfastly. Why would a young man spare his friends' pockets, but not their necks? Who else was there? George Lavender, of Smithfield Market. A laughable character in many ways, hateful to others, it was true – but could a scrawny pile of twigs like that work for the Society? It was a sure way to cut his own neck, but still ... not impossible. Then there was the Duchess. Gabriel shook his head. That chinless looby, Mister Rettipence from the Royal Exchange, who arrived every Sunday night at Clap's, wringing his hat in his hands, unable to look anybody in the eye. Not only that: he had a wife and two children. All of which left the last man Gabriel had seen: the beautiful stranger sitting high in the gallery, watching the dancing below, a gentle look on his face and a clean, carefree smile.

Gabriel shook the memory from his head as they drove down Fish Street towards the bridge, Henry still snoring in the back of the cart. The image of the young man had joined Gabriel in his dreams, for shame, and they had been sinful together. Smooth skin, athletic proportions, long, muscular legs. Could such a pretty fellow be a rat? Impossible, he wasn't even a fully inducted molly yet. Gabriel had asked Jacky about him at the end of the night and got little sense for his trouble. Thomas True was the man's name, apparently, and he'd only arrived that morning. A rector's son of all things, soon to be a chandler's apprentice on the bridge.

Thomas True.

Gabriel imagined the curls of blonde hair around his ears. He would have smooth hands and square fingernails. Gabriel looked at his own calloused fingers with a groan. The young man would have a lean stomach too, he knew it, and shoulders round as apples, and smooth—

Henry snorted and sat up, coughing. 'Where am I?' he said, smacking his lips and kicking Gabriel's tool bag away. 'Get off me, foul wench.'

Gabriel squinted. 'Fool.'

Henry climbed onto the bench beside him.

'Why we heading to the bridge, Gabe? We should have been on the scaffolding hours ago.'

'It's all agreed with the foreman: dusk still comes late this time of year, and we can work past dark. Reckon with you and Bet having a baby, we'd better find some new work – said so yourself.' He nodded over his shoulder, and Henry reached back to pull up a placard. There were words daubed across it in clumsy blue letters:

MR. GRIFFIN AND MR. SYLVA

QUALITY MEN

AVAILABLE NOW, ALL OFFERS

Henry chuckled. 'All offers, Gabe? What we after, work or women?' He held the board above his head, waving as they rolled past a gaggle of cockle-maids. 'Henry Sylva does a solid job,' he called to them. 'They don't call me Hardwood Henry for nothing.'

The women threw fistfuls of cockles at him, their shells clattering against the cart. He shook his fists at them in mock outrage before turning back to Gabriel.

'Here, where did you go last night? No lies – I heard you sneaking out. That's why I ended up in trouble. Thought I might follow you to a tavern for a few beers.'

'Supposed to wet the baby's head after it's born, not before.'

Henry tipped his hat to a pair of market-garden ladies carrying truckles of herbs. 'The wetter the better.'

Gabriel drew the cart up on Fish Street Cross, the roar of the river assaulting his ears, along with the caterwauling of so many fish sellers and wherrymen.

'Never mind where I was,' he said, climbing down to a tying post, fetching the sign to set against the cart. 'Had some work to do, that's all.'

'Whatever you say, Gabe. I'll fetch us some beers for the heat.'

Gabriel rubbed the sweat from his face. It was too hot for a man of his size, though his leathery skin proved he'd suffered the same torture for approaching thirty summers. He pulled the wide brim of his hat over his eyes and peeped at the crowd streaming from the bridge. London had been baking since morning, the August air vinegary with the stench of rotting meat and sweaty armpits. The sun burned white as a blister, and the houses and shops quivered in the oven as tumbril carts and carriages clunked by, heavy and sluggish with their goods. He pitied the poor horses gasping for water and fetched a bucket on a long rope from the back of the cart, making his way to the wharf. London Bridge loomed above him, offering a little shade, while below, the water thundered its vast mass between the struts. He set his heels against an iron loop and braced himself as the bucket hit the surface, pulling hard with the flow.

No, he thought, *none of them fellows in the gallery are likely to be Martin's rat.* One of the others then? There were hundreds of mollies in London, and more molly houses opening every week. Yet Martin had been clear: the rat was sitting in the gallery, right where those particular mollies were enjoying the show. Gabriel hoisted the bucket, carrying it back to Peter, who instantly plunged his long nose inside for a gulp. Gabriel patted him on his flank then went to stand beside the sign on the cart, nodding to passers-by.

P'raps Martin got it wrong, he thought. *P'raps he saw someone else, or got confused. Was only a young lad: a know-nothing, know-all, like most men his age.*

He leaned against a broken post, pushing the point deep into his backside for a much-needed scratch.

'Something in your eye, dear?' came a voice from the crowd.

Gabriel groaned. It was Nelly Fump, only without her ringlets, jewellery, makeup and gowns. In the daytime, he was plain old Nelson Fump, though he could hardly be described as such: his round body bedecked in a profusion of brocade and embroidery, set off with an enormous periwig and lace ruffles. The man fanned himself, wrinkling his pert nose at the painted sign.

'My goodness, Mister Griffin, has it come to this?'

Gabriel scowled. 'We're offering carpentry, nothing else.'

'Pity. Still, I'm sure we've got a few things in need of a good hammering on Covent Garden if you ever fancy a few shillings.'

'Leave the poor man alone,' said Mister Vivian, appearing with a wheelbarrow full of goat hair. His cheeks dripped with sweat and white powder. He caught sight of the sign and looked at it, concerned.

'Dear me, Mister Griffin, there are laws you know.'

Gabriel huffed, turning the sign around. 'Get away the pair of you, I'm not on the door now, I'm working.'

'Well, if you must hang about by London Bridge, dear,' said Fump. 'Such a common molly market these days. Scandalous place to be, I should say.'

Vivian frowned, patting his neck with a handkerchief before wringing it out like a washing rag. 'London Bridge, dear? A molly market? It never is.'

'It is indeed! Sweet Jacky told me ... I mean to say,' Fump added with a conspiratorial wink, 'Master Jack Huffins.' He cocked his head to the crossing. 'The filthy knave says there's no better way to pass an afternoon than parading across the bridge, watching men shoot between the legs.'

Gabriel rolled his eyes and inspected the crowd, unsettled by Fump's loud voice. His was an amusing act for Mother Clap's Molly House, but for the bustling streets of London on a Monday afternoon, it was far too much ribbon and song.

'Got to work,' he said, catching sight of Henry returning with two slopping jugs of beer. 'Be off with you.'

Mister Vivian spoke discreetly now. 'We shall do as you say, Mister Griffin, but tell us first about this Society stooge poking about Mother Clap's. Fellow calling himself...' he looked around '...the Rat. What is it all about; are we to worry?'

'Gossip,' said Gabriel. There was no sense telling his friends what he'd heard, not yet anyway, for they were liable to fret and, in their fretting, turn the whole situation into a riot.

Mister Fump pursed his lips. 'You are so secretive, Lotty. There must be *something* going on.'

'Call me Lotty in daylight once more and I'll knock your teeth in.'

'Good gracious,' said Mister Fump, clutching his companion's wrist. 'Mister Griffin is a rampant bear in the daytime. Protect me – I shall be bitten!'

Henry arrived, setting the beers on the cart and turning to Fump and Vivian with a curious frown. He took in their patterned stockings, buckled shoes, powdered faces and ornamental wigs and stuck his fists to his hips. 'Morning, ladies; fayre's back in town, is it?'

'Bitch!' said Fump, marching away as Vivian hobbled after him with the wheelbarrow.

Henry watched them go, clicking his tongue. 'If I didn't know better, Gabe, I'd say that was a pair of pretty fellows, like what the Society's hunting down.' He raised his eyebrows, shaking his head. 'That's something I'll never understand. Fellows lusting after fellows. What's there to play with on a man, eh? Apart from the obvious, but...' He mimed being sick, swigging the thought down with a hefty slug of beer. 'Still,' he added, fetching the board up to his chest, 'I don't care what they get up to, long as they pay on time.'

'They only wanted to prattle,' said Gabriel. 'No work.'

'Ah well, no matter. This is a good idea of yours, Gabe. Not done this since our old men kicked the bucket.'

He held his thumb up to a gentleman and his wife, who stopped momentarily to read the sign then rushed away towards the bridge as soon as they saw Gabriel with his shirt hanging open. Henry lowered the board, dejected.

'Gawd Gabriel, do yourself up, will you? What sort of customer's gonna go for a carpenter looking like a seven-foot bear?'

'Hello there,' said a young man with a bright smile. He was making his way over the road, a woman walking with him, her gloved hand rested on his arm.

Gabriel lowered his jug of beer from his mouth, spilling half of it down his front. It was Thomas True.

CHAPTER SIXTEEN

Gabriel caught the young man's eye momentarily then looked away, shielding his burned face with his hand. How ugly he felt, how round and clumsy and red. The young man was crunching an apple, his lips pressing against the flesh of the fruit as juice dribbled down his chin. Gabriel tried to speak, only for a tingling pain to dash across his ribs. A pain it was, though not an unpleasant one, rather like his heart was about to sneeze. He covered the patches of sweat beneath his arms and pulled his hat low.

'Good day, Mister True.'

The young man coughed up a chunk of white apple, as his companion looked at him in surprise.

'Sir,' she said, 'you know my cousin?'

Henry folded his arms, looking at Gabriel with a puzzled expression. 'Ay, you two know each other?'

Gabriel realised his mistake and shook his head in a panic, struggling to think of an explanation.

Mister True cleared his throat. 'Why, yes, of course we know each other. This is Mister ... er—'

'Griffin,' said Gabriel.

'Yes, Mister Griffin is a...' he looked down at the sign '...carpenter who did...' his eyes goggled at Gabriel, desperate for help.

'Carpentry,' said Gabriel.

'Yes, he did carpentry for my father,' said Thomas.

'In Highgate?' said Abigail.

'Of course in Highgate, where else?'

'Ay, in Highgate it was,' said Gabriel.

Henry knitted his eyebrows. 'When were you in Highgate, Gabe?'

Gabriel batted him away. 'Long time ago.'

'Oh, it was a very long time ago,' said Mister True, 'but my father says it's the finest shelf in the rectory.'

Henry snorted. 'A shelf? Must have been back in them lean days when you was saving up for the babe. All the way up the North Road for a shelf, ha ha!' He slapped Gabriel on the back, catching sight of the sign and grew solemn. 'Not so funny now I'm in the same spot.'

'Oh, you poor thing,' said Abigail. She went to touch Henry's arm, then saw his grimy coat and thought better of it. 'Are you both very poor?'

Henry hunched over and walked in a circle with an invisible bowl out-stretched. 'We are the poorest carpenters in all of Christendom, good, generous lady. Not a penny to rub together for a new wangle-hammer.'

Gabriel imagined running off the edge of the wharf into the river. He tried to look away from Mister True's face, yet he could not help himself. He was the most beautiful man – indeed the most beautiful *thing* – he had ever seen.

'Did you hear that, Cousin Thomas?' said Abigail in a fit of empathy, tears brimming in her eyes. 'Not even enough for a wangle-hammer.' Suddenly, a burst of sunshine lit up her face and she patted Thomas's arm. 'I have had an idea!'

She whispered into Mister True's ear, concealing her lips behind her hand. The young man looked sideways at Gabriel, giving little shakes of his head, yet before he could speak, Abigail was instructing the carpenters to visit Squink's Candles on the bridge the following week, that they might discuss a considerable amount of work on her father's property.

'It's perfect; both of you are desperate for paid work and we are desperate for carpenters; we have your lodging money now, Thomas, so I'm certain we can agree a rate between us.'

Gabriel listened in horror. He shook his head, but Henry cut across him before he could speak. 'Happy to talk terms, mistress, especially with such a pretty lady to bring us our beers, eh Gabe?'

Gabriel met Mister True's eyes and felt his heart stop. He could not think, was not breathing, felt himself plummet like a hammer through scaffolding. What was happening to him? He reached out to nothing then placed his fists inside his coat for precisely no reason, then wiped his face upwards as no man had ever done. This perfect being in front of him with so many colours of gold in his hair and those grey eyes – he never knew there could be beauty in grey eyes – and the smattering of freckles running over his cheekbones ... these details of the man's face left him transfixed, and...

Henry pulled Gabriel to the cart by his shoulder.

'What's wrong?' he hissed. 'You're as red as a radish.'

'Don't know.'

'Get yourself in order, these good people are about to give us work!'

Gabriel nodded, clearing his throat and turning back. 'We'll take the work.'

He made the mistake then of looking at Mister True's lips and had to bowl away to fetch the bucket, annoying old Peter, who was still enjoying his drink. Henry was just arranging a good time to visit the candle shop when a little boy came running up.

'Oi! You the Holborn pullers?' said the urchin, a dribble of slime running from his left nostril.

'Ay, that's us,' said Henry.

'You're needed; right away.'

Gabriel stepped back around the cart, his heart heavy. Usually, he would have chosen anything to avoid such a grim responsibility, but one more moment spent in the company of Mister True and he would have gone mad with embarrassment.

'Tell 'em we're on our way.'

Gabriel climbed onto the cart and tipped his hat to the young man and woman who stared up at him with expressions of concern.

'Enough mucking about, Henry. Business can wait. A body's in the ditch.'

CHAPTER SEVENTEEN

'Saint Peter's arse,' said Henry, slinging a coiled rope over his shoulder. He stepped carefully across the beam spanning the upper reaches of the Fleet Ditch. 'The stink's worse than ever down here.' He looked up at Gabriel, who was climbing after him from the open window of the warehouse, balancing a hooked pole on his shoulder. 'God tell me, what sins did our fathers commit to bequeath us this responsibility?'

It was one of London's grimmest jobs, dredging bodies from the ditch, yet somebody had to do it or the cut would clog. Besides, Gabriel and Henry were grateful for the few shillings they received for the nasty work.

Gabriel found the oak beam with his toe. He steadied himself, holding on to the slimy bricks and looked down at the gunnel of filth, which bubbled and wrinkled below their feet.

'Hush yer gums. We'll pull the body out and get back to the cathedral.'

He held out his pulling pole and found his balance. One slip and he'd fall into the soup, never to be seen again.

Henry tied his kerchief across his nose. 'Watch your feet now, Gabe, the damned thing's slippery with shit.' He stretched, reaching out to the wall on the opposite side of the ditch, tied his rope to an iron loop, then tossed the loose end below. The rotten carcass of a cat swam under their feet, its paws sticking up to the sky.

'Poor fellow,' said Henry. 'Must have eaten some of Bet's soup.'

Just then, a cloud of gas rose from a popped bubble and passed the groaning spectators. It reached a raven perched on an overhanging beam, which squawked and plummeted into the filth.

'There!' shouted a little girl, pointing to where the insensible creature had landed. 'It's a finger!'

Gabriel looked down and felt his heart twist. The girl was right: in the crook of the bird's wing was a human hand, poking through the surface of the ditch. It was covered in weed and grime. Gabriel's stomach tightened – he recognised it: those fingers had gripped his shirt the night before. He held his breath and readied himself for a new vision of horror, then looked up at the bridge to see a fierce-looking woman standing amongst the onlookers. She gave a regal nod. Mother Clap was dressed in a plain black suit with a high collar, her hair pulled up into a tricorn hat. She offered a consoling smile and stepped back.

There was a jostle in the crowd and two more spectators filled the empty space. Miss Squink was nibbling her lip, still gripping Mister True's arm, both of them looking down with horrified expressions. Gabriel swallowed his rising panic. The young man agitated him – the mere sight of his hands gripping the railing, the tight pinch of his waist broadening to the span of his shoulders.

'Body's half sunk,' said Henry.

Gabriel forced himself to concentrate, removing his eyes from the bridge. The dead hand sailed slowly towards the Thames, the open fist curled as though gripping an invisible cup. He remembered that hand too well, could feel it still, tearing at his arms to get away.

Henry was sliding towards the middle of the beam, steadying himself with his pole. 'Let's land this fish. I'm in no fit state.'

Gabriel thrust his pole as deep as it would go into the ditch until the hook found the unmistakable solidity of a human corpse. He pushed down with all his strength, the body tugging the hand below the surface. Gabriel nodded to Henry, who steadied himself then thrust his pole to the same spot and levered it up and down with groans of effort.

'There, Gabe,' said Henry. 'Got him.'

Gabriel flexed his shoulders, then heaved as hard as he could, steadying his boots as they slipped on the paling. The crowd gasped as, inch by inch, a shoulder pressed through the surface of the ditch, then an elbow, then a hip – and then the body screwed over and a full arm and torso resurfaced, partially clothed. Up came the pelvis in torn breeches, the ladies on the bridge feigning to look away. Gabriel glanced up to catch Mister True covering his eyes, while his woman friend stroked his arm for comfort.

'Here he comes, poor sod,' said Henry, a vein popping in his forehead. 'Easy now, Gabe, don't break the neck.'

Gabriel gritted his teeth, forcing himself to draw a lungful of foul air, ready for the last pull. He shut his eyes and grabbed the metal ring on the bricks by his shoulder then, with a roar like the Tower lions, dragged the pole with one arm to horrified exclamations from above.

Martin Lightbody appeared as though borne from Hell, his mouth filled with foaming liquid, eyeballs staring through a yellow membrane of urine-stained fat. Gabriel shut his eyes as he looped a rope around his back.

'Martin,' he muttered to himself, 'what did they do to you?'

CHAPTER EIGHTEEN

Gabriel and Henry hoisted the corpse through the wharf window then laid it out on the warehouse floor and sat themselves down on buckets, sucking air through cloths doused in vinegar.

'Young,' croaked Henry, touching the body's shoulder with his toe.

'Ay.'

'A boy, really. Barely a beard on him, look, Gabe.'

'Ay.'

'That exotic woman was there again in her strange garb. Reckon she kept looking at you.'

'Didn't notice.'

'Same as last time we pulled a boy with injuries like that.' Henry grimaced, looking at the slice across Martin's throat, the blood stains on his groin. 'And the time before that. Seemed to know you, I'd say.'

Gabriel rose suddenly, kicking his bucket across the floor. 'What if she did? There's the body, now we can go.'

Henry pulled his gag under his chin and picked up a fresh bucket. He sluiced the body a second time, the water running across the lad's face, his eyelashes dancing in the flow. He sucked air through his teeth, crouching down to take a closer look at the cut in his neck, the blood at his crotch.

'Reckon it's a pretty fellow by them mutilations. Another sodomite, sent to Hell by the Society; God forgive him.'

Gabriel furrowed his brow. 'Ay, God forgive him.'

'You recognise the face?'

'Why would I recognise the face?'

The silence hung between them, heavy with a hundred unspoken questions. Gabriel's mind was an inferno, horrible thoughts screaming out from the flames. Martin had been right: Mother Clap's had been infiltrated by the Society, and this spy, this *Rat*, must have silenced him. He kneeled down, pressing his fingers inside the lad's pockets, then stood up and moved to the wall for some privacy.

'Where do we take him?' said Henry. 'Usual?'

'Ay. You go back to work before we're given the boot; I'll manage it alone.'

Henry came over and placed his hand on Gabriel's shoulder. 'You alright, Gabe?'

'Ay.'

Henry nodded without another word, leaving for the cathedral. He wasn't gone a minute before a long shadow drew across the warehouse floor. Mother Clap was standing at the open doorway, smoking a pipe.

'Another one. Reckless boy, never cautious.'

'Young'uns shouldn't be cautious, or nothing would change.'

'Have you seen 'em? Dancing through the streets in their dresses, drunk on wine and their own pride? Daring ordinary folk to have a problem so's they can rail against it.'

'Only being themselves. No crime in that.'

'No crime,' said Clap, bending down to close Martin's eyes. 'Brave, if you like to see it that way, but dangerous an' all. It's innocence what kills you when yer different, not guilt. Gawd bless him, he lived longer than some.'

Together, Clap and Gabriel rolled the body up in a tarpaulin and carried it quickly to the cart.

'Walk on, Peter,' said Gabriel, and the horse shook his feathered hoofs and plodded away from the miserable ditch, up Gray's Inn Lane to the outskirts of the city, where a gentle track led around Black Mary's Hole to the shallow foot of a hill. Behind it stood a great pile of rubbish shaped like a sugar loaf, and behind that the crumbling walls of an abandoned chapel. There, they dug a hole between two rows of shallow mounds and placed the sleeping boy beside his friends, covering him over and saying a prayer.

Clap sat beneath an ancient oak tree, throwing stones into an empty grave. She fished a pie from her coat pocket.

'Eat, Lotty, you need some vittles after all that digging in this heat.'

He took the pie from her, gobbling it down before sitting on the opposite side of the grave, remembering a pond that used to be here, and even though there was nothing now but a hole, he imagined seeing his younger face reflected in the ripples of green water. It was a day long ago, when he and Henry had first discovered the chapel and climbed its walls before throwing rocks into the water to see who could make the biggest splash. Later, Henry had left, and Gabriel had sat alone in the grass, tormented and desperate. Even then as a boy, he knew he was too large, his head too fat, his veins too proud, his upper lip growing unsightly rabbit fur at the corners. He had done something terrible to Henry – something so sinful and embarrassing, he should have drowned himself.

Gabriel shook the painful memory away and looked at Clap. 'You got it wrong.'

'Wrong? Clap's never wrong, presumptuous cow.'

'Martin wasn't killed for dancing in the streets.'

'Only my guess,' said Clap with a shrug. She pulled up her petticoats and crossed her polished boots, the buckles twinkling in the sunshine. 'What was it then? Sucked on the wrong soldier, did he?'

Gabriel reached into his coat pocket and pulled out a slip of damp paper.

'What's that then?' said Clap, standing up to get a closer look.

'Found it in his breeches. Got a quick look before you showed up.'

Clap took the paper, unrolling it with her close-clipped nails, her clever eyes sliding from word to word as her face grew grim. The words on the note were stained by the water from the ditch, yet still legible:

Watch Your Mouth Molly. This Rat Bites

CHAPTER NINETEEN

The Black Bull Inn served some of the finest roast pork and potatoes in Herefordshire, not to mention their famed fritters and honey, so it was a welcome pleasure after a taxing day for Justices Grimp and Myre to settle in for a banquet beside the grumbling fire.

'The best possible outcome,' said Spiritus Grimp.

'Undoubtedly,' said Praisegod Myre.

'Certainly, the old man was guilty.'

'Certainly, he was.'

'Poor soul.'

'*Wretched* soul.'

'A particularly unrepentant sodomite for so advanced an age. Thank goodness we found him.'

'A lifetime of sin.'

'Eighty-four!'

'Eighty-four, and no more,' said Myre, chuckling to himself as he peeled a strip of skin from the cheek of his piglet. He sucked it into his mouth like a toad's tongue. 'If the good people do not delay.'

Justice Grimp looked out through the tavern window to the village green, which was quite empty in the dusky light, but for a gibbet, which stood unloved beside an empty casket.

'They ought to have hanged him by now. Perhaps they disagree with our judgement? Were we too harsh?'

'It is God's judgement, not ours. Let them carry out the deed in their own good time. For now, we have a visitor.'

A figure had appeared through the tavern door, shrouded in a camlet cloak. The Rat inspected each stool, table and cubby then approached with shifting, suspicious eyes.

'Justices?'

'You are most welcome,' said Grimp, examining the new arrival. 'And you are our friend?'

'I am your servant.'

'Prove it,' snapped Myre.

Justice Grimp held up his hands with a calm smile. 'Forgive my colleague, dear Rat. These are treacherous times; we see more than our fair share of knaves and ne'er-do-wells in our line of business, such is our burden. Our friends at the Society tell us you bear their mark, may we see it?'

The Rat showed them, exposing a symbol, drawn in blue ink.

'Well, well,' said Justice Grimp, inspecting their informant's face and clothes. 'What a queer creature you are.' He sat down, beckoning the Rat to follow. 'My colleague and I have been speculating as to whom our precious informant might be.' He tittered to himself, shaking his head. 'I concede neither of us was expecting you.'

Myre was busy forking a boiled eyeball from the piglet's skull. He popped it into his mouth and crushed it like a grape. 'Indeed.'

The two men duly smacked and slurped their way through their meal while the Rat looked on in silence. When at last the men had finished eating, they pushed their pigs' heads away – skulls picked clean – retrieved their quills and papers from their cloaks, and sat ready to consume their spy's intelligence.

Grimp's belly was full, yet his expression was hungry. 'We haven't long, and doubtless you will be missed in London. You do your soul great good by meeting with us, the Lord have mercy.'

'And justice?' said the Rat. 'Will she have mercy on me too?'

Myre coughed. 'She? She? God shows *His* mercy where it is earned. What ails you?'

'Murder. Already, terrible violence carried out by the Society hounds, and more to come.'

'These men you sympathise with, these sodomite evildoers, will die quicker and happier with a beating or a stabbing than they will at Tyburn. Besides, the sooner they die, the fewer sins to answer for in Hell. Do not see it as violence, dear Rat, consider it clemency. Now tell us what you know.'

The Rat looked from one to the other, then spoke in a whisper.

'Very well then. I was there, this Sunday past.'

'Where?' said Myre, readying his quill.

'A molly house on Field Lane, named Mother Clap's.'

Justice Grimp scratched the name into his notes, his tongue bitten at the corner of his mouth. *Mother Clap's...* he wrote. 'I have heard the name. So, it exists?'

'There are many such places in London, but hers is the biggest, boldest, and best loved. Hundreds go there, every Sunday night.'

'The Lord's day too, shameful creatures!' Grimp licked his lips. 'Why do they go there particularly, is it the size and quality of the men, perhaps...?'

The Rat gave him a level stare. 'She keeps pretty fellows safe.'

'We shall see about that,' chuckled Myre, the feathery tip of his quill tickling the hairs in his nostrils.

'She pays the marshal to keep his guards away.'

Myre slammed down his knife. 'Damn it, Marshal Queed! The very custodian of the law, the very *captain* of the king's good justice taking bribes?'

'Calm, calm, dear friend,' said Justice Grimp. 'Allow our Rat to speak.'

'I can give you names, if you have the money?'

Justice Grimp raised a finger, reaching into his pocket for a purse. 'As agreed.'

The Rat took the purse and tipped the coins onto the table. 'That is half the amount. So I will give you half the names.'

'Shrewd little Rat,' said Myre with a thin smile.

Grimp dipped his quill. 'That will do for now, and once the Society confirms your intelligence, you shall have the rest.'

The Rat began listing mollies, Myre scribbling them in a column of squirled letters. Deep in thought, Justice Grimp's eyes rose from his papers to the gibbet outside, where the villagers were at last hanging the elderly convicted sodomite from a makeshift noose. His expression grew in excitement until, by the end, he was grinning, ear to ear.

Myre held up his hands when the Rat was finished, then tore a crackled pig's ear from his plate, nibbling at it thoughtfully. 'A beast-like confederacy. Such ugliness, never encountered before.'

Grimp rubbed his legs. 'What a pretty society they sound with their peacock feathers and frilly gowns.'

'Such brazen mockery of the faith.'

'Little wonder the Society begs us to hasten our hooves to the great Sodom; I pity these men terribly.'

'Pity not the men who throw themselves into Hell,' said Justice Myre.

Grimp licked his lips with a look of abject sorrow. 'You do realise what will happen to these friends of yours, gentle Rat?'

'I do.'

'All of them will hang, God willing; it is the righteous thing to do, yet I confess, I'm not sure my conscience could carry such horror. Such things we do for money.'

'It's not the money I do it for,' said the Rat, picking up the purse.

Myre rapped the table with a snarl. 'Then why, vermin?'

The Rat looked through the window to the dangling body of the executed man. 'I have my reasons. But if I am to continue this work, I will need greater compensation.'

'More, greedy Rat?'

'Not for me. I was spotted by an over-curious molly boy and had no choice but to have his throat cut.'

'A mucky business, this,' said Grimp. 'The Society ought to carry out its work for its own reward.'

'The hounds need feeding, good Justice, or who knows which of us they'll bite next. Besides, there's another molly who may cause us some difficulty.'

'Meddlesome he-whores.'

The Rat nodded. 'Griffin's his name. Lotty when he's at Clap's. A giant, big as a bear. They call him the molly guard, and he is on my tail.'

CHAPTER TWENTY

Uncle Squink was standing proudly behind a peculiar wooden apparatus consisting of a cantilevered frame with sets of hooks, carefully dipping rows of candles into the molten wax. The whole room was filled with the putrid stench of mutton fat, the fresh air from the open window instantly lacquered with sticky grease.

'Now then, do you see how carefully I lower the donkey?' said Uncle Squink. He held up a finger. 'It is vital, good Apprentice, *vital*, that we should maintain a dry wick, lest our good customers complain our candles are difficult to light, wasting their precious stubs.'

Thomas felt Abigail's elbow jab his ribs and he looked up. 'Yes, Uncle,' he said. 'Very good, absolutely.'

Uncle Squink raised the donkey on the other side, the cantilever mechanism lowering the respective candles into the bubbling liquid. It was mesmerising, watching them grow fat, skin by skin, as the translucent wax wrapped their spindly bodies in fresh coats.

'These are not attractive candles,' declared Mister Squink in one of his characteristic outbursts, as though responding to some imaginary insult. 'Yet, do not presume they can be trifled with. They cannot be! Even the meanest tallow candle might offer light to a man's dying flame, or illuminate the face of a pretty girl on her wedding night. There is no such thing as an unimportant candle, Nephew Apprentice. No such thing!' He licked his lips, his face lit up like a Bedlam lunatic as the candles slipped and dipped in unison. 'What do I say, good daughter?'

Cousin Abigail sat up and recited the family motto with prim solemnity: 'Every candle matters, Father.'

'So it does,' replied Mister Squink, checking the tin below the pot was emitting just the right flame.

Precisely what 'the right flame' was, Thomas couldn't say, nor had he managed to count how many dips were necessary for each type of candle, nor had he yet been allowed to lay a single finger on the nodding donkey with its rows of hooks. He looked over at the loom where Aunt Squink was busy making wicks, and wondered if he wouldn't prefer to learn that part of the process instead, enjoying the threads as they passed over his fingertips. In truth, his heart wasn't in candle making at all, but if he was to stay on the bridge with his kind relatives, there was no choice but to feign interest. Which was difficult when his head was filled with so many exciting visions. Every time he closed his eyes, peacock feathers and dancing shadows paraded around him in a circle, flashing bare thighs and bare chests as his feet tapped a rhythm on the floor. No Wednesday had ever felt so far from a Sunday, and he felt as though every minute of the sluggish day was encased in opaque wax. There were other less titillating visions: a hook on a pole pulling a mottled arm from thick sludge. A startled face, screaming through a beer of yellow bubbles. The huge man, Mister Griffin, dragging the boy's body up with inhuman strength, his rippling arms tugging at the pole with a hard, muscular grip.

'Thick and firm!' came a voice, snapping Thomas from his daydream.

'Pardon?'

'The twin pillars of the chandler's art,' said Uncle Squink, rounding the donkey to thrust a freshly dipped candle into Thomas's lap. It was hot still from the well, burning his legs.

Thomas nodded, holding the candle in his hands, smoothing the velvety wax with his fingertips. 'Thick and firm, Uncle.'

'You see?' said Uncle Squink, lifting a pair of candles from their dandle-hook and pointing them at his wife. 'I told you, he's a natural. Observe the lust in his eyes. His parents' blood may run hot for Christ, but Thomas clearly has a passion for a good, sturdy candle.'

'I can see,' said Aunt Squink, without looking up. She gave a thin smile to her threads. 'How fortunate we are to have Thomas with us.' She raised her eyes. 'My sister has written to express her relief after your unexpected departure from Highgate, nephew. She asks me to watch over you closely, to protect you from any sinful temptations.' She rocked her foot against the pedal, the loom clunking as she held his eye. 'What temptations might those be, I wonder?'

Thomas looked up from his candle and blinked. 'I don't know. She thinks of London as an evil place. I concede I left without telling my parents, or they might have kept me from my passion.'

'Your passion?' said Aunt Squink, resting the machine. 'What passion is that?'

'Candles, I told you.'

Uncle Squink was quite overcome with emotion. 'Have a care, sweet Nephew, or I shall ruin the tallow with my tears. My goodness, my goodness.' He patted his eyes with his shirtsleeve. 'To hear a young man speak with such fervour about my life's work, I could dip myself in this very wax and set fire to my hair with happiness!'

Abigail jumped up with an excited glint in her eye. 'One moment,' she said, clattering up the stairs. Three heads followed her footsteps across the upper floor, then back down again, where Abigail reappeared, carrying her silver tray. 'Father,' she said, clearly giddy with excitement, 'I have created some very fine decorations, if you would like to see them. I found that by cooling the wax against pewter, it allowed me to—'

Uncle Squink was in no mood for distractions, and he cut her at the quick. 'Hush Abigail, please. Leave your fancies for another time.' He caught the pain in his daughter's face and softened. 'Forgive me, my darling, but you must allow the menfolk to do their essential work before troubling us with your fripperies. What do you say, Thomas?'

Thomas remembered Nelly Fump at Mother Clap's, defending the value of finer things.

'I believe Abigail's decorative animals and flowers are very clever. She clearly takes after her father, who must have taught her most assiduously over many years.'

'Assiduously?' said the man, looking between his nephew and daughter before straightening his long body so his red wig brushed the beam above his head. 'Assiduously, I did!'

Thomas continued. 'And I wonder whether her fripperies might look rather attractive on some of the more expensive candles?'

'Will you listen to the boy?' said Aunt Squink. 'Candles are messengers of God's light, a most precious gift bestowed on us by his grace for the illumination of our penitence. Attractive?' She looked nervously about the room. 'Good Nephew, we are not Catholics.'

'I am sure you're right,' said Thomas, plucking one of Abigail's creations from the tray. 'Only ... did the Lord in his wisdom not dress the world with pretty flowers and gentle creatures too, that we may nurture and enjoy them? I only wonder whether a few of the same might make Uncle's candles – the thickest and firmest candles in all of London –a perfect reflection of God's bounty?' He held the warm candle to the flame below the pot then, ever so gently, lifted it to the light and pressed the feet of the little woodland creature into the soft wax, adding two dainty flowers above its sniffing nose. 'Perhaps this little fellow likes the smell of tallow,' he said with a happy chuckle.

Abigail squealed with delight, while her mother laid her scowling eyes on a cross hanging above the doorway. Just then, the bell rang in the shop downstairs.

'That must be our visitor,' she said, bustling from the room with a disapproving look.

Her husband, however, padded to Thomas as though approaching the altar. 'Surely this boy is the very trinity of piety, passion and art,' he said, his palms pressed together in prayer. He kneeled at Thomas's feet, turning his face up to a shaft of light that beamed from the window. 'Show me the way, sweet boy. I do believe you are an angel.'

CHAPTER TWENTY-ONE

Up Giltspur Street went Gabriel, through Pye Corner to Smithfield Rounds, filling his nostrils with the stink of roast meat. He pulled his hat up to look where he was going, the heat from the firepits scorching his face. He pushed his way through huddles of hungry mouths, making his way from stall to stall, searching for a singular face amongst the meat-sellers and butchers.

He was passing a ring of dung carts piled high with steaming straw, when a woman approached him carrying a basket of hot pies. 'Lamb and pepper?' she said in a heavy Irish accent. 'Goose and gravy?'

'Not hungry.'

'So says Hungry Hill himself!' said the woman, looking under the brim of his hat. 'Ye will have a pie now.'

'Get off, woman,' said Gabriel, pushing her away. He marched as quickly as he could past a long row of trestles piled high with frowsy bacon, then passed the crooked mouth of Chick Lane, where the measly pork and neck-beef stood out in wooden platters. He approached a stewhouse where the flies hung about the piles of meat like vibrating jackets, sporting carrots for necklaces. A table of likely-looking drovers were sitting close by, stuffing their mouths with chunks of grey meat.

'More over here, stupid child,' shouted one of the men, his voice slurring. He must have expected the food to drop from the sky, for he didn't chew more than three times before shouting again: 'More over here, stupid girl, or are you deaf?' He leaned across the table to a pair of women in straw hats, their blouses crawling with lice and screaming children. 'Treat 'em hard, fine ladies, the girl's a terrible chore.'

The larger of the two ladies leered at him with a toothless grin.

'You say right, sir. I'll say she lacks a strict father, though her brother does his best, funny sort of lad he is.' She laughed merrily. 'We only comes here to watch the beating they gets from their customers. Better than fightin' cocks it is.'

Just then, a flap flew open in a nearby hut with a burst of steam, and a little girl in a long apron and cloth cap skidded backwards. She stumbled, just managing to keep a platter above her head, the dish piled so high with slices of meat they hung over the edges like tongues. She made her way between the tables, circling them in all directions, hopping over outstretched feet, throwing slabs up to elevated plates with a long knife.

Gabriel slid onto a bench and watched as the girl made her way towards the impatient man. When she arrived, the man stuck his leg out and tripped her into the mud. Instantly, she was surrounded by a carpet of stray cats, which crawled over her, hissing and tearing the dropped meat with their teeth. The man leaned back, roaring with laughter, tears bursting from his eyes as the women slapped his arm in fits.

'By the saints!' said the younger of the two. 'Ain't that the funniest thing we've seen all day? Look at them cats, they'll be eating the girl when they finish the lamb!'

Gabriel was already half up from his seat when the flap snapped open again, emitting a spindly young man in an apron spattered with grease. He carried a long carving knife in his hand, the blade of which found its way to the neck of the oaf.

'Help her up.'

Gabriel lowered himself back to his seat. This must be George Lavender's twin brother – there was a striking resemblance to the intemperate molly, from his wide-set features to his gangly legs and arms, yet his movements, attitude and voice were of another man entirely.

'Wouldn't touch the little rat,' said the oaf, glancing to his lady friends with a brave smile.

The young man pressed the blade deeper and the crowd grew quiet.

'Told you to help my sister up. Then you can beg her forgiveness, or I'll slice you up like the rotten sack of gristle you are.'

The girl managed to scramble up from the brawling cats. 'It don't matter, Georgie. Don't fight.'

Gabriel looked again at the face of the spindly gentleman and realised to his surprise that it was George after all. The transformation was extraordinary; like the stem of a flower without its petals, he stood there, gruff and straight as a pole. He beckoned his sister to stand behind him then pressed the knife against the oaf's jugular vein.

'Be a good sir. Say you're sorry to my sister.'

The man was about to laugh, when he caught sight of the glint in George's eye and thought better of it. He gulped and nodded.

'Forgive me, little girl,' he stammered, 'you tripped over my boot.'

George grunted, flicking the knife so it drew a squirt of blood, which slapped the women across the face. A gasp went around the crowd of onlookers.

'Try again or you're a dead man.'

'You wouldn't dare,' said the oaf as a bead of sweat trickled down his face. 'You'd hang.'

'So hang me.'

Gabriel could see George meant what he said, as could the oaf, who apologised profusely, explaining in hurried detail that his wife had been caught up an alley with a sailor that very morning, and he was drunk and very sorry for himself and unhappy with women generally. The confession earned him the disgust of his admirers, who spat on him and knocked his drink across his legs.

George pulled the blade back, kicking the wretched creature as he stumbled away, crying for his own bad fortune.

The little girl took George's hand. 'I dropped the best cuts; only scraps now.'

'Never worry,' said George, patting her tangles. 'I'll get back to the kitchen and see what I can cook up later. Ma needs feeding by now, hey?' He turned to his customers and announced the kitchen was closed, all meat off, and by the solidity of his voice, they did not protest.

Gabriel turned away, trying to get his thoughts straight. Of all the things he'd expected from George Lavender, bravery wasn't one of them, nor sweetness to a younger sibling. Still, he could not help but notice the artful way the young man had handled the knife at the man's neck. Poor Martin was murdered with a long, sharp blade just like it. Ay, everyone had a table knife to eat, but the cut in the boy's neck was clean, made with a single swipe, and there was no tearing of the skin, even though the gash was deep. A butcher's knife then? Or a carving knife.

George's voice came from behind Gabriel's back. 'You there. I said no more food.'

Gabriel turned to face him and tugged the brim of his hat. 'Afternoon, Lavender.'

George's face flattened. He grunted and marched over, still clutching the blade, and by the look of rage in his eyes, Gabriel was next for a shave.

'Dumb old horse, what're you doing here?'

'Martin Lightbody. Pulled from the ditch.' Gabriel looked at the knife. 'His throat was cut.'

'And? Poor Martin, whoever he was. I barely knew him.'

'Reckon you might have killed him.'

George snorted. 'Me? Kill some lad – what for?'

'Money,' said Gabriel, glancing at the hut. 'Or shame.'

Just then, the little girl poked her head back through the flap. 'Georgie, who's that you're talking to? Ma needs us.'

George narrowed his eyes. 'I'd not risk the noose and leave my sister alone.' He looked around with a suffering breath. 'You'd better come in.'

Gabriel followed him through the curtain to a large stove with a griddle pan caked with an inch of fat. Beyond it, there was a room barely the size of a pig pen, where a low bed of straw lay in the corner, butted against a makeshift wall of wooden slats. The little girl was sitting on a stool beside the bed, carefully tipping spoonfuls of broth between the teeth of a recumbent skeleton. At first, Gabriel thought it was a very elderly woman, what with her sunken eyes and hollow cheeks, yet as his eyes grew keen he realised her hair was black, while her face – though riven with pain – was not much older than his own. Her eyes rolled and she smiled, coughing broth down her chin.

'A visitor, Georgie?'

'Careful, Ma,' said George, gently propping her up. 'Take your food before you speak.' He gave Gabriel a bitter look. 'This giant looby says I'm a killer; one of my molly friends got his throat cut last week.'

The woman wiped a brittle arm across her lips. 'It's only your dear Duchess who visits me, none of your other friends.' She met Gabriel's eye, struggling to lift her face. 'You the molly guard then? Heard about you.'

Gabriel frowned, uncomfortable speaking in front of the woman and child. What was George thinking, sharing their secrets so carelessly?

'You know about us?'

'What there is to know.'

'You know...' Gabriel cleared his throat uncomfortably '...what George is?'

'I do,' said the woman, her eyes fierce. 'He's my son.'

She struggled to lift herself higher, reaching out her hand, but she was too weak to keep it aloft, so the girl helped her.

'Come close, molly guard,' said the mother.

Gabriel stepped to the side of the bed and kneeled down, taking the woman's brittle hand in his own. He searched her face, finding wisdom and kindness beneath the sallow skin.

'You keep my boy safe,' she said.

'Don't know about that,' he said. 'Got to find a traitor though, or I reckon we'll hang.'

'Find him then,' she said resting her head back with a rattling breath. She looked at her two children. 'Keep my George safe, molly guard. Or nobody will be here for Annie by winter.'

Gabriel told her he would do his best, then stood up and beckoned George to follow. Together, they made their way out, walking in silence between the stalls and carts, coming to a stop by the entry to St Bart's Hospital.

'Nasty place to live with an ailing mother and child. Disease and stink everywhere.'

George looked back towards the shack and shrugged. 'Better than some. You live in a marble palace, I suppose?'

'Won't live anywhere soon. Been told to leave Red Lyon Street in a few weeks.'

'Well, you're not staying here, great stinking cow.'

'No need.' Gabriel paused. It was then that an idea came to him, only partially formed. What if he set a trap for the Rat? It would take time, and he'd have to keep it a secret, but it might just work if all else failed. He eyed George suspiciously, waiting for his full attention, then spoke as clearly as he could so the young man wouldn't miss a word. 'There's an abandoned chapel out by the dump at Black Mary's Hole,' he said. 'Same place me and Clap bury our molly martyrs. I'll be there a month from now, if you need me.'

George snorted. 'And why would I need you?'

'Treacherous times. Can't trust nobody.'

'And me a suspect, what a jest.'

'And you a suspect, ay.'

George arched an eyebrow, a cloud slipping over his eyes. 'I could have drowned Martin in the ditch for all the times he laughed at me. Called me names, pointed out how skinny I am, like I don't look pretty in my gowns.'

A pair of drovers passed them by, too close for comfort. Gabriel spoke quietly: 'Martin confided in me last Sunday night. Next morning, I'm pulling his body from the ditch. Never seen a lad so scared. He saw someone he knew, meeting with the Society. Saw them again at Clap's too. Won't say more than that, but I reckon someone's taking bribes to hand our names over for hanging. The Rat, so he calls himself.'

George's eyes flitted between Gabriel's. 'Then I'll show you.' He scrabbled in his apron. 'They want me dead an' all. You'll be pulling me from that ditch next.'

He held up a torn piece of paper. It bore the same handwriting as the one Gabriel had found in Martin's pocket.

You're Next Molly Boy. The Rat's Hungry.

George's bravado was gone now. He looked fearful, just as Martin had the day before he was pulled from the ditch, and Gabriel had a vision of a red line slicing across his neck.

'When did you get this?'

'Found it this morning. Tucked under a dish.'

'Whose dish?'

'Annie didn't recognise him. I only saw the note when I was throwing the bones away, so I asked her who it was. Some man, she said, with a pointed snout and dead skin under a hood.'

Gabriel thought of the deathly figure standing on the gangway at Clap's.

'A hood? How about a cloak?'

'Might have been. She said he stank of rotten meat, even in this place. I caught the note before Annie saw it, praise be.' He held Gabriel by the wrist. 'I ain't been a friend to you, Lotty Lump. You don't like me, neither. Only molly who does is the Duchess, but she's afraid.' His smile turned bitter. 'Saintly Mister Rettipence, sticking with his sad little family in their smart house on Camomile Street, them children of his cosy as kittens while we starve. That's when he ain't travelling, of course, important merchant as he is.' He wiped his nose. 'All that money wasted on the wife when all I get is tatty gowns and wigs. Ain't fair, if you ask me.'

'Life ain't fair for mollies; that's why we say our promise.' Gabriel held out his hand and nodded. 'Together.'

'Ay, always together, whatever that means.'

George stepped closer to Gabriel, careful not to talk until a pair of beggars had passed them by. 'Thomas True. That's your rat. New molly, only just christened. Cocky little prick if ever I met one, playing all innocent, but I can smell a liar from a mile off. Saw him at the exchange on Sunday night. Got myself knocked out by them Society hounds, but when I came round, he's standing right there in the middle of 'em, bold as brass. So I get up and run off, but he follows me, thinking I'm blind, and turns up at Clap's not half an hour later.' George narrowed his eyes, nodding meaningfully. 'There wasn't a scratch on his pretty face. Ay well, pretty he might be – I've seen you making sheep's eyes at him – but true? Don't make me laugh.'

CHAPTER TWENTY-TWO

George Lavender was right about one thing: Gabriel had been watching Thomas True. Was he a fool not to see the young man as a suspect in his hunt for the Rat? But the lad was new to Mother Clap's; how could he be giving men's names away to the Society? And surely he wouldn't be handing threatening notes to Martin and George before he'd ingratiated himself. No man could be so clumsy. Besides, Mister True was not evil. Gabriel could feel it deep in his bones; there was something pure and good in the man, something innately kind.

Henry and Bet had been quarrelling all night, so he slipped away from Red Lyon Street without them noticing, hiding his face from the moonlight beneath the drooping brim of his hat. Across High Holborn he went, bowling from shadow to shadow into Lincoln's Inn New Square, crossing to the bog houses on the opposite side of the court. Mister Spue was in residence, for a sprig of ivy had been placed on the door of one of the bog-house stalls and whispering could be heard coming from inside. There was a sort of rubbing sound and a regular yelping. Gabriel waited patiently, watching the square to make sure no guards were about. Eventually, the door opened and a sorry-looking gentleman departed in funny jerks, his knees apart.

'Enter,' said a voice, followed by a curled finger.

The stall was tiny, its floor drenched with piss, while the cesspit below stank.

'Apothecary Spue,' said Gabriel as he entered the stall. 'You took my money for a witch's potion.'

The man looked up from his bag. 'Mister Griffin, how nice to see you again; has the past month treated you kindly?'

'Your remedy didn't work.'

'It had no suppressive effect?'

Gabriel wrung his hat in his fists, looking at his boots. He thought of the sinful dreams he'd been having about Mister True. 'I'm worse than ever.'

'Is that so? It's done the trick for other fellows, I assure you. Still, you are a very large man. Did you insert it twice daily as instructed? Crouching helps.'

'I did.'

'All the way up?'

Gabriel shuffled uncomfortably. 'Ay.'

'And my remedy had no effect at all?'

'Made my arse itch.'

The apothecary waggled his finger. 'Sodomitical tendencies are symptomatic of a lifelong disease, Mister Griffin. It is not a mere distemper or blistered finger. Still, Apothecary Spue does not give up so easily.' He opened his case, rifling through the bottles, stretching his face as he peered at their labels in the scant light. 'Rubbing mercury?'

'Burns like Hell.'

'That is the purpose, dear fellow.' He pulled out a metal ring the diameter of a parsnip. 'How about this?'

Gabriel kicked the floor. 'Too tight.'

'Goodness me, is it really? Let us see, let us see.' He rummaged deep in his bag, pulling out a little jar of pine needles. Gabriel grimaced and the apothecary gave a little chuckle. 'They cause some irritation of course, which is part of the remedy, and passing water is a problem...'

'You have any cures that don't make a man want to hang himself?'

Mister Spue folded his arms. 'Mister Griffin, my curatives are designed specifically for a man riddled with your peculiar sexual perversion. Lord knows the sins you might have committed without my ministrations these past three years. Still, I have one last tincture that might just quell your desires. I rarely use such old-fashioned remedies, but you are an old-fashioned sort of a man. A few drops of this should turn a horse into a tortoise.' He took out a glass bottle, filled with a resinous liquid and held the swirling mixture to his eye. 'If it worked for the monks, it ought to work for you.'

'What is it?'

'A little camphor.'

'Ay?'

'And chasteberry – monk's pepper as it was known in old Harry's day.'

'And?'

The apothecary smiled, leaning in conspiratorially. 'I added a little dilution. Vrina Vulpis.'

Gabriel frowned. 'Fox piss?'

The apothecary gave an encouraging nod. 'Half a crown will see us right, Mister Griffin; two spoons daily or...' he looked Gabriel up and down '...on demand.'

Gabriel jangled the last of his week's money in his pocket and gazed at the tincture. Might it save him at last? After a lifetime of torture, might he be free of his disease? The oil was glutinous and pale green with little black and yellow lumps floating in it.

'Two shillings.'

'Oh, very well, very well. By Christ, here I am keeping my patients healthy, only to have my pockets picked.'

Gabriel moved to the spyhole in the door and froze: a shadow was crossing the square in a long cloak.

'Who is out there?' said Spue. 'The guards?'

'Just the night watch,' said Gabriel, inspecting the apothecary in the darkness of the stall, wondering whether he could be trusted. He decided to take care. 'You heard any of your other molly clients talking about a rat?'

Spue frowned. 'I am a medical man, sir, not a ratcatcher. Why do you ask such a thing?'

Gabriel went to push the door open. 'No matter, best be getting home.'

'I shall go first,' said Spue, pushing past him. 'You must wait a few minutes, or we may arouse more than your devilish loins.'

The apothecary slipped from the stall, hurrying into the night with his tinkling potions while Gabriel sat on the bench, deep in thought. He held up the apothecary's bottle, watching the tincture swirl inside the glass and sniffed the sour liquid.

A vision of Mister True appeared before him in the darkness, and he quickly slugged a measure of the potion to quell his excitement. He heaved and swallowed vomit. The cure hadn't worked, for the young man was still there, looking down at him from the corner of the stall, a spot of apple flesh sitting on his lower lip.

The white of his parted teeth, the square chin, the faint dusting of freckles across his cheekbones.

Gabriel reached out, tracing the contours of his face. He breathed heavily, his hands brushing the man's ribs. A gulp. A pulsing neck. A clean, muscular chest. Gabriel took another slug of the revolting potion then threw himself back. It was hopeless. These were not the usual visions, well worn and easily dismissed; not the shirtless masons from the cathedral, nor the soldiers with their swords unsheathed; nor the butcher with powerful fingers buried in meat. The usual cast of seductive players had been usurped by *him* ... Thomas True turned with a smile, then stripped away his clothes as Gabriel felt an explosion of biting pleasure and the bog-house door swung open with a bang. Three pairs of hands reached inside and grabbed him by the coat. Gabriel struggled but he was sick from the potion, and with much shouting and kicking he was pulled out and thrown to the ground.

'What is this?' he demanded as a boot collided with his head.

The men rolled him onto his stomach, his teeth biting the gravel, and as he craned his neck he noticed the outline of the cloaked figure watching him from the shadows of a passageway on the far side of the moonlit square.

The Rat held his gaze, then turned and melted into the dark.

CHAPTER TWENTY-THREE

Gabriel ignored the watchmen's insults as they trundled through the sleeping city. After an eternity, they arrived at the Poultry Compter, passing through a stone porch with an iron grating. Three knocks were given, and the captors waited. At last, the door swung open and Gabriel was bundled into a dank cell.

'Filthy buggerantoe,' laughed the gaoler, slamming the cell door with a jeer. 'Watch yer backsides, good thieves, this one's another pretty fellow, the great beast.'

The bolts clanked shut and the cell turned black, but for the faintest light through a low grill in the wall. Gabriel huddled against the bricks, listening to the whimpering of his cellmates. The air was a poison of tobacco, sweaty toes, putrid breath, puss-riddled carcasses and filth. The restless men shuffled, pressing together for warmth. Those manacled to the corners pulled rags over their legs with their toes, while roaming shadows loomed between the prisoners, shards of glass between their knuckles, threatening murder if a shilling wasn't paid. Gabriel parted with the very last of his money.

'Be merciful,' came an old man's voice, rattling his chains by Gabriel's side. 'What use is there in killing me? No point hurting a poor old bag of bones, I'll be dead soon anyways. Here, I will pay you when my good wife collects me in the morning. She will have a pie for you, kind sir. Now, please, won't you take that piece of glass from my neck?'

Gabriel saw the goblin shift. He pressed his foot between the stumpy legs with a low growl. 'Touch the old beggar and I'll boot your cherries to your jaw.'

'What's it to you, filthy madge?' said the prowling shadow.

'Don't want his blood on me, do I?'

The goblin considered his prey, then moved off to another victim.

The old man struggled to his knees, clasping his hands together. 'By the saints, is there any man so fortunate as Old Bob Buckleburn this night? I swear, I thought he would cut my throat, but I shall see my darling wife on the morrow thanks to a kindly giant.'

Gabriel huffed, turning to face the bricks, but the beggar spoke on:

'Sir,' he said, 'did I hear the turnkey call you a sodomite? I'm sure he did. Caught on Sodomites' Walk, was you? Or searching for love under the arches at the exchange? No fear, gentle giant, I am a friend, you can trust Old Bob. My dear wife will feed us both come morning and we can share a drink together if you'd brave Alsatia?'

Gabriel shuddered at the name. Once a religious sanctuary for men escaping justice, Alsatia was now the heart of London's criminal society – and the fabled home of the spider children known as the Blackguard. 'Not likely,' he said, rolling over.

'Then let me give you the only precious thing I own,' said the man, huddling against Gabriel's back and cupping a cold hand to his ear. 'I am locked up in here because I know something, you see. I know a secret, a funny old tale, if you'd care to listen?'

Gabriel nudged the man away, preferring the chill of the flagstones to his cellmate's faint warmth. Still, the man tugged at Gabriel's shoulder. 'I know who you are, Lotty Lump. Recognised you the second the cell door opened. Dark times, dark times.' He shuffled closer. 'It was at Miss Muff's on Whitechapel – I'd been there a few times, preferring the quiet to all that commotion at Clap's. Besides, it was too painful to see my darling with a younger molly. Anyways, I come out of Muff's for a little puff on me pipe and I sees a young lad in the stable yard. Skinny little thing he was, by the name of Martin Little-something.'

Gabriel turned over. 'Lightbody?'

'Yes! Martin Lightbody, that's the one. Martha Moggs they call her. Like I say, young as anything and not too smart. Part of that gang of brave bone-heads who like to go trolling through the streets in their gowns like they want a beating.' The old man's head shook in the shadows. 'I would have done the same their age, I confess, yet still it frightens me, by Christ; it frightens me to see 'em goading the Society, thinking it won't bite us all back.' He prodded Gabriel's side. 'That's what's happening now, I suppose.'

'What is?'

'I heard what happened to poor Martha. You dredged her up from the ditch yourself with her throat cut, ain't that right?'

Gabriel whispered, 'Get to your point, or I'll silence you myself.'

'I'd seen her, hadn't I? Martha, outside Miss Muff's. Only, she wasn't alone. I went over to the stable she was hiding in and saw her talking to someone I thought I recognised. "Get back inside," they were saying. "Find out their names and bring them to me."'

Gabriel rolled over, their noses almost touching. 'You mean Martin Lightbody was playing spy for the Society?'

'I don't think so.' The old man's voice fell fainter still, his beard tickling Gabriel's ear. 'Martha was telling them "no" – quite bravely I thought. You can imagine my bones a-shaking while I listened with these cloth ears of mine. It was so terrible dark in that stable, I couldn't see much, but I could see enough.'

'Who was it?' said Gabriel, straining his eyes as black shapes swam around them through the darkness. 'Who was Martin talking to?'

'The Rat,' said the man. Then he gave a dry chuckle, clearly sensing Gabriel's quickening heartbeat. 'So you heard it too, did you? News travels fast along the ivy trail, don't it?' His eyes grew wide. 'I saw the Rat alright, and how I wish I hadn't, or I wouldn't be chained up in this place. I reckon I was spotted, peeping from that other stable. One moment I was back home in Alsatia enjoying one of my lady's pies, the next I was beckoned by a queer-looking fellow with a face like death itself, then shackled up and dragged to Hell.'

Gabriel kept his voice low. 'Did you see the Rat's face?'

The old man opened his mouth to answer, only for his eyes to bulge and with a loud rattling of chains, he was yanked across the floor. Gabriel wrenched at his shackles, listening helplessly as the old man was murdered beyond his reach, sobbing for mercy until his miserable screams were drowned in blood.

'Timothy,' was his final breath, 'Timothy, take care.'

Shaking, Gabriel waited all night for a slice at his own throat, managing to grab a stray shard of glass, brandishing it till morning. It was so deadly cold, the wet stones of the cell echoing to the sound of men's sobbing and screaming and snoring. Gabriel could feel the Rat gripping him as tight as the shackles, the mystery of the traitorous molly looming large above him, more terrible than any shadow-cloaked assassin. For this was a man who threatened hundreds of lives, including his own. Who was he? And why would he do something so wicked to his friends?

Eventually, enough pale light slipped through the grate to illuminate the old man's corpse, his eyes and gaping mouth fixed in everlasting be-wilderment as though asking Gabriel a question. There was little to tell which of the other cellmates were responsible, all of them cast in the same character of villainy, all of their hands filthy with blood.

Duly, the bolts on the cell door clanked open and the men were led out to have their shackles struck off, then to a paved yard to stretch their legs, craning their necks to the pale sky. Like mice in a box, they trudged in a circle, spitting grey slugs of phlegm up the garrison walls until, finally, they were shepherded into a cellar to eat.

Gabriel sat on a bench beside a long table and stared at his bowl. Had the old man really spied the Rat? If so, the knowledge had surely killed him. Gabriel shuddered, forcing himself to swallow the bowl of slop. The constable's polished shoes clapped the stones as he paraded ceremoniously between the tables, huffing and tutting at his captives before settling himself into an elbow chair with all the majesty of a king.

He quickly dispatched his business, most of the men being regular guests, and finally came to Gabriel, the last prisoner to be heard.

The constable yawned, peering at a note. 'Griffin's the name, is it?'

'Ay. I did no wrong.'

'That so?'

'Was just passing through Lincoln's Inn. Stopped for a piss in the bog house.'

The constable laughed, slapping the arms of his chair. 'Never gets old no matter how many times I hear it: "But sir! I was only walking past the bog houses when I happened to drop my drawers. I did not mean to sit on the man's cudgel. I thought it was a wooden spoon and my arse a mixing bowl!"' He wiped tears from his face, his cheeks flushed. 'I have a good mind to send you to the pillory. Why, I would be the envy of every constable in London, catching a sodomite the size of you. Sadly, on this occasion, I must do as I am told.'

He stood and made his way from the cellar, beckoning Gabriel to follow. Outside, beyond the stone porch, a broad man in a crimson doublet was waiting, one of his eyes yellow and swollen.

'What's this?' asked Gabriel, catching sight of the man's sword. 'That's a marshal's man. Ain't I free?'

'No man is free, only waiting to be captured,' said the constable. Then he turned to the guard: 'Now then, good fellow, here's your swarthy buggerantoe, delivered fresh and steaming, as requested. Tell the marshal Constable Kirby did well.'

The guard grunted, clasping a gloved hand on the dagger at his hip, kicking Gabriel's heels. 'Move.'

Gabriel's body had never ached so hard, his bones deadly stiff. As they turned a corner, an old woman came scurrying along, carrying a basket of pies. She had a hopeful look on her face, eagerly craning her neck to the gaol. 'Bob,' she was saying to herself along with prayers to her papist saints. 'My Bob, will they let him out today?'

She caught sight of Gabriel, her neck springing up like a startled goose. 'Now will you look at that big bullock. If it isn't Hungry Hill from Smithfield. I know that face, so I do. You pushed me away. Here, is that why you're for the pillory, is it? Saints save ye, I say. Serves you right.'

They left her at the compter, then marched all the way to Clerkenwell, past the workhouse and to the Black Horse Tavern. A pair of the marshal's men stood aside – one with a patch on his eye, the other with splints on both legs – admitting Gabriel into a low-ceilinged saloon with a riveted door. The guard removed his glove to reveal a hand covered in burn marks, and knocked on the door with a wince.

A voice came from within, high and reedy like split bone: 'Enter.'

The door swung open to reveal a table groaning under a mass of gold coins.

'Ah,' came a voice from behind the treasure. 'My, what a grizzly bear you are, Mister Griffin. I was warned, but I didn't believe you could possibly be such a size, least of all a man of your habits.'

Gabriel peered around the desk to see who was there, then felt a tug at his breeches and looked down to find a short fellow, barely higher than his navel, staring up at him. Though Gabriel had heard much about the city's chief law man, he was taken aback by his appearance: squat, with eyes drawn out to the sides of his head, long hairs growing from his pink cheeks like the whiskers of a cat. He wore a tricorn hat and a buff doublet matched with a tinsel cloak buttoned over his left shoulder. There was a long dagger in his belt, the point of which dragged over the floor with a scratching sound as he walked, while his pointed boots were strangely padded, as though his feet were raised upon concealed chopines.

Never had evil worn such a ridiculous costume, yet Gabriel kept his face straight, for he sensed he was about to be placed in grave danger.

CHAPTER TWENTY-FOUR

Marshal Queed looked up at his visitor with clever, fidgety eyes.

'Look at this! Why, if it isn't Mother Clap's very own molly guard right here in my office. Tell me, did you enjoy a comfortable night at my pleasure?'

Gabriel balled his fists, willing his heart to slow. Here was the devil responsible for the pillorying and hanging of so many men. Here, the architect of London's terror, and yet for all the world, he had the appearance of a merry uncle.

'Ah well,' Queed continued, waving the guard out of the room, 'you are entitled to a little sulk after a night in the cage. Won't you join me for a drink?' He waved Gabriel to sit before slopping red wine from a pewter jug into a pair of cups.

Gabriel sat down, eyeing the man suspiciously. 'What am I doing here, Marshal?'

Queed waved his hand. 'A casual meeting between friends.'

'A threat more like.' Gabriel gestured to the guard outside the door. 'I give you what you want or I'm back in the compter. You had a man killed last night just for talking.'

Queed appeared shocked. 'Did I?' He raised an eyebrow. 'I heard about the old bugger, God save his bones. You are mistaken, however; I had nothing to do with his killing.' A shriek rang out from the window behind him. 'I am questioning a few of your cellmates as we speak, though none seem willing to enlighten us. I have a more persuasive contraption on order from Greece, you know. Certain to loosen men's tongues.' He reached across the desk and cleared a valley in the pile of golden coins. 'Mother Clap tells me you are searching for our Rat?'

'She lies.'

The Marshal's smile vanished. 'Who is it? Tell me. They must be stopped.'

Gabriel had learned to read men like the marshal, and he was surprised to see him so agitated. Agitated men, Gabriel knew, are frightened men, and frightened men are dangerous.

'What do you care if mollies get murdered by the Society? That's what you want, ain't it? It's your noose at Tyburn, after all, your pillories, your prisons.' Gabriel had to keep his voice steady. 'Your laws.'

The marshal wriggled back, clicking his tongue. 'You flatter me, Mister Griffin. I am merely a puppet.' His lip curled. 'A poorly paid one at that.'

Gabriel looked at the gold coins. 'Looks like it.'

'Ho, ho, Mister Griffin, these are merely the spoils of a business I run in what little spare time I am afforded by His Majesty the King.' He inspected his fingernails. 'The grand idiot. My function as city marshal offers me nothing but headaches and sleepless nights. Still, Providence intends to compensate me for my considerable services to the community. Good deeds remain good deeds, whether a man profits from them or no. This money is paid to me by dear friends, for my protection.' He gave an impish smile. 'Your beloved Mother Clap included.'

Gabriel snorted. 'The mother of mollies giving money to the law? Never. You don't even know where Clap's is.'

The Marshal tilted his head, walking his fingers across the desk. 'Along Field Lane, about halfway to Saffron Hill, through a hidden doorway poorly disguised with ivy, along the gangway, up the steps, around the warehouse to the stinking backside of High Holborn. Through a door of rose-stained glass to a sodomites' sanctum of drink and debauchery.'

Gabriel sat in stunned silence. 'You've been there?'

'Certainly not, but my guards have, to collect my garnish.'

'Then the Rat is one of your guards under cover. They've been threatening mollies, blackmailing them into passing names to the Society, cutting boys' throats.'

'I wondered the same thing,' said Queed, 'yet no, it is not one of my men, thank goodness. I have brogged, boiled and burned the lot of them to test the theory. There was a time I knew every scoundrel in the city. This Rat, however, is being protected by a far greater power than me. I'm told there's a pair of pious justices heading to London post-haste with a growing list of mollies and molly houses that they intend to shut down.' He turned thoughtfully to the window as another cry rang out, then fixed Gabriel with a squint. 'If I have to raid them all, I will betray my own business interests; a most unedifying prospect for a man of principle.'

'You'd lose all your money, more like, and your little empire will be blown asunder – your protection racket will be revealed in the light of day. You'd hang with the rest of us.'

Queed sprang from his chair and shot around the desk. 'Tell me who the Rat is. Don't test my patience.'

Gabriel thought about his six suspects: Sweet Jacky, George Lavender, the Duchess, Fump and Vivian, and yes, Thomas True.

'Told you. Don't know.'

Queed stamped his foot in frustration. 'Those magistrates are drawing closer every hour. Don't you fear them? You will be the first to hang, I shall make sure of it. Find me the Rat, and I will protect you, Mister Griffin. A little grace while you carry out your investigations. You will be spared for so long as your search continues.'

'What if I don't?'

The marshal stepped back. 'Then you will hang for sodomy tomorrow morning before the sun rises.' He laughed at Gabriel's silence. 'I am often impressed by the courage of he-whores. Hardly the prancing pretty fellows of popular imagination. But you will work for me, Mister Griffin. Or should I say Lotty? One way or another, you will do as you are told.'

Gabriel felt a dagger between his shoulder blades and realised the guard had re-entered the room.

'Muff's,' he said.

'I beg your pardon?'

'Last night in the cell, the old man said he saw the Rat at a place called Miss Muff's. You know what happened to him after that.'

'Indeed I do. What is this Muff's then?'

'New molly house, up Whitechapel way. Never been.'

'Well then,' said the marshal, 'perhaps it's time you did.'

CHAPTER TWENTY-FIVE

'Push, my darling,' said the Duchess of Camomile. 'You are doing so terribly well.'

It was the following Sunday, and the mollies were huddled on the floor of Miss Muff's molly house, encouraging Lavender as she panted and cried out, her legs jacked apart. Nelly Fump was head and shoulders deep inside her petticoats, her feet sticking out like a rabbit in a hole.

'Push harder, you lanky sow,' came her voice, 'he's coming!'

The scene was all pandemonium, draped with hot towels, Sweet Jacky gripping brave Lavender's hand, encouraging her (through fits of laughter) to persevere through the pain of her labour. Fump reappeared from within the stricken molly's petticoats, her face shining bright pink.

'That's it. You can do it! Last effort my dear, push with all your might and we shall have our birthing.'

Lavender rolled her eyes. 'Must I?'

'You must!' declared Fump, slapping her around the face.

Lavender tutted and resumed her lowing, grimacing quite convincingly as she bit down on a wooden spoon. With an almighty effort, she bucked her hips and gasped in relief as a young lad from Wapping named Daniel popped out of her ruffles: 'I am out!' he declared.

Lavender lay back, her brow mopped by her attentive companion the Duchess, while Nelly Fump bent the newborn lad over her knee and slapped his buttocks, mollycoddling him against her stuffed bosoms with much maternal cooing. Meanwhile, Sweet Jacky retrieved the purple ribbon that ran from Lavender's petticoats to Daniel's naked belly button and gnawed through it with her teeth.

Thomas – or rather Verity True-tongue by her new molly name – looked on in complete puzzlement.

'I wonder who will birth me?' she mumbled to herself somewhat sulkily, looking hopefully at her friends, yet they didn't seem to hear her, and she found herself hanging in uncomfortable silence. It had become her usual treatment over recent days, people behaving as though she wasn't there. She told herself she must be imagining it, yet when she touched Sweet Jacky's shoulder, she was shrugged off. Well, they were busy after all.

Duly, Miss Muff appeared – huge and whiskered in gold leather buskin boots and a fur-trimmed gown. She gladly christened the new arrival Daisy Dandy-legs, on account of her muscular calves, and paraded her around the molly house to applause, before dressing the babe ceremoniously in a sarsnet robe.

The uninitiated Verity True-tongue couldn't help but wonder what Cousin Abigail would say if she'd seen these grown men rolling around on the floor pretending to give birth to a squealing baby almost six feet tall. She laughed at the idea, suddenly desperate to tell her all about it, just to see the look on her face.

'Noisiest birthing I ever did see,' said old Vivian Guzzle, tutting at Nelly Fump, who was folding her midwifery towels into a cloth bag. 'Get off the floor, good woman. Lord, why must we play at such ridiculous games?'

'Ridiculous games?' said Fump. 'Birthings are a molly's rite of passage. First, we are born, then we are married, then we must ourselves birth a new molly into this unforgiving world.'

Old Vivian gave a deep groan and lowered her clicking skeleton into a cushion beside Verity. 'Do not look so confused, Miss True-tongue,' she said, with a kindly tap on her knee. 'A molly marriage is a pleasurable thing, not to be rushed.'

'It is an honour,' said Fump. 'We christened you already, so we may birth you soon as you are trusted.'

'Am I not trusted still?' said Verity, looking around the faces of her friends.

Lavender snorted from the floor. 'Not likely, Rat.'

Thomas was struck dumb. He sat up, staring at the faces of his friends. 'What did you just call me?'

The Duchess petted Lavender. 'That is rather harsh, my duckling. Such allegations are serious.'

'They are,' said Lavender with her nose to the ceiling, 'and I say it again to anyone listening.' She clapped her hands and raised her voice. 'Verity True-tongue is my guess for the Rat. Has to be one of us, according to Lotty Lump, and if it is, I say it's that prim bitch sitting right there.'

Fump covered her mouth with her bejewelled fingers. 'Oh, stop this, please. I trust Verity fully, as her friend and mother. Lavender, why not have a twin birthing tonight and we can get poor Verity married before her breeches burst, poor thing? Then she may prove to us all that she's a thumping great molly. I mean, look at this face.' Fump gripped Verity by the cheeks. 'So innocent. Come darlings, let us turn her into a princess tonight. If there is no other advantage to being a molly, at least we have our magic?'

Verity nodded, only to be met with dead stares and muttering. She sat back, a horrible sickness growing in her stomach. She had listened to people's stories and laughed at their japes, she had been nothing but kind and complimentary, yet all she'd been given in return was chilly indifference and hidden sniggers and was now accused of something clearly quite awful.

Damn them, she thought, growing uncharacteristically peppery as Sweet Jacky fell across her lap. The freckled molly swung her legs in the air with a cackle.

'Nobody marries the new mollies but me!' she said. 'When Verity's ready, I shall have the pleasure. It was I who found her, after all.' She waved her hand around the small parlour so all could hear. 'Listen up, I say. If anyone lays a finger on my Verity True-tongue I shall cut their throats. Rat or no Rat, she's mine to ruin, you hear? Speaking of which...'

She rolled to the floor and crossed the parlour to Daisy, leading her to a side room and slamming the door to an instant bumping and hooting.

'Will you look at that?' said Fump. 'Born one minute, married the next.'

Lavender's wide mouth turned down. 'Ain't fair. Why am I always mother? I should like to marry one of them new mollies myself. Sweet Jacky has a pretty face for all them freckles, but my legs are the longest in London.'

Fump laughed, nudging Verity. 'Long and spindly as canes, dear. If she stands overlong in the nursery gardens, slugs climb up her breeches looking for runner beans. Needless to say,' she added with an academical frown, 'they are not disappointed.'

Lavender sprang up with her claws out, only to be pulled back by the Duchess who spoke in pathetic whimpers: 'My darling, I married you only last month and we are companions, is that not enough?'

Old Vivian smoothed her skirts across her petticoats and spoke in a sage voice. 'The appetites of young mollies are seldom satisfied by a mutton molly of your years, Duchess Prune. Forgive me for using your original name, yet a prune you were christened all those years ago, and a prune you remain, my darling, no matter your smart address. Your face is as wrinkly as a dried plum, and your plums are as dusty as walnuts. Alas, it comes to us all.'

The Duchess looked terribly hurt. 'I am a man of middling years, it is true, yet I love my Lavender dearly.' She kissed her young companion's cheek. 'With age comes comfort and respectability. My own dear Polly Pieface showed me as much when I was a young thing myself.'

'Ah yes!' said Fump, snapping open her fan. 'Gawd bless the stringy bitch. Where is she, for that matter?'

The Duchess fiddled with her lace gloves, a fretful look in her eyes. 'I don't know; I was wondering the very same. I do hope she's alright.' Her face grew thoughtful. 'Dear Old Bob, he did look after me, you know; I should never have hurt him.'

Lavender Long-legs spoke harshly, her temper bare to the bone as rude noises rang out from the closed room:

'She was here with us a fortnight ago. We all saw her, heading out for a puff on her pipe. Hope it choked her too, then she won't be staring at me and my Duchess any longer with them jealous eyes of hers.' She sat up, indignant, warming to her theme. 'I stole the Duchess from her, and what of it? I think it was a shameful thing – such an old maid as she with a powerful and handsome molly of the exchange.'

The Duchess blushed and wiped her nose on her cuff. The banging from the closed room ceased and the door swung open, emitting a blotchy-faced Sweet Jacky with her petticoats over her shoulders.

'P'raps that's what happened then,' she said, rejoining the chatter as if she'd never left. 'Old Polly Pieface fancied a puff on poor wee Martha Moggs' pipe while she was at it – the dirty ferret always did like 'em young. They went out to the yard at the same time, I saw them both, and neither of them came back. Next thing you know, one's disappeared, the other's dead in the ditch.'

Fump pointed an accusing finger at Sweet Jacky. 'I saw you watching them two weeks ago, I remember. You had one of your mean looks. Why?'

'How should I know? Lord, if this Rat ain't got everyone slanting their eyes at trusted friends.'

Lavender tutted, folding her arms. 'I already told you who the Rat is.'

She pointed the toe of her slipper at Verity with a meaningful glare. 'She's sitting right there.'

'Bitter suspicion,' said Fump, hugging Verity close. 'All these nasty rumours and hurtful allegations – this is what they want. The Society would love nothing more than to see us turning on each other. Why, we would be doing their work for them.' She gave Verity a kiss on the cheek. 'Now, what do we say, everybody? Or have we forgotten so quickly? Together...'

The sparse crowd dotted around the parlour of Miss Muff's answered dully, staring at Verity with hostile faces.

'Always together.'

From there, the night grew in discomfort and drunkenness, only Fump and Vivian offering Verity occasional smiles and friendly scraps of conversation, yet even they seemed a little distant, while Lavender made sure to mingle with all the mollies in the room, glancing in her direction with whispers, eruptions of laughter and sly pointing.

Verity settled deep into the cushions and sipped her spiced wine, trying her best to look indifferent to her notoriety; but eventually she grew tired of being glowered at and made her way out to the yard, feeling the eyes of every molly on her back.

It felt good to escape the smoke and heat, to be away from them all. Barely two weeks ago, she had longed for company; now she found herself missing solitude. She checked to make sure she was alone. There was nothing but the sound of a distant bell, so she folded herself into the privacy of a bricked-up window, tugging off her shirt to enjoy the cool air.

Alone, half dressed, half molly, Thomas allowed the welcome breeze to ruffle his hair and brush across his naked skin. He stretched his legs, running his toes over the rough bricks. Rejection was nothing new to him. They would come to trust him in time, if he remained patient.

He swung his legs down and was about to go back into the parlour when the door opened, and Fump and Vivian emerged, arguing with each other as they made their way across the yard to the gates. They were through the bolted hatch barely a second before the rest of the mollies piled out, singing and waving their wigs and caps above their heads, twirling in a line around the yard with their petticoats lifted to their knees. Sweet Jacky spotted Thomas in the window and pulled him out by the fingers.

'Come along, Verity,' she laughed. 'Stop sulking, you handsome cove, we have decided to trust you after all, on condition you come a-cater-wauling with us; let's dance through the city and show 'em just how scared we are. They can't throw us all in the ditch, and if they do, we'll go down singing!'

CHAPTER TWENTY-SIX

Verity lagged behind her drunken friends as they danced into the city without a care for their necks, flashing their gowns and dipping curtsies, daring scandalised men to challenge them. People slammed their shutters closed as the merry troupe clattered and howled their way through Whitechapel. A few of the more sensible mollies peeled off from the group, hopping down alleyways to remove their gowns before trouble started. Sweet Jacky harangued them for their cowardice, though she forgot them quickly enough, duly rolling over Lavender's back, before collapsing in uncontrollable fits of laughter. 'Come and take us!' she sang, twirling about so her petticoats blew out like a tulip. 'We are not afraid of you. We are young and brave. We are the future!'

Newborn Daisy swigged her wine and screamed in admiration of Jacky's bravery, then sprang one-legged over a tying post, and dashed ahead, lifting her petticoats to her waist. Even the sensible Duchess danced beside Lavender, checking nonetheless to make sure they were not being followed.

To Verity's surprise, it seemed they were perfectly safe, as if they were shielded by their own righteous audacity, so she followed closer as they marched on towards the turrets of Aldgate, noisy as a peal of bells.

They stopped beneath the teeth of the portcullis while Jacky bit her petticoats in her teeth and took a piss. Verity was exhilarated to have such wild friends; how far she felt from Highgate now! Yet she was ashamed too, for she was still wearing her usual clothes. She wanted to be one of them more than anything in the world, to be trusted by them and accepted fully, yet at the same time she felt another kind of shame, for she could envisage manacles, chains and nooses hanging around them like so many bell ropes and she was fearful of being seen.

They struck up a new song as they marched on, then as they passed the corner of Shoemaker's Row, Lavender stopped and looked around, tripping over her own shoes.

'Wait! Where is my Duchess?'

The molly was nowhere to be seen, so they retraced their steps and discovered her halfway up a side street, attempting to shrink away unnoticed. She might have managed it too, if she hadn't stumbled into a discarded bucket, which clattered across the road.

Jacky shook her fist. 'Ho there, old prune, where do you think you're going?'

The Duchess froze. 'You are all mad!' she hissed back. 'You have a smart mouth, Sweet Jacky. The air has sobered me up, thank Christ. You'll get us all arrested – or worse. I am known hereabouts; I have a wife and children to think of.' She looked at her beloved Lavender and reached out her hands. 'Please, my petal, bid me a pleasant farewell, I am leaving you now, sweet sorrow, yet only for the night. Go home to your dear mother and sister before they lose you.'

Lavender lifted her broad face, swishing her petticoats in frustration. 'I fancy some more caterwauling. You're such an old bore.'

The Duchess was already removing her gown and wig, revealing a suit of smart clothing. 'We're fools to be abroad like this,' she said, peering up at the windows. She shook her head, shielding her face. 'What am I doing? Oh by the saints, what am I doing? I am a stupid man.'

'You're no man at all!' said Lavender, her ringlets flapping as she hopped in frustration. 'I'll bet your wife knows exactly what you are. If you can't get your worm up for me, I doubt you'd do any better with her, the tufty old fish.' She folded her arms. 'Oh, fine then. Abandon your Lavender, go back to your wench, see if I care. But don't come a-sniffing for me again, do you hear? Give me my gown back.' She clicked her fingers.

The Duchess did as she was told, removing the last of her garments. In his everyday garb, respectable Mister Timothy Rettipence of the exchange looked entirely ordinary with his round face, thinning hair and timid eyes, which peeped from behind his cheeks as though they were afraid of his own nose. He handed Lavender his gown before accepting a slap, then staggered up an alleyway towards Camomile Street.

Lavender rounded on Verity now. 'I don't know what *you're* smiling at, Thomas Rat,' she snapped, snatching up the Duchess's gown and throwing it at her feet. 'Join in or admit who you are.'

Verity looked at the gown, crumpled and tatty, trimmed with lace like a dowager's nightshift.

'I don't think I can; it won't fit me.'

Sweet Jacky pulled off her wig, shaking out her red curls. 'Just put the damned sack on and we can have our night. Or are you a traitor like Lavender says?'

Verity picked the gown up, twisting it in her hands. She wanted to please them so desperately, yet she felt more uncomfortable than ever. She looked up at the houses and noticed people milling about further down the road. 'I have changed my mind,' she said. 'Can I not be a molly in my normal clothes? I haven't been birthed yet.' She looked back to see a large shadow moving across the mouth of the gate. 'I'm not ashamed, only a little afraid.'

'No,' snapped Lavender, folding her arms, her toe turned out. 'Put it on or bugger off.'

Verity bit her cheek. She felt in her bones that there was something wrong about the night, something manic in the behaviour of her friends after so much drink. Yet, how could she ask them to trust her if she didn't trust them? They shamed her with their triumph. She looked at Sweet Jacky, her first friend in London – her first male friend in her whole life – imploring her to understand. Yet Jacky scowled and turned her back in exasperation. Lavender did the same.

Daisy came back, twirling in her gown. 'Come on, Verity,' she said with a hiccup. 'I'm doing it, why not you?'

There was nothing else for it. After all those years imagining what it must be like to have friends, Verity supposed it must come with some risk, so she stepped into the gown, biting her wobbling lip as she tugged the loose material over her shoulders. Tears pricked her eyes, yet when she looked up, Jacky was grinning at her, proud as a father watching his son's first play with a sword.

'You see, Lavender? Told you she's a true molly.'

Lavender frowned. 'Any man can wear a gown.'

'In a molly house, perhaps, but a Society stooge would rather die than get caught in public like that. See how suspicious you are, daft frog? Ain't Verity True-tongue the prettiest molly in all London – myself excluded?'

'Flat as flagstones,' said Lavender, 'with an ugly lump in her petticoats and pasty pancakes.'

Verity peered down at herself and couldn't help but laugh. The skirts and petticoats swished around her ankles as she turned in a circle, while the bodice hung hollow where her breasts might have been. She looked again at her dear friends and thought of her mother and father in their precious rectory. How irrelevant they suddenly seemed, and how distant were the stocks and the graveyard, so many countless miles away, across woodlands the size of continents, along roads that might climb forever up endless hills before reaching her miserable childhood. They could not hurt her now, not with her friends to protect her, not when she was free.

The four mollies linked arms, passing along Fenchurch Street, swinging their caps and singing, laughing so hard they gasped for air, tripping over themselves, until Verity caught her toe in the hem of her dress, and they clattered together in one single heap, squealing and squawking like chickens.

'Nasty he-whores.'

They scrambled to their knees and looked up. Four men were leaning against the wall of a tavern, its windows shuttered. The gang sidled into the road, spacing themselves apart. It was the Society hounds with blotchy, unshaven faces, each carrying a wooden club barbed with nails. Without a second's delay, Lavender jumped to her feet and ran, only to be tackled to the floor with a winded thump, her arms pinned behind her back.

Verity froze.

'Hell's teeth,' said the chief dog, stepping away from his friends. 'What do we have here then? A full set of brazen bugger-boys, out for a parade. We was told you'd be coming this way, but I never thought I'd see such a pretty pageant.'

'Too pretty for you,' said Sweet Jacky, spitting at his feet. 'I know what you're about.'

The man sniggered, swinging his club to his shoulder. 'Thought you could walk through London dressed like that? You should watch your tongue.'

Sweet Jacky turned in a circle, shouting so every window and alleyway could hear. 'You don't scare us. We do what we like with our bodies – they're ours to own.'

'Shut yer mouth,' croaked Lavender, still squashed beneath her assailant. 'You'll make 'em angry.'

The leader of the mob looked at his friends with a wink, then turned back to the mollies, swinging his club between his legs. 'Dirty madges, get up. You'll take my cudgel, barbs and all.'

Jacky laughed. 'Bird-witted sister-whores! We're free men, and better men than any of you. Why, there isn't one of your fathers we haven't raked.'

One of the brutes smashed his club into the ground, the sharp nails digging three inches into the hard dust. 'What did he say?'

Verity wanted to run, but her feet were no less pinned to the ground than the man's club. Her legs trembled as the men drew closer. The leader of the gang set his feet wide, grinding his teeth. He cocked his head.

'Take 'em off.'

Verity did her best to steady herself as she removed her gown, thankful she was wearing her everyday clothes underneath. Jacky tugged off her own dress in a flash, standing defiantly with her arms outstretched, her impressive cudgel hanging like a bell clapper between her legs.

'See that? My club's twice the size of yours.'

Poor Daisy was struggling to unfasten her gown, whimpering as her fingers refused to do as they were told. 'Please, what are you going to do? I'm not a molly. Let me go.'

Lavender was skinned to nothing but her stockings, covering her long body like a bashful heron.

'Now,' said the young man, tensing his legs. 'Run.'

'No!' said young Daisy, tripping on her petticoats. 'Don't hurt me. I told you, I'm not a molly. I was tricked.' She looked at Jacky, bewildered. Suddenly, she seemed incredibly young, her bluster gone. 'I don't know who they are. I was at the Talbot Inn on the Strand. Huffins tempted me with wine. I want to go home to my pa; he'll be waiting for me. I want my pa, I beg you.'

The man nodded to one of his friends, who stepped forwards and grabbed the lad by his wrists, dragging him screaming into Mincing Street, his voice reeling as he disappeared behind a pile of bricks. His cries rang out from the darkness:

'It's all true then?' he screamed. 'You told me I was safe. You said they wouldn't get me!' His voice choked. 'You said ... No, no ... please!' There came the inevitable thud, the cries for his father, the inhuman bleat of someone unable to calculate their own agonies.

Thomas was Verity no more. Shaking, he watched helplessly as Daisy's feet poked from behind the wall, heels bouncing to the sound of each thump, until at last, with a wet smack, the weeping fell silent.

The leader of the pack lifted his club. '*Run*,' he repeated. '*Run*.'

The instruction hung in the air for a moment, and then the gang charged like bloodhounds, each fixed upon the tail of a molly. Thomas shot away instantly, pelting over the ground towards a passageway, his naked heels pounding sharp stones. He skirted around a corner, only to tangle his feet in a discarded cloak and come crashing to the ground.

Thomas waited for the blinding flash of pain, for the feeling of his own skull being splintered by a nail, his brain skewered, yet nothing came, and he wondered if death could possibly be so kind. Seconds passed, and in his bewilderment, he opened his eyes to see a huge, black figure looming over him, shadowed below a low-brimmed hat.

Thomas spoke in a shaking voice. 'Mister Griffin? You saved my life.'

The molly guard's eyes were filled with thunder. 'Go home.'

Thomas struggled to his feet, clutching himself with sprained fingers. 'I thought I was going to die; I don't know how to thank you.'

He brushed himself down then looked up, only to find himself alone, his voice echoing against the bricks. The man had vanished.

CHAPTER TWENTY-SEVEN

'I am so deathly tired,' said Grimp, as they rumbled their way along a rutted lane, banked with cropped hedgerows. He sighed, watching Myre rummaging in his cloak. 'What have you got there, dearest Praisegod?'

'A letter from the Rat, sweet Spiritus. Our informant has more squeaking to do.' He tutted as he read the paper, slamming his fist against the side of the carriage. 'Christ's teeth! The fool has been spotted.'

'By whom?'

'By two more mollies.'

'Dear, oh dear. So the game is up?'

'Thank heavens, no.' Myre roved his eyes over the letter like black beads. 'Our cunning friend had the older one's throat cut in the compter before he could betray us.'

'And the other?'

'The other was young and foolish. Threatened to expose the truth and demanded more money, so he's been clubbed to death on Fenchurch Street by the Society hounds.' Myre closed his eyes and rubbed the bridge of his nose. 'Still, our informant grows nervous.'

'How so?'

'Apparently the city marshal has recruited a spy of his own.'

'A spy! Who?'

Myre turned the letter over with a frown. 'The Griffin character mentioned at our last meeting.'

'The molly guard from Mother Clap's?'

'The very same. He was seen entering the Black Horse Tavern in Clerkenwell, from where the marshal runs his more casual business affairs.' Myre's face grew from sullen to sunny, his fingers tickling the letter like the belly of a kitten. 'Oh you clever little Rat, you! Devious little vermin.'

'What's that? Clever you say? Devious?'

Myre held the letter to the light and read aloud. '"Do not fear, Justices, I have a plan to catch Griffin in a trap. Once the molly guard is captured, he will perish for sure, never to be found so deep below London, not even by the marshal, and then our work will be secure, and your path to the door of the molly houses will be clear, every parlour fully stocked with he-whores to save from their sins."'

Grimp frowned. 'A risky business, this. We had better stay away a little longer.'

Justice Myre agreed. 'Our Rat requires further funds to deal with this Griffin character once and for all. I say we offer the necessary benefaction and introduce our own expertise to ensure the job is done properly.' He reached into his pocket and pulled out a purse of bright-green velvet. 'The trap requires a little payment, and I think the investment is wise. We shall send it ahead, along with details on how to make contact with our trusted associate, the assassin, advising in the strongest possible terms that he is employed for this most pressing matter.'

'The assassin; are you sure?'

'Never more. Mister Griffin will be dead within the week.'

CHAPTER TWENTY-EIGHT

There was only one tower of scaffolding left to dismantle from the cathedral, a single elevation reaching up the far west end of the nave. It had been left until last so a remaining mason and his apprentice could fix a broken stone in the pediment. After thirty-five years, the work on the building was almost complete, and only a small number of scaffolders were required to remove the final timbers. More craftsmen and their wives had arrived at the churchyard that morning to witness the historic moment, climbing up the ladders to have one last look, laughing and singing, and shouting their blessings for a job well done. Sir Christopher Wren was there too, of course, riding his basket up and down the walls attached to a rope and pulley, sparing his old legs the climb. His voice could just be heard by the onlookers, complaining that the stones had not been laid to his design. 'Ugly great wart!' he was saying to himself, punching the walls with his liver-spotted fists. 'Blasted clumsy carbuncle!'

Gabriel and Henry ignored the fuss.

'P'raps we should cut a few throats ourselves,' said Henry. 'We'd make a good trade on the pulling then.' He gave a grim chuckle. 'I could think of a few knaves London could do without.'

Gabriel ignored him, swinging to the next piling. They hadn't spoken properly for days; longer than they'd ever been without words in all their thirty years of friendship. He concentrated on his work as Henry whistled to himself, pretending to inspect a lashing that had been shrunk and washed white by the rain.

'Listen Gabe, I know you're angry at me. I begged Bet to let you stay.'

Gabriel removed his hat, wiping sweat from his brow. 'That ain't why I'm angry.'

'Why so moody then? You should be happy after my good news this morning. I sorted us some grift, but Gabe says "no" without explaining why. Your sign did the trick; now we've got some solid work on the bridge. Them candle folk have the money.'

Henry waited in vain for a response. He couldn't understand what the problem was; not that he'd ever truly understood Gabe Griffin, even as boys playing together by the ponds out by the chapel ruins.

It had been their own secret place, long before women and babies, maybe a year or two into their apprenticeship. They used to visit the chapel grounds to drop huge rocks into the water and fish for tiddlers and hide from passing carts while assaulting the drivers with childish insults. They had shared secrets and plans with each other and once – Henry laughed to himself at how innocent and foolish they were back then – Gabriel had played like a maid and kissed him on the lips. Henry had pretended to be asleep, waiting for Gabe's breathing to grow heavy, then as his friend was dozing in the sunshine, he'd crept behind a wall to hide. Gabriel had woken a little while later, and Henry was just about to spring out from behind the wall to surprise him when he'd stopped himself. Gabe was crying. Henry had looked on mystified and unsettled as his friend grabbed fistfuls of wet shale from the pool, scratching his teeth and lips until they were raw and bloody.

No, Henry Sylva had never understood Gabe Griffin, yet he so desperately needed to if they were to stay in business. He climbed through the scaffolding. 'We have work now, Gabe. It's been a nasty time, but things are looking up, aren't they? A new baby coming into the world. We can teach him to tie knots and hammer nails! A grand few weeks of nicely paid work on the bridge? Say we'll take the job. Funny folk, I know, but deep pockets, and free candles to boot. Bet's warmed by that prospect, I can tell you. Why, Red Lyon Street will glow brighter than a priest's parlour. And you...' Henry tapped Gabriel's cheek '...you are going to meet someone special, just like Em. That good lady is up there looking after your Dot till you join them, thinking how daft you are. You're a man, Gabe, no need to be a spinster!'

Gabriel cleared his throat and tried to speak but couldn't. He sniffed and found himself coughing as motes of ash clung to his throat and the insides of his nose. He looked down to see a cloud of white smoke at the feet of the scaffolding, a crowd staring up at them, waving their arms. More men were jumping from the lower regions of the structure and running away, while ladders fell back, splintering against the paving slabs.

'Fire,' murmured Gabriel.

'Eh?' said Henry.

'Fire!' bellowed Gabriel, as distressed voices drifted up from the gathering crowd below. He caught sight of other men lower down the scaffolding, clinging to trusses while flames licked at their heels. There was a sharp crack as the lashings gave way beneath them and a walkway swung out like a gangplank, toppling to the ground. Gabriel looked away, unable to watch the men fall to their deaths, while Henry jumped to the ladder. 'Not that way!' said Gabriel, clutching Henry's collar. 'If we go down, we'll roast on the flames. Have to go up!'

So they climbed, ignoring the screaming from the men below, holding each other against the copings as the timber shuddered and gave way around them.

'Hold on,' said Gabriel, jumping to reach the lip of the pediment. Henry clung to his legs as the scaffolding peeled away from the cathedral in a slow arc, smashing to the ground in a mass of burning splinters and old rope.

Gabriel fixed the muscles in his fingers and peered down beyond Henry's swinging legs to see bodies strewn over the steps far below, their limbs bent in strange configurations. There was a figure in a dark cloak moving amongst them, turning their cracked heads to check their faces.

Gabriel's fingers slipped as Henry called up: 'Pull, Gabe, God blast you! Imagine we're on the ditch and pull!'

He flexed his shoulders and imagined his hands were cast in iron, setting each muscle to work in turn, flexing from his fingertips to his shoulder blades as he craned upwards. He snarled and gritted his teeth, rising inch by inch until he could reach the pediment with his knees, lifting himself the rest of the way with the last of his strength. Henry clambered up after him, the pair of them panting as they stood against the carvings of rampant horses, peering down at the devastation below.

It was a sorry sight. A number of men had lost their lives to the flames and the deadly smack of the paving. Gabriel leaned his back against the carved legs of a saint and sucked lungful after lungful of burning air.

'Hell's teeth,' said Henry. 'I reckon God wants every church on this spot to go up in flames. All them years of work and it burns down on the last bloody strut?' He gulped at the sky, where scraps of smouldering splinters drifted to the heavens, still smoking. 'Call yourself a benevolent God, you great jinglebrains?' he shouted. 'Why burn your own house down now, eh?'

Gabriel was searching the people below, looking for the mysterious figure in black. 'Ay,' he muttered, 'why now?'

Part Three

CHAPTER TWENTY-NINE

Two weeks had passed since the horrors of Fenchurch Street, and after another Sunday night at Clap's, Thomas was suffering a terrible headache. He held his throbbing skull. He was fast growing tired of Verity True-tongue and her late-night adventures, making a fool of herself with frantic dancing and clumsy flirtations. He'd arrived home at dawn, and now it was late morning, the outside world clattering and shouting, and there was an almighty racket coming from downstairs, with every kind of banging and rapping and slamming. He rolled over, trying to remember what had happened. The hall had been quieter than his first visit, the rumour about the Rat having spread quickly through the community. Verity was a suspect still, of course she was. Thomas cradled his head and groaned, remembering a drunken argument he'd had with Lavender Long-legs, the pair of them shouting horrible names at each other on Field Lane while Jacky and the Duchess tried to pull them apart. Vicious toad, that George Lavender. If anyone was the Rat it was him.

Thomas rolled onto his back and splayed his legs out, cooled by the summer breeze.

'Morning, matey,' said a voice from the window, and Thomas jumped in shock. He rubbed his eyes, thinking he must have been imagining it: a man was peering in through the hole in the wall, grinning at him. 'Late night?' he said, gesturing a fistful of nails at the empty jugs strewn around the bed.

'Yes,' said Thomas, cupping his groin as he crossed the room. 'Who are you?'

'Henry Sylva. Have you forgotten our meeting a fortnight back? We're here to fix up the building.' He waggled his hammer. 'Carpenters, like.'

'Oh yes,' said Thomas, leaning out through the hole to see if the man was floating. Indeed he was not, for his shoes were rested on a wooden platform fixed to the side of the building. Thomas jumped back with a startled gasp. A second man was climbing up the side of the building, a rope coiled around his huge shoulders. It was Mister Griffin, the molly guard.

Thomas ran to the bed to fetch his shirt, finding his stockings by the broken desk, but in his haste he managed to put both feet in one leg, and his arms became trapped in the shirtsleeves, so he found himself standing in the middle of the room, staring at the molly guard, trussed up in his garments like a Bedlamite.

Mister Sylva hooted. 'Will you look at that, Gabe? And I thought you were the worst-dressed man in London.' He cast his eyes around the garret suspiciously, leaning inside. 'I reckon there's a wench hiding in here somewhere.' He winked at Thomas's bare backside. 'She's missing out, my friend!'

Thomas hopped to the side of the room, pressing his front against the wall, his hands over his rump.

'Good morning, Mister Griffin,' he said over his shoulder. 'What a fine day it is, such a summer we're having.'

Mister Griffin looked at him with a dark frown on his handsome face, then lowered himself on his winch without a word. His work mate followed him with a cheery wave, and after much struggling, Thomas was able to tug his limbs out of his clothes and rearrange himself, before heading down to greet his aunt and uncle.

As he descended, he met Cousin Abigail on the landing, carrying a tray of miniature creations: a songbird with a seed for a beak, a hedgehog with prickles of thistle spines, and the most intricate creeping vine of ivy leaves.

'Don't you love them?' she said, looking at him hopefully.

'I do,' he said. 'I think they'd sit very nicely on the votive candles; what do you think?'

'Yes, that's perfect. How clever you are.'

Thomas left her in the workroom and made his way to the shop floor, which bustled with so many customers he had to breathe in to squeeze past. All the while, the house rattled and banged to the infernal noise of the builders outside. He thought of Mister Griffin, and squirmed with embarrassment to think of himself tangled up like that with his pale body exposed. Thomas shook the thought from his head and made his way to the back window where Uncle Squink was standing, looking out at dangling ropes and elm trusses.

'Little did I imagine,' croaked the man, in a reverential mood, 'that the arrival of my dear nephew would herald such a glorious epoch for Squink's Finest Candles of London Bridge.' His eyes glittered as he stared through the dusty window. 'We have never sold so much stock in all these years. I have been a fool, neglecting my own art. You have shown me a better way, my sweet apprentice. Thank goodness I had the sense to send for you.'

'I have seen the books,' said Thomas, ignoring his uncle's new version of events. 'Takings are up threefold on last year. Yet, I wonder...' He rubbed his chin. 'No, it is a silly thought.'

Uncle Squink took his nephew by the hands. 'Tell me, what has that mind of yours dreamed up now?'

'Well, the candles are so pretty, all covered with blossoms. I thought they might be ... scented?'

Uncle Squink stumbled backwards, clasping his hands as tears sprang from his eyes. 'My God! Scented candles. You are an artist, Thomas True, an apostle in wax, bringing the good news to chandlers everywhere. I have a vision...' He stepped back to the window, beams of light circling his crown as he turned to face the packed shop. 'One day, candles shall be more than mere sources of good, Christian light; they shall be luxury items like ornaments, every shape and colour, and, yes! every scent. They shall burn in thousands of homes the very length and breadth of the country, filling rooms with their glinting glow.'

Just then, there came an ebullient cry from the shop door, a man appearing from the bridge with a towering wig of peacock feathers in blue curls.

'Candles, darling, I must have them all!' Mister Fump pushed his way to a counter. 'I shall buy one as a gift for my sister. They won't have them in Buckinghamshire and she loves her figurines.'

Mister Vivian entered behind him. 'What is the point of a candle if you can't melt it?'

'You are a philistine, a cretin, and a bore,' said Fump. 'If I didn't know better, I should think you were Scottish.' He craned his neck, wiggling his beringed fingers at Thomas and his uncle. 'Come here, fine gentleman, I am eager to be served.'

Mister Squink hopped excitedly, rushing off to greet his customers, Thomas stepped aside just as Mister Griffin pulled the window open. He climbed into the shop and walked straight past Thomas to the shop door, his bag of tools slung over his shoulder.

Thomas watched him go, desperate to follow him onto the bridge.

Should he not thank the brave and handsome fellow for saving his life on Fenchurch Street? Besides, he had a compulsion to spend time in the company of that solemn face. He simply wanted to be near the man, and almost as soon as the thought had formed in his aching head, he found himself dashing out of the door and onto the crowded roadway.

CHAPTER THIRTY

The master carpenter, Dick Jenings, had concluded the fire at the cathedral was an honest accident: some wayward spark catching the sun-baked scaffolding like dry twigs. Gabriel knew better. That cloaked figure was no imaginary vision. Someone was trying to kill him. The Rat knew who he was and must have guessed his intentions.

Glad to have escaped the candle shop, he made his way along High Holborn, passing over the Fleet Ditch. The sun burned the back of his neck so he stopped for a rest beneath a tarpaulin. London seemed busier than ever, the crowd pressing past him like one mass of coats and baskets. For a moment, he thought he saw someone staring directly at him from the opposite side of the street, but they were immediately obscured by a cart, and when it passed there was nobody there. Gabriel growled, wiping sweat from his brow. His eyes had been playing tricks on him for two weeks now, his every nerve sensitive to the slightest movement. Was he being followed by the marshal's spies? Is that who the cloaked figure was?

Trouble, thought Gabriel, the word conjuring up the image of Thomas True: the fool standing half naked with his clothes on backwards, his body braided with plump muscles like a young sailor. Yet Gabriel had been surprised to see pale scars running across his back ribs. Had Mister True been lashed as a boy?

He walked around the bent elbow of Snow Hill, past Cock Lane, shielding his eyes. News of another murdered molly had spread fast as fire. Daisy was dead now too, the same night as her birthing, and the mollies were fearful.

Above his head, a window slammed shut, sprinkling grit around him as he stepped inside a shrinking alleyway, dipping under shirts hung from twine. He slapped through a puddle and went to turn left when his shoe met something hard in the dirt. He lifted his boot to see a flash of polished silver, the edge of something metallic cutting up through the sludge. Gabriel bent down and pulled it from the sucking ground. It was a silver disc the size of his hand, and when he buffed it on his sleeve, he saw that it was a badge with an inscription: *FREE WATERMAN*, the letters circling the

St George's Cross. It had the number *6363* engraved below, and at the very bottom of the disc, a pair of dolphins leapt up from the silver sea.

It was a Thames waterman's badge. Whoever had lost it would be unable to carry passengers. Likely drown in rum and debt within days. Gabriel rubbed the badge on his hip, then looked about. There was no sign of a waterman, and it was rare for them to climb so far from the river. Whoever it was, they must have dropped it on their way to a tavern or bawdy house. Gabriel held the badge up to the meagre light of the alleyway, grimacing at the sight of his own bloated reflection. Mister True forced his way back into his imagination, and Gabriel fished the apothecary's tincture from his pocket and was about to take a slug when a patter of footsteps came up the passageway. Gabriel spun around on his heels, yet there was nobody there. Gabriel stepped through a curtain of hanging sheets, the dripping swags closing behind him with a flutter. There were footsteps again, and a shadow. Gabriel's heart quickened.

'Anybody there?'

The end of the alleyway was bent, buildings half crumbling. Gabriel quickened his step, for there was something moving behind a torn tarpaulin up ahead.

'I see you.' He craned his neck, watching as the lurking figure shifted. 'You following me?'

He took another few steps as the figure shifted, and Gabriel found himself overcome with rage.

'Rat!'

He leapt forwards, tearing back the material to find nothing behind it but a sagging fence. For a second, he thought the skulking figure must have been a phantom, until he pressed on the wooden slats and they opened onto a steaming swamp. There was a shed half sunk in the filth like a wrecked ship, its door swinging closed.

He pulled his head back through the slats and stowed the waterman's badge in his coat pocket. The passageway was empty still, only the sound of a barking dog, a baby crying in some distant hovel. Whoever the Rat was, they were playing games with him now. Enough. He set off, eyes stinging with sweat as he climbed down through a maze of alleyways.

'Duchess,' he said, 'let's see what you have to say.'

CHAPTER THIRTY-ONE

The Royal Exchange was always busy that time of year, the favourable winds having blown ships to London from the Indies, the Middle Kingdom and the Americas. Advertisements hung on every pillar, while the perimeter of the grand façade was troubled by fruit sellers and beggars. There were the strutting Italians in their flouncing shirts and Dutchmen in thrum caps, Frenchmen shaking their heads in furious agreement, yet no sign of the Duchess, or to use his proper name: Mister Timothy Rettipence.

Gabriel passed around to Kidnapper's Walk where the plantation traders set their traps for lost boys and girls for slaves and whores. Still, no Rettipence. Gabriel took a moment to himself, thinking about his own trap. He'd allowed the time to pass, waiting for the right opportunity to slot the next piece into place. Perhaps this would be his opportunity. He would listen closely to what Rettipence had to say, sure to choose his own words carefully.

He pushed back to the courtyard, glad as ever to have the advantage of height. After three orbits, he was ready to give up, when Mister Rettipence appeared right in front of him, speaking animatedly to a wealthy associate about investments in a new shipping route around the Cape.

Gabriel blocked their way. 'Afternoon.'

Mister Rettipence tutted. 'Oh, do get out of our way, barbarian oaf, whatever you're selling, we don't want it.'

Gabriel refused to move, holding his arm out so they couldn't pass. 'I said, afternoon.'

'Zoods, these primitive savages,' said the second man, puffing out the gold buttons on his waistcoat. 'Where on Earth do they import them from? Move aside, alien beast, or you'll taste the kiss of an Englishman's cutlass.' For the first time, he looked at Gabriel directly, expecting to see a face rather than a stomach, realising there was far more to the man than he'd bargained for. His tufty eyebrows sprang up to his periwig. 'By the heavens, he must be a giant from the New World.'

Mister Rettipence looked up from his ledger with an impatient huff, catching sight of Gabriel and instantly turning pale.

'I ... oh ... It is ... ah,' he said, before suggesting his friend take a walk to the offices on the opposite side of the exchange so matters might be drawn up. As soon as the man was gone, he turned to Gabriel with his cheeks puffed out. 'What are you doing here?'

'Reckon you might know who the Rat is. Reckon you might *be* the Rat.'

'Preposterous,' said Rettipence, struggling to keep his voice low as people milled around them. 'Is that the way it works, eh? Clap sends her troll out to threaten us? I have a wife and two children, you know.' He pushed his thumbs through his buttonholes. 'Timothy Rettipence is a respectable man.'

'Ay,' said Gabriel, 'that's what I say to meself every Sunday night. There goes the respectable Duchess Prune with her lips stuck to Lavender's backside.'

Rettipence's eyes bulged. 'Why me? Whatever makes you think I should want to mix with the Society hounds? I do not need bribes, Lotty Lump, I do not require power, I have no vendettas to settle. I value my privacy.'

'Martin Lightbody pointed you out the night before his throat got cut. You, Lavender, Jacky, Fump, Vivian, and the new lad, True.'

'Thomas True,' nodded Mister Rettipence. 'My darling Lavender met him right over there through those arches, the night he first arrived in London. He was invited by Sweet Jacky, that cocky little cutpurse. Did Lavender tell you what she saw?'

'Mister True was exploring the molly market at night. I hear he got himself into some bother with the hounds.'

'And managed to get out of bother with not so much as a bruise or a cut on his pretty face.'

'Ay?'

'Well then, there you are. Most suspicious.'

'Lavender escaped too.'

'With a lump on her beautiful face the size of an onion.' Mister Rettipence pulled his chin into his neck. 'And twice the size of your brain, I should say.'

He stepped around Gabriel, barging between a pair of spice merchants, and turned the corner, jumping as Gabriel stepped out from behind a pillar.

'You're the easiest of all of them to blackmail. So much to lose.'

Rettipence looked around for a way to escape then gave in. 'You can blackmail me anytime you like, molly guard – you won't be the first,' he said in a defeated voice. 'But nobody, not even the Society, could threaten to shame me more than my own sorry heart. I am tortured every single day and every single night with terrible feelings. Crimes committed against my own soul, my own family, my own body. I know people laugh at me – you must know what that feels like – but none of them laughs so loud as I do when I catch sight of myself in those places, dressed up like an old maid. Why, that silly, womanish thing they call the Duchess is almost as whimsical as the man standing before you today.' He held out his hands. 'The Duchess or Mister Timothy Rettipence, it really doesn't matter which you laugh at, which you threaten, or which you blackmail, both of them are pathetic and both are doomed.' He stepped closer. 'With the dreams I have every single night of my life, I deserve to hang, and soon I expect I shall, with the way things are.'

Gabriel gripped him by the arm as he tried to go. 'I spent a night in the compter with Old Bob. I hear the two of you were lovers before Lavender came along. I listened to him crying out your name while they cut his throat. He was about to tell me about the Rat. I'm thinking, maybe he did.'

Mister Rettipence blanched. 'My name? As they killed him? My poor Bob. I guessed he was dead. I wish I'd told him what he meant to me.'

'Then I'm right. You're the same Timothy he spoke of that night?'

'I am. It was a long time ago when he took me under his wing. I was a young man then, and he was much older. He taught me so much about truth and kindness and patience, and now I hope to do the same for my Lavender, even if it means taking the noose for him. Is that such a suspicious thing? Some think I'm a sordid, pathetic creature. Do you?' He shook his head. 'It isn't like that. Youth is attractive, it's true, but even with my wobbles and wrinkles I can offer a young molly what I was given myself: a little wisdom, a little hope, a little comfort. Love, you might say.'

Gabriel shrugged.

'I see it's an alien concept to you,' said Mister Rettipence with a sour smile. 'Together, always together, that's what they cry. There's a joke. Together till you're an old man past his best years, and then you are adrift, nothing but a target for mockery. Oh what do you care, you are young and strong still. Listen to me; I know my Lavender is not the Rat, and nor am I.' He reached into his pocket and pulled out a slip of paper. 'Our housemaid found this under our front door the morning after the ambush on Fenchurch Street. Much persuasion it took to convince my wife it was posted to the wrong address.'

Gabriel opened it, a chill running down his spine.

You Were Right To Leave. Coward. Beware The Rat

Mister Rettipence shook his head. 'I was lucky to get away. Poor Daisy, she was too confident. Take the note if you like. I shall call on you if I hear any more; what is your address?'

So, Gabriel's trap was about to gain a new part, just as he'd hoped. He imagined his scheme taking shape in his hands like a model made of doweling. He took a breath, checking they weren't being spied on then spoke clearly so he couldn't be misheard. 'I'm on Red Lyon Street for now, but I'll be gone from there soon.'

'Where will you go?'

'Warehouse by the Fleet Bridge,' he said. 'The one with the blue doors. Keep our pulling ropes and poles in there. Might as well stash meself by the stink an' all.'

'The sacrifices we make.'

Gabriel nodded and moved away, but then turned back, struck by something the man had said. 'You reckon you'd take the noose for Lavender?'

'I would not let her swing alone. Some say those words for fun, but my poor Bob taught me the promise before anybody else did, and it is written onto my heart.'

Gabriel heard the words that filled the man's eyes with sorrow. He nodded, finishing the phrase for him:

'Always together, Mister Rettipence. Have a good day.'

He left the exchange, his mind reeling with doubts and questions. Still, his plan was forming, and after meeting Rettipence, he was certain it would work. It was a last resort and required careful preparation, yet with a few morsels dropped here and there, the trap would soon be set.

First, however: the waterman's badge.

CHAPTER THIRTY-TWO

Gabriel battled his way to Tower Hill. He stood for a moment, allowing the breeze to cool his pits. There were fifty or more boatmen along the wharfside, playing cards, drinking and laughing, and he was just looking at the badge, wondering whether he had the strength to speak to them all, when his shoulder was grabbed by a raven-haired man with coal-rimmed eyes and the waterman's livery of a scarlet doublet.

'My saviour! You found it, so you did.'

Gabriel held the badge close to his chest. 'You know the owner?'

'I do,' said the man with a deferential bow. 'That is the property of Apollo Rawhead, I could not mistake it.'

'How do you know?'

'When a man has lived with an object for so many years, then every corner, every scratch, every dent is no less familiar than his own mother's face.' He reached out with black fingernails. 'Give it.'

'Tell me your name first.'

'I just told you. Apollo Rawhead.'

'Ay, and what's the number on it?'

The waterman scratched his head, looking to the sky, deep in thought. 'Well now, can Apollo remember? It's been his badge since he was a tiddler. Still, you're right to be careful, Apollo appreciates it very much. Too many rogues around these days.' He tugged the skirts of his doublet, brushing his stained fingers over the filthy material as though it were finest silk, then recited the number. 'Six three, six three. Now, will you complete your good deed and return the badge to its rightful and most grateful owner?'

Gabriel stared at the man, then looked around the wharf, not sure who might be watching, but certain someone was.

'Should have taken better care of it.' Gabriel slapped the badge into the waterman's hand and turned away too quickly, his head spinning.

'Look at you,' said the boatman. 'Melting like a mountain of tally wax in the hard sun, poor fellow. You must accept my apologies for dragging you all this way from Highest Holborn on my account. Here...' He stepped up, taking Gabriel by the elbow. 'Allow me to give you a trip downriver, by way of a reward. No payment requested nor taken, upon my honour.'

Part of Gabriel wanted to refuse, but another part had caught the scent of something – something he couldn't help but follow. The waterman would not be told, and soon Gabriel found himself being led to the Tower Stairs and into a waiting wherry.

'Easy, Mister Griffin,' cried the boatman, settling his oars. 'You wouldn't want to fall in now, would you? I'm sure you'd drown.'

Gabriel caught the flash of a long knife at the man's hip. He had a sudden thought: how had the waterman known his name? And how had he known that his badge was discovered in High Holborn? It could have been lost in a hundred places, surely? Gabriel gripped the sides of the boat and was about to climb out when there came a sudden clattering down the stone steps above their heads and to Gabriel's astonishment, none other than Mister True leapt across five feet of open water with a yelp and a happy laugh, landing feet first in the wherry boat.

'Mister Griffin, there you are!' he cried, all arms and legs wiggling over the sides like an upturned woodlouse. 'I saw you leaving the shop, then lost your tail. I'm so pleased I found you.'

CHAPTER THIRTY-THREE

They were already halfway across the river, harried by the trailing wakes of passing boats. 'Why, Apollo Rawhead is lucky to have such a fine gentleman as Mister Griffin riding in his little boat. Truly he is a blessed Charon.' He turned his coal-blackened eyes to their stowaway. 'And you too, Mister True.'

They skulled upriver, Gabriel watching the Tower slip away as he tried to think. A pair of apprentices in high spirits called over to them: 'Oi, you mother-pimps, you sister-stallions, you cockbawds!'

'Why are they shouting at us?' said Thomas, craning his neck as one of the lads flashed his pimply backside.

'River wit,' said Gabriel. 'A fool's custom, old as London itself.'

Apollo gave a deep nod. 'Ay, a fool's custom it is. After all, there ain't a custom that wasn't invented by a fool, and not a fool who doesn't love a custom.' He rested his oars. 'Hey ho!' he shouted to his fellow boatman, splashing water into the air as they rocked and rolled. 'Control them boys in your puny galleon; I've got a pair of fine lords aboard my ship, can't you see?'

The other boatman watched Apollo with a curious gaze. 'Wherryman, where is your badge?'

Apollo held it up as they sailed by, spitting a gobbet of phlegm expertly into the passing boat.

Soon, they were as far from the sloping banks as they could be, the fat river flattening out to broad banks as the oars clooped through swirling water.

'What's this?' asked Gabriel. 'Why are you passing the stairs? I never needed to go this way.'

Apollo continued with his sculling, deep sorrow in his eyes. 'Ah now, this part of it does cause me grief. I do feel badly, Mister Griffin. And poor young Thomas True here will regret jumping in the boat, I'm sure. I wonder, does he comprehend it yet, the pretty flea?' He fixed his eyes on the young man. 'His dandy shoes never to touch cobble again?'

'What do you mean by that?' laughed Thomas. 'Mister Griffin, what is he talking about?'

Gabriel sat up straight, holding the sides of the boat. 'So, it was you following me today?'

Apollo lifted his hat with a wink. 'Depends where you were followed. Come on now, no trouble, it'll be kinder on you both to stay calm.' He pulled the knife from his pocket, turning it in his fingers as he spoke. 'She's an old blade. Some take her gentle as a kiss between the ribs, crying softly for me to do it quick. "Will it hurt badly?" they say. While others make a terrible racket, fighting till their fingers are ribbons and their whole body is sliced up like lamb.' He cast his eyes over Gabriel. 'They told me you was large, but never so large as this. If I'd have known, I'd have charged them double.' He pulled a pea-green purse from his pocket and bounced it on his palm. 'Should have two of these just for you, Mister Griffin; and another for your bitch.'

Gabriel jumped forwards, snatching at the knife, but the boatman was too quick for him.

'Sit back! My God, Mister Griffin, you will drown us all if you move so sudden. Sweet shit,' he clasped his heart, 'how I hate the water.'

'What sort of a wherryman hates the water?' laughed Thomas, looking between the men with a confused frown.

Gabriel studied the man's costume, caked in blood. 'He ain't a wherryman.'

'Ay, 'tis true. Though I couldn't tell you who I am most days. Last week I was an apprentice farrier, the week before that, a porter from Dublin. Today, you may call me Apollo Rawhead, for that is the fool what lent me his clothes, and he shan't be missed by all accounts.'

Thomas scrabbled backwards, pressing his slender back between Gabriel's legs, and spoke from the corner of his mouth. 'Mister Griffin, I believe he intends to kill us.'

Gabriel tried to think. At any second, the killer would lunge at them with his knife, and if they weren't stabbed to death, they would all end up in the river. Gabriel peered over the gunnel to the water where the green mud lay barely an inch below the surface, puckered like a toad's back. The rogue was right – they would never swim through it.

'The big one knows it,' said the man. 'There's no escape, molly boys.'

Thomas gulped. 'Mister Griffin is not a molly, nor am I.'

Gabriel hushed him, holding the man's eye. 'I'll pay.'

'How kind,' said the man, holding out his calloused fingers.

Thomas gripped Gabriel's arm. 'Don't pay him, Mister Griffin. We'll overcome him and fetch a constable.'

The man laughed. 'I'll slit your pretty gizzards and say you fell in, a-coddling like two young sweethearts. Even if you get back to land, I reckon they'll believe me before you.' He lifted his eyes to the heavens. 'Oh, sweet Lord, with their fudgelling about in their breeches and drinking of their tongues, and touching and squeezing, it was all I could do to pray they would answer my begging, but, oh! they was gripped, I say! Gripped in the tight fist of the dark angel.'

'Liar,' said Thomas. He tried to stand up, almost capsizing the boat. 'Help! Thief!'

Gabriel reached into his coat and pulled out his purse, fumbling the small, glass bottle with it. The boatman instantly snatched away both, lifting the bottle to his eye with a merry wink. 'What do we have here then? A little tipple?'

'It's a potion, that's all. Hand it back.'

'Oh ay, what sort of a potion?' The man pulled the cork from the bottle for a sniff. 'Phwoar, what foul poison is this?'

Gabriel held his eye. 'Aphrodisiac.'

'An aphrodisiac, says the giant?' The boatman looked at Thomas. 'You must be a very brave boy to play with a cannon like that.' He held the bottle up to the light, inspecting the glutinous yellow liquid, before scrabbling forwards and thrusting it at Gabriel. 'You drink some, first. Show me it's safe.'

Gabriel took the bottle and swigged a measure of the foul liquid, holding it in his cheek as he struggled to keep his face from gurning.

The wherryman watched him with a sceptical eye. 'Does it work?'

Gabriel leaned back. 'Ay,' he said, hoping the assassin wouldn't notice the slur in his voice. 'Would make a tortoise fuck a horse.'

The wherryman roared with laughter, grabbing the bottle back and swigging half of it down in one go with a smack of his lips.

'Well then, boys,' he burped, cupping his groin. 'I think it's working already. I think we need a little privacy, don't you? Satisfy my curiosity, then we'll see about making a bargain.'

Gabriel held Thomas in silence as the boat slid beneath a gangway. It was silent in the shadows, but for the sound of a distant songbird and the soft lapping of the water. Thomas began to sob, understanding what was about to happen.

'Please,' he said, as the boatman began to unbutton his breeches. 'I don't want to.'

'Hush, pretty lad, you've done it before, I wager.'

'Never.'

The assassin spat into his palm. 'God should forgive a fellow a little mis-adventure, don't you think? Come closer now, pretty lad.' He looked down at himself, impressed. 'Your potion works, Mister Griffin. Will you look at this pole? I've not been so glorious in months.' He grunted at Thomas, his eyes glittering. 'Well then, boy, have at it.'

Thomas shifted forwards and lowered his head, but found himself overcome by the stench and leaned over the side of the boat, retching.

'I'll do it,' said Gabriel, pushing past him.

The assassin held out his knife, flashing light into Gabriel's eyes. 'Hold up a second,' he said. 'I'll slit you up nicely if you bite me, then I'll cut the boy up before tipping you both overboard. How do you fancy that? Off we go then, giant, I'm ready to dock.'

Gabriel took one last breath, almost vomiting at the stink. He was about to lower his head when a deep rumbling sound rose up and the assassin dropped his knife into the water, curling up on the prow, clutching his stomach.

'The potion,' he squealed, 'it's poison!'

Gabriel lunged at the man, gripping him around the neck and they scrabbled together as the boat tipped and swung. Thomas realised what was happening and joined the fray, until suddenly the assassin's head collided with a pier strut and he lost his balance, falling over the edge of the prow with a splash into the shallow water. The stricken man stared up, his hair swimming around his face in tendrils.

'Save me,' he said. 'If I move, the mud will swallow me up. Here, take my ankle.' He waggled his foot, yet even as he did so, the mud sucked at his heel.

'Forget your damned foot, take my hand,' said Gabriel, reaching out.

'Not likely!' said the assassin, the mud sucking at his ears. He had the green purse clasped to his chest. 'You will steal all my money. Pull me in by my leg and I'll share it with you.'

It was impossible. A touch of the assassin's ankle or a mere tilt of his boot and his head would be gobbled up by the green mud before he could blink. Not even a man of Gabriel's strength could save him then, not without ropes and a pulling pole. Gabriel reached down, clicking his fingers.

'Enough, damn you, what's worth more? Those coins or your life?'

The man's eyes were peering through an inch of water as he kissed his lips to the surface like a fish. 'Do you take me for a fool?' he said. 'You would snatch my money and drown me.' He began to panic as he felt his legs sink. 'This is their fault!' he gasped as the slime drew fingers over his eyes. 'The Rat. The Society. The Justices. I should never have gone to...' His nostrils sucked in water, spurting and wheezing until, with his final breath, he spoke a single word: 'Alsatia!'

Quickly, inexorably, the mud ate him up, first hands, then feet, then legs, head and torso, until all of him was consumed by the loamy depths, but for his erect prick, which slipped out of sight last of all, root to winking tip like the mast of a sinking ship.

CHAPTER THIRTY-FOUR

Gabriel and Thomas sat together, each lost in his own thoughts, as the boat drifted back into the sunshine. When after an hour or so they met one another's eye, Thomas exploded with a hysterical laugh and jumped to his feet.

'We will hang. We killed a man. Murder!'

'Hush your gums,' said Gabriel. 'We were defending ourselves. Didn't kill him, did we? He fell in.'

'What was in that potion? You poisoned him, then drowned him.'

Gabriel looked at the bottle, still a quarter full, and sniffed it. 'Not poison; medicine.'

Thomas pushed back with his heels, holding his hands out with a terrified expression. 'Please, Mister Griffin. Am I next? Will you murder me too? I shan't tell a soul what you did, not a soul. If you must kill me, do so quickly, I beg of you, not in such a peculiar way. Or take me back to shore and turn me in. Only ... no!' He covered his face with a whimper. 'I couldn't bear the pillory; I am not brave enough to survive it. I will pay you, Mister Griffin, anything you ask.'

Gabriel gripped Thomas by the belt of his breeches and forced him to sit down. 'I'll throw you overboard if that's what you want; or you can sit quietly while I think.' He looked at his fingers, still pasted with the assassin's slime, and wiped them on his breeches then peered along the flat water to where the river bent its belly towards the bridge. He had an idea. He took off his coat and donned the boatman's scarlet doublet, the shoulders and arms ripping at the seams.

'What are you doing?' said Thomas.

'Hold on. There ain't much time.'

Water flew behind the boat in waves as they raced upriver, driven at such an almighty clip they could have shot past any galleon at full sail. Thomas watched the muscles in Gabriel's arms tensing, his shoulders snapping firm and round as cannon balls, ripping the fabric of the boatman's doublet with every heave.

'Where are we going?' he shouted as they dashed past Pelican Stairs.

'The bridge,' said Gabriel, forcing the boatman's hat onto his head, though it was several sizes too small. 'Now lie flat so you're out of sight.'

Thomas did as he was told as the bridge hove into view against the orange sky, its stone legs assaulted by a thundering cascade of water. With an almighty roar, Gabriel doubled his efforts, wrestling against the river as they flew towards the bellowing cataracts. 'When I tell you,' he shouted, 'take a deep breath. Deepest breath you ever took.'

'We'll crash!' shouted Thomas. 'If we pass under the bridge in this direction we'll be smashed to pieces!'

'You think that assassin's body won't be dredged up sooner or later? You think the other boatmen didn't see us with him? If we want to live, this is our best chance. We have to make it look like he foundered.'

Thomas nodded as Gabriel fought to drive the boat towards the booming rapids. The bridge loomed over them like the walls of a great castle as the stern nosed into rolling glass.

'Now!' bellowed Gabriel.

The river chewed the boat up like a biscuit, breaking over the gunnels in a wailing hurricane of white water. They were flung hard against the side of a towering strut and tumbled, sinking as the bridge disappeared in a wall of foam. They touched hands as they spun in a plunging screw, clinging to one another, blinded by their own clothes until the waters grew dark. Gabriel opened his eyes and saw the dim outline of Thomas's face, the laces of his shirt drifting in ribbons through his hair. They lay still on the riverbed, encased in a blanket of velvet loam. Gabriel blew out his final breath and, wracked by pain, felt the twitch of Thomas's fingers, and to his surprise, felt sad to die.

CHAPTER THIRTY-FIVE

Thomas exploded to the surface with an almighty gasp. He coughed, flapping about in circles before swimming to the wharf, dragging himself up by his elbows and knees. After much spluttering, he collapsed at the summit of the steps.

'Mister Griffin?' His teeth were chattering, his fingers numb against the stone steps. 'Mister Griffin, where are you?'

He climbed a little further, coughing up buckets of brown water. There was such a storm in his skull, he could barely make sense of what had happened.

'Oh dear. We killed a man. Murder.'

He slapped onto the wharf, finding his skin raw but his bones miraculously unbroken. He cradled his knees and wiped a film of green slime from his cheek, searching the surface of the water for his friend.

There was nothing to see but the roar of the rapids between the cataracts, pieces of the boat drifting downriver.

Thomas imagined Mister Griffin's lifeless body far below the surface: heavy and huge as a boulder. Their eyes had met down there in the privacy of the riverbed, and he felt sure they had exchanged a secret. Mister Griffin had cradled his body, and he had softened to it, ready for death. It felt as though they belonged in that moment, that they could simply open their mouths and breathe.

Thomas pulled a length of twine from his tongue, gagging as a long weed slid up his throat. He remembered the force of a kick as he'd risen from the riverbed.

'Thank you, Mister Griffin, you saved my life again.' He smiled. 'If only I could find a friend so brave as you, I should make him my companion.'

Shoeless with raggedy clothes dripping on the cobbles, he limped over the wharf with a sorry heart towards Darkhouse Lane.

'Wait,' gasped a voice from his back.

Thomas turned to see an arm slap onto the wharf, followed by a pair of muscular shoulders. Mister Griffin climbed into view then collapsed, water gushing from his nose and mouth. Thomas ran back to the stairs, rolling his friend over to help him breathe, tugging vegetable peelings and fur from his nostrils.

'Come along, Mister Griffin, that's right, choke it all up.'

It might have been an hour before the huge man stirred. It often seemed he must have drowned after all, for Thomas was forced to check his pulse more than once. Yet stir he did, just as the moon cut free of the bridge, and Thomas helped him up, carrying as much of his weight as he could manage. By the time they'd passed from Fresh Wharf to Thames Street, Mister Griffin could walk unaided and after a gruff 'thank you' he staggered ahead, leading them away from the river.

'Come,' he croaked, 'follow me.'

Thomas followed along as they trudged through lightless alleyways, down street after bewildering street, until at last they arrived at Covent Garden. The piazza was empty, its extremities haunted by skulking harlots who whistled and cooed at them as they passed.

'Where are we going?' Thomas asked. 'To hide perhaps? Or to pray?'

Mister Griffin turned with a grunt. 'Pray to what?'

'Well, to God, of course. Or to a saint perhaps. Is there a saint for drowning? Nicholas, I think; he looks after sailors.' He waited for an answer, yet none came. 'I won't tell a soul what happened on the boat, you know. I shan't say a thing, I swear it.'

Mister Griffin walked on, water spurting from his boots. Thomas grew peevish in the silence. Was there really nothing to say, after everything they'd been through in the past two hours? He was about to voice his frustration when he collided into Mister Griffin's back. They were standing outside a small shop with a brightly lit window, casting its happy glow to the gravel at their feet. Behind the glass stood a display of periwigs of all styles, each individually coiffured and coloured. Mister Griffin rapped on the door and stood back.

'Hello?' came a timid voice from within. 'Who goes there?'

'Open up,' said Mister Griffin. 'It's me.'

'My goodness!' came the man's voice. 'Frank, it's Lotty and a friend, come to see us without warning.'

'Well then, let them in,' came a second man's voice.

'And what of my face?'

'Well there isn't much you can do about it.'

'I suppose you're right. They shall have to see me at my worst.'

With that, the door swung open, revealing Mister Fump in a banyan of purple silk, a turban on his head the size of a footstool, and upon his dainty feet, slippers with curled toes, which jingled as he ushered in his dripping visitors.

'Enter, enter! My goodness, Lotty, squeeze past me but don't marry me. Oh, Mister True, how pleasurable to have you in our sweet sanctuary.'

The shop was a merry little place, filled from floor to ceiling with row upon row of periwigs, ribbons, powders and bows. The walls were painted with roses, while a small but ferocious fire burned beside an assortment of dozing chairs. Mister Vivian appeared through a velvet curtain with a bowl of steaming water, setting it down before the hearth. Thomas shivered in the sudden heat, his clothes hanging from his pimpled skin like wet crepe.

Mister Fump looked them up and down. 'Just look at the pair of you; whatever happened?'

'We were in a wherry boat,' said Thomas, 'and there was an awful man who—'

A hand clapped over his mouth and Mister Griffin spoke up. 'Never mind what happened. Do you have wine and clothes for Mister True?'

'Wine we have,' said Fump, with a suspicious eye. 'Clothes however...' He gawped at Thomas's open shirt and hanging sleeves, exposing more than they covered. 'I confess, he looks rather smart to me.'

'Clothes,' said Gabriel. 'Now.'

'Oh, very well, though I shouldn't think any of my shirts are suitable for either of you – they are far too fashionable.'

'And far too large,' added Mister Vivian, placing a pair of silk robes beside the fire. He pulled a set of shutters across the shop window. 'Come along, dearest, let us give these two some privacy.'

Thomas and Gabriel stood alone in a puddle, their faces lit by the crackling fire. With a mumbled apology, Thomas moved to the corner of the room and began removing what remained of his clothes. He watched Mister Griffin do the same on the opposite side, moving behind an assortment of horsehair perukes. The long mirror above the fireplace betrayed him, for Thomas could see the man's entire body: huge shoulders rigid beneath the thin gauze of his wet shirt, the golden skin of his forearms covered in dark hair. He was feeling around his neck with a worried expression, searching the floor, then his pockets.

Thomas tugged his breeches down, keeping his voice light as he played the voyeur.

'It is ever so nice of Mister Fump and Mister Vivian to help us.'

'Ay,' said Mister Griffin distractedly, turning his wet breeches inside out and staring inside them.

'They look very different as men, don't they?'

'Ay.' The man was holding his boot upside down now, poking his fingers inside it.

'Do you think your plan has worked? Are we safe and—'

'Enough, Mister True.'

And that, evidently, was that. Thomas kicked away what was left of his stockings and threw them in a ball into the fire. The scraps fizzled and hissed as the flames ate them up. Mister Griffin seemed to give up on his search, whatever it was for. He stepped onto the rug in front of the fire and peeled away his translucent shirt. Thomas watched him from the corner of his eye, biting his lip. He had never seen such a muscular back, the man's flesh cobbling as he wrung the material dry, sending sparks barrelling up the chimney. The steam varnished the giant's muscular chest as he leaned against the chimney breast, pulling his breeches down to his ankles and folding them over the back of a chair. Thomas admired his mighty calf muscles and a pair of impossibly powerful buttocks, which shone like boulders in the flickering light. *Turn*, thought Thomas, and the man did with his arms above his head, his spine pattering with a series of dull clicks.

'Christ Almighty!' exclaimed Thomas in an unintentional hoot of shock, knocking his head against a cupboard and falling to the floor.

Mister Griffin looked down with a frown, balling his stockings. 'Trouble,' muttered the man. 'Trouble.'

'You're quite right,' said Thomas, picking himself up, suddenly feeling overcome by the heat. He turned to the wall to spare himself more excitement, for he felt certain he would faint. 'I am trouble, always have been, it's my constant worry. I didn't mean to behave so foolishly on the boat. That's just my way though, I'm afraid, causing a fuss everywhere I go. I sometimes think I must be mad, always saying and doing the wrong thing.' Thomas attempted a carefree laugh. 'You're such a great beast of a man, Mister Griffin, running about, saving everybody. You must be used to people staring at you? I don't think I've ever seen a man so large.'

Mister Griffin gave a humph, pulling the robe around himself, his vast frame wrapped in silk like a pink apple. Thomas folded his arms to cover his nipples, more ashamed of his body than ever. He dashed to the chair and slipped into his own robe as quickly as he could, pulling it up to his neck to cover his slender chest.

'You're not like me,' he said. 'I'm too skinny, that's my problem. I do what I can to lift heavy things and eat twice as much as any man I've ever met – though it's mostly fruit – but still here I am with barely a hair on my chest and all my veins and bones showing through.'

The fire popped, and Mister Griffin glanced across the room with a curious expression. 'Look alright to me.'

Thomas gave a shy smile. 'You're a quiet man, Mister Griffin. I like that. So very large. Isn't it strange that I'm stuffed with so many words, when you have none?' He laughed at his own jest, then straightened his face under the man's flat stare.

They were trapped in silence once more, and Thomas found himself growing peevish again. After all, had they not survived their adventure together? Was he not worth a few kind words? Lavender Long-legs must have dripped her poison into Mister Griffin's ears, the same as everybody else. He was just about to say so, when the man surprised him, speaking in a soft rumbling voice.

'I know I am ugly.'

They stared at each other; Thomas astounded by what he had heard. He shook his head. 'No, Mister Griffin, you are beautiful.'

Just then, Mister Fump stepped back into the room, clapping his hands together with a whistle. 'Well now, look at you both standing there like a pair of shy schoolboys. My, my!' He plucked at the cord of his robe. 'The fire is too hot, don't you agree? I have an idea. Instead of wearing our night clothes, perhaps we ought to steam together naked, like Turks in a hummum? Wonderful fun, so long as we cover the chairs.' He looked between the men hopefully. 'Now come along, both of you, surely mountainous Adam and fair Eve can keep a little snake company?' He gave Thomas a wink as he opened his robe, only to snap it shut again as his companion walked in with cups of steaming wine.

'Put it away, dear, they've suffered enough.'

Duly, they settled in front of the fire, Thomas curling into a low chair with his bare feet to the hearth. Slowly, he roasted and relaxed, his breath thickening to the back of his throat, while the hard wood of the chair pinched his ear, as warm and welcome as any pillow. With a cosy smack of his lips, he forgot where he was and fell into a deep and exhausted sleep.

CHAPTER THIRTY-SIX

'I can't believe it,' said Mister Fump, jumping as the wind rattled the shutters. 'You honestly think the *Rat* is one of our own dearest boys from Mother Clap's?' His face was solemn for once. 'Surely not.'

'Has to be,' said Gabriel, keeping his voice low as Mister True muttered beside him, deep in slumber. The young man's words were only just audible above the crackling of the fire: 'Tie them by their necks,' he was saying, 'drop them in rows.'

Gabriel shifted in his chair and gave Fump and Vivian a serious look. 'Martin told me the night before we found him in the ditch. Said it was one of the six of you sitting up in the gallery. He got a note. George Lavender got one too.' And Rettipence. Don't seem likely it's him, far as I can tell.'

Mister Fump shook his head. 'A molly could never be so wicked.'

'Nonsense,' said Mister Vivian. 'Anyone can be wicked; it only takes practice.'

Gabriel sighed. 'Queed says I have to find the Rat, or we all hang.'

Fump gasped, gripping his companion's hand. 'Lord save us, we'll perish.'

Vivian waved him away. 'Gabriel dear, they cannot hang a man unless a witness catches him in the act of sodomy. Anything less, and it's the pillory, and even then, they require evidence. This Rat can give all the names he likes to these *justices* – they can't do a thing.'

Gabriel shook his head. 'There'll be raids. Don't know when exactly, but Queed says they're planning a sweep of the whole city. Every molly house in London will be purged. They have names, and if mine is on the list, yours will be too.' Gabriel paused as Thomas stretched his arms and turned his face into the chair with a dimpled smile.

'Tie their necks,' he said in a dreamy voice again, just loud enough for Gabriel to hear. 'Drop in rows.'

Gabriel gave him a lingering frown before turning back to Vivian. 'You think them justices won't have witnesses? Men and women ready to testify against us for a shilling? The Society supplies what the law demands. If it wants us hanged, then hanged we'll be, sodomy or no.'

Fump raised his cup. 'Then I choose sodomy! We must tell our friends at once.'

'Hush,' said Gabriel. The walls of the shop were thin. 'Do that and there'll be panic across the city, spreading fast as the Great Fire. Accusations, arguments, betrayal...'

'Betrayal?'

Gabriel didn't want to admit such a thing, but the evidence of his work on the door of Mother Clap's had taught him that injustice does not make men kind. 'Ay. Mollies turning on each other, betraying friends. I'd be doing the Society's work for them if I shared our secret.'

Mister Vivian nodded. 'Then you must work with the marshal. I never thought I would say such a thing. Find the Rat before it's too late.' He leaned in, checking Thomas was still asleep. 'What do you know so far?'

Gabriel shook his head. 'Hardly anything. Only that the Rat must have been at Mother Clap's the night Mister True arrived, and if Martin was right, it has to be one of the six of you.' He gave his friends an apologetic look then cast his eye to Thomas. 'The Rat was at Miss Muff's on Whitechapel too, I reckon. The hounds had been warned the mollies were going that way, and when poor Daisy was clubbed to death, she cried out to someone there. I heard her.'

'What did she say?'

Gabriel chose his words carefully. '"You told me I was safe. You said they wouldn't get me."'

'So Daisy was in the pay of the Rat.'

'Seems so. Threatened, I expect.' Gabriel took a deep gulp of hot wine and told his friends about the figure he'd seen at the bog houses and below the burning scaffolding, then his night with Old Bob in the compter. He relayed his conversations with Lavender and Rettipence and, though he'd promised himself he would be discreet, he told them about the assassin in the wherry boat.

Once he was finished, Vivian poured them all a fresh cup of hot wine and lowered himself back into his chair. 'Who do you think it is then – the Rat?'

'How should I know?' said Gabriel. 'Could be one of you.'

He laughed, yet the two old men exchanged meaningful looks, speaking without words, as companions do.

'We weren't going to show anybody, dear,' said Fump, reaching up to a trinket box on a shelf and opening it up. 'But since others have, we might as well.' He held out two slips of paper.

Gabriel already knew what he'd see, yet the words chilled him to his bones in spite of the burning fire. He read Mister Vivian's first:

ALWAYS TOGETHER?

He turned it over, sniffing the paper to catch a peculiar scent, then read the second note:

SOON PARTED.

'You needn't look so concerned, sweetheart,' said Fump. 'We've been threatened so many times before. Ugly notes through our door, nasty heckling in the street. Why, those windows have been smashed more times than we have.'

Gabriel rubbed his eyes, thinking as the room went dark. The time had come to add another piece to his trap. He felt like a worm, yet there was only one way to be certain, and even his good friends Fump and Vivian must play their part in unmasking the Rat. He stared into the fire as Thomas stirred beside him. There wasn't much time, so he spoke quickly, making sure the old men were listening to his every word.

'I'll have nowhere to live soon. No time to find anywhere, neither. Got to move out from Red Lyon Street by the end of next month.'

'That's less than four weeks away. Where will you go?' said Vivian.

'Up by Clap's I reckon, in the wood stores by the steps. Should do me right for a few days at least.'

'How very arboreal of you,' said Fump. 'I do enjoy the scent of timber on a man, but you can stay here.'

'Rather be alone. But thank you.'

Vivian turned his eyes to Thomas, who was stirring again. 'What of our young friend here; has the Rat sent him a note?'

'Don't think so,' said Gabriel.

'Only Mister True and Sweet Jacky spared then. You know, there are those who might say our Rat is right there, sleeping like a lamb.'

The three men settled into a thoughtful silence as they sipped their spiced wine and watched the flames dancing in the hearth.

'He ain't wicked,' said Gabriel. 'Foolish though.'

Vivian gave a slow nod. 'Tyrants conjure the Devil; fools follow him.'

Fump tore off his turban in a fit, speaking in an outraged whisper. 'Listen to the pair of you condemning the poor creature. Honestly Viv, dear, you're as bad as Lavender, shame on you.'

Mister Vivian supped the last of his wine and rose unsteadily from the chair. 'Time for my bed.'

Fump batted him away irritably. 'Ignore him Gabriel, he's rotten drunk. You're still a young man yourself, barely six or seven years between the pair of you. I fancy you make a handsome couple. There, I said it! He, the beauty, you the brawn.'

Vivian chuckled, leaning down to give his companion a kiss. 'And not a brain between them. Goodnight, my darlings.'

Fump emptied his own cup and stood with an exasperated puff. He turned to Gabriel with a twinkle in his eye. 'Listen to me, won't you? Listen to your kind, wise, sensible Fump? Do as I say, I implore you. Be stupid, strong and beautiful together and save our lives? Make Mister True your accomplice and find this Rat before it's too late. I am brave enough to admit it: I am frightened.'

Vivian poked his head back into the room in amazement. 'The two of them working together as accomplices? Are you mad?'

'I expect I am, fifty years cutting your toenails.' Fump scratched his bald head with a yawn. 'The pair of them are accomplices anyway after all that splashing about in the river. Gabriel can't possibly catch the knave alone, can he? I say get to know this pretty new arrival of ours, my dear; *watch* him, and you'll soon see he can be trusted. Perhaps you might conjure up some sort of a plan with his help?'

'I already made one.'

'Is that so?'

'Started laying a trap a couple of weeks back. Nobody knows what it is, only me.'

Mister Vivian re-entered the room in a nightcap. 'What sort of a trap?'

Gabriel emptied his cup, 'If I told you, I'd have to break your necks. But if nothing else works, our Rat will reveal himself sooner or later, without even knowing it.'

'Oh, this really is too thrilling,' said Mister Fump, only to be hushed by his companion, for Thomas was blinking and stretching his legs, lifting himself up in his chair with a groan.

He looked around, his hair poking up in tufts. 'Where am I?'

'Aha!' said Fump. 'Orpheus has returned from the underworld. Oh, to dance with you in your dreams.'

Thomas rubbed his eyes. 'Hello Fump, hello Vivian.' He turned to Gabriel. 'Did I miss anything?'

His question went unanswered, the pair of peruke-makers ushering their young visitors from the shop in ill-fitting clothes, and before they could say their goodbyes, Gabriel and Thomas found themselves standing on the piazza, blinking in the dawn light. Covent Garden was already bustling with traders, their wagons rumbling over the cobblestones as Gabriel cleared his throat, searching his neck for his locket. It must have been left on the riverbed. Would Emily and Dot be angry at him? he wondered. He dismissed the thought, summoning the last of his energy.

'Mister True,' he said, scratching his head.

'Yes, Mister Griffin?' Thomas stretched his arms with a deep yawn.

'Would you...' Gabriel's voice trailed off.

'What is it, Mister Griffin?'

Gabriel shook his head, rubbing his brow. He walked away and then turned back. 'I'd like to know you better.'

'Really?' said Thomas. 'We can talk tomorrow morning at my uncle's house. My cousin and I will be working on some new candles together and you'll be right outside our window.'

Gabriel shook his head. 'Best we don't speak at the candle shop at all. People can't know we're acquainted, not after today. Dangerous enough as it is.'

'But they're my family.'

'You're a molly now, Mister True. Ain't nothing is so dangerous as your own family. Meet me Sunday after church. Steps of St Paul's.'

CHAPTER THIRTY-SEVEN

'Constable,' said Justice Grimp, 'take the stones away, please; this is a pillory, not an execution.'

The mob was in a frenzy, hurling anything they could find at the guilty woman's face, her nose, mouth and eyes clogged with dung and rotten vegetables so that she could hardly breathe. The constable edged across, shielding himself with his arm as he scraped the filth away with a stick. The woman gasped, shaking her head so the stocks rattled.

Justice Grimp grimaced. 'Perhaps it would be better if she died this afternoon, rather than starve to death when they cast her out. She will be branded a witch by dusk.'

'Let the king's justice take its course for now,' said Justice Myre. 'Then God's justice may follow.'

They turned back towards the inn as a post boy came running over from the track. He was brandishing a letter: 'Justices Grimp and Myre?'

'The very same,' said Grimp.

The post boy removed his hat with a bow. 'A letter for you, post-haste.'

Myre snatched it away and tore it open. 'The Rat,' he said, before reading it aloud in a simmering rage.

Dear Justices,

I write to you with disappointing news. My attempt to rid us of Mister Griffin failed, his strength on the scaffolding at the cathedral proved beyond doubt that the Devil possesses him.

Meanwhile, I met your assassin in Alsatia as instructed. He took a wherryman's life and his badge then lured Griffin to a watery grave. Amateur. I can tell you that grave now holds the bones of your assassin, while Griffin still walks.

No fear, I have more names to share, and more molly houses for your good, Christian mission, Heaven praise the Society and praise His Majesty the King. I shall enclose the names and places in return for a generous payment in recognition of my most dangerous work.

Heed this message well, good Justices, and do not deny me my worth, for I believe Mister Griffin is a cunning and deadly sodomite, for he has kept his counsel and stalks me daily, growing nearer the truth each hour. He is now very close indeed to discovering my identity, yet I have covered my tracks thus far, and I am sure he will not unmask me before your raids.

I must implore you: hasten your journey to London, for soon, all may be lost. The Devil burn them in Hell.

Your most faithful servant,

Rat.

Justice Myre handed the letter to Grimp, then collected a rock from the ground. 'Damn you foul sinners!' he bellowed, stumbling as he punched the air. 'Must the Devil have all the guile? Must Heaven recruit fools?' He pushed his way through the crowd to the stocks, raising his rock, flinging it at the woman's head. 'Have that, demon. Take your misery to Satan and deliver a message to him from Praisegod Myre. Tell the dark angel I shall not stand for his cunning. His army of whores and sodomites shall be choked and burned, or let the demons fling my bones to oblivion.'

The post boy stood beside Justice Grimp, watching as Myre marched from the pillory to start an argument with the trunk of an oak tree. 'The man's prattled in the head,' he said.

'Yes,' replied Grimp, his attention back on the letter. 'Justice Myre is indeed quite mad. He carries the sins of the world like chains at his feet.'

'Is he fit for the law?'

'Fit?' said Grimp. 'Fit? That man has enforced the laws of this realm for more than fifty years. As God's missionary, he has brought enlightenment to Africa, Asia, the Indies and Norfolk. His father was a bishop, his mother a saint, his brother a lord, his sister the wife of the king's chief cutler. He has personally advised no fewer than four sovereigns by written correspondence, and not one of them has seen fit to respond, let alone disagree with him.'

'What's any of that got to do with him having an argument with a tree?'

'Stupid boy,' said Grimp. 'Why shouldn't he argue with a tree if he chooses? What's the tree ever achieved?'

The post boy wandered back to his horse, scratching his head as Grimp called Myre away.

'Come along, old man. The Rat is quite right – nasty little vermin – we must away to London, there isn't a moment to lose.'

CHAPTER THIRTY-EIGHT

Gabriel made his way along Hart-Row Street, the menacing towers of Newgate staring down at him as though death had been baked into every brick. At the southernmost end of Jackanape's Road, the tightly packed houses burst open, revealing the splendour of St Paul's Cathedral towering above him. With all the scaffolding down, the great lump of Portland stone looked very grand indeed. 'Pa,' said Gabriel, taking it all in, 'we finished the job; you'd be proud.'

He looked across the courtyard, shading his eyes as he searched for Mister True, and felt giddy. There was a lump in his throat and his new waistcoat seemed to crush his chest. He rubbed his neck, missing the weight of his locket, and wiped his clammy hands on his breeches. He would question the young man, to test his story. He would not look foolish. He would control himself.

The churchyard was dozing in dappled sunlight, street sellers hiding in the shade of their stalls while visitors mingled, lifting their sunburned noses to gape at the majesty of the new church. Gabriel stopped beside the west gate, admiring the stonecutters who were still working on one of the statues on the roof.

'Aren't they brave?' came a voice at his side. Mister True was dressed in a smart green coat and cream breeches, a compact peruke fixed neatly on his head. 'Good day to you, carpenter. How goes it?'

Gabriel grunted, watching the artisans swinging their ropes about the soaring stones. 'Knock it off. This place is too busy to talk. This way.' He made his way towards the cathedral steps, ascending to the great doors. Inside, the air turned chalky and cool.

Thomas shook his head in wonder. 'I've never seen anything like it. I heard tales, of course I did, and watched them building the dome from Highgate, but by Jehovah, it's magnificent. Father's quite mistaken; he says cathedrals are papist devilry. I believe it's church envy, don't you? His rectory's barely the size of a chicken coop compared to this. Besides,' he added, brushing Gabriel's hand with his knuckles, 'I don't believe the Devil could build something so handsome and grand ... nor so quiet.'

Gabriel tugged the collar of his shirt. 'Dome's a fraud; all for show. Nothing underneath but a pile of bricks and timber planks.' He pinched himself through his pockets, annoyed at himself for being so sharp. 'That where you grew up then, was it? Rectory in Highgate?'

'Yes,' said Thomas. 'Father built a tower on the roof, but we all know it isn't really a church. He's the schoolmaster there too. He taught me to love the law, our rightful king, and God. In that order.'

Gabriel regarded Thomas's pleasant face, keeping his voice low. 'Decent man, your father?'

'Oh yes,' said Thomas as his grey eyes followed a column up to the heavens. 'Very decent.'

'Wouldn't be too keen on his boy going to Clap's then.'

'No, of course not.'

'Unless there was a good reason to be there.'

Thomas didn't seem to have heard him. He was talking to himself in an almost imperceptible voice. 'Devil child,' he was saying, stroking his arms, lost in a memory. For the first time, Gabriel saw the smile fade from Thomas's face. He was wincing and shrinking as though taking blows from an imaginary belt.

Gabriel watched him, remembering the scars running across the young man's back.

'Strict man, your pa?'

Thomas nodded. 'He beat me. They all did. How did you know?'

Gabriel raised his eyebrows. 'Quiet men like me notice things, I suppose. I'm ugly, but I ain't stupid. Remember that, Mister True.'

They passed to the far side of the north transept, where Thomas paused, staring up at a statue of Christ.

'The Bible says: "he who spares the rod, hates his son". Dear Father must love me very much.' He placed his palms together and spoke in the solemn burr of a provincial clergyman. '"Oh Lord, what did I do to deserve such a demon for a son?"'

Gabriel thought of his own father, with his patient smile, and whispered a prayer to him, his voice drifting into the cool stone. 'Amen.'

He guided Thomas to a doorway at the far side of the cathedral, passing through a tight passageway to a spiral staircase that climbed interminably through the bones of the building. Eventually, short of breath, they stepped onto a gallery circling the interior of the dome as tiny people milled about below them.

Thomas whistled. 'I've never climbed so high. What if I slipped?' At that, he leaned over the edge of the gallery, lifting his feet from the stone slabs, balancing his stomach on the railings. 'Perhaps God would rather I did.'

Gabriel gripped him by the tops of his breeches and threw him against the wall. 'Idiot,' he snapped before he could control his tongue. Suddenly, all the worry and sadness and frustration he'd been storing up for so long blew out of him. 'Must you act the fool like the rest of them young mollies? Larking about with no clothes on, dancing and arguing at Clap's, jumping into other people's boats, caterwauling about in public dressed in gowns? Or is there a serious man hidden somewhere inside that addled brain of yours?' Gabriel could not stop himself from saying it out loud: 'Or are you the Rat? Is that how it is?'

Thomas shook his head, his eyes brimming. 'You think it too?' His chin puckered. 'I thought you wanted to spend some time together as friends.' He pushed Gabriel away and righted his peruke. 'I don't know anything about your Rat. How could I? Nobody talks to me, only my pathetic spinster of a cousin. I have no friends and nobody trusts me. All I know is that some traitor has sent three men to Hell.' He turned to the stairs then looked back at Gabriel with a sniff. 'Is that where they are, do you think? In Hell? I mean, do you think we will burn for being mollies?'

Gabriel shushed him as a lady stepped through the doorway in a curled wig and frilly cap. She stared at them over a long, pointed nose before bustling away. Gabriel moved Thomas further around the gallery.

'Might as well stick your head in a noose talking like that with people around.' He rubbed his eyes, thinking of Fump's suggestion that they work as accomplices. 'You're a good man, Mister True, I believe that, but I can't trust you to help me find the Rat; it ain't no use.'

Thomas's eyes grew wide. 'Is that why you asked me here then? You can trust me with anything, Mister Griffin. I have never once told a lie.'

Gabriel huffed and checked the gallery. There were various people now, standing at the far side of the circular walkway, some of them pointing down at the people below their feet, others staring goggle-eyed at the oculus above their heads. He took a deep breath, rubbing the bridge of his nose. Fump was right though, he desperately needed help, and who else could he turn to?

He leaned on the balustrade, speaking in a low whisper. 'This false molly working for the Society, passing our names to a pair of murderous justices; from what I know, he was at Mother Clap's the night you arrived, and at Miss Muff's when you went caterwauling through London.' Gabriel read Thomas's eyes. 'I ask you one last time: is it you?'

'How can it have been?' said Thomas. 'I've not even had my birthing yet.' He blushed. 'Or my marrying. I hardly know anyone in London.'

'Ay well, just as I thought. Has to be one of you though. Damn Martin for running away before telling me. You've met 'em all. Lavender, the Duchess, Sweet Jacky, Fump, Vivian.'

'They're all true mollies. I've seen them sporting together.'

'Men go a long way for the right money. Any of them might have been bribed or blackmailed.'

Thomas thought hard, a crease running across his brow. 'Then whichever one of them it is, we'll unmask him together; we have to.'

Gabriel felt his temper soften, relieved to see the young man's sincerity. 'Ay.'

Thomas drew closer. 'The Duchess left us on Fenchurch Street after Muff's, didn't she? Snuck away before we were attacked, which seemed odd to me at the time. Still, she has family. And Lavender can be heartless, but I believe she loves the Duchess.'

Gabriel looked out across the nave. 'Ay, she does.'

Thomas's nose wrinkled. 'And why would Lavender put herself in such danger, anyway? She was genuinely terrified when the men came for us with those clubs. Little Daisy is dead, of course. I shall never forget her screaming.' He moved his hand over the balustrade and touched Gabriel's wrist. 'I've had nightmares every night since then. I can't walk in the dark anymore, and there's no one to talk to about it.' He sighed. 'What about Sweet Jacky?'

'Ay, there's always Huffins.'

'I don't think she's evil; she returned my purse.'

'Bet he stole it first.'

'That's even more honest, wouldn't you say? She was confident, mind you, dancing through the city as though she hadn't a thing to fear. The rest of us were scared, even though we pretended not to be, but not Jacky. It was like she knew something we didn't.'

'Jack's always been reckless. If he's not at Clap's he's waving his cudgel about on Sodomites' Walk.'

'We'll have to make a plan to interrogate him, Mister Griffin; where is it you live?'

Gabriel turned his face, remembering his trap. Mister True had given him the perfect opportunity to add another vital piece. 'Have to leave my lodgings in a few weeks.'

'Where will you go?'

'Just out there in the churchyard I reckon.' Gabriel kept his voice light, careful to make sure Thomas was listening. 'There's an empty store by the railings on the south gate, where the old chapter house used to be. Got some old barrels of gunpowder in there from the demolition. Nobody checks it no more.'

Thomas looked up at Gabriel, his grey eyes shining. 'I think it's sad for you to sleep alone like that. Do you not have a wife to look after you?' He bit his lip, fiddling with his cuffs. 'Or a companion?'

'Had a wife once.'

Suddenly, Thomas gave a grunt, his face shooting upwards. For a moment, Gabriel thought he was climbing over the edge of the walkway, but then he saw a dark shape rushing behind their backs, and before he could move, Thomas gave a startled scream and flew over the railing headfirst. Gabriel shot his hand out just in time, clutching Thomas's fingers as the young man dangled a hundred feet above the distant tiles.

'Help me!' cried Thomas, struggling to hold on as the sleeve of his coat ripped at the shoulder. Gabriel was just in time to see a cloak disappearing through the doorway to the gallery stairs. With a heave, he pulled Thomas to safety, then ran to the door, but it was too late.

'My God,' said Thomas shakily, when Gabriel returned. 'That was him, wasn't it? That was the Rat?'

'Ay.'

Gabriel tentatively wrapped his arm around Thomas's shoulders and the young man clung to him, burying his head in his chest as his heart pounded. People stepped around them, muttering to each other about public decency, but Gabriel didn't care. If the Rat was down there, scurrying back to his lair with his latest plan foiled, he could not be with him on the gallery, quivering like a startled chick in his arms.

Beyond any doubt, Thomas True was innocent.

CHAPTER THIRTY-NINE

'I worry for you, Thomas,' said Abigail. 'These mysterious friends of yours, they seem rather dangerous.'

It had been barely two hours since his adventure at the cathedral, yet here Thomas was, dipping candles in the shop.

'London is a dangerous place, Cousin,' he said. 'You told me so yourself when I arrived. I merely slipped, that's all. But what a thing to say. How many men can claim to have swung their feet so high above the ground? I must be the closest thing London has to an angel.'

Abigail smiled. 'You are an angel, you have made us all so happy. Not like those common brutes tearing our home to bits.' She looked over at the gap where the wall used to be, for now there was nothing between the room and the outside world but a few timber scantlings. The smaller of the two men, Mister Sylva, was on his leather swing, his powerful arms controlling the rope. Abigail watched him closely. 'They spend every day dangling against our home like monkeys. Look at that one now.' She glanced up to make sure the workman could hear her then turned her back to him with a huff. 'I don't know where the ugly one is; he hardly ever seems to do any work. I heard them arguing about it, you know. Like a pair of little boys they were.'

Thomas bit his tongue. He knew exactly where Mister Griffin was at that very moment: still searching the perimeter of the cathedral to find traces of the Rat. It had been a wrench for Thomas to leave his new friend, for his every nerve tingled for more adventure, yet Mister Griffin had ordered him away with such a ferocious look, he had done as he was told. What a pity, he had rather enjoyed their time together. He turned back to the donkey and tilted a row of candles carefully into the molten wax. *I would gladly fall off that gallery a hundred times,* he thought to himself with a smile, *if Mister Griffin would put his arms around me again.*

Abigail caught his eye and giggled. 'What are you making doe eyes at now, sweet Cousin? You're as bad as Father, treating those candles better than me.'

Thomas gave her a shy smile and fetched three boxes of 'citrus spring' pillar candles decorated with daisies. They required careful embellishment, Thomas and Abigail working in silence, lost in their own thoughts. Once they were decorated with birds and flowers, Thomas ran them down to the shop, where he was immediately pounced upon by a gang of baying customers.

He returned covered in scratches, his peruke on the side of his head. 'Your father demands more,' he said, hanging a rack of freshly dipped candles from hooks on the ceiling. Abigail did not respond.

'Cousin, did you hear me?'

He sat beside her at the table and waited for her to speak. Eventually, she put her sculpting needle down and met his eye, wiping away tears. 'I would never survive if I lost you,' she said. 'You are my oldest and only friend. You go out, and I have no idea where you are. I worry for you every day and every night, thinking you won't come home. Still,' she sighed, 'I suppose I must lose you sooner or later.' She wiped her nose. 'Have you fallen in love? ... You have, I can see it.'

Thomas wrinkled his nose, failing to hide the shy smile growing steadily across his lips.

'Oh, Thomas!' said Abigail, taking his hands as her wax miniatures scattered across the floor. 'You are so cruel to keep it from me. You have that look boys get when they're silly for a girl. I've seen it before – though it's never been for me.' She lowered her eyes to the table and bit her lip before scooping the spilled decorations into her lap. 'I suppose your sweetheart is very pretty.' She frowned, little creases hatching over the bridge of her nose. 'Not plain like your cousin Abigail. My arms too large, and I'm far too tall and my middle is too thick.'

Thomas lifted her from her chair by her hands. 'I promise you, dear Abigail, that no matter whom I marry, you will be the only woman I love.'

She squealed with delight. 'Me? Do you mean it?'

'I do, though I shall have competition. You'll find yourself a wealthy husband soon from all those admiring men downstairs, and he shall make you rich and happy.'

Abigail sank back to her seat. 'Our candles do not appeal to men looking for a wife. And the rest...' She looked out at the carpenter Henry Sylva, who was still dangling on his rope, a chisel between his teeth. 'The rest do not appeal to me. Do you remember the summer I visited you when the ponds flooded, and we sailed leaves across the water with those little seeds for sailors?' She clapped her hands to her face. 'Oh my goodness, what did we call it? Captain Dandelion and his ship, the *Holy Ghost*!'

Thomas smiled, remembering the warm sun on his back, the feeling of his knees tucked into his stomach as he reached out across the pond, nudging the stalk of an intrepid oak leaf into the water. The rush of kinship as he'd caught sight of his cousin waving at him from the far bank. The little galleons would take an hour or more to cross the pond, and while they made their valiant way past drifting twigs and quacking sea monsters, he and Abigail would tell long stories about the seedling sailors on board, the battles they fought with enemy ships, the hand-wringing, cheek-clutching distress if they sank, and the leaping joy if they bobbed their way to dry land.

Thomas met Abigail's eye, and as they shared a secret smile, he felt a warm rush like toasted bread beneath his ribs. 'He is very handsome,' he said, staring at her with all the hope in his heart. 'My love.'

They sat, contemplating one another, the room holding its breath. Thomas was about to say more when Abigail's face cleared. She picked up a wax ladybird with great concentration as she muttered a little song to herself, dipping her brush in cochineal.

'Won't you say something to me?' said Thomas.

She raised her eyebrows. 'I have so many things to say, I really don't know where to begin.'

'Cousin Abigail,' said Thomas, his voice unsteady. 'Do you understand what I mean?'

Abigail lifted the brush, singing her little tune as she ran her fingers around the creature's shell.

'Cousin Abigail,' repeated Thomas, reaching out to touch her fingertips.

Abigail slapped the beetle down. 'Yes, Cousin,' she said, before adding, in a nonchalant manner: 'I have told you before, I know you better than anybody in the world and always will.'

They stared at each other across the table and in a moment they were together, embracing and whispering, and anyone who'd seen them playing pirate ships on the pond all those years ago would have said they'd never been apart.

Meanwhile, beyond the room, Henry winched himself out of sight, tutting at the behaviour of artisans. He took the chisel from his teeth and threw it to the roof, then looked out across to the City, wondering where on Earth Gabriel had gotten to this time.

CHAPTER FORTY

The marshal turned upon his chair as Gabriel stood before his desk. 'Mister Griffin,' he said from a raised pile of cushions, 'I was starting to wonder where you were. You must have unmasked the Rat to be darkening my door. Tell me, who is he? We shall beat a confession from the little devil by lunchtime and suck out his bone marrow for supper.'

'I don't have him and I won't be finding him neither; I'm finished.'

Gabriel had been wrestling all day and night since the incident at St Paul's the previous Sunday. Already Martin was dead, so too Daisy and Old Bob, now Thomas was at risk, having almost drowned in the river and toppled from the gallery. Not to mention the men burned to death on the scaffolding and scattered over the steps of the cathedral. Gabriel was the common factor in all cases; it was time to let another man do the hunting.

The marshal wriggled on his cushions as the lowing sound of cattle rang through the windows from the yard outside. 'What do you mean, you're done?'

'The Rat knows I'm following him. It's too dangerous.'

'Are you sure?'

'Ay.'

'Dear, oh dear, Mister Griffin, a dangerous business indeed. I quite understand your caution.' Queed settled back, kissing his fingertips as the terrible bellowing outside grew louder. It sounded like a bull being butchered. 'However, I must ask whether it's your own neck you're worried about, or someone else's?' He arched his eyebrows.

'Eh?'

'Another fellow maybe? A pretty young molly, just come to town perhaps?'

Gabriel looked around the room at the guards. 'What you on about?'

Queed scratched his whiskers and yawned. 'Dear, oh dear, I have been up since the early hours, you must forgive me. What I am proposing to you, Mister Griffin, is that you have been seen by my guards fraternising with one of your chief suspects – Mister True, of all names. They were *his* lovely legs swinging over the drop at the church, were they not? Then the business on the river. You were seen climbing into a wherry with an unlicensed boatman, only to smash into the bridge and – lo and behold, it's a miracle! – reappear on the wharf with no boatman to be seen, only Mister True, dandling half naked on your arm.'

'Mister True ain't a suspect. Not anymore.'

'And why not, pray tell?'

'You reckon he pushed himself over them railings?'

The marshal tilted his head. 'He might have done. Men do the most impossible things to hide their secrets, you ought to understand that.'

'He ain't the Rat, I know it.'

'Then who is?'

'Told you: I don't know and I ain't about to find out.'

The marshal slammed his fists on the desk. 'Damn you, Mister Griffin, for thinking me a fool. You won't catch the traitor for me? We shall see about that.' He hopped from his chair to the window. 'Come here,' he said, beckoning Gabriel to stand by his side.

Gabriel felt a dagger at his back and did as he was commanded, rounding the desk to look out. He froze at the sight that met his eyes. There was an enclosed yard at the back of the inn, with tethering beams for horses. To each of the beams was tied a man, lashed by their arms so that their joints were popped white, near tearing through the skin. Some were unconscious, others staring up at the window, pleading for mercy. There were barbed shackles around their ankles, while in the centre of the yard stood a large metal bull, a sort of statue made of polished bronze with a burning fire below its belly. There was steam rising from its nostrils as a deep lowing sound emanated from its open mouth like a horn.

'My latest acquisition,' said the marshal. 'An antiquity imported from Greece, no less. I am quite a collector of such contraptions.' He tapped the window with his fingernail as the moaning of the metal beast grew in volume and pitch. 'A very clever instrument, certain to strike fear into any man who hears it.'

'How's it making that noise?' said Gabriel, not sure he wanted to know.

'Ah! That is a fine question. It was designed for the Sicilian tyrant, Phalaris, so the merchant tells me. There is a man inside his belly, you see, and as the wretch screams for help, so the particular arrangement of pipes inside the bull's head turn his agony into music. It is really quite artful.'

The bull gave a long, high-pitched bellow, its voice breaking into a distended sob and Gabriel stood back, sickened. 'Monster. Who is in there?'

'Oh, just a petty thief.' The marshal pressed his face to the window like a child at a pie shop. 'By way of encouragement to the rest. Who else do we have down there? Let me see: a couple of survivors from the fire at the scaffolding. What is another little scalding to them, eh? They claim not to have seen who lit the flames. Then we have a boatman who passed you on your little trip down the river. He has confirmed the identity of the assassin, so we shall spare him the worst.' At that, he waved to a guard, who duly took a dagger from his belt and stabbed the man in the heart. 'Your assassin was known to us and had many masters. Two of them: our friends the travelling justices.' He moved along the window. 'Ah now, these two hounds were on Fenchurch Street clubbing your molly friend to death. They're yet to enlighten me, but by the looks of their breeches I suspect the crying bull is jogging their memories.'

Gabriel looked across at them all, overcome with horror. None of them would have been there if it weren't for him. They were not alone in their misery. Gabriel could see the lifeless remains of two more men spread out like butchered pigs upon a carpenter's block, their bellies sliced open.

'The corpse of your assassin gave us no particular clues,' said the marshal, holding up a small bag of green velvet, caked in mud. 'Only this purse with a little treasure for our troubles.' He held the purse up with a chink of coins. 'The man he killed however – the true Apollo Rawhead – his body was found washed up on Temple Stairs, by sheer good fortune.' He pointed at the second cadaver. 'He gave us a little more information from his clothes. A clue, you might say, to the Rat's identity.' He pushed a slip of paper into Gabriel's pocket. 'There you are, my good ratcatcher. You may look at the clue later.' He faced Gabriel with a quizzical expression. 'Tell me, by the way: what did you do to the assassin before you drowned him? I wager it wasn't the fish that undid his breeches, you rogue.'

Gabriel spoke in a wooden voice as the bull let out another blast from its mouth. 'He tried to have his way with Mister True. He opened his breeches up and demanded pleasure, then fell in and drowned. We didn't kill him.'

The marshal frowned. 'I believe you, Mister Griffin, though I doubt the courts would be so indulgent. I couldn't make head nor tail of it. Ah well.' He raised his hand and signalled to the guards outside. Duly, they emptied the bull's stomach of its roasted contents, then dragged the two hounds towards the open hatch as they begged for their lives.

'They're bad men,' said Gabriel, 'but still, they don't deserve to die like that.'

He felt his arms gripped by the guard and he was forced back to his seat. After a moment of hollow silence, the room shook to a series of blood-curdling screams, which duly turned into the ever-louder moaning of the metal bull.

'Very good,' said the marshal, fixing Gabriel with a charged look. 'I wondered whether it could fit more than one man.' He tugged his waistcoat over his belly and began polishing his buttons with a handker-chief. 'They will burn like that for eternity anyhow. What is a few extra minutes to warm them up? You mollies have your pretty peacock plumes, after all. Well, this is my fancy show.' He cupped his hand to his ear as a second wave of bellowing rattled the windows. 'So, let me ask you again, and this time I would like you to consider your answer more carefully. I cannot use my guards to find the Rat – a little too on the nose – and I cannot use my own spies, for I would lay myself open to blackmail. I wouldn't like that very much. So, will you catch this Rat for me? Or will I lock you in my bull with Mister True?'

Gabriel said nothing, desperate to cover his ears.

Marshal Queed raised his eyebrows, stroking his long whiskers. 'Or shall I dig up your wife and daughter and feed their bones to my dogs?'

The chair narrowly missed the marshal's head as it flew across the desk, smashing through the windows beyond. In an instant, the guards were at Gabriel's neck with their knives, holding him back as he kicked the desk over, coins ringing against the walls.

Queed picked himself up from the floor, brushing himself down with a chuckle. 'I suggest you channel that anger towards the Rat, Mister Griffin. One stab to the heart, and our little problem is gone. I can handle the justices, and you can go back to your sordid life.' He pointed at Gabriel's pocket. 'Now, take that money and that clue, and find the Rat, there's a good elephant.'

CHAPTER FORTY-ONE

The carriage shot at incredible speed along the narrow country lanes, slewing like the tail of a snake behind rampant horses. Where the roads grew tiresome and winding, the carriage ploughed directly across the fields, never minding the bushels, bales and livestock, which flew in all directions to make way for the charging vehicle; for nothing, *nothing* was allowed to slow the justices' progress towards London.

Inside the carriage, hidden behind punctured screens of tin, sat Justices Grimp and Myre appraising the Rat.

'Say that once more,' said Grimp.

The Rat nodded at the papers in Justice Myre's hand. 'You have all you need. I am done.'

'All?' said Myre. 'All?'

'Yes. Names and places as promised. I am finished; the marshal is growing angry, so I'm told. He'll find me soon and there are fearful rumours about the things he does to his enemies. They say he feeds his victims to a monstrous bull and roasts them all on a spit.' The Rat gulped. 'Countless men are dead, including two of the Society hounds, their corpses black as coal dredged from the Fleet yesterday morning. Meanwhile, Gabriel Griffin is cunning and—'

Justice Grimp raised his hand for silence. 'My sweet Rat, these men you mention may well be finished, but you, most certainly, are not.'

'But there's nothing left for me to do.'

'Nothing?' shouted Myre. 'Nothing! With Griffin so close to scuppering our raids, and the Devil still spreading his evil seed?'

Grimp squeezed Myre's arm. He took the paper. 'Surely you are not suggesting that every molly in London is on this list?'

The Rat was about to argue, when the carriage pulled to a juddering halt, Justice Grimp yanking down the screen to find out what was going on. With much calling to the driver and bashing of Myre's cane upon the roof, it transpired that they had passed into a particularly tight junction, their passage being blocked by a second carriage, which refused to make way.

'Then tell the other carriage to back up!' yelled Grimp, waving his hands through the window. 'We must pass. We are representatives of the king's justice, on urgent business. Urgent business, I say!'

They heard the driver hop down from his seat to remonstrate with his counterpart. For some minutes, the men argued with ripe language until, at last, the driver returned with good news: the other carriage was content to make way for the cost of five shillings, an offer the magistrates, in their haste, felt compelled to accept. They moved off, taking the dry ditch to make space for the blockage, drawing alongside the second carriage so the fee could be paid. Myre pulled the screen down, jangling the coins in his fist.

'Ho, ho!' came a sprightly voice, a plump-faced gentleman appearing through the window of the second carriage. 'Good day to you fine fellows. I thank you for your patience with my driver. He is a stubborn brute; I shan't be riding beneath him again. Why, my dear business partner, Mister Vivian, shall be outraged to hear of this when I return home to Covent Garden.'

'Lord, spare us,' groaned Justice Myre.

Grimp studied the man with a look of appalled fascination. 'Who are you? What is your name?'

'Why my name is Mister Fump, of Fump and Vivian's Finest Perukes. You must recognise me.' He turned to show off his profile. 'You see? There isn't a pamphlet worth reading without our wares on display. Well, never mind, never mind. It is essential to remember men before meeting them and advisable to forget them as soon as they depart.' He waited for some response, yet on finding none, he continued. 'Such a darling day for travelling, don't you agree? I wish I could roll up the fields and take them home for a new waistcoat. I do believe the sky is bluer than—'

'Where are you going?' interrupted Grimp. He offered his most benevolent smile.

'To visit my sister in Buckingham. She is unwell with her stomach, poor dear. If she isn't falling over she's belching. Why, they've banned her from church, and the cat's grown vicious. How I shall miss our home, yet it is indeed a relief to get away for a few days, and is that not the tragedy of London? One must live there to appreciate the joy of leaving.'

Inside the dark carriage, the Rat pressed back into the shadows, while Myre grew impatient.

'Shut him up. We must go.'

'You are a wise man indeed, Mister Fump,' said Justice Grimp. 'I assure you, when we arrive in London, we shall certainly pay your little shop a visit. Covent Garden, did you say?'

'That's the one. Oh, what fun we shall have. I do believe you are precisely the sort of fellows we like to welcome into our sanctuary.' He winked, tapping his finger against his nose. 'If you understand my meaning?'

'I believe I do,' said Grimp, his face a picture of affection, while below the carriage window, his fingers scratched curls of varnish from the door.

'Wonderful, wonderful,' continued Mister Fump. 'Well then, if you have the token, I shall instruct my coachman to remove himself from your passage.'

Justice Myre leaned out with the coins, ready to pass them over the gap, only for Fump to fumble them to the ground.

'Oh, will you look at that! "Butter fingers Fump" they call me, for a number of good reasons.'

He opened his carriage door and climbed to the ground, fetching the coins up before climbing inelegantly back to the running board. As he did so, he poked his head directly into the justices' carriage, looking around at the sparse interior.

'Really, gentlemen, what a puritan little trundle-coffin you have here; you might as well be travelling in a crypt...' He stared at the piles of law books at their feet and then noticed the collars at their necks. Bewildered, he blinked, the blood draining from his face. 'You are ... travelling justices?'

'We are.'

'On your way to London?'

'Indeed.'

Fump eyed the men in a state of agitation, then peered into the opposite corner of the carriage. His eyes popped.

'My goodness,' he said, 'what on Earth are *you* doing here?'

CHAPTER FORTY-TWO

Lotty scanned the sparse crowd from the secrecy of the pit beneath the stage, peering through the gaps between the wooden slats. It was the quietest Sunday night she'd ever witnessed.

'Empty your cups, sweet harlots,' shouted Mother Clap from above with the customary stamp of her boot. Dust fell between the boards as Lotty watched the few mollies in the hall. Many were dressed in their usual clothes, looking nervously towards the entry in case a pack of constables burst in. Mother Clap's voice echoed around the cavernous space. 'Pull up yer skirts, push out yer paps. Show us yer arses, you're at Mother Clap's...'

There was some desultory applause, joined by laughing and jeering from a few soldiers who may or may not have been mollies.

'Whoever you love, whoever you are, we will always be righteous ... always be free ... and...'

More dust fell through the gaps as Clap stamped her boots to the lonely beat of the drum, for even the fiddler had decided to stay away. Lotty spoke the words with her.

'Always together.'

A trap door opened, and Mother Clap fell through, frozen in her pose like a dropped statue.

'Where the bloody Hell have you been?' she said, clambering from a pile of sacks arranged to break her fall. She pulled her waistcoat up and marched off.

'Don't ask.'

'Oh, but I do ask.'

She passed into a warren of dimly lit corridors then up a set of narrow stairs, Lotty squeezing behind her.

'Who is our Rat? I'll skin the damned bastard alive.'

'You sound like Queed.'

'Oh, Queed's got nothing on me when it comes to torture. Tell me the name and I'll cut the devil's balls off and feed 'em to the Tower lions, so help me God.' She punched a panel in the wall, swinging it open to reveal a view of the hall from above. 'Look at that. Emptier than a nun's cunny, damn it.'

Indeed, the hall appeared even more barren from above. Lotty swept her eyes across the gallery to see Mister Vivian sitting alone, while Thomas True was crossing the empty hall dressed as Verity, her yellow gown far too large for her frame.

Clap slammed the panel shut. 'Cowards, the lot of 'em. One rumour and they all stay home with their wives, playing family.' She stomped to the end of the runway and struck her heels against the balusters of a makeshift staircase, sliding to the floor below. 'Must have lost half my takings this last month.'

They reached the end of the passageway and turned down a dark corridor striped with poles of horizontal light. She stopped, pressing her eye to a coin-sized peephole.

'Bloody empty,' she said, moving to the next.

Lotty followed her, peeping inside a softly lit room with Turkey-work cushions scattered across the floor. There were shelves stacked with various paddles, wooden cudgels and bottles of oil, yet the chapel – as it was called for the act of marrying – was empty, the bedclothes unruffled.

Lotty pulled back. 'I'm struggling, Clap. The marshal says I have to find the traitor, but it takes time.'

Clap moved to the next peephole. 'Ah now, look at this. Much better, my darlings, work up a nice thirst.' She stood back. 'Struggling, you say? Takes time? Oh dear, well, never mind, eh Lotty? Least you tried yer best. It don't matter.' She folded her arms, her brown eyes shining through the darkness. 'I suppose that's what we'll be saying at Tyburn is it, when we're standing on the edge of a cart with a noose around our necks? "Don't worry about the drop, ladies. Lotty did her best searching for the Rat, but she couldn't quite manage it. Let's all meet up in Hell for a nice chocolate."' Clap spoke in an angry hiss, lest she disturb the lovemaking on the other side of the wall. 'Send us all to our deaths, would you? Ay, how blessed we are to have a seven-foot goose for a molly guard.'

'Want to find the Rat, course I do, but—'

'But nothing. You already told me it's one of them six mollies.'

'I've spoken to them all, only one left. Sweet Jacky Huffins, the Tower pickpocket. Been searching for her all week but I reckon she's fled.'

Clap narrowed her eyes. 'That freckly bitch?' She took off her hat and raked her fingers through her curls. 'She's a trick, but a traitor an' all? Can't see it. She might pick pockets for a living, but she's the most honest crook I ever met. Survivor like her, she's smart enough to lie low till the Rat's caught.'

'Might be right. Don't see how it's Lavender either. She's bitter—'

'She'd make a lemon wince.'

'But not so bad when she's sober. She got a threatening note, just like Martin Lightbody did, before he ended up in the ditch. So did the Duchess, and Fump and Vivian.'

'P'raps the Rat sent a note to himself to knock you off the trail? Clever vermin.'

Lotty rubbed her face. 'It ain't Fump and it ain't Vivian, they've got nothing to gain, and I can't see the Society choosing a molly like Lavender or Rettipence. One's a loudmouth, the other's a coward. They'd be dead in the ditch soon as they talked to me, but both are still walking.'

'More than walking,' said Clap, gesturing to the spyhole further along the wall. Lotty joined her and peeped through, instantly wishing she hadn't. There they were, the Duchess and Lavender, fooling about clumsily on the floor, their bodies entangled in a mess of pimply buttocks and creased linen.

The Duchess was begging between kisses: 'It is too dangerous, Lavender, we should not be here.'

'Say more, brave master,' Lavender replied in a breathless voice, lifting her petticoats, 'all this peril turns me hot.'

Lotty took her eye from the hole and murmured: 'Ay, the Duchess left Fenchurch Street before the hounds attacked.'

'Just in time to save her own skin.'

'She only did what any sensible molly would have done. Besides, young Daisy cried out to the Rat just before she was killed. The Duchess was away by then. Fump and Vivian weren't there either. They left Muff's long before.'

Clap thought it over, inspecting Gabriel's face. 'Most of my mollies reckon Mister True's the Rat.'

Lotty shook her head. 'Was with him at the cathedral Sunday before last. He almost got tipped over the gallery. Saw the Rat escaping afterwards. Mister True's innocent.'

Clap gave a knowing smile, moving to the next peephole. She pressed her hands to the partition and looked through.

'Maybe you're right, maybe you're wrong. Still, I know a thirsty molly when I see one, and that lad ain't innocent.'

Lotty joined her and saw Thomas dressed as Verity in the chapel room, sitting on the edge of the bed. She was fiddling nervously in her gown of yellow cotton, the lace sleeves hanging around her arms like daffodils.

Clap tapped her finger on the wall. 'Verity True-tongue, ain't that what they christened her?'

'Ay.'

Lotty watched as the molly stood up from the bed and sidled to the door, her hands on her lower back. She ruffled her skirts to her waist then twisted into a stretch and rested her weight on one leg in the pose of a contrapposto statue.

Clap gave a soft laugh. 'Looks like she's ripe for a marrying to me.'

Lotty's heart ached, angry at herself. Mister True had cooked up a foolhardy plan without her knowledge: Verity True-tongue would tempt Jack to the chapel room then question him about the Rat and somehow force him to confess in a careless fit of passion.

It would never work. Jack Huffins was a child of the streets, far too canny for such a simple ruse, yet perhaps – just perhaps – Jack was the Rat after all, and if so – Lotty gulped as Verity slipped from her gown and stretched out, naked and vulnerable on the bed – there was no finer bait.

CHAPTER FORTY-THREE

Verity waited alone on the bed, her gown strewn on the floor, her wig flung to the side of the room. It was a very clever plan, she was sure of it. She'd told every molly she knew that she wanted to marry Sweet Jacky that night, and that she would be waiting in the chapel room for her induction. Mister Griffin said it was a stupid idea and a thin chance, not even worth a try, but Verity had insisted.

The blue chapel was larger than she'd imagined, and it smelled funny, of sweat and oils. Standing up, she wiggled her toes on the rug covering the grimy boards and cleared her throat, then made her way to the opposite side of the room and stretched, inspecting her slender chest, hating the sight of herself. Mind you, some of the other mollies seemed to like the way she looked. Strange, the things men find beautiful. And women too, for that matter: only the previous day, Abigail had taken her cousin's arm and told him how much he had grown – then squeezed his flesh as if it were a piece of fruit and said he was quite the man now. Verity stared at her reflection, turning from side to side. All she saw was ugliness.

She shivered in spite of the sweltering heat and hunched her shoulders, listening to the muffled cries coming through the walls from the neighbouring room. She felt sick, almost fetching her gown from the chair and escaping, yet she had to be brave. It was her idea to make this sacrifice, and surely Mister Griffin was impressed by how brave and serious she was.

She walked across the room and stroked a painting with her fingers, feeling it bow at her touch. There was a rustling noise on the other side, and some low, murmuring conversation. Lotty would be there with Clap, watching to make sure she was safe. She stood back. The painting was of a man wearing the skin of a woodland creature, sprawled beneath a tree. There was a spear through his chest, his flesh being torn apart by the bare hands of a pack of rampant women. Verity imagined Sweet Jacky tearing his own body to pieces as she begged her to stop. What would be done to her, she wondered. Would it hurt?

She stretched her hands to the ceiling, going over her plan, simple as it was: she would pleasure Jacky one way or another, and then at the last moment of bliss, offer to be a second Rat, and in her frenzy, Jacky would explode with an unbridled confession. It would work, Verity was certain of it. What could possibly go wrong?

Suddenly, the door burst open and Verity spun around, ready to welcome her prey, only to see a pair of shirtless soldiers swinging bottles of rum over their heads. They took one look at the young, naked molly and grinned. 'What do we have here, then?' said the taller of the two. 'A milky white maiden, ready for the lay.'

'Skinny runt,' said his grimy companion. 'They're saying out there she's a rat or sumfing.' He smeared sweat from his neck with a dirty rag. 'Still, I reckon she'll take it.' He waggled his eyebrows.

'I'm waiting for a friend,' said Verity, hearing the thump of boots departing on the other side of the wall.

'And you found two of 'em, lucky bitch,' said the large soldier, unbuckling his breeches while his friend tugged off his turkey-leather belt. 'Lusty he-whore, we'll pay you well.' He kicked the door shut with his heel and prowled around the room, his arms outstretched. 'Been a long time since we tasted the kiss of a he-whore, ain't it Jeremiah? But we ain't mollies, you hear?'

Verity held up her hands as the men approached. 'Please,' she said, 'I don't want to.'

'Nice,' said the grubby man, scratching his chin. 'I likes it when they beg, takes me back to Kingston, it does—'

The man's head shot forwards, smacking the wall by Verity's shoulder.

'Here, what's this?' said the second soldier, before flying sideways and landing on the floor with a thud.

Verity crouched down, covering her face with her arms as Lotty towered over her. She felt her hand gripped by a set of rough fingers and was helped up. 'Just in time,' said Lotty. 'Looks like Jacky ain't coming.'

The drum thudded beyond the chapel door as both men sat on the bed side by side.

'Was worth a try,' said Gabriel.

'I suppose,' said Thomas, covering his naked lap with his daffodil gown. 'You were brave.'

'I was stupid, as always.' Thomas pushed back to the corner of the bed, hitching his knees to his chin. 'I suppose Jacky wasn't tempted. I can't say I blame her.'

'Then she's a fool as well as a traitor,' said Gabriel. 'Any molly would be lucky to marry you.'

They met eyes and Thomas bit his lip then stretched out his legs. 'Do you think so?'

Gabriel coughed. 'Ay.'

'Here we are then.'

'Ay, here we are.'

'Alone in a chapel room.'

Gabriel felt for his locket, remembering it wasn't there anymore. The apothecary's tincture had taken its place. He fiddled with the bottle, turning the glass in his fingers. Should he drink some more? He looked at Thomas's legs, his supple arms behind his head. His pale, dimpled face and blonde crop of hair. His yellow gown across his groin. It was no use; he could drink a lake of the stuff and it wouldn't soften his urges. Only thing it was good for was making men vomit.

He reached over to the wall, scratching a beam with his thumbnail. 'Damp,' he said with a tut. 'The wood's gone soft.'

Thomas looked up through his eyelashes. 'Has it?'

Gabriel made a gruff noise deep in his throat and stood up, but Thomas spoke: 'We could marry?'

Gabriel looked over his shoulder. 'Eh?'

Thomas shrugged. 'We could, Mister Griffin, if you wanted to.'

'I can't...' said Gabriel, his voice trailing away. 'I ain't ever...'

Thomas climbed from the bed and took the man's fingers to his lips, soft skin meeting rough. He moved closer, pressing their bodies together. 'Touch me.'

'I can't.'

Thomas looked up with a dimpled smile, his grey eyes shining in the amber light.

'Touch me.'

He reached for Gabriel's face with trembling fingers and kissed him, light at first, then held his parted lips at his closed mouth. Gabriel did not move. His hands swung at his sides, heavy as church bells. Thomas shivered. 'Do it,' he said, and Gabriel felt a hand tracing inside his shirt, up to his chest, where it rested, as though praying to his pounding heart. He gulped and pushed Thomas away, yet their tongues touched and Gabriel moved his balled fists to Thomas's back and felt them open out and hold him, just as he'd dreamed. The valley of a bent neck, the hot prickle of alert skin. Thomas gave a moan as Gabriel devoured him, wrapping him up in his arms and scooping him to the bed, where they fell together, ropes snapping beneath the mattress. The scratch of hair over smooth muscle; the weight of Gabriel's body burying Thomas in fur. Gabriel rose up, snapping the lace from around his neck, and held the bottle of poison to the flickering lamp. The viscous oil swirled as he poured it into his palm and threw the bottle to the fire with a smash, then cradled Thomas as they joined in a slow, panting prayer. They kissed each other from collarbone to jaw as they twisted tight as rope, all the tears and sweat wrung from them to the beat of their wet bodies. They could have stayed that way forever, yet with a buck of their legs and the hissing of dark oaths, their eyes locked hard into one another's shock and the small room burst with a flash of bright stars as there came a sudden bang and the door slammed open.

They looked up from the bed, panting, and there stood none other than Jack Huffins, staring down at them with a face as white as wax, the bloody stump of his tongue wiggling and flapping at the back of his gaping mouth.

CHAPTER FORTY-FOUR

Gabriel and Thomas jumped from the bed instantly, scrabbling for their clothes. They stared in horror at the young man's once-handsome face, now blanched in agony, the raw wound of his mouth yawning wide and hollow as red spittle hung in strings from his chin.

Thomas stood against the wall, unable to look. 'My God, what have they done to him?'

Jack staggered inside, reaching out for Gabriel's hands, his throat gargling. There were cuts on his lips and all up his arms. His loose shirt was stained with streaks of fresh blood, still seeping through. Gabriel took him by the shoulders as Clap appeared at the door, surrounded by mollies.

'What's going on in here?' she demanded, staring at the back of Jack's head. 'What's all that terrible grizzling for?' She gave a cheerful laugh. 'Jealous I expect, finding Lotty alone with Virgin Verity here. No wonder she looks so pale after marrying an ox like that. Ah, let 'em play, ye nasty whore.' But then Jack turned to face her and she recoiled. 'Lord Jesus,' she said, 'where's yer tongue?'

Gabriel took Jack by the face, holding him gently so their eyes could meet. 'The Rat did this to you. That right? Rat got your tongue, did he?'

At first, the young man shook his head, then tried his best to form shapes with his mouth, yet his lips had been so expertly slitted that they flared out in tabs. His eyes grew angry – wild with frustration and terrible pain, and he flew at Thomas, punching the wall and gesturing at him, beating him around the shoulders and face with his fists.

Thomas managed to get away, hiding behind Gabriel. 'What have I done?' he said. 'Why is he pointing at me like that?'

'Don't know,' said Gabriel, noticing the faces of the mollies staring into the chapel through the door.

Clap was amongst them, her eyes boiling. 'Seems like Jacky's got something to say, Verity True-*tongue*,' she said. 'Why's she pointing at you?'

Thomas looked at her, his eyes balling. 'I don't know, I really don't.'

Lavender stepped through the door and pointed a long finger straight at him. 'Thomas True,' she said. 'Thomas Rat.'

Behind her, the collection of mollies repeated the words: 'Thomas True, Thomas Rat, Thomas True, Thomas Rat.'

'No,' said Thomas, pulling himself behind Gabriel. 'It isn't me. I told you.'

There came a ripping sound from the far wall and Gabriel spun as Jack bent double beside the painting. His head hung low to his ankles, curls of red hair dangling to his shoes. He smacked his arms against the wall a second time then straightened up with an anguished howl and ran to Clap, scratching at her to understand. He must have realised it was hopeless, for he grabbed his blood-soaked shirt and tore it open from neck to navel, revealing his naked chest covered in slices that smiled and kissed, exposing the white bones of his ribs. And they were not only slices – for now Jack had received his own note from the Rat, written into his flesh with a knife. It was a single word:

REPENT

Gabriel sprang at him but was too slow, for Jack was still quick on his toes. He tore at the painting and jumped through, then down the secret passageway. By the time Gabriel had reached the hatch at the back of the building, the tortured man had disappeared into the stews.

CHAPTER FORTY-FIVE

'Time for me to go,' said Gabriel.

'You're not serious,' said Henry, steadying himself on the pulley. 'It's not even lunch.'

They were swinging below the candle shop, the Thames charging barely twenty feet below their boots. Henry whacked a fresh peg into a support beam then cracked his neck. 'I might as well take all the money as well as all the work.'

'Got to find a new home, ain't I?' said Gabriel. 'You and Bet want me out from Friday.'

Henry's shoulders drooped. 'Still no luck? Can't be so hard for a man to find lodgings in London.'

'I ain't living in a hovel.'

Henry held his mallet like a purse. 'Well now, Gabe Griffin has expectations, that it? Years of living like a hog, suddenly it's curtains and tassels and fine glazed windies?' He pushed away from the bracings, admiring Gabriel's work. 'Ay well, we're making good progress on the job. Got to take the tiles off the roof and replace them purlins, I reckon. Empress Squink says she'll pay us what we need to get it all done. Lord, we're in the wrong business, Gabe. Should be sticking silly flowers on candles. They're making a right mint up there; listen to all them stomping feet.'

'They can keep their candles,' said Gabriel. 'Just fashion for fops is all. Won't last. Here, I'll check them tiles before I go.'

He winched himself up the side of the shop, nodding at the young Squink woman, who watched him ascend with a hostile expression, then past the workshop, where the dipping donkey stood idle, up past the sleeping quarters to the garret. Thomas was waiting for him there, leaning out of the newly installed window.

'Hello,' he smiled, his cheeks dimpling. He gave Gabriel a secret kiss on his cheek.

'Not here,' said Gabriel, flushing.

'Time for the lions?'

'Ay, meet you under the arch.'

Ten minutes later and Gabriel was pushing his way across the teeming bridge. He reached St Magnus Church and waited for Mister True in the shade of the old stones. He watched people bustling by and caught sight of St Paul's peering down at him over the rooftops. He imagined himself standing on the balcony below the dome, looking out across London. *Might just work*, he thought, going over the details of his secret trap. The pieces were all in place now; all he had to do was set it in motion at just the right moment. Gabriel shielded his eyes and looked back towards the bridge as Mister True approached.

They made their way towards Tower Hill, speaking under their breath as Thames Street narrowed around them.

'You'll be homeless soon,' said Thomas, kicking a stone into a bucket thirty yards away to cheers from a group of children.

'I will.'

'Where will you go?'

'Told you. I'll sleep in the old gunpowder stores by the cathedral, while it's warm and dry.'

'Isn't that dangerous?'

'You're the only one who knows I'll be there.'

They linked fingers, covering their hands with their coats as they stepped onto Tower Hill, the imposing castle draped with bright scutcheons, dozing in dappled light. Gabriel scanned the crowd, searching for Jack's face as he spoke. 'How long you in London for?' he asked, trying not to sound bothered.

'I don't know,' said Thomas. 'I should like to be here forever. Safe with my companion.'

Gabriel tutted. 'Who's that then?'

'You, I hope.' Thomas laughed. 'When you love me.'

Gabriel lowered his head. 'Don't know what love is, Mister True, not since I lost my family.'

They walked on in silence, Gabriel feeling every pair of eyes following them across the open grounds. He wondered whether Emily and Dot could see what he was doing. His parents too. Was his father looking down on the chapel room when he sinned? He let go of Thomas's hand and when he spoke, his voice came out sharper than he meant it to and his words were clumsy. 'This ain't love, whatever love is.' His words hung between them unanswered, and then he added: 'It don't matter.'

They circled the castle, scuffing stones with their shoes until, on the third lap, Thomas gave a dejected sigh.

'I know what you mean, Mister Griffin, about it mattering. It's so busy in London, it's impossible for anything to matter really. Here, nobody cares who you are, not even your closest friends, and maybe that's for the best.' He looked at the barrels busy with apprentices and soldiers gambling and drinking. 'I suppose men like us are safest when we're forgotten.'

But that wasn't what Gabriel meant, and he was about to tell him so when their eyes met and they stared at each other in that pale-blue silence beneath the looming stones.

'I just can't say it, Thomas. I can't.'

'You don't have to.'

'I want to, though.'

'So do I.'

'Stop!'

Gabriel had shouted the word, and Thomas looked at him, puzzled. 'I don't want to stop, I—'

'Not you,' said Gabriel, barging past him, pointing as he thundered, 'Stop that man.'

A figure had passed through the Tower gates. Jack Huffins' clothes were filthy and he was stooping, yet with his freckles and curls of bright-red hair, it was definitely him.

'Hold it,' Gabriel boomed.

The man looked back and instantly hobbled away, clutching his ribs.

'So that's your game, is it?' said Gabriel, pressing through the crowds huddled around the Byward Tower. 'I'll make you talk somehow, Jack Huffins.'

He waited just inside the gate and looked around. There was a large cage, prowling with lions: one crouched upon its belly in the pose of the Sphinx, another lying on its side, ribs swelling and departing like menacing bellows. The third stared majestically at her audience with eyes like cups of liquid gold.

'Where did he go?' said Thomas, craning his neck to peer over the heads of the crowd.

'Only one way in, one way out, far as I know,' said Gabriel. 'He's trapped.'

They toured the rest of the cages, searching for their prey. There was a leopard sleeping behind a log, and a pair of plump owls with eyes like saucers. One was the size of a bear cub, the other barely larger than a tea pot.

'They look like us,' said Thomas with a hoot so convincing it elicited an answer from the larger bird. He smiled. 'I learned to speak like the birds in the attic at home.' The bird blinked. 'His Majesty says we should split up to find Jack. I'll go that way towards the Tower gates, you circle around and he won't get far.'

'Ay,' said Gabriel, tracing his eyes along the ramparts of the perimeter walls. When he looked back, Thomas was already gone. The crowds were growing thick in expectation of the midday show, so he pressed through, shielding his eyes from the sun so he could check their faces.

Ten minutes passed and he was just thinking Jack must have slipped through some unknown thief's exit, when he caught a movement in the corner of his eye and glanced back at the lions to see a figure moving quickly through the hordes, covered in a long cloak.

'The Rat,' he said to himself, marching from the bird cages, pushing people out of the way as he ploughed through the yard. The figure turned, sensing movement, and Gabriel caught sight of that strange visage, the distended face stretched back from the pointed nose. 'Stop,' he called. 'Stop that man.'

The crowd paid no attention to him, for the lions were on their haunches now, flashing their incisors and shaking their heads. Something had excited them, and the crowd was packed around their rattling cage. Gabriel craned his neck to get a better look. Jack was there, right beside the bars, staring at the hooded figure, who was closing in on him.

Gabriel yanked people back by the collar, ignoring their protestations. 'Hold it there,' he said, yet his voice was lost beneath a bellowing roar as the male lion rose up on his hind paws, brandishing his talons as the females threw themselves against the walls of their shuddering cell.

Jack was shaking his head, his eyes fixed upon the concealed face of the hooded figure, who was almost upon him. At the last moment, he caught sight of Gabriel, the bloody stump flapping in his toothless mouth as he tried to scream for help. Others did so on his behalf, for the hatch in the lion cage was open, the bolts pulled back.

'No!' shouted Gabriel, turning around to see where Thomas had gone.

No sooner had he spoken, than Jack's arm was torn clean from its socket, his body crashing against the iron bars with a winded moan, only for a second lion to pounce upon him, clamping her jaws around his skull, and before anyone could pull him back, his screaming face was bitten off like the belly of a pear.

All was pandemonium, the crowd trampling on each other to get away, streaming around Gabriel like rapids. The lions feasted on their prey, their mouths stained crimson, with curls of red hair and scraps of scalp hanging from their snouts.

The guards took position at the arrow loops in the battlements, firing at the beasts, who came growling, bounding over bodies directly to where Gabriel was standing.

'God save us,' said Gabriel, turning to run, yet he was too slow, and the lion was upon him in a second, pinning him to the ground, stretching its jaws to the sky with a deafening roar. It braced its hind legs and lifted its paws ready to gut its meal.

'Mister Griffin!' said Thomas as he threw himself across Gabriel's stomach. The beast's claws cut through his coat like so many daggers through butter. Gabriel was pinned down by the weight of the animal and he saw Thomas's face, grey in shadow against his own. 'Take the lash,' Thomas was saying to himself. 'I am a sinner.'

It was the end for them both. Surely they would die this time. Gabriel readied himself for the feeling of a lion's incisors crushing his legs. He found Thomas's hand gripping his chest and held it tightly.

'Mister True,' he said, 'yer a good man, I know it. Don't know what love is, but I can learn.'

Yet Thomas didn't hear what he said, for the noise of screaming was too loud and there was nothing but kicking feet and the sight of the wild animal ranging above them, her golden eyes pricked with a single black dot of drugged savagery. She shook her shoulders and yawned, then gave a high-pitched squeal as an arrow bolt shot through her neck and those brilliant, deadly eyes grew faint as she fell, lifeless, to the ground.

Part Four

CHAPTER FORTY-SIX

Gabriel took the bowl of vinegar from Bet. 'Ta,' he said, his hands shaking so badly the liquid spilled to the floor.

'It ain't nothing,' she replied, looking at the wet boards with a weary frown. 'Don't think I'm bending down to wipe up yer mess, though. I'll never get up again.' She sat heavily on a cushioned chair. 'Mary's tits, Gabe, this ain't no baby, it's a cannon ball.' She reached up for his hand. 'Actually, pull me up, will you? I need to go.'

'Again?'

'Ay, again, dumb idiot. Lord how men suffer a woman's comfort, and all without sympathy. Steady your hands.'

He placed the bowl and rags on the side and pulled the piss pot over with his toe. 'Take your time,' he said. 'All that weight in your belly, you must be hungry.'

'Could eat a cow and still have room for cheese, but can't eat a bean without being sick. I swear,' she said with a burp, 'that child must be smoking a pipe down there.' She passed a noisy stream of water. 'Reckon he's using my belly for a tavern; takes after his pa.' She grimaced. 'Lord don't he kick me about, violent little cove. Won't be long now, though, and I do love the little turnip already, God save us.' Deep creases lined her brow as she lifted herself back up. 'I've been hard on you this past while, Gabe, but I see what it means now, to care for a babe. Different ain't it, from other loves?'

Gabriel thought back to the moment he first saw little Dot, staring up at him from the blankets. Was that love he felt? Or terror?

'Ay, it's different.'

Bet nodded across the room to the partition, where spots of blood were leading a path around the door. 'He seems a smart fellow, your friend. Not a crusty carpenter, that's for sure.'

Gabriel helped her back to the seat. 'Name's Thomas True,' he said, 'if you can believe that.'

Bet whistled as she fell back, her arms dangling either side of the chair. 'Friend of yours, is he?'

'From the job on the bridge.'

'That so?' She leaned sideways, trying to catch a glimpse of their visitor beyond the partition. 'Here, Mister True, thank you kindly for the work. My Henry was dreadful worried about the baby coming, and you won't find a better carpenter than my boys.'

Thomas's voice came through the partition, shaking. 'My pleasure, Mrs. Sylva. Mister Griffin, might you assist me? I'm afraid I am dripping blood on your floor.'

Bet peered up at Gabriel. 'What happened?' she whispered.

'Fell on a nail,' said Gabriel. 'Didn't want to get us in trouble with his relatives, so he asked if he could come here so we could fix him up.'

Bet nodded suspiciously. 'That right, is it? Looks like he's been in a fight with a lion. Well, you'd better get in there and sort him out before Henry gets back. He's all for clubbing you on the noggin for leaving him with all the work these past weeks.'

Gabriel helped her stagger to the bed for a rest then crossed to the partition and closed the door quietly behind him. Thomas was sitting backwards on a chair beside the window. The wound from the lion's claws flashed across his skin in three bright-red stripes.

'Lucky you had yer coat on,' said Gabriel, resting the bowl on the floor behind him. 'That lion wanted us both for supper.' He kneeled down and dipped the rags in the vinegar.

Thomas hissed, his fingers gripping the back of the chair. 'It hurts.'

'It will. Hold still.'

Gabriel carried out his work in silence, the room listening patiently to the tinkle of warm water and Thomas's whimpering. The horror at the Tower had been too much. The open shell of Jack's faceless skull. The way he'd turned with his hands outstretched, pushing his fingers inside the twitching cavity of his own head, touching the tubes of his nose with his fingertips. The scraping sound of the lion's teeth on bone. It was shocking beyond any capacity for shock, and there was nothing Gabriel or Thomas could do but keep company with their own minds, growing still whenever the memories grew too large for them. This they did every few seconds, taking it in turns to disappear, before coming back to life with a jolt.

'There,' said Gabriel when he was finished at last. 'Patched up.' He tucked in the loose ends of the bandages and smoothed the folds over the

man's bare ribs so they didn't catch. 'Only a scratch really, not deep.' He
touched a pale patch of skin, drawing his finger down its path as Thomas
quivered. 'These old scars – where they from?'

'My childhood,' said Thomas. 'I used to hide under a wall behind the
graveyard. Boys would pull me out and toy with me. I don't talk about it.'

Gabriel leaned in and kissed the broken skin, then took a damp cloth
and washed him. By now, the room was painted with slices of orange light
stretching from the window to the bed, while Bet could be heard in the
next room, snoring like a happy dog.

Gabriel turned Thomas to face him. 'Better?'

Thomas sniffed. 'Yes, Mister Griffin. Thank you.'

'Say Gabriel.'

'Hey?'

'Call me Gabriel. If you want to.'

'I do.'

They held each other and Gabriel huffed, looking down at the stable.
He wished his locket was pressed between them, yet Emily had made her
feelings clear. From the second Thomas had arrived she had begun to grow
faint, and now she had abandoned him completely, taking Dot with her.
He smelled Thomas's hair and rested his cheek on his head.

'We should go before Henry gets back.'

Thomas pulled away and collected his clothes from the floor, twisting
his torso to test the tightness of his bandages. He dressed and wandered
across the room, idling beside the cot.

'Whose bed was this?'

Gabriel stopped by the door, carrying the bowl of rags and vinegar.
'Never mind about that,' he said, turning away. 'Bet can use it, soon as her
babe is born.'

'You say you don't know what love is, but you loved them very much, I
can tell.'

Gabriel turned back and paused, for there was Thomas, leaning over
the cot and inside it: a vision of his baby daughter, lying inside the cradle
just as she had been before, yet now her dimpled hand was gripping
Thomas's finger, and upon her face there shone a little smile. It was
Gabriel's own smile, and for the first time, he recognised himself in his
daughter's face. Thomas brushed his fingers through the air as the baby

responded with kicks and claps, no movement in the blankets, no sound of clapping.

'Don't,' said Gabriel, as Thomas walked from the cradle to the bed and sat down beside Emily's ghost. The spectre of the grey-faced woman turned to the young man with an expression of deep interest.

Gabriel threw the bowl to the floor and stepped forward. 'Will you do nothing you're told? I beg you, come away from there.' He strode to the bed and yanked Thomas up.

'Ow!' said Thomas, gripping his ribs. 'Stop that, you're hurting me.'

'I told you to get up.'

'Mister Griffin, you're shaking.'

'Ay, I'm shaking.'

Thomas took him by the face but was pushed heavily against the wall. A voice came through from next door. It was Bet.

'Gabe? You alright in there?'

Gabriel looked at the ghost of his wife on the bed. Her expression was a mix of fury and disgust. Already, she was fading. Dot was in her cot also, her eyes blinking, and then they were gone again. He turned his back on Thomas, remembering the miserable night on the tower of St Paul's before they'd met. He thought about so many nights, so many moments, across so many days since Thomas had arrived, and fiddled with his cuffs, ashamed of himself.

'You keep asking about love, Thomas. Everything I love gets ruined, everything I love dies. I'm a curse.'

Thomas lifted himself up from the floor and gave himself a shake. 'So am I. We're two curses together.' He stepped gingerly towards Gabriel, then jumped into his arms and kissed him, and they lay together on the floor. As they married, Thomas wondering why he enjoyed the pain, Gabriel staring at his wife's bed in lustful shame.

It was Thomas's turn to wash Gabriel. He did so, drawing swirls in his fur, then dried his back with aching arms and dressed him. As he held up the man's huge coat, he saw something poking out of the inside pocket. 'What's this?' he said, pulling out a slip of paper, stained brown.

'A clue,' said Gabriel. 'Been too scared to show it to anyone till now. Not a nice prospect. Marshal Queed's men found it on the body of the real boatman.'

'The man our assassin killed for his identity?'

'Ay, the same. Must have hidden it in his pocket before his throat got slit and his boat stolen.'

'Well then, what does it say?'

'Look.'

Thomas took the note out and spread it flat on the wall so he could read the faint letters. 'Is this the Rat's handwriting?'

'It is.'

Thomas read aloud. '*White Friars* – some sort of monastery, is it? And a man's name: *Ned Skink.*' Thomas frowned at the scrawled letters. 'That it then? The Rat's real name is Ned Skink?'

Gabriel took the paper, holding it up to the dusky light from the window. 'You think I'd be standing here if it was?' He wrenched open a cupboard. 'White Friars ain't no monastery and Ned Skink ain't no man, not since the first plague. Here, catch.'

A hammer flew across the room and Thomas caught it by the handle with a dry slap. 'Where are we going?'

'Just like it says,' said Gabriel. 'White Friars – or as the villains like to call it: Alsatia. The deadliest place in all London.'

CHAPTER FORTY-SEVEN

Some three hundred yards west of the Fleet Ditch skulked Hanging Sword Alley: a dismal-looking crack between two dismal-looking buildings that led to London's most infamous district. There, no constable dared tread, for he would never come out again, and even the worst villains of the city kept their distance, for it was the home of sin itself, the very den of vice and evil.

Thomas gulped. The sound of a familiar chiming rang from the grim faces of the blackened buildings, their walls plummeting into darkness. Gabriel took Thomas by the wrist and entered the flagged passageway, his hammer outstretched. They made their way past pipe-smoking skeletons and phantom wives, then turned a blind corner through haunted twittens and snickets, pressing beneath a running walkway to what appeared to be a dead end.

Gabriel ducked under a toppled strut and halted. 'Damn it, what way did we come in?'

'I don't know,' said Thomas looking back with a shiver. 'I can hardly see a thing.' He cupped his hand to his ear and listened, for there was the ringing again, drifting in ominous peals from somewhere out of sight. He followed the sound, tracing his eyes along a crooked wall into a yard, and in a deep corner beside a pile of empty bottles lurked a half-concealed door. It was an unspectacular object on first glance, yet when Thomas stepped closer for a better look, he realised that each of its four panels were in fact perfectly rendered individual doors in their own right, only a quarter the usual size. He looked at Gabriel, who was standing back, rolling the handle of his hammer with a doubtful expression on his face.

'Not going in there,' he said.

'Why not?' said Thomas. 'Where do you think it leads?'

'Don't know, and that's enough reason to leave it alone.'

Thomas shook his head. 'That's the saddest thing I ever heard. You have to open doors, or you'll only ever see what people *want* you to see.' He looked back at the door and crinkled his nose. There was certainly something shifty about it. After all, don't all doors have certain ways about them? Certain characteristics ingrained in their faces, just like people, betraying the character of whatever they're trying to hide? Some are jolly, some smart, some inherently hospitable, others elementally hostile – and this particular specimen, with its peeling paint and queer construction of four little handles and four sets of brass hinges, gave the overwhelming impression that it was downright impish, certainly volatile, and very much hoping to be opened.

So, Thomas gave it a shove and it did open, all as one. He looked back at Gabriel with a triumphant nod, then stepped straight through. They were standing at the apex of a long, sloping corridor, the green-painted walls lit with a glimmeration of lanterns no larger than crab apples. The door slammed shut behind them, making Gabriel jump.

'Turn back, I reckon,' he said, but Thomas was already marching off to the sound of the ringing bells, his heels bouncing happily as he swung his arms like a marching soldier. Gabriel took one last look at the closed door behind him and whined. He gave a troubled sigh and followed down the passageway, which twisted and tightened, as such passageways often do, until they were forced to crawl through a space the size of a drain, which tightened until Gabriel was wriggling on his stomach, following the soles of Thomas's shoes.

After some time, Thomas stopped and gave a soft whistle. 'Well now, will you look at that?'

Gabriel shuffled beside him and stretched his eyes wide in astonishment. Ahead of them, the passageway opened onto a vision, something like an old engraving of a forgotten London, long before the Great Fire. It was a buried lane; an entire street of half-submerged houses and shops either side of a cobbled thoroughfare, while every building was no larger than a child's playhouse, fully a quarter their usual size, each with its own pigmy door and soft-glowing windows of little panes, while the avenue was lit with torches on poles no higher than a man's waist. There were no horses, for there simply wasn't room for them, in fact there was nobody there at all. Gabriel searched the queer terrace, noticing the various doors, which were only half closed, while the first-floor windows had the corners of their blinds caught between them, as though they had been pulled shut in a hurry.

'Who goes there?' he said, shimmying forwards on his belly. He reached his hammer into the deserted street and tapped on one of the tiny doors, withdrawing his hand with a snap. 'Answer.'

There came a buzzing sound from within the property, and shadows moved beyond the blinds.

'You've done it now,' said Thomas, 'I made that mistake once with a wasps' nest in the woods at home.' He winced. 'I was pulling stingers from my backside for days.'

Gabriel groaned. 'Told you, Thomas, we should have gone back.'

'And miss seeing this? It must be a pixies' lair. Look at those windows, aren't they funny? I do believe they're made out of the bottoms of jars. And there...' Thomas chuckled, unable to conceal his delight. 'The little roofs, they're tiled with seashells.'

'Ay,' said Gabriel, staring from property to property. 'Heard about this place. Never thought I'd see it with me own eyes.'

'What is it then?'

'Glasshouse Yard, home of the Blackguard.'

The phantom bell returned as little hands brambled across the yellow lights of the windows, the avenue filling up like rising water to the sound of gathering whispers.

'Answer me,' said Gabriel. 'Who goes there?' He crawled from the mouth of the passageway and crouched in the lane, shoulders buffeting the tangled vaults. There was a shift at the far end of the avenue, where the small beams and little slatted walls became mud. For the briefest of moments, the silhouette of a person appeared, with a cane and a funny hat, and then they were lost, consumed by a ball of shadows. 'Stay back,' said Gabriel, his words ringing up and down the length of the avenue. A huddle of figures nestled together and grew up ahead, then came on as one crawling mass, moving towards them like a bristling ball of crystal spiders. 'By God's soul, save us,' said Gabriel, crouching with his hammer raised, trying to stuff himself back into the tunnel. 'Get back, Thomas. Get back.'

'I can't move,' said Thomas. 'You're too big.'

And with that, Gabriel swung his hammer into the oncoming mass and with a battle cry they were engulfed.

CHAPTER FORTY-EIGHT

They awoke, side by side at the bottom of a funnel of blackened bricks on a bed of crushed glass.

'Thomas?' said Gabriel, his voice echoing. He struggled against the lashings around his arms and legs.

'Gabriel?' said Thomas. 'You're awake.'

'Ay, are ye hurt?'

'No, I'm not hurt. Are you?'

They stared up the sides of the looming walls to a disc of blue sky hundreds of feet above their heads. They were at the bottom of a huge chimney, trapped like mice in a well. There was a scuffling noise behind them.

'Dear, oh dear,' said Thomas sitting up with a stretch of his arms and legs. 'What a pickle. Do we call for help?'

Gabriel glowered at him. 'You mean you ain't tied up?'

Thomas wiggled his ankles and waved his hands. 'Apparently not.'

'Hell's bones, hush your yapping then and untie me.'

Thomas bit his bottom lip. 'I don't really know if I should. They seem to want you tied up at the moment.'

Gabriel stared at him, incredulous. 'Eh?'

'Look,' said Thomas, pointing to the walls.

Gabriel turned his head as shapes grew out of the brickwork. The chimney was encrusted with a roiling tapestry of a thousand button faces. 'The Blackguard,' he said, in a fearful mutter.

'What are they singing?' said Thomas, as the creatures made an inhuman, metallic sound, the perfect symmetry of...

'Chiming,' whispered Gabriel. He stared in disbelief at the soot-covered children, who twitched their joints with deliberate jerks, their bejewelled rags catching dashes of light, spearing the cavernous space with stolen beams.

Thomas raised the hammer Gabriel had given him and stood up. 'Who are you?' he said.

The chanting stopped and the carpet of heads grew still. A voice spoke, sharp as a pin.

'We's the Blackguard, ain't we, conker head? And this be the great chimney of Glasshouse Yard. No growners allowed.'

'No growners allowed,' repeated the chorus of children, and their chant whistled to the top of the chimney then down again at enormous speed.

'I see,' said Thomas, turning in circles to find the origin of the voice. 'Are you our friend or foe?'

'We ain't friendly nor foely, ye grand idiot. That's our tradition.'

Gabriel rolled over, sliding down the glass shingle. 'Why you tied me up like a fly then? I ain't no threat to the Blackguard.'

Thomas lowered the hammer. 'Gabriel's right; we mean you no harm.'

The nest convulsed with the sound of laughter, the pixies flashing their pink mouths and nattering to one another.

'Them dumb loobies ain't meaning us no harm, says the pretty one. How would Thomas Trumper and Grubble Griffin harm the Blackguard, we should like to know? Not like they can drown us under the Bridge like they did that nasty wherryman.'

Thomas clapped his hand to his mouth. 'How do they know about that, Gabriel? They can't have—'

'The Blackguard knows all,' said the voice. 'We's the memory of London, so we is. Oh yes, silly Thomas, we hold the knowledge.'

Thomas peered up at the children's faces, though he might as well have searched for a stitch in a blanket. 'Which of you is speaking?'

'There ain't one Blackguard, any more than there's one molly man. And that's your answer, duff-ears.'

Thomas put his hands to his hips. 'Listen here, you pack of imps, tell me where to find Ned Skink's right away.'

'Bugger off.'

'You have to help us, or our friends will hang.'

'It be so.'

'Why have you tied Gabriel up? He isn't any trouble.'

'He is.'

'Is what?'

'Trouble.'

'How so?'

'We know.'

'What do you know?'

'Everything.'

Gabriel spoke in a low voice. 'Easy now, Thomas.'

Yet Thomas wasn't listening. 'You don't know everything, that's ridiculous. You can't know anything about me, for a start.'

'Oh, we do.'

'Well, then, prove it.'

And so the voices began a solemn chanting to that familiar, unsettling chime, like woollen mallets on copper:

'Thomas True from Highgate flew
On a postal coach he drew
Down to London Bridge to dwell
With candles, lies, and love to sell
Mother Clap's and vermin tales
Tumbles over lofty rails
Through the streets he bravely pranced
As dreams of friendship dipped and danced
Lost in veiled sincerity
That molly christened Verity
Moulded fashions up for sale
With artful, lonely Abigail
Praise for her, yet sin for him
He drowned a man who could not swim
A grieving heart he thinks to mend
Yet still the lions ate his friend
And now he wonders what to do
When true is false and false is true
For Tyburn waits to kill the cat
Who dares to stalk the hooded Rat.'

Thomas gaped in wonder as the children recounted his adventure. 'Incredible,' he said to himself. 'Gabriel, did you hear that?'

'Ay,' said Gabriel, his voice reflective. 'Ay, I heard it.'

'They've been following me all along. I sensed it.'

'Following you?' snapped the voice. 'The Blackguard follows nobody, weasel bum. We's the living chronicle of old London.'

'A chronicle? You mean ... you record history?'

'No stories, only what happened.'

Thomas knitted his brow. 'And you see everything?'

'Every thing and every nothing.'

'How?'

'Most people choose to forget; we choose to remember.'

'Well in that case,' said Thomas, feeling a rush of excitement, 'you can tell us who the Rat is.'

'Wasting yer time,' said Gabriel, rolling about like a frustrated caterpillar. 'They like to gabble but only for gold.' He managed to sit up. 'Well, we ain't got no gold, ye hear? Not a damned penny.'

A whisper circled the brim of the chimney before slipping down the funnel in a wave. 'Don't want gold,' said the voice. 'Thomas already gave us that.'

'Did I?' said Thomas. 'Oh well come along then, tell us who Daisy cried out to before she died. And who tipped me off the gallery at St Paul's. Who is giving men's names away to the Society? Who is the Rat?'

The voice spoke in a trilling cry. 'As if we would tell you that, you massive carrot.'

Thomas kicked his foot in frustration, spraying beads of glass against the bricks. 'But you just said you could.'

'We *could* ain't we *would*, tufty-head! Besides, yous already know the answer, if you'd only listen to yerselves.'

Thomas scratched his chin, staring at the funnel of faces surrounding him. 'God bless you children, I wish you would help us save our friends from hanging; they are good men.'

A fresh whispering started halfway up the walls, the agitation amongst the children splitting them into a pair of rings, which moved up and down the chimney like a gulping throat, the sound of their voices jumbling together until they rang less like a bell, more like the howling of a February wind. The commotion settled some fifty feet high before drawing slowly back down again, when at last the voice spoke in a fatigued croak:

'Our knowledge goes back to ancient times, Thomas True. But we ain't got no knowledge of good men.'

Thomas thrust his hammer into his breeches. 'Well I am hardly innocent myself, I know that, but I'm kind when I can be. Won't you save my life?'

The voice was silent for a moment. 'Ain't much value in a life, sir. If there was, we wouldn't be orphans.'

Thomas crouched down beside Gabriel. 'This is such a lot for my brain,' he whispered. 'What do I do?'

Gabriel looked around at the myriad faces and realised their expressions had changed from black to gold, like the molten scales of a dragon's skin. 'Keep talking,' he said, 'them spiders seem to like you in favour of every other soul in London.'

Thomas raised himself to his feet and pulled off his peruke. 'Whoever you are, come along, show yourself; I expect you're the grandest Blackguard of all.' He gave a knowing smile, suddenly realising that he had indeed given them a gold coin before. 'I should like to see your green pendant again.'

The funnel hissed like steam, not a head turning in sequence, only the boiling mass of rebellious children. At last, they flattened to the walls, spitting a single child in a *plop* to the middle of the circular space. The little creature wore a ripped doublet gemmed with shards of broken glass, their pendant glittering amidst tight curls of black hair. They were perhaps six years old, though terribly small for their age, with intelligent eyes that stared out from their soot-coated face, bright and beautiful. Thomas extended his hand and smiled. 'Good day, little thing,' he beamed, 'I believe we met on my first night in the city.'

The urchin gave a low bow, reaching into their pocket, and pulled out the half-guinea: the very same coin Thomas had given them beside the exchange on his first night in London. 'Kind Thomas,' they said, 'I return this to you.'

Thomas bowed, taking the coin. 'Won't you keep it?'

The child shook their head. 'Money ain't valuable if alls you do is keep it.'

'Then tell me your name.'

'Nobody ever gave me one.'

'Well,' said Thomas, 'I shall call you Glimmer if I may? Yes, that suits you nicely. Glimmer Littlethorn.'

The urchin screwed up their face like tissue as the choir of Blackguard children sang the name in a delightful peal. It was as though wind was blowing through a forest of crystal leaves.

'Keep going,' muttered Gabriel. 'Ask 'em again about the Rat.'

Thomas took the hammer from his belt and rested it on the ground. 'I beg you, help us find the Rat. It's very important.'

Glimmer hopped away from him. 'Why should we help you, when nobody helps us?' They looked around at their friends. 'Even if we did, who would remember that we helped?'

'I would.'

'So says everyone who visits us with a beg for something they wants, but they never do. Soon as they're rich or safe, they forget, and there they sit all cosy by their fireplaces in their silks, happy as pigs, while we watch 'em through the windies, shiverin'.'

Gabriel tutted, wrenching his arms against his ropes. 'Don't reckon they know anything about the Rat; they're making it all up.'

'Not true!' said the child, and so bridled, they turned to their cohorts and began a long and evidently arduous consultation. Every Blackguard orphan partook in what appeared to be some form of referendum, whereby glass pellets dropped from the summit of the chimney via their heads like beads through a living machine.

At last, Glimmer returned. 'We'll tell you some of the truth if you want to hear it, but only if you promise to give us something.'

'What would you like?'

'What we never had before.'

'Go on.'

Glimmer edged closer, eyes glowing. 'Already told you what it is.'

Thomas nodded solemnly, tracing his mind over what the children had told him. What could they possibly want, if it wasn't gold? And then he remembered: *we ain't got no knowledge of good men.* He understood the children well; after all, he'd been looking for precisely the same thing all his life. 'Very well then, little friends,' he said with a deep breath, 'I gladly give you myself as a good man, and perhaps one day you'll give me my own in return. How does that sound?'

The bricks shivered in a dainty rippling of green and blue shapes, then with a sudden crack, the entire funnel was lit with an iridescent mosaic of moving peacock feathers, climbing in a repeating pattern towards the distant sky.

Thomas and Gabriel stared up in amazement.

Glimmer gave a bow. 'Looks like we accept your gift, Kind Thomas. Do not let your goodliness go rotten, or we'll take your life as a forfeit.'

'A Devil's bargain,' said Gabriel. 'They mean to kill you.'

Yet Thomas took no notice and kneeled before the child. 'As my name is Thomas True, I will not disappoint you, I promise you, and if you see everything, you'll know I have nothing to hide. Quickly now, you must help us.'

The child considered for a minute then spoke in a song, moving their arms and legs in such a way as to chime the scales of glass in a rhythm.

'You search for the Rat.
A man, mostly that,
With faces, not one, but a few.
They crawl foul and pretty
Across this cruel city
First truth, but treachery too.
A tragedy hidden
Banished and bidden
A molly, discovered and lost
With an envious eye,
He'll kill then he'll die
And together – the Rat is the cost.'

Thomas waited for more, yet already the bricks were thinning into bald patches. 'I don't understand it at all,' he said, stepping towards the child as they sprang away like a flea. 'A man, mostly that? Banished yet bidden? Foul and pretty? It doesn't make any sense.' He looked up to find all of the children had melted away. He put his head in his hands, desperately trying to remember the rhyme, repeating it as the words echoed up the funnel.

A heavy hand rested on his shoulder.

'Did well,' said Gabriel, the lashings in lengths around his feet.

'I don't think so,' said Thomas. 'I thought they would help us more than that.'

'P'raps they have,' said Gabriel, 'p'raps they will some other day.' He pulled Thomas to his feet. 'Still, it's a dark bargain you made, you'd better take care not to break your word.'

'Oh, that's nothing to worry about. I only promised to be myself.'

Gabriel cocked his head, pointing to the far side of the chimney. 'Look.'

There was a small doorway in the black bricks, a path snaking through the mounds of glass shingle. Thomas looked at Gabriel. 'Was that there before?'

'Don't think so.'

'Then where do you think it leads?'

'Don't know,' said Gabriel. 'But that's enough reason to go through any door, ain't it?'

Thomas grinned and took his arm. 'It most certainly is.'

CHAPTER FORTY-NINE

Ned Skink's was less a tavern than a cellar with a puddle of piss for a floor. Thomas and Gabriel swam to a dark corner where a tallow candle stank up the air. They spoke as quietly as they could, their words lost beneath the hollering of an ancient pie woman selling her wares from a dish.

Gabriel caught her eye as he leaned in, wondering if he'd seen her somewhere before. 'This has to be the place,' he murmured. 'Boatman met the assassin here, I'd bet on it. His body was pulled from the river just down from here by Dorset Stairs. Question is, did the Rat come here too?' Gabriel inspected their fellow drinkers. Men with noses like plums, women staggering about with skirts lifted to their patch-plastered cheeks. Toothless skeletons picked sodden crumbs from the puddles, while a bald woman in rags plucked milky slime from the corner of a sleeping man's mouth and sucked it from her fingers like cream. Gabriel heaved and took a glug of sour beer, thinking of his kindly cellmate at the compter. 'Reckon Old Bob would have been glad to leave this place for the next life.' He pulled the boatman's note from his pocket. 'Hell can't be any worse.' He stared at the paper, the letters squirming in the flickering light.

'Ho!' came a voice beside their table. 'Pssst...'

Gabriel and Thomas looked up to see the pie woman holding out her dish.

'Be off with you,' barked Gabriel. 'We don't want your mangy pies.'

The woman huffed. 'Now, handsome sirs. Won't you at least glance at me pies, I'm certain you won't be disappointed.'

Thomas shook his head. 'Good lady, we do not want your pies. Here,' he said, fishing the half-guinea from his pocket, the glint of gold catching every eye in the room.

Gabriel snapped Thomas's hand closed. 'What are you thinking? Put that away or we'll be garrotted.' He turned to the woman. 'No pies. Be off with you.'

'Modder Mary!' she hissed in an Irish accent so thick it could turn the Ottomans Catholic. Her eyes darted down three times on stalks. 'Will ye look at me pies, ye great mountain o' stupidity?'

Gabriel followed her gaze to the dish in her hands, where a splash of gravy had been painted into the shape of an arrow. The woman swivelled her hips, directing them towards a curtain hung across a buried doorway.

'Aff I go then,' she said in an unnaturally loud voice. 'No pies for sirs today. Why, old Treasa's so tired she'll have a sleep so she will, afore she goes a-pie-selling on Fleet Street.' With that, she turned and slipped through the doorway out of sight.

'They're all mad in Alsatia,' said Thomas, catching the murderous glances of the men who had arranged themselves to bar the exit. There was a narrow fellow at a neighbouring table, nursing a drink, his hat pulled low over a distended face. He slugged some beer and as he did so, the skin around his lips peeled off and fell like rotten fish into his cup. Thomas gulped. 'Perhaps we should follow the pie woman after all.'

'Ay,' said Gabriel, 'let's see what she has to say. Reckon I may know her.'

They stepped through to the cubby, finding the hag buried into the deepest corner of the snug. 'Come in,' she whispered, 'and pull a stool up tight, both of ye.'

She took in her visitors, her face glowing like a bearded swede beneath her loose cap. 'Sit close, good gents, close as ye can, so's no one can hear what we're about.'

Gabriel remembered. 'You're the pie seller I saw after my night in the compter, and at Smithfield Market.'

'Just so,' she said. 'Charmed to meet you again, I'm sure.' She patted her pinny and sat back. 'Treasa Buckleburn's the name.' She checked they were alone and leaned in. 'Heard ye both gabbling to each other about my Old Bob and a Rat.'

Gabriel and Thomas exchanged looks.

'Maybe we were.'

'Definitely you was,' she said, her eyes drifting to the candle as they filled with tears. 'Heard ye say his name just now, so I did. Wasn't *Old* Bob to me of course. To me, he was my husband, sure enough. Knew him since I first came here from Cork to work the nursery gardens.' She smiled to herself, counting out her favourite memories. 'Saved me, he did, from a rotten marriage to a violent fella past Rotten Row.' She picked up one of her pies and began stuffing it into her mouth. 'Heard ye say his name, whoever you are, then I thought to myself: "Treasa, if that isn't the big lump o' lard they kicked out the compter the morning Bob vanished. Maybe he knows what happened to make ye lonely.'"

Treasa chewed like a cow on cud. 'Don't furrow that brow at me, you grumpy old barrel, I don't expect ye to give me good news. Sixty years I waited to lose my Bob and now it's come. He couldn't stop himself, so he couldn't. I'd beg him to tell me why he kept going to them places.' She spat a gobbet of gristle to the floor. 'Sodomites' Walk, you lads call it. Sodomite's Grave more like.' She drew her fingernail down the side of the candle, rubbing molten wax between her fingertips. 'Now don't look so fearful, boys. I learned to spot a molly over the years and I'm no member of the Society, no thank you. Never begrudged my Bobby, he was a rosy sort of a husband now, never unkind. Besides' – she licked the pastry and wax from her fingertips – 'I prefer a cunny anyways, only there ain't no molly houses for that.'

'No hangings neither,' said Gabriel.

'Too true,' said the woman. 'You boys have all the fun.' She took a second pie, nibbling its crinkles like a squirrel on a nut. 'Well, I was a fortunate wife, so I reckoned, free to do as I pleased, no screaming babes or lusty boozer for a husband.' She rolled her eyes. 'Till the Duchess comes along, that is.'

Gabriel sat up. 'You knew the Duchess well? Old Bob told you about her?'

'Ay so,' said the old woman, resting the pie as her face hardened. 'Mister Timothy Rettipence. Merchant's secretary now, so I hear, with a proper wife and children dressed up all smart for church. Nothing more than a lowly apprentice clerk when I first laid eyes on him, the little beggar.' She gave Gabriel a meaningful look. 'Nought unusual about a crusty molly showing a fresh lad how to roll pastry, I suppose, though it raised my old Celtic suspicions, I must say.' She sucked the juice from the pie, licking gravy from her whiskers. 'We know how to spot an English devil, so we do; years of practice carved into our bones. Well, my Bob disappeared for days on end, coming home so sozzled he walked like a monkey and spoke as much sense. Over time, Mister Rettipence grew wise and wealthy, and my husband grew old and tired. That's what happens, you see, boys.' She held her hands out like weighing scales. 'Young men grow middling, middling men grow decrepit, and that's when the Duchess got himself a young bitch of his own.' She held up her hollow pie crust to the candle, moving it around in her fingers. 'So the world turns.' She took a long, troubled breath and tapped her visitors on the knee. 'Don't think me bitter, my lads. I hope ye live long enough to know what it's like to disappear, though you needn't worry about that too much: men don't perform the trick so well as women do, not even mollies. Still, a little disappearing has its benefits, long as ye ain't alone.' Her face went mystical at that, sitting back in the dark cubby with her eyes nowhere on Earth. 'Ay, long as ye ain't alone.'

Gabriel leaned in. 'Bob told me he saw the Rat, that's why they killed him. He was trying to save us, I reckon.'

The candle sputtered. 'Bob told me about it too, surely enough, just before they took him to the compter.' She raised her chin slowly, her aged face carved in every line by the guttering flame. 'Said he saw someone at the molly house on Whitechapel.'

'That's right. Miss Muff's.'

'That's it, so.'

'Who did he see?' said Thomas, wiggling excitedly on his seat.

'Didn't tell me.'

Gabriel thumped the back of his head against the wall in exasperation. 'God's bones.'

'They came here, though,' said Treasa, brushing crumbs from her chest.

Thomas reached out and gripped her by the wrists. 'Who came here?'

She checked the entry, moving nothing but her eyes. 'A boatman with a badge,' she said. 'They dredged him up the day after, just down by them slippery steps. And two others. A pirate with long hair and coal-rimmed eyes.'

'The assassin,' said Thomas.

She laughed. 'Ack, that's a good name for him, I should say.'

Gabriel forced his voice to stay calm. 'And the third? Who was it?'

'Strange-looking fellow,' said Treasa, resting her eyes beyond the cubby. 'Such sallow, bloodless skin he has, all sweaty like bacon rind. Pinched out like someone pulled him from the womb by his snout. I remember yer assassin calling him "the Rat" and having a good chuckle about it.' She lifted from her chair, freeing herself of Thomas's grip, and nodded to the tavern parlour. 'Seems the right name for him, so it does.'

Gabriel frowned. 'Woman, you talk like he's still here.'

'Sure, he is. Or at least he was a minute ago. You was sitting right next to him. Why d'you reckon I pulled ye away?'

Gabriel shot out to where they had been sitting. Thomas came after him, leaping over stools to the tavern doors, but they were too late, the Rat was gone.

'I saw him,' said Thomas, 'just as you called us in, I looked straight at him.' He shivered, remembering the buried eyes, the skin falling from his lip. He huddled close to Gabriel. 'I saw his rotten face. You wouldn't forget it.'

Gabriel nodded, scratching his head. 'Remember the Blackguard riddle: "With faces, not one, but a few. He crawls foul and pretty." He's wearing a mask, whoever he is. And not one mask, lots of 'em.' He growled. 'God burn his blood.'

He turned to go, then caught sight of something under the stool where the man had been sitting. He bent down to fetch it up, pinching it between his thumb and forefinger to let the juices from the floor slide away, then turned it over. It was a silver tobacco tin, shallow and flat with bevelled edges.

Treasa gave a croaking gasp, stepping away with bulging eyes. 'Him!' she said. 'It's him. I told ye!'

Thomas took the tin, turning it against the light. 'Who?' He opened it up. 'There's nothing inside.'

'The inscription, ye fool,' said Treasa. Three initials had been punched through the metal.

$$\text{T. A. R.}$$

'Do you know somebody with those initials?' said Thomas.

The woman nodded, her face seething.

'She does,' said Gabriel. He took the tin and held it up to the burning lamp on the wall so the letters glowed. 'So do we. Timothy Rettipence.'

'That's him,' said Treasa, her fists balling. 'Must have a second Christian name beginning with "A", the grand queen. That's yer Rat, I knew it all along. All my Bobby did for him, only to end up dead on some compter floor. I could stab his bloody eyes out, so I could.'

'Might be a coincidence,' said Gabriel, doubtfully.

'No,' said Thomas, standing apart. 'Look.'

He was staring at the opposite wall, where the initials had been projected in reverse three feet high as though daubed across the wooden panels in rippling flame.

A.A.T

CHAPTER FIFTY

Gabriel and Thomas were dripping with sweat, dashing as fast as they could along the Strand.

'We should be going straight to Camomile Street,' said Thomas. 'That's where Rettipence lives.'

'Ay, but he won't be back from Alsatia yet. Knows he's been spotted, doesn't he? Reckon that'll make him rash. Our friends are in danger.'

The peruke shop on Covent Garden was strangely quiet as they approached, while the display window was in complete disarray, the periwigs strewn about like so many squabbling hens amidst tangles of ribbon and spilled powder. The door, meanwhile, stood open.

'Where has everything gone?' said Thomas. 'Have they abandoned shop?'

Gabriel turned in a circle, searching the piazza, and saw Mister Vivian walking amongst the crowd. He looked older than ever with a crooked back and frail, shaking legs, his thin hair blowing like lamb's wool from his naked head. He was passing from person to person, tugging on their sleeves like a lost child. Gabriel and Thomas approached him.

'Mister Vivian,' said Thomas, 'what are you doing out here alone?'

The old man shifted around, looking at them both as though they were strangers. 'Tell me, gentlemen, have you seen him?' He stared up at Gabriel with pale, watery eyes, his chin shaking.

'Come home to your shop,' said Gabriel, leading him by the elbow. How thin the man was, his bones sharp inside his hollow sleeves, the flesh of his face shrunk to his skull so that every dent and curve was visible through his transparent skin.

'What's that?' said Vivian. 'What did you say? My, my, my. Where is he? Have you seen him?'

Gabriel and Thomas guided him carefully inside and settled him into one of the armchairs.

'Where's Fump?' said Gabriel, sitting beside the old man. 'Is he unwell?'

'Unwell? Oh my darling Fump, unwell, unwell. He shall return to me, do you think?'

'Return from where?'

'From where, indeed, sir, from where indeed.' Mister Vivian gazed across Gabriel's shoulder, his drooping eyelids filled with tears. 'My sweet love, my gentle companion, where have you gone?' He pulled one of Fump's pink periwigs from a shelf and cuddled it to his chest. 'He left a fortnight ago and hasn't returned. I expect he will come home this evening. Have you seen him? Yes, yes, he will be back, eating our cupboards bare and making my life such a trial, such a trial.' He stopped still, his eyes going blank, and for a moment he seemed dead, yet with a rattling breath he blinked and continued with his rambling. 'He has been gone for two weeks, my dears, two whole weeks and not a word since. I confess when he left, I thought myself relieved, Lord forgive my folly.' He pressed his uncut fingernails to his face, staring in disbelief. 'If anything has happened to him I shall never forgive myself, but he does try my nerves, you know, and we had a row about something silly, what was it? Oh yes, too much money spent on your uncle's scented candles, my boy, that's what it was.' He gave Gabriel a curdled smile. 'Why are the angriest arguments over the most trivial things? Now I cannot sleep in fear of missing his return. Have you seen him?'

Thomas took Vivian's hand. 'Where did Mister Fump go to?'

The old man sank deeper into the chair, staring out from the crimson cushion like a corpse in an open casket. 'He was visiting his sister in Buckinghamshire, my dear,' he croaked. 'Not for this long though; I haven't been alone for so many days, not in fifty years.'

Gabriel cast his eyes around the shop, realising for the first time that Fump, who delighted in mess-making with his friends, was in fact the cleaner and tidier of the two, and without him, sensible Mister Vivian had unravelled completely. Perukes lay in heaps across the floor, curls and switches bedraggled like the tentacles of stranded octopuses, and there was a grimy film of dust already coating the mantelpiece and shelves. He remembered his own quarters after Emily had left him. It was an unfathomable emptiness: a chilling realisation that one's existence had become so entirely grown-through with the roots of another person, that without them, it was impossible to stand.

'Have you heard from him since he left?'

The old man sprung up. 'I did, young man. Indeed I did!' He searched between the cushions and drew out a bundle of papers wrapped in string. 'I received this from him the day after he departed, nothing since.'

'A letter,' said Thomas, taking it from the man's shaking fingers. He lifted it to the light of a candle burning on the mantelpiece and read...

Dear V,

I have arrived in a little town named Newport Pagnell, where I shall spend the night. It is a jolly enough place but if you were here there would be more to look at. We had quite a downpour earlier. I am in terrible danger of catching a chill. I shall warm myself by the fire, for what might happen if my letter were drenched? I must turn in as soon as I have finished my coffee. How I shall miss my home then, but I must watch the time before I retire to the land of nod, for I have not enjoyed a good sleep in ages.

I have a young and lusty driver assisting my passage, who I have not used before and shan't use again. He has good haunches but a smart mouth, which got us into a bit of a pickle earlier at a turnpike leading onto the North Road. We found ourselves in A Terribly embarrassing impasse with two justices travelling the other way.

Well, I made friends with them, dear, as I always do, yet I had the most unexpected surprise!

Gabriel took the letter and read the second page.

There was a mysterious creature riding with them in the carriage. They jumped from their skin when I spotted them. The creature bears more than a little attention, mark my words. Very suspicious travelling companions, very strange indeed. That is to say, I shan't reveal the identity of the animal.

We drew away in opposite directions, my poppet, I being the very epitome of discretion. Yet, much to my surprise, the justices are here, my darling! Here, in this very inn, I thank you! They must have gotten lost for want of a map, this being the wilderness, and followed after me.

I know how tiresome you find me, my sweet Viv, so forgive my hot words. Wait faithfully for my return, for I believe I shall have much to say. It is dreadfully hot and the candles are mostly lit, so I shall lay my sheets at a careful distance from the flames, so I might sleep in gentle safety and appear to you, should you care to read this letter carefully, very soon.

Gabriel frowned, turning to the third and final page.

I bid you goodnight, my friend!

Gabriel hummed to himself. 'Strange letter, even for Fump.'

'I agree,' said Thomas. 'There's something curious about the phrasing; it sounds like Fump in parts, yet in others not at all.'

Gabriel re-read the words, some shouting out from the pages, while others were cluttered and jumbled, shrinking back as though attempting to hide in the paper.

'Where is he?' asked Mister Vivian with a yawn, his eyelids growing heavy. 'Where is my Fump?'

Thomas gave Gabriel a knowing look. 'Who knows where he is, but we might guess what he saw. Or whom. Mister Rettipence must have been away from London to make a trade.' He rose from the chair, speaking low so as not to wake Mister Vivian who had fallen into a rattling stupor. 'If Fump saw him then he'll be dead by now.'

A cloud covered the sun in the piazza, turning the interior of the shop grey. Gabriel held the letter closer to the candle, the heat of the flame sending an ache through his fingernails. 'It just don't quite add up,' he said to himself thoughtfully. 'At the exchange, Rettipence didn't act like a guilty man. He got a note himself, and he went home from Fenchurch Street before the ambush, so who was Daisy talking to?'

Thomas shook his head in frustration. 'All lies, all subterfuge. He wrote himself the note as a diversion, knowing you'd come to question him sooner or later. Perhaps he knew you were watching him that night on Fenchurch Street, went home to Camomile Street then dashed out again, knowing exactly where the attack was going to be. Maybe he wasn't there at all, and Daisy was confused after so many knocks to the head.'

Gabriel rubbed his brow, his tired brain making his words come out short. 'You're making stories to fit stories, Thomas. Don't be so quick to judge.'

'Quick? We have to be quick, or we'll all swing. Why must you be so slow?' He tapped Fump's letter, which glowed beside the candle flame. 'I suspected the Duchess and Lavender from the start. I'll bet they're companions in deceit as well as in bed. They've both been accusing me to cover their tracks. George was at the exchange the first night I went to Clap's and the Society hounds let him go, remember? Just like he escaped them on Fenchurch Street.'

'Careful,' said Gabriel, inspecting the illuminated page a second time. 'He could say exactly the same thing about you.'

'The nasty little liar,' said Thomas. 'That's it, I'm sure of it. Both of them are the Rat.' He marched to the door. 'Come on, let's get a mob together and hunt them down. We've got our hammers. I'll stave their heads in.'

Gabriel glared at Thomas, surprised. 'You would see two men lynched for a tobacco tin and speculation?'

Thomas held up the tin. 'I would see them face justice on this unquestionable evidence. They have treated me cruelly, and now I know why. Or have you forgotten what they're chanting about me in Mother Clap's?'

'It ain't fair on you, but you're no better than them, condemning men because you don't like 'em. No better than the Society neither.'

Thomas crossed his arms. 'And you're just another London molly, telling everyone to be cautious and scared when it's time to act. You can hide away in those empty quarters on Red Lyon Street all you like, wishing your wife and baby were back to keep you hidden from yourself, but I intend to—'

Gabriel slapped him across the face.

Thomas staggered back, gripping his cheek. He landed heavily on the floor. With tears in his eyes he stood up, wincing as the bandages pulled at the wounds on his back, and was about to yell at Gabriel when he caught sight of the page of Fump's letter, still resting beside the candle.

He hooted with mocking laughter. 'There,' he said. 'You're just like the rest of them; you don't trust me, but will you trust Mister Fump?'

Gabriel looked at the page. A brown mark was worming its way through the paper, forming a gentle scroll. It was a pair of symbols spreading out like feathers. He recognised them before they were complete.

T. R.

Gabriel turned to Thomas. 'Forgive me, I—'

'Leave it,' said Thomas with a chop of his fingers. 'It doesn't matter.

Fump was trying to warn us before it was too late. Perhaps it already is.'
He marched out to the piazza, swinging his arms. 'Come on.'

CHAPTER FIFTY-ONE

Mistress Rettipence arranged her skirts as she took her visitor in with a fretful smile. 'You say you work with my husband at the exchange?'

Thomas nodded, crossing his legs then uncrossing them again. He looked towards the parlour window to see Gabriel standing across the street, keeping watch outside. He swallowed his anger at the man, forcing himself to focus. 'I do. I am an apprentice clerk.'

'How lovely.'

She was forty years old, or thereabouts, with a round, intelligent face. She looked Thomas over, sipping from her cup, before giving him a cautious eye. 'Do you live in London, Mister True?'

'I do indeed, on London Bridge.'

'Oh, how lovely. Beyond the chapel?'

'The north side, of course.'

'Of course. I hear the air is the cleanest in London.'

'And the noisiest.'

'Ah.'

The clock chimed on the mantelpiece, motes of dust floating through the room as carriages trundled by outside. Camomile Street was a busy thoroughfare, yet the smell of food and the sight of smart hats passing by was a world away from the common crush and clatter of the bridge.

'Will Mister Rettipence be returning soon?' asked Thomas.

'I should ask you,' said Mistress Rettipence, meeting his eye, 'since you are also employed at the exchange.'

Thomas was about to summon an answer, when a housemaid bustled along the hallway beyond the parlour, opening the front door. 'Good day to you, sir,' came her voice.

Mister Rettipence stepped into the hallway, brushing dust from his shoulders. It was all Thomas could do not to wring the man's neck right there and then. The merchant removed his long coat and hung his hat on a peg. Thomas coughed, and the man turned around, jumping so high that his head was momentarily rehatted. 'Why, good afternoon,' he said, flicking his eyes nervously to his wife. 'Do we have a visitor, my darling?'

'We do. Mister True, your apprentice colleague from the exchange.'

Thomas stood, brushing down his breeches. He smiled, raising his eyebrows.

The befuddled man cleared his throat, pulling at his kerchief. 'Good day, sir.'

'Good day.'

The man's wife gave him a quizzical look. 'Mister True brings glad news, so he says.'

'I do,' said Thomas, holding the man's eye. He was so tense, he was forced to expel a little energy by tapping his toes.

Mister Rettipence looked between his visitor and his wife, stammering as sweat dribbled from his peruke to his eyebrows. 'Are the children in the nursery?'

'They are, dear, shall I call them?'

'No,' said Mister Rettipence, 'leave them where they are.'

Yet it was too late, for the man's loving brood had heard him enter, and soon there was the sound of little shoes clopping down the stairs, a boy appearing with long curls of black hair, followed by a girl who was so much the picture of her father, she might have been a walking miniature of him, her blue dress trailing a pair of long strings behind her.

'Ah, my beautiful children,' declared Mister Rettipence, forgetting his agitation in a moment. 'Come here, come here, your father must have his kisses!'

The little boy stood by his father's side, offering his wet lips to his pa while staring at Thomas with shy fascination. He held a wooden soldier in his hand, brightly painted with a green tunic, while his sister was duly hoisted to her father's hip and dandled there with hugs and kisses. She giggled uncontrollably, clinging to a doll with a daffodil ribbon tied around her ringlets. It was a charming scene indeed, and Thomas was forced to harden his heart.

'Mister Rettipence, I believe you left this behind.' He presented the tobacco tin, turning it to catch the light.

'What is it?' said Mistress Rettipence, looking at her husband. Her face would not have been more astounded if Thomas was holding a chicken.

Mister Rettipence paid no attention, wholly distracted by his daughter, who pulled against her reins, skating her feet across the floor with hoots of laughter.

'What was that?' he asked.

'Do you not recognise it?' said Thomas, struggling to hide the smirk on his face. 'You left it at Ned Skink's Tavern this afternoon. In Alsatia. It has your initials on it, see?'

The man's wife spoke first, looking at the tin in Thomas's fingers. 'It's a rather tatty thing, Mister True. I don't think that can be my husband's; he wouldn't have been in a tavern, let alone Alsatia; he doesn't drink. He's a very sensible man, aren't you, dear?' Her eyes darted to her husband, who had shuffled his children behind his legs. 'My darling, are you unwell? You're shaking.'

Indeed, the white powder on Mister Rettipence's face could not be distinguished from his ghostly skin.

He turned to his wife, speaking in a sombre voice. 'Please, my darling, won't you take the children from the parlour, there's a good woman. I have some business to discuss with my young colleague.'

There was an exchange of private looks, and the dutiful lady nodded, bidding Thomas a curt 'Good afternoon.' She collected the children, assisted by the housemaid, with all sorts of fuss and noise, the children protesting and sneezing and stamping their little feet, while the two men stared at each other without saying a word.

When they were alone at last, Mister Rettipence closed the parlour door, turning to face Thomas. 'Do you threaten me?'

Thomas stepped towards him with the tin, letting the lid fall open. He drew his finger over the letters in reverse and spoke in his deepest voice. 'Rat,' he said.

Mister Rettipence took the word like a nail to the head. He stared at the punctured metal, his answer escaping his lips like a final breath. 'Yes. Yes. It has arrived at last.'

'Disgusting liar.'

'I am.'

'Shame on you.'

'Shame on me, yes.' Mister Rettipence raised his hands, moving away, then in a dash tore open the parlour door and bolted into the hallway.

Thomas sprang after him, only to catch his fingers in the slamming door, squealing as he toppled backwards. He jumped to the window and called out to Gabriel: 'He's off. Catch him!' then scrambled up and tore open the parlour door, collecting his hat from the hallway.

'Are you leaving so soon, Mister True?' said Mistress Rettipence from the top of the stairs.

'I am chasing your damned husband!' replied Thomas.

'My husband? He only just arrived home. Where is he going?'

'To Hell!' shouted Thomas. He tugged down his waistcoat and exploded from the house, fast as a musket ball, onto the busy street, leaping over puddles, riding the backs of carts, somersaulting donkeys as he closed in on his prey.

In seconds he was past Gabriel, swinging his arms and pounding his feet against the soft dirt. Mister Rettipence looked over his shoulder with a terrified squeal, his peruke flying off as Thomas gained on him, spiralling around a clot of chair-men on Wormwood Street, and soon, they were slipping over Moor Fields, barely three yards of rutted grass between them. Thomas reached out, yet just as his fingers were about to grip the man's collar, his shoe got caught in a divot, and he crashed to the ground with a winded thump.

Mister Rettipence turned, panting. 'Why are you chasing me?' he said. 'What have I ever done to you?'

Thomas was about to answer, when he felt the ground quake, and he looked up to see a huge shadow lumbering over him straight into their prey, flinging the man to the dirt. Thomas laughed, rolling onto his back with his arms and legs spread wide.

'That's it, Gabriel,' he said, gasping for breath as the clouds slid across the blue sky, 'don't let him go. We caught him. We caught the Rat!'

CHAPTER FIFTY-TWO

The infamous Sodomites' Walk was little more than a high wall running between the upper and middle parts of Moor Fields. One side faced the City, all innocence, yet the other – cloaked from prying eyes – was as busy as the bridge, with a constant traffic of male pedestrians, wandering up and down its length with furtive glances and winks.

'Don't kill me, Gabriel, I beg you!' said Mister Rettipence as he was dragged around the back of the walk and thrown against the bricks. Men around them craned their necks to see if the noise meant danger or sport. He clasped his hands together. 'Please, take what you want. Let me go, I won't say a word.'

'Can't,' said Gabriel. 'You'd only go squeaking to your friends at the Society.'

He held the pages of Fump's letter out for their captive to see. 'Seems you were spotted by Fump. Your initials were concealed here, just like they're punched into that trinket of yours.'

Mister Rettipence shielded his face. 'I don't know what you're talking about.' He caught sight of the tobacco tin in Thomas's hand. 'Before you kill me, let me hold Bob's gift one last time. I have been searching for it.'

'Ay, ye lost it at Ned Skink's,' said Gabriel, taking the tin from Thomas. 'Careless Rat.'

'Ned who? Careless Rat? Oh please, what are you saying?'

Thomas snatched the tin back and threw it into the man's lap. 'Coward. Running away from me instead of admitting what you are.'

'I know what I am,' said Mister Rettipence, turning the tin in his fingers with sniffs and kisses. 'I don't deny it.'

Gabriel was struggling not to beat the man's head against the bricks. He thought of Martin in the ditch, Daisy clubbed to death on Fenchurch Street, the men burned alive on the scaffolding at St Paul's, the drowning in the river, Jack's terrified face bitten away by the lions, and every other life the vile creature had doubtless put to death. 'Why did you do it?'

'You ask me why?' sobbed Mister Rettipence. 'I cannot say why; I have always simply felt this way, for as long as I can remember, even as a tiny boy. Oh my poor son, my poor daughter, what will become of them now?'

'You should have thought of that sooner,' said Thomas, turning away in exasperation. 'A traitor all his life and he begs for sympathy. Well, at least he admits it.'

'Hush your gums,' said Gabriel, crouching beside the sobbing man. He gripped him by the chin and forced him to look into his eyes. 'What are you talking about feelings for?'

The man sniffed. His legs and arms were shaking violently. 'Only what you know already. That I am an inveterate sodomite. I admit it, I cannot hide the truth any longer. I always have been, and I cannot stop it, though Lord I have tried, God save my soul, I love it too well, like other men love their women, I cannot help myself. It is a symptom of the mumps in childhood, I heard, and over-kind mothers. Whatever the cause of my malady, the apothecary Spue cannot cure me.' He scratched between his legs with a wince. 'Will you murder me now, or take me to Newgate?' He righted himself against the wall and gave Gabriel a look of complete surrender. 'I must say, Mister Griffin, I never thought it was you.'

Gabriel frowned. 'What does that mean?'

'I knew there was a Rat; Lavender told me about it, and everybody knows, but I never suspected you.' He turned to Thomas. 'We all suspected him, of course, who wouldn't? Still, you've revealed yourselves to me now, you may as well hurry up and slaughter me, just as you slaughtered the others.' And with that, he cowered against the wall, covering his face.

Thomas looked at Gabriel. 'What is he going on about, the sneaky little vermin?'

'Don't know,' said Gabriel, pulling Fump's letter from his pocket for a second look. His eyes slid over the strange writing. 'Damn it, Gabriel, you fool.' He reached down and yanked Mister Rettipence to his feet. 'Stand up man, and quit yer crying; you ain't the Rat, and nor are we.'

CHAPTER FIFTY-THREE

'For goodness sakes,' said Mister Rettipence, his fitful hands spilling hot coffee from his cup. 'How could you take me for the Rat, of all the mollies in London? Clap and the marshal have entrusted our lives to the pair of you, have they? By the beggar's boils, we are doomed, all of us.'

Thomas kicked the man under the table. 'Stop lying and confess. It was you who set that false boatman on us, wasn't it? You who led us towards the Fenchurch mob. And it was you who tried to tip me off the gallery at St Paul's.'

Rettipence turned to Gabriel. 'Mister Griffin, won't you call off your dog? I can hardly stand its yapping.'

Gabriel sighed. 'Ay, stand down, Thomas. Don't you see? We got it wrong. We're no closer to catching the Rat today than we were a month ago. God save every molly in London.'

They were sitting at the back of the Little Devil Coffee House by Moor Fields, their conversation lost under the clatter of cups. Mister Rettipence took another sip of his drink, the black liquid spilling over his sleeves.

Gabriel gave a long, regretful sigh. 'Tell us, Timothy Rettipence, do you have another Christian name?'

'No, of course I don't,' said the man. 'One is quite enough. Why?'

Thomas placed the tobacco tin onto the table, jabbing the letters with his finger. 'Then what about these letters?'

'Well,' said the man, running his fingernail over the clumsy inscription, '"T" is for Timothy, you are quite correct about that, then "A" is for *Amore* – Bob was a hopeless old romantic – then "R" is not for Rettipence. It is for—'

'Robert,' said Gabriel. 'Old Bob's Christian name.'

'He was a dear man. Kind to me when I was learning how to live my double life.' He smiled wistfully at the tin. 'When I heard what happened to him at the compter, I couldn't bear it. He was my first sweetheart and my second father. I was his apprentice in love, in a funny sort of a way. I don't think ordinary people would understand, but that's how it was all the same. He was angry at me for falling for a younger man, but he was never bitter.'

'Unlike Lavender,' said Gabriel.

'Yes. George Lavender. God knows why my heart clings to him so, such constant humiliation he brings me. I thought I could teach him some of the wisdom Bob taught me, yet still I find I am the apprentice.' He looked at Thomas. 'Your world is so different to mine. All this dancing through the streets, sporting in parlours where everyone can watch. I used to envy you, then after a while, I realised none of you were happy, not truly. Pride was once a personal thing; now it feels like a performance, all for show, and what sort of currency is adoration when men are still hurting?' He laid the tin down, stroking the lid. 'I cannot lecture you, I am a coward.'

'Look here,' said Gabriel, smoothing Fump's letter over the table. 'Vivian received this. Now Fump's disappeared. Read it.'

Mister Rettipence did as he was instructed, turning the pages over as he went. 'Well,' he said once he was done. 'A strange letter as you say, even by Mister Fump's standards.' He lifted the page with his initials on it, staring hard with a wrinkled brow. '"R.T."' He scratched his fingernail over the marks. 'How did these appear?' Gabriel did not need to answer. 'Lemon juice, I expect.' He held the page to the window. 'Burned over a gentle heat to bring out the code, very neat. We get all sorts of secret messages through the exchange. Pirates, smugglers, Jacobite spies. Things have moved on a little since crudities such as this, yet Fump wouldn't have had access to ferrous sulphate.' He sniffed the paper. 'It's scented.' He turned it against the light before pressing it flat on the table along with the other two pages, tracing his finger gently over the letters. 'Aha,' he said with a satisfied nod. 'Yes, I see it now.' He squinted with the unblinking eye of a physician at his spyglass. 'It is very fortunate you didn't burn the letter for longer, Mister Griffin.'

Thomas and Gabriel watched as the man squashed some coffee grains into a fine dust and swept them into the open tobacco tin, clicking it shut. 'Let us see.' With a gentle movement of his hand, he used the tin as a shaker, sprinkling the grains over the pages. 'It seems some of the words in Mister Fump's letter are sticky with resin or gum. Very clever, Mister Fump, very clever indeed. I suppose he might carry such materials with him for gluing wigs onto bald heads.' The corner of his tongue poked out of his mouth as he leaned closer, tapping the back of the paper with his fingernail. 'Now we shall see what you are trying to tell us, Mister Fump.'

He reached out and clicked his fingers. 'Mister True, may I have your shirtsleeve.'

Thomas wrinkled his nose. 'I beg your pardon?'

'Tear off your shirtsleeve and give it to me, quickly.'

'I will not; why should I?'

Gabriel rolled his eyes. 'Do it, Thomas. An hour ago you were bent on hanging the man. Can you not spare your blasted sleeve to catch the Rat?'

Thomas grumbled to himself about capsized boats, lions and shirt-sleeves, yet with a glower and much sulking, held out his hand for Gabriel, who promptly tore it away right up to the shoulder of his waistcoat.

'Thank you,' said Mister Rettipence with a little chuckle at Thomas's expense. 'You have shapely arms, young man, perhaps you will start a trend.'

He held the sleeve over the steaming coffee pot until the linen was sufficiently damp with heat and moisture, then placed it gently over the pages and patted it down. 'Observe,' he said, and sure enough, a selection of Fump's written words rose through the linen while others lay dormant, revealing a hidden message...

Dear V,

I have arrived in a little town named Newport Pagnell, where I shall spend the night. It is a jolly enough place but if you were here there would be **more to look at**. We had quite a downpour earlier. **I am in terrible danger** of catching a chill. I shall warm myself by the fire, for **what might happen if my letter were drenched**? I must turn **in** as soon as I have finished my **coffee**. How I shall miss my home **then**, but I must **watch the** time before I retire to the land of nod, for I have not enjoyed a good slee**p** in **ages**.

I have **a young** and lusty driver assisting my passage, who I have not used before and shan't use again. He has good haunches but a smart mouth, which got us into a bit of a pickle earlier at a turnpike leading onto the North Road. We found ourselves in **A T**erribly embarrassing impasse with two justices travelling the other way.

Well, I made friends with them, dear, as I always do, yet I had the most unexpected surprise!

There was a mysterious creature riding with them in the carriage. They jumped from **their skin** when I spotted them. The creature **bears** more than *a* little attention, **mark** my words. Very suspicious travelling companions, very strange indeed. **That** is to say, I shan't **reveal** the **identity** of the animal.

We drew away in opposite directions, my poppet, I being the very epitome of discretion. Yet, much to my surprise, the justices are here, **my darling!** Here, in this very inn, I **thank you!** They must have gotten lost **for** want of a map, this **being** the wilderness, and followed after me.

I know how tiresome you find me, my sweet Viv, so forgive **my** hot words. Wait **faithful**ly for my return, for I believe I shall have much to say. It is dreadfully hot **and** the candles are **most**ly lit, so I shall lay my sheets at a careful distance from the flames, so I might sleep in **gentle** safety and appear to you, should you care to read this letter carefully, very soon.

I bid you goodnight, my **friend**!

'Thank goodness we didn't kill you, Mister Rettipence,' said Thomas, absorbing the words as quickly as his sleeve. 'We never would have found the message with you in a ditch.'

Mister Rettipence gave Thomas a narrow smile. 'I am humbled to be of service to you, Mister True.' He pulled the sleeve from the paper, draping it carefully over the back of his chair.

'Still, I don't understand, why doesn't he simply tell us who the Rat is?'

'Was thinking the same,' said Gabriel. 'P'raps he was planning to, then realised his letter might be intercepted. P'raps he wanted the drama of telling us in person.'

Thomas shook his head. 'This Rat has it all his own way.' He went to fold his arms, accidentally knocking his cup over, boiling hot coffee flooding the pages of Fump's cryptic letter with a wave of black liquid.

Gabriel reached out to grab the papers before they were ruined, yet Mister Rettipence held his wrist.

'Wait,' he said. 'That's precisely what Fump instructed us to do. Drench the paper in coffee and watch the pages. Observe.'

The coffee had covered the paper entirely, yet as it soaked through, so the water began to brown and pull away in crinkled lines, rejected by a pattern of curls and hatches. Soon, Fump's writing had been washed clean, leaving nothing but a pale image glowing in the translucent tissue.

'First he used gum,' said Mister Rettipence, raising his eyebrows in admiration. 'Then wax.'

The three of them looked down transfixed as a new set of hidden letters rose through the liquid.

$$S F$$

$$M$$

'Add those to the burn marks,' said Mister Rettipence, 'and there you are.' He sat back in wonder. '*T.S.F.R.M*. The Society for the Reformation of Manners.'

'Ay,' said Gabriel. A shiver ran down his spine as the coffee thinned. Something had been etched above the letters. A face in wax, its eyes black, jaws yawning. He thought again of the Tower lions, yet this was a different creature.

Thomas leaned in. 'I can't make it out. Looks like an old man, screaming.'

'Not a man,' said Rettipence with a dry chuckle, quite in his element. He tapped the image. 'I should say that is a stoat.'

Gabriel couldn't help but laugh. 'First a rat, now a stoat?'

'Rats may be hated in England, and for good reason,' said Mister Rettipence, 'yet they are venerated in the East. After all, they are God's best-travelled and most secretive animals. I believe our traitor must have a wicked sense of humour to call himself such a name. Still, I say to you' – he tapped the picture – 'that is a stoat, which just happens to be...'

'The Society Mark,' said Gabriel, remembering it from pamphlets he'd seen at church.

Thomas pulled the page closer. 'Why would the Society choose a measly stoat for its totem?'

Rettipence wagged his finger. 'Ah, but if you spent any time at the exchange, you would understand instantly. Stoats are also known as ermine.'

Gabriel sat back, impressed. 'The most valuable pelts in Christendom.'

Mister Rettipence nodded. 'Revered from Rome to Constantinople for their snow-white fur, which bears not even the slightest blemish.' He met Gabriel's eye. 'The Society fancies itself pure, while we sodomites are—'

'The dirt that stains them, ay, but not many in this world can afford ermine. The king, right enough, but it wasn't His Majesty riding in that carriage, I'll bet.'

Thomas sat forward. 'Perhaps the Rat wore the symbol on a chain, or on a keepsake, like Mister Rettipence's tobacco tin?'

Gabriel scratched his whiskers. 'P'raps.'

'But we already have the answer,' said Mister Rettipence, bringing Thomas's sleeve from the back of his chair. 'Look here – Mister Fump is quite clear about it.' He traced over the words with his finger, reading them aloud in a reverential whisper:

'a Young ... R.A.T ... their skin ... bears ... a ... mark ... That ... reveal ... identity.'

'That's it,' said Gabriel, slamming his fist on the table. 'The Rat has the Society's mark painted on his skin.'

'He must do,' said Mister Rettipence. 'Such unsightly scars, yet sailors have been returning from the New World, inked from head to toe with sirens, sea monsters and bare-breasted Molucca maids.'

Gabriel nodded. 'Seen 'em like painted pots. Often fancied one myself. Still, a likely disguise for any villain.'

'Well, I can tell you one thing: George Lavender has no such mark on his body, and neither do I.'

'Nor I,' said Thomas.

Mister Rettipence and Thomas turned to Gabriel with raised eyebrows.

He tutted. 'Course I don't. Nothing on me but hair. Rat won't admit to having the Society mark on him, anyways. Could still be any of us. We ain't proved nothing.' He waved his hand at Rettipence. 'I don't believe you're our traitor, but we only have your word for George Lavender.'

Mister Rettipence bristled. 'Well for that matter, I have never seen you out of your clothes, Mister Griffin, nor has anybody unless Mister True can correct me?' He looked at Thomas, who blushed.

'Gabriel has no mark.'

Mister Rettipence gave a pert look. 'I see. Congratulations, dear fellows.' He looked at Thomas. 'Forgive me, young man; it seems I have treated you unfairly.'

Thomas shrugged. 'I'm quite used to it, though perhaps you might ask your darling Lavender to stand off?'

'I shall try, though she won't listen to a word I say.'

'Ay, well.' Gabriel stood up, scraping his chair over the tiles. He found his heart quickening, his breath short. Now, at long last, it was finally time to put his plan into action. After weeks of waiting, the trap was ready to be set. He collected his hat and nodded at Mister Rettipence. 'You must go immediately to Smithfield. Tell Lavender to stay safe with his ma and little Annie. And Thomas, go back to Vivian on Covent Garden at once. Tell him the same: he must stay safe. Tell him we'll search for Fump tomorrow, soon as I've snared the Rat.'

Thomas and Mister Rettipence looked at each other, astounded.

'What are you talking about?' said Thomas.

Gabriel had never felt so grubby in his life, yet it had to be done without feeling. 'Just tell 'em, alright? Say the molly guard's been setting a trap all along.'

Thomas wrinkled his nose. 'You never told me about a trap.'

'Never told nobody, not even the voices in my head, not even the good spirits watching over us. But by this time tomorrow, I'll know who the Rat is once and for all.' He stepped back from the table. 'First, I've got to get home and pack up. Time's up for me on Red Lyon Street. At midnight tonight, I'll be sleeping safe and sound, getting some peace at last.' He gave them both a meaningful look. 'You know where.'

With that, he collected his coat and moved through the coffee house, praying they'd remember everything he'd told them. Time was running out and this was his last hope of unmasking the Rat once and for all.

'Ay,' he said to himself, stepping onto the street, 'I'll catch you now, whoever you are.'

CHAPTER FIFTY-FOUR

So the time had come at last. Time for a revelation, time to bid farewell.

Gabriel stood in his quarters, looking at his undressed bed and the empty cot. He gave a deep sigh, trying his best not to think too much. He took one last look out of the window to the yard and raised his hand to old Peter the shire horse then turned to face Emily's bed. 'Time to go,' he said, though she was already long departed.

There came a bang and the partition wall blew in, scattering the room with shards of wood, and there was Henry, swinging a long-handled mallet over his shoulder. Bet was fussing about behind him, arranging Dot's cradle with blankets, ready for the baby.

'Little one'll be happy in that,' said Gabriel. 'Warm as an angel's pocket in there.'

Bet looked up. 'Ay Gabe, you didn't have to share it.'

'Don't want the babe getting cold toes.'

Bet gave him a soft smile, leaving the room. Gabriel beckoned Henry through the hole, speaking in a hush.

'You understand what I'm asking you to do? If ye care for me at all, you'll make no mistakes.'

Henry checked over his shoulder then looked back with a whisper. 'Tonight?'

'Ay, tonight.'

'Still don't understand—'

'No need to understand, just do as I ask.'

'The abandoned chapel, where we used to play?'

'Ay,' said Gabriel, jerking his head to the corner of the room where one of his old coats was lying on the floor. It was buttoned up and tied at the sleeves with string, stuffed with old linen sheets. 'Lay it under the window. Keep it in the light of the moon, then hide yourself.'

Henry stepped through the hole in the partition. 'Till morning?'

'Till morning.'

'That'll be me in the doghouse with Bet. What is all this about, Gabe? What are you involved in?'

'Don't bother yourself with that. Got the signal?'

'Ay,' said Henry, cocking his head to a bag hanging from a hook by the fire. 'Pilfered two flares from the old stores, just like you asked me to.' He leaned in with a wink, speaking from the corner of his mouth. 'Gawd, I've missed a thrill like that, sneaking about like we used to. Remember all the thieving we'd do!' He gave Gabriel a nudge with his elbow. 'Tested one last night, lit up the sky just like they did back when our pas were blowing up the old cathedral.'

'Send it up if someone comes sniffing,' said Gabriel. 'I'll take another.' He held Henry's eye. 'Reckon that stuffed coat of mine might end up with a dagger in its back.'

'And if it does?'

Gabriel thought back to the day he visited Smithfield Market. 'Then a skinny rat called George Lavender will be holding the blade. He's the only one thinks I'll be there. Knock him out and tie him up. Send the flare, and I'll race to you, fast as I can.'

Gabriel took a steady breath and gave a final look around his quarters then stepped through the hole in the partition, grateful not to use the door. He crept to the bag by the fire, took a flare to his coat pocket and slipped into the night.

Down Red Lyon Street he went to the Fleet Ditch, where he entered the warehouse beside the bridge. Cautiously, he edged through the darkness to where he and Henry kept their ropes and pulling poles and stood still, listening for footsteps. All was quiet, nothing but the sound of the ditch beyond the windows and the drip of water from the roof. He fetched some kindling from the far corner, checking it was still dry, then laid it carefully on a tarpaulin beside a second stuffed coat and breeches, just like Henry's. 'There you go,' he said.

Treasa the old pie woman emerged from the shadows. A smile spread over her wrinkles. 'Evening, Mister Griffin. I'll take my shillings first.'

He handed her the money, repeating his instructions for the night to come. 'If you want to help me catch the Rat, do as I say.'

'You can trust Treasa, right enough. I'm no stranger to peril, living in Alsatia.'

'If he comes, light the kindling on the warehouse roof. As much as you can, so I can see it from my lookout.'

'Not before I've bashed his brains in.' Treasa held up a rolling pin, long as her arm. 'Been wanting to long enough.'

'I don't reckon you'll get a visitor, but if Timothy Rettipence is the traitor after all, then he'll come sneaking here tonight to do me in. He's the only person in the world thinks this is my hideout.' Gabriel looked around the warehouse, stepping to the large window and leaned out, holding his breath against the stink below. It was the perfect place for the Rat to kill him unseen, then roll him into the ditch. He thought back to his conversation at the coffee house that afternoon. Whoever the Rat was, they'd know by now that a trap had been set, but they'd have no idea what it was. Tonight was their last chance to kill him.

'Good luck,' said Gabriel, 'and take care.'

'You can trust me,' said the old woman, collecting the kindling and sinking back into the darkness.

Gabriel climbed through the window, shimmying along the lip of the ditch so he wouldn't be seen, then tangled his way back up to Field Lane and along to the hidden doorway camouflaged with ivy. The lanterns beyond were lit, just as he'd asked them to be. He took one down and made the solemn walk to the wooden steps then up the gangway some hundred yards till he reached a shed stacked high with logs. He stepped inside, breathing in the familiar scent of sap and sawdust.

Mother Clap's face shone out. 'All set?'

'Ay, all set.'

'Pity Mister Vivian, if he's the Rat.' She stood, kicking the stuffed coat and breeches lying huddled against the logs. 'You reckon this'll work?'

'The traitor's clever, whoever they are. If it's Vivian, he'll have seen me coming up here already from across the way. Made sure to light myself as I walked. Might be watching the shed right now. You leave and head back to the molly house, and he'll think I'm bedded down for the night.' He hung the lamp by the door and collected a bundle of his old clothes, deposited earlier that day. Clap had stuffed them well, he thought, with his barrel chest and belly. He sat them against a pile of logs. 'Don't hurt to give a shadow.'

'Where's this flare then, eh?'

Gabriel reached into his coat and pulled it out. He held her arm as she took it. 'You strong?' he asked.

'You ugly?'

Gabriel smiled. 'You'll have a quiet night, Clap. No chance it's old Vivian.'

'One thing I learned when I was young: there's good people out there, but there ain't nobody honest. Not one. I can't see Vivian as the Rat, but if it's him ... well, you won't need to answer the flare. He'll be hanging from this gangway soon as I see him come up them steps.'

She stepped out of the shed, her boots thumping along the gangway back to the hall. Gabriel waited before moving to the back of the shed, lifting away a pallet. The hole he'd cut in the floor was just large enough for him to squeeze through. He lowered himself to the brackets below, counting them as he swung deftly through the struts, then clambered up a ladder and over the roofs to the courtyard of the Swan Inn. No heads turned as the black shadow slipped down the wall from sill to sill, then through the crowd to the streets of High Holborn.

He moved as quickly as he could towards St Paul's, his nerves jangling like keys in a cup. He felt dread, for the trap was almost set, and now all he had to do was watch and wait. He was certain of it – never more certain of anything in his life – the Rat would strike that night, and in striking he would be snared at last.

CHAPTER FIFTY-FIVE

The Rat waited for the city to sleep.

For the shadows to run long.

For the lights of the houses to flicker out.

Until there was nothing to be seen but the faint outline of a sleeping metropolis beneath God's yearning sky.

It was warm, though the air which had burned brown all summer was at last promising rain, praise Heaven. The long cloak was a blessing rather than a curse.

After weeks of toil, the justices were drawing close; very soon the great reckoning would put this nasty episode to bed. It had been an exciting prospect at first, to cleanse one's soul of all sinful impulses by carrying out a virtuous crusade against the sodomites. Playing the trusted friend had been difficult at times, though fascinating too, poking inside their hidden world and exploring their putrid little lives. Yet now, the risk had grown intolerable.

Gabriel Griffin had been careless enough to let slip where he'd be sleeping following his eviction from Red Lyon Street. Stupid oaf, meddlesome troll, it was time to get rid of him once and for all. He would be sleeping now, vulnerable and alone in that secluded place, exposed and defenceless as a child. No need for an assassin or complicated schemes this time, no need for the hounds. Unlike Martin, Daniel, Jack and the rest, Lotty the molly guard would be a clean kill.

'Sleep gently, Gabriel Griffin,' said the Rat, moving silently through the lightless city, 'I am coming for you.'

Gabriel broke the lock on the railings and passed quietly inside, checking to make sure the watchman was away from his post. He would be carrying out his checks on the far side of the cathedral, smoking his pipe on the steps of the north transept. The terraced sheds and offices of the former workers' yard were once crammed with piles of wooden planks and stone blocks, yet now they stood empty, ready for their demolition. Gabriel crossed past the timber stores and the old astronomer's office to the dry-houses where a few damp barrels of gunpowder remained from the demolition of the old church. They were retained in expectation that further smaller buildings would one day require demolition. He looked around to make sure he was alone and stepped inside. There it was, just as he'd left it that morning: a stuffed dummy, laid between two barrels, a pair of his old work boots poking out as though he was sleeping on his back. And by the door, a barrel of explosives, frothing with sawdust. He looked around the scene, begging with all his heart that it would remain undisturbed. Only one man thought he would be sleeping there, and if Thomas was the Rat, skulking through the city in his long cloak, then Gabriel would rather be blown to smithereens than live with such betrayal.

He stepped back from the stores, knowing there wasn't long until midnight, and hurried between the tool sheds, covering himself with a black tarp, then crossed to the double doors in the south transept. He'd tampered with the lock earlier that day, preventing the key from moving the bolt. The door swung open with a creak and Gabriel slipped inside, climbing with acid in his belly as the scratch of his feet echoed up the stairs.

It had once seemed a childish plan, hardly likely to work, yet as he ascended through God's great palace, he felt certain the Rat had taken the bait and was already tracing through the city with murder on his mind. One of his traps was about to spring, but which would it be?

The Rat stopped and checked to make sure the way was clear. The narrow alleyways were empty, while the overhanging buildings gave enough cover to make sure nobody could follow such a winding route.

It was not a pleasurable thing to commit murder. Such killings had been necessary at first, to silence men and boys too stupid to salvage their own souls. Martin Lightbody, that reckless sinner, who took the bribe and gave names, only to streak about the city, threatening to expose the Society's spies unless he was given more money – he had to be hunted down, his neck cut. Yet, it was a terrifying business, watching the blade slice into his neck as he'd cried for his ma. The Rat banished the thought. As the justices said, it was clemency not violence. Then there was Daniel, that forsaken young man sent into the molly houses to clear his father's debts. It was a dreadful thing to watch the clubs raining down on his body. A quick death, mind you, unlike poor Jack Huffins, who lived a full week without his tongue before the lions silenced him, once and for all. Framing Rettipence had almost worked, thieving his precious tin and leaving it in that squalid tavern...

The Rat smiled. None of it mattered now. Gabriel Griffin would be dead within the hour, then the way would be clear for the justices to demand their raids, and the marshal would be forced to comply, while the Rat ... the Rat would slip away as though nothing had ever happened, and return to a godly life, safe in the knowledge that London was purged of sin, and the righteous had been spared.

Across the city, the bells of countless churches were chiming a quarter to midnight, and there loomed the great dome of St Paul's.

'Good saints and apostles,' said the Rat, hurrying onwards, 'smile down on me tonight.'

Gabriel leaned against the balustrade high on the perimeter of the dome and followed the lanes below. Was he there, the Rat? His nerves skittered at the thought of it: a pair of eyes looking back at him from within a black hood. Gabriel could sense him amidst the cluttered stews, jagged lanes, and buried streets. Where was the Rat coming from, he wondered? A smart residence on Camomile Street, perhaps, or Smithfield Market? Or was it Covent Garden? Gabriel steadied his breath. *Or the bridge*, he thought, chewing his lip.

He circled the walkway, tracing his eyes along the Thames, then marked the three locations again to be sure he had his bearings. Below him on the south side of the cathedral, he could make out the slanted roofs of the dry-stores where he'd left the dummy amongst the barrels. There was no movement as far as he could make out, no sign of anybody approaching the railings, thanks be to God. He moved around to the west side of the dome, the city stretching out to St James's Park and beyond, where the Thames curled away into the distance. Gabriel stopped and scanned across the flat roof of the Fleet Prison to the stacked warehouses that ran either side of the ditch. Treasa's torch was flickering on the roof, but no beacon, not yet. Gabriel ran his eyes across the sloping rubble to the north of the city, where the open square of Gray's Inn Gardens sat like a footprint amongst the surrounding buildings, then further to the fields beyond. Somewhere amidst that tree-spotted patchwork, behind the faint mountains of rubbish, was the abandoned chapel. 'Will you send up your flare, Henry?' he asked, leaning out as a cool wind blew through his shirt. He hoped so, for even though he bore George Lavender no spite, he liked the young man least of all. Yet still, Gabriel thought of the sick woman in her bed, and the little girl who would doubtless perish without the care and protection of her brother. 'Ay,' he murmured, chastising himself, 'don't let it be George, neither. Don't let it be any of 'em.'

He stepped a little further around the dome, following the black cut of High Holborn, before settling his eyes on a cluster of shrouded buildings. 'Field Lane,' he muttered to himself. There was no sign of arson, no flames burning between the huddled roofs. *Careful, Clap*, he thought. *If the Rat pays you a visit, he'll be smart and cruel, no matter his years*. He shook his head, tutting. 'I know it ain't you, Mister Vivian. Forgive me.'

There came the sound of bells, chiming a quarter to midnight, and Gabriel lowered his head and recited a prayer. His chest felt tight as he clasped his hands together. 'Please Lord, I beg you; I ain't asked for much and never got nothing I wished for. You weren't listening when you took my family. Please listen now.' He turned and stared up beyond the curve of the dome to the cross above, glittering gold against the heavens. 'End this tonight, will you? Don't think you like the Rat any more than we do. Don't think you see evil in my friends. Ain't we all good fathers, good sons, hardworking men like the rest of 'em?' He opened his eyes. 'Ay,' he said, dropping his hands. 'You ain't listening.'

So, with a deep breath, he began his slow patrol, anxiously orbiting the dome as he rested his eyes on each of the traps, waiting for one of them to snap.

The dry-stores, the ditch, the chapel, Field Lane.

The dry-stores, the ditch, the chapel, Field Lane.

The dry-stores, the ditch, the chapel, Field Lane ...

The Rat snuck closer, treading lightly. Griffin must be sleeping barely ten yards away on the other side of the open entrance. So close, so unguarded, such a fool. Softly, softly, moving silently around obstacles, careful not to trip, certain shapes took form in the gloom, and there he was, the outline of a recumbent man, nestled almost out of view. 'I found you, Mister Griffin. Now go to Hell.'

The last chime of midnight was still hanging in the air when the dome of St Paul's flashed orange. Gabriel spun around, the stones jumping under his feet to an almighty explosion, a huge ball of orange flame rising into the sky. 'No,' he said. 'No.' He ran around to the south side of the cathedral and bellowed as his eyes fell on what was left of the dry-stores. Nothing more than a burning crater now, surrounded by shards of splintered barrels and smouldering wood.

'Please,' he shouted, spinning around, hoping to see a flare above the ditch, or from the abandoned chapel, or from Field Lane. Yet there was nothing, while below him, an inferno raged and crackled, more barrels bursting into the air.

The trap had worked, just as Gabriel had planned. The Rat had tried to kill him.

And the Rat was Thomas True.

CHAPTER FIFTY-SIX

Thomas could not sleep, thinking about Fump's cryptic letter and Gabriel's promise to catch the Rat. He felt a little frustrated to be in the dark. Why had Gabriel kept his plan a secret? It hurt. He could accept such callous mistrust from the other mollies, they were a suspicious lot anyway, but for Gabriel to be so sly – that made his heart ache and left him feeling foolish for thinking they were better friends. He sat up in bed, looking around the moonlit garrets. It must have been almost midnight. He kicked his sheets away and padded to the window, pulling open the shutters. The scaffolding was still in place, ready for the roof to be retiled. Thomas reached out and tested the poles to see how sturdy they were, then pulled himself out of the window and landed like a cat on the shaking boards. He laughed to feel the night wind ruffling his open shirt and peered down to the rushing water below. The river was dark blue, swirling with frothing eddies as it dashed between the cataracts. He edged along the gangway, following the guy ropes with his fingers, then climbed up the ladder to the very top of the roof as it wobbled against the timber frame. He settled on top of the tiles, crossing his legs beneath him, and looked around. It was so peaceful on the roof, nothing to fear, nothing to fret about, only the twinkling sky and the happy moon. He leaned back and filled his lungs, tracing the far horizon, where the distant trees fringed Highgate. He smiled privately, closing his eyes to picture his favourite face. 'My Gabriel,' he said, brushing the rough tiles with his fingertips, imagining they were stubble. He rolled his head and looked out to the northwest of the bridge, where St Paul's hunkered amongst the rooftops like a giant, swimming in the stew. Gabriel was there now, sleeping below that grand palace, his handsome head rested amongst the barrels. 'My companion,' said Thomas, hugging his knees to his chest, enjoying the sound of the words. 'We shall live together one day, you and I, in a small cottage somewhere smart.' He smiled, imagining them both suspended high above London, halfway between the cathedral and the candle shop. He could wait for the next day, when doubtless all would be explained to him and somehow, the Rat would be snared. Then Gabriel would be free to talk about happier things. Thomas clasped his hands together and prayed. There was so much he wanted to talk about. Gabriel's childhood, what plans he had for the future, where his new lodgings might be and ... was there any room for a second man to lodge with him?

He climbed to his feet and stepped gingerly to the edge of the roof, scattering chips of old tiles to the river below. His head whirled and he almost fell forwards into empty space, swinging back from the precipice just in time. He wiped his brow and laughed, only to be cut short by an almighty flash as the sky turned yellow. He turned his face away, then looked back to see a ball of flame shooting into the sky from the cathedral. The distant air warped and the roofs sprayed their tiles in an oncoming wave as his face was slapped by a hot, harsh wind. He jumped down to the scaffolding and climbed back inside his room. In his panic he didn't know what to do. He paced the room for sometime, emptied his bladder into the chamber pot, then paced again. Was this the plan? Should he go and check on Gabriel? Or would he once again be messing things up?

Ten minutes later he'd made a decision and was clattering down the stairs as Abigail came running up.

'Did you see it?' she said, her eyes wide.

'Yes, an explosion.'

'We must go.'

They ran down to the shop together, where Mister and Mistress Squink were already filling baskets with candles. They collected as many as they could, then rushed out to join the throng of people hurrying over the bridge. They could not go quickly enough, for Thomas felt a deep sickness in his stomach, sensing somehow that this would be the most terrible night of his life.

Gabriel, he thought. *Gabriel!*

CHAPTER FIFTY-SEVEN

Gabriel crashed his way down endless stairs to the doors, running into the churchyard, which was strewn with rubble from the explosion, half-ripped planks shot like spears through broken windows. The watchman was running in all directions, shouting instructions to church men and neighbouring residents, who were throwing pails of water into the boiling flames. They might as well have been thimbles for all the good they were doing. Amidst the shrieks, ringing bells and dancing shadows, Gabriel pulled his hat low and passed what was left of the dry-stores. Indeed, there was nothing left of them at all, except for the remains of so many barrels and the scorch marks stretching their black fingers across the burned gravel.

Already, a curious crowd was gathering around the railings. Gabriel pushed through them to the lanes beyond, pounding his boots to Thames Street in the direction of the bridge. Thomas would be almost home by now, having lit his dastardly flame in a hidden corner of the stores then fled in good time before the explosion. Safely ensconced and thinking Gabriel dead, the treacherous little Rat would wrap himself in his blankets and doubtless fall into a contented sleep, happy as a pup. Gabriel wiped his eyes with the back of his wrist, furious at his own passion, for it was one part rage, one part heartbreak.

The alleyways around Thames Street were teeming with people, hustling and bustling through the dark lanes to see what had happened, while above them, people were leaning from their shutters, calling out that the Great Fire was back, and that all of them were sure to burn. Gabriel passed Bell Alley and was approaching St James Garlickhythe Church when he caught sight of four faces, lit up bright as brasses by the tall windows. It was Thomas and the Squinks, rushing with the rest of the city towards the cathedral. Gabriel pulled back into a doorway and listened as they approached.

'Do you really think they'll want to buy candles?' asked Uncle Squink, wrapping himself in his cloak. 'It might not be proper.'

'Pish to *proper*!' snapped Aunt Squink. 'A fire burning at the cathedral and what do we have here?' She lifted her basket from beneath her cloak, shouting louder than any cockle-seller. 'Miniature replicas of the very same church, crafted by expert hands, complete with a burning wick in perfect commemorative mimicry of the Great Explosion.' She tilted the basket so all could see, and before she could tilt it back again, various hands were inside it, plucking souvenirs out like so many plums. 'You see?' she said. 'By the end of the night, we shall have made enough money to pay Mister Sylva for the new roof.'

'How clever you are, my darling,' said Uncle Squink. 'Who could have guessed Thomas's creations would inspire people to collect candles like relics?' He looked up at the turning seam of smoke stretching like a vast beanstalk into the sky. 'Praise God for gifting us such glory.'

'They are not my creations,' corrected Thomas, following behind his aunt and uncle. He squeezed Abigail's hand. 'My cousin is the true artist, I am merely the architect.' He traced the chimney of smoke back to its origin. His mind was caught in a tug-o-war, certain Gabriel was safe, certain he was dead. Surely, he'd been on the tower rather than sleeping in the dry-stores? Or was he somewhere else entirely, snaring the Rat just as he'd promised? It didn't matter, so long as he was safe.

The air was thick with falling ash, and Abigail coughed. 'Were you awake when the explosion happened?' she asked privately.

'I couldn't sleep.'

'I thought it must be the end of days at last; that all our sins had finally blown up like a volcano.'

'It was gunpowder, I'm sure.'

'Gunpowder, where?'

'Barrels of gunpowder kept in the stores from the demolition. A friend told me about it; he was sleeping there.'

Abigail covered her mouth with her hands. 'He must have been killed!'

'Do you think so?'

Abigail shook her head, gripping Thomas's arm with both hands. 'Oh no, I'm sure I'm wrong, don't worry.'

Thomas nodded as they passed a square church, its tall windows lit up like a lantern. He felt an overpowering urge to go inside and pray before they reached St Paul's. 'Abigail,' he said, 'I should hold back a moment to compose myself. Will you tell your parents I ... I forgot my coat and had to run home?'

Abigail kissed his cheek, taking his basket of candles. 'Of course, dear Thomas. Though you must find me when you're finished.' She stared up at him, her eyes filled with tears. 'I'm frightened.'

Thomas squeezed her hand. 'So am I.'

They embraced and parted, Thomas holding back as he watched the Squinks turn the corner to St Bennet's Hill. When he was sure they were out of sight, he pressed his way through the oncoming hordes to the pedimented doorway of the church, where a gang of fire wardens were rolling out a water pump on a wooden trolley, ready to take it up to the cathedral. He pressed back to let them pass then stepped into the abandoned nave.

Gabriel watched the fire trolley race by, then followed Thomas inside the church. He looked around at the soaring windows and chequered flagstones, spying Thomas kneeling in the chancel, his head bowed. *Ay*, thought Gabriel, swallowing hard, *you had better pray for your soul, the place you're going*.

He pushed his shoulders back and with a long breath to steady himself, approached the Rat.

CHAPTER FIFTY-EIGHT

Thomas allowed his tears to roll freely down his cheeks as he whispered his prayers, shaking his white knuckles so God might hear him more clearly.

'Please Father, let Gabriel be safe, do not let him die. I think I would die too. I know my feelings are sinful, but I love him more than the world, I don't know why, but it's not an evil feeling, it's a good feeling, and I mean you no harm. I pray, I pray, I pray—'

'Pray all ye like,' came a rumbling voice by his side. 'Ye failed.'

Thomas opened his eyes and saw Gabriel standing above him. He sprang up and threw his arms around him. 'You survived! Thank God, thank God!' He pulled back, wiping his eyes and grinned. 'I thought you were dead, but I didn't want to believe it. Did you catch him?'

Gabriel's eyes were like iron bolts. 'Ay.'

'Well then,' said Thomas looking around the church, 'where is he?'

Gabriel nodded. 'Here.'

Thomas laughed, turning in a circle, then laughed again, only for his happy smile to fade under Gabriel's glare. 'What do you mean?'

Gabriel was trembling. 'Enough, Thomas True. Even yer name's a lie.'

Thomas tried to take his hand. 'What are you talking about?'

Gabriel gripped him by the wrist. 'I tricked you, just like you tricked me. I caught you in my trap. Devil.'

Thomas gaped. 'What is this? You're hurting me, let me go.'

'Hurting you? Hurting you? Could hurt you worse than this and it wouldn't measure half the pain you've caused the rest of us. Slicing boys' necks, beating their heads in, cutting their tongues out, burning innocent men alive, making fun of old friends even when they defended your name, and you...' He pushed Thomas to the flagstones and stood over him, jabbing his finger. 'You talk about hurt?'

Thomas scrabbled backwards on his hands and knees, lifting himself up against a column. There was a candlestick by his side and he snatched it up. 'Get back. You're mad. Were you hit by the explosion?'

'Bet you wish I was.'

'What's happening? I thought you were my friend.'

'Thought I was a fool, more like,' said Gabriel, marching up to Thomas and grabbing the candlestick. He flung it against the wall with a clatter. 'Rat.'

'No.'

'Rat!'

'No!'

Gabriel reached out and clamped his hand over Thomas's face and drew his fingers across his lips. 'Where's your mask now, eh?' He knocked Thomas to the chancel, standing over him with his fists clenched.

'What's happened to you?' said Thomas, cowering on the steps. 'I saw the explosion from the bridge and came straight here.'

'When do you stop, eh? Do you lie in your prayers? In your dreams? Do you lie to yourself?'

'When have I ever lied?'

'You got away from them hounds at the exchange; funny that. George said it didn't make sense, and he was right. Why didn't they beat you, Thomas, like they beat the rest of us?'

'I've no idea.'

'Ay, course you don't. They let you get away on Fenchurch Street an' all.'

'I was about to be clubbed, you saved me.'

'They didn't chase you at all, they ran after the others, but they let you go. I found you in that alleyway on your own, hiding from nothing.'

'That isn't what ... no, that's not right.'

'Ay, it's right. And the assassin: he knew exactly who you were.'

'How could he have done?'

'You jumped in the boat, just as he expected you to.'

Thomas edged away on his hands and feet. 'This isn't happening, it's a nightmare.'

Gabriel followed him, flexing his fists. 'The assassin knew your name.'

Thomas's eyes were wide, the print of Gabriel's hand still marked on his face. 'What are you talking about?'

'He'd never seen you before, then soon as you jump in the boat he says "and you too, Mister True".'

Thomas blinked. 'Did he?'

Gabriel mimicked him, unable to control his bitterness any longer. '"Did he?" Ay, he did. Hell's arse, you'd lie to the ghosts. You'd lie to God himself, thinking to hoodwink a mind reader. You're not real, Thomas True, you're an empty lie.'

Thomas could hardly speak. 'Everything I do is wrong. Whether I'm honest or deceitful, I still get a beating, I'm still hated.' He turned over to hide his face. 'What have I ever done?'

'Save me the performance,' barked Gabriel. 'I thought you was a good man, I stood up for you, confided in you. Got that wrong. Never met anyone so cunning.'

'Is there no hope for me? Does it matter what I do or say? I think I'll always be punished.' Thomas turned back over. 'Very well then, I'm the Rat. Now tell me why.'

'I will tell you.'

'Do it then. Tell me who I am. I'd like to know.' Thomas jumped to his feet, snatched a Bible from the lectern and threw it at Gabriel's face. 'Beat me with that, why don't you? It was good enough for my father.'

Gabriel stepped back. 'You spoke in yer sleep at Fump and Vivian's.'

'Did I?'

'Ay, ye did.'

'And? Will you condemn a man to the gallows because it suits your story and you don't like him? Eh?'

Gabriel gave a snort, jabbing his finger. 'You were describing men being hanged, Mister True.' He turned away picturing that night like a shifting tapestry projected on the church wall: Thomas in the dozing chair in Fump and Vivian's shop on Covent Garden. His pale hair was matted from the river, his eyelashes fluttering as he described tying men around the neck, letting them drop in rows. 'Ay,' said Gabriel, catching sight of Thomas laughing. 'Is this funny to you? I've seen what the marshal does to his enemies.'

Thomas crouched down, hitting his head with his fists then exploded up again, charging towards Gabriel with his teeth bared. 'Candles,' he shouted. 'Candles, you stupid man.'

'Eh?'

'I must have dipped a hundred of them that day before joining you on that blasted wherry boat. Tying them by their wicks, dipping them in wax.' He punched Gabriel's chest. 'Let the marshal torture me,' he said. 'This is worse. What else do you have against me, clever Mister Griffin, eh? Come on, what other reason do you have to condemn me after everything we've been through together? Show me how fragile we were, how little I meant to you.'

'I can,' said Gabriel. He backed away to a pillar, wringing his hands. 'You wasn't thrown over them railings at the cathedral. You must have thrown yourself. Don't know who the figure was in the cloak. Reckon you must have enough accomplices at the Society. And that's when I told you where I'd be sleeping tonight. You're the only one I told about the dry-stores, Thomas, the only one who knew about the gunpowder, and look what happened.' He pointed to the high windows, where the sky flickered orange.

Thomas staggered backwards. 'That's why you told me where you'd be sleeping?'

'Ay.'

'I thought you were sharing a private thing with me. All the while, it was a trap.'

'Didn't think it was you I'd catch.'

'You never trusted me? It was all a lie?' Thomas shrank, tears filling his eyes. He leaned over and coughed. 'I have never had a friend.'

'You lied to me.'

'Never once. Not a single one.' Thomas leaned against the wall. 'I came here to escape my father, thinking I might make friends with other men who shared my feelings. I expected them to love me and treat me better. I thought they would be kind to me, but all anyone has ever done is doubt me, abuse me, ridicule me, force me to do things I didn't want to do. You frightened me more than the Society ever did. At least they're honest enough to say it: they hate me, and so do the mollies. You hate me more than any of them, because I love you.' They stared into one another's eyes. 'I do.'

Gabriel lowered his head. 'Stop it, please.'

'And you love me too. In spite of everything, I know you do.'

Gabriel bent down and collected the Bible from the floor. He placed his hand upon it and spoke slowly. 'I have told you more than once, Thomas True. I do not know what love is. There was a time when I thought maybe I did.' He looked up. 'Not now.'

Thomas stepped towards him, nodding. 'You always suspected me, didn't you?' He gave a bitter smile. 'Deep down, I've always been the Rat.

Everyone thought so.' Thomas looked past Gabriel to an invisible space, as though meeting the eye of some hidden observer. 'Yes, everyone.'

Gabriel pointed to the door, unable to look at him. He never wanted to see that face again, nor hear his voice. 'Go. I won't stop you.'

'Go where? This is my home.'

'You don't belong in London, Thomas, never have. Go before I do the right thing and turn you in.'

'I would turn myself in if it made you happy. I have been in the stocks before.'

'And I bet you deserved it. Queed will skin you alive to get the truth out of you. He'll make a game of it, roasting you till your screams whistle. Go.'

'You'd let me escape, even though I'm the Rat?'

'I would, ay.'

'Then I was right. You do.'

Gabriel slammed the Bible back on the lectern. 'Do what?'

'Know what love is.'

'Just go!' Gabriel ripped the lectern from the floor and threw it to the ground. 'Get out of this church, out of London, out of me.'

Thomas covered his face with his arms. 'I knew I loved you the moment I saw you, Gabriel Griffin. When you dropped that hammer. You almost killed me, but I felt something happening. I felt it, same as you.'

Gabriel shot across the nave, grabbing Thomas by the throat. 'Leave tonight,' he said through gritted teeth 'Never come back.'

They kissed, holding each other's faces as they wept. Above them, small hands began crusting the arches of the windows, growing in across the sky like time-sped twigs until the glass was blinded by a thousand faces. Gabriel pushed Thomas away, wiping his mouth.

'How could I ever love a rat?'

Thomas clutched his chest. 'This is the last time we'll speak.'

'I wish you were dead.'

Thomas felt the words like a slap. He looked up and noticed the faces staring in through the windows. 'Our Blackguard friends,' he said. 'We should have listened to them, don't you think? They were right, after all. There is no such thing as a good man.'

And with that, he walked past Gabriel and left.

Part Five

CHAPTER FIFTY-NINE

A week had passed since their parting, and Gabriel had become as much of a ghost as his wife and daughter had ever been. He stood in the gallery of St Paul's beside Henry, only half aware of the voices around him. He was drowning in deep sorrow so that the whole world felt muffled behind thick glass.

They had been called back for a new job at St Paul's, the ruinous project refusing to end its demand on the city's time and money. The astronomer Wren himself was at war with the commissioners on almost every finishing detail, from the iron railings in the yard to the paintings, soon to be daubed on the interior skin of the dome. In the case of the latter, the architect was so angry he'd threatened to stab his own eyes out with the artists' brushes sooner than look at the 'meagre sketches' being displayed on the plaster ceiling from spandrel to oculus. Still, just like any parent, it was time for the great master to stand back and allow his creation to ruin itself: the monochrome murals would go ahead and the artist required scaffolding to reach his great canvas.

'A big job this,' said Henry, staring up from the gallery, his hands on his hips. 'Only just done on the bridge, finished the tiles yesterday, and now we're back here again. Lucky the place wasn't turned to rubble by that explosion; they say it was Wren's revenge for them railings!' He laughed. 'Good riddance to them Squinks anyway,' he added, avoiding Gabriel's eye. 'That family ain't right, none of 'em, especially that young fellow. Don't blame you for keeping your distance.' He cleared his throat and looked down to the nave far below. 'Lost my head for heights, I have, ever since that fire on the scaffolding. Still, money's good when the baby's almost due. I say we take the work, Gabe, don't you?' He looked at his friend, shocked anew by the transformation that had come over him in just a few days. He seemed to have lost half his size and his eyes were dark. He elbowed Gabriel in the ribs. 'Wake up, friend. What say you? Take the job or no? I say we take the job.'

Gabriel grunted.

Henry rolled his eyes. 'Very well then, I'll sort it. That's Dick Jenings over there, let me circle round and tell him we're good for the work.'

Gabriel watched his friend orbit the gallery, his head swimming with exhaustion from a lack of food and sleep. A week tormenting himself in the abandoned chapel had left him broken, the air cold at night, damp in the morning. Besides, how *could* he sleep, knowing he'd allowed the Rat to escape? How could he dream when Thomas still haunted his every thought? How could he eat a morsel of food knowing that Thomas had betrayed him, and (somehow far worse) he had betrayed Thomas? Again, he stumbled over his reasoning like a drunkard in a bottle shop, salving his own sickness with the sure evidence – the absolutely certain evidence – that Thomas deserved to be accused, deserved to be banished, that he had never belonged in London or in his heart in the first place. He held his calloused fingers out, counting out the facts one by one.

Thomas True had escaped the hounds multiple times without a scratch. Ay, that was beyond doubt, yet … can a man not be lucky?

He can, but what about the molly boy, Daisy? He had cried out during his beating: 'It's all true!' Gabriel had thought nothing of it at the time, until he'd sprung up in his makeshift bed in the chapel, the dead boy's voice crying out from the shallow graves. 'It's all … True.'

Or was that merely a coincidence? What court in the land would convict a man on wordplay? Ay, but the assassin on the wherry boat had known Thomas's name, and how could that be explained? Gabriel rubbed his head. The Rat was collecting molly names, that's how. Had he mentioned Thomas to the killer?

What else then? Thomas had been suspiciously keen to blame Mister Rettipence after discovering the tobacco tin. He must have planted it in Ned Skink's tavern himself when they were sitting there, then pretended to find it on their return to the table. Only … no. They only went back to find the tin because the pie woman had seen the Rat sitting beside them.

The coffee shop, then. Gabriel leaned his elbows on the balustrade, rapping his head with his knuckles. Thomas had knocked his drink over Fump's letter on purpose; he must have done. Surely no man could be so clumsy; it was the only piece of reliable evidence they'd found. Gabriel let out a long breath, remembering Thomas's clumsiness, his hapless ability to say the wrong thing, jump to the wrong conclusion, be in precisely the wrong place at precisely the wrong time at every given opportunity. He was the very epitome of clumsiness, and if that letter had been a cheque for a thousand pounds written in the dust from a butterfly's wings, Thomas would undoubtedly have sneezed it into oblivion, to his own detriment.

He watched Henry on the far side of the gallery, shaking hands with Jenings, then realised he was standing exactly where Thomas had fallen, right beside the door to the tower stairs. A figure had rushed behind Thomas as he'd tumbled. Gabriel leaned over the balustrade and opened his fingers, imagining Thomas hanging there still with a terrified expression on his face. He met eyes with his own imagination and felt the deep aching in his heart grow deeper still. It yearned for Thomas to be innocent, yet the man had confessed.

He had to, for nothing could undo one simple fact, one unquestionable piece of evidence that proved beyond a doubt that Thomas True was the Rat: he was the only one who knew about the gunpowder stores. Not the warehouse by the ditch; Treana had confirmed she was undisturbed until daybreak. Not the abandoned chapel where Henry had spent a lonely night before making his drowsy way home to a very angry wife. Not the woodshed where Clap had kept her secret vigil from eleven o'clock to the small hours, no sign of a rat. Only one place had been visited that night: the gunpowder stores, and only Thomas had been beckoned there by Gabriel's trap. Gabriel had told him about it right there in that exact spot below the dome.

'Ay, it'll be a flying scaffold I reckon...'

Gabriel looked up. 'Eh?' he said, expecting to see Henry standing beside him.

'...same as before, spanning east to west, up to the ocklebuss if that's the name. The hole up the top, like...'

Gabriel scanned the circular gallery, spying Henry forty feet across the gallery on the opposite side. He was pointing up at the dome, Jenings following his finger with a concentrated frown.

'Reckon the spars can rest on the gallery stones...'

Henry was talking in a casual voice, yet his words seemed to be carried around the stones by some peculiar magic. Gabriel shifted and Henry caught sight of him, raising his hand. Jenings did the same with a friendly nod then spoke out of the corner of his mouth. 'Your man Griffin up to the job, Sylva? Looks like he belongs in the funny house to me.'

'Gabe's fine,' said Henry. 'He's suffered these past three years. Still, if he's weak, I'll swap him for a better man. I've got a few lads lined up.' He lifted the plans to cover his face, and when he lowered them again, Gabriel was gone.

CHAPTER SIXTY

Gabriel rapped on the door of the candle shop then rapped again. He could hear raised voices from within, so he knocked harder, shaking the wood in the frame, and duly the door snapped open, a pair of long faces poking out.

'What? Who?' said Mistress Squink, her beady eyes hawking about the busy bridge as though Gabriel wasn't there. 'We're closed.'

'Griffin!' said her husband, fighting with his wife to open the door all the way. 'Come to inspect Sylva's work have you? I am delighted with the results.'

He ushered Gabriel inside as Mistress Squink rushed about the place, tidying things away on the shelves, which were poorly stocked of candles. Gabriel wrung his hat in his hands, looking about for Thomas.

'Mister Tr—' The name caught in his throat like a fish hook. 'Is your nephew here?'

Mistress Squink paused her tidying and looked up with a scowl. 'Nephew Thomas? Do not speak that name in this house.'

Mister Squink shushed her with a flap of his hands, giving Gabriel a sorrowful look. 'He has abandoned us, Mister Griffin. You hardly know him, yet I do believe he is the messiah of candlemakers. We were touched all too briefly by his majesty, and now...' the man raised his eyes to the freshly plastered ceiling '...he has ascended.'

Gabriel froze. 'He is dead?'

'Worse,' scoffed Mistress Squink. 'He's in Highgate. Left in the middle of the night, while we were sleeping. Nasty little knave.' She bustled around a barrel of dried rose petals. 'Stole our daughter while he was at it! Here,' she peered into Gabriel's eyes like an idiot confused by a painting. 'What's the little rat stolen for you to come snooping about our shop? We paid up and he's no responsibility of ours, so think again if you're accusing us of anything, you hear?'

Gabriel shook his head. 'Nothing's stolen. Reckon I left some tools on the scaffolding is all. Wondered if I could look.'

'Ay well, scaffolding's still up there till you bother to take it down.'

Gabriel gave a bow and moved past them, squeezing up the stairs through the building. As he passed the chandlery on the first floor, he saw the donkey standing untouched, half-dipped candles dangling in desultory rows. On the next floor up there was a parlour room, set out more like an office with a table and chairs, then above that the Squinks' sleeping quarters and at the very top, Thomas's garret room. Gabriel pulled himself into the lofty space and looked at the naked bed and empty writing desk. What did he hope to find there? A letter of confession perhaps, or an explanation? An apology? There was nothing, only the faint memory of Thomas's bare footprints running to the window. He followed them, looking out at the river as it thundered below. The dust on the gangway was soggy from the spray. Gabriel pulled the window wide open and climbed out, trusting Henry's lashings as the boards bowed under his weight, then swung effortlessly up to the roof. He frowned, for the tiles were not new at all. Henry had been uncharacteristically dishonest, charging for fresh materials when in fact, he had simply flipped them over. Irritated, Gabriel wrenched one up and inspected it. Moss was still clinging to its crumbly edges. He tutted and went to drop it over the edge before noticing something. Part of the weathered surface had been painted white. He levered the next tile from its nails, laying it so the weathered side was facing the sky, then did so with all the others and stood back with a long, sullen breath. He stared at the painted words and knew beyond any doubt that he had done a terrible thing. He kneeled down and traced his fingers over the words, understanding that Henry must have seen them and covered them over. He heard shouting, dogs barking, street vendors calling out their wares, and allowed his eyes to trace across the city to the Highgate Road climbing up through the valley to the horizon. He chewed his lip and gave a long, aching groan. What had he done?

THOMAS TRUE

&

GABRIEL GRIFFIN

ALWAYS TOGETHER

CHAPTER SIXTY-ONE

Justices Grimp and Myre could taste London as they approached the valley above the great Sodom. At last, they were almost ready for the purge.

'My dear Praisegod,' said Justice Grimp, 'I must concede I am weary. So many weeks from home, so many foul creatures to save, so much pressure, always pressure, to move on to the next den of sin; I find myself quite exhausted.'

Myre grunted and gave his associate a prickly glance from beneath his bushy brows. 'Artless, unsophisticated Praisegod, the Lord looks down in wonder at our tireless mission, yet we are but kittens, licking at the Devil's salt, which doth gush forth from his engorged evil like a torrent. How many souls have we saved these past twelve months?'

'Thirty hanged, I should say. Pilloried? Perhaps fifty-two. Whipped or banished: seventy at the last count. Still, we are but caterpillars nibbling the tips of the vine while the root of sin presses thick and hardy into the fundament of God's green land.'

Myre drummed his bony legs. 'Yes, deep indeed, and thick, my goodness me.'

Grimp crossed his legs and sat back as the view beyond the carriage windows turned from field to brick. 'We shall dig out the nest with Christ's good spade soon enough; for now we must breathe steadily and take succour, for the reckoning awaits. Remind me: where are the marshal's offices?'

Justice Myre took out a crumpled letter and unfolded it. 'The Black Horse Tavern, Clerkenwell. God burn the little shrew. I shall break his damned neck.'

'I tell you, we must be calm,' said Grimp, taking the letter and smoothing it out. He read the marshal's words for the umpteenth time, his eyes growing hot as they flicked from side to side. It was a most presumptuous correspondence, stating that their brave Rat had been unmasked by a man named Gabriel Griffin. The marshal asserted, amongst so many doubtful claims, that he had no idea who Mister Griffin was, while their Rat (Mister True) had been forced to flee, meaning they must (must!) postpone their raids. After all, stated the marshal in his pathetic scribble, the sodomites had taken flight in fear, and the justices were certain to raid nothing more than hollow taverns, unpatronised and perfectly deserted. Better to wait a few weeks, suggested the marshal; better to hold fire and castrate the Devil once he had grown back to his full tumescence.

Grimp lowered the letter and peered out. 'What on Earth is Queed talking about? Who is this Thomas True fellow, and why does he call him the Rat?'

'That Griffin fellow must have snared the wrong man,' said Myre. 'Thomas True is one of the names on our Rat's list.' He fumbled a ledger from his pocket and flipped past many hundreds of men. He tapped his fingernail on the sinner in question and spoke in a merry quiver, his eyes like burned raisins in cake. 'Queed thinks he has foiled us, gaining precious time to cover up his treason. He is in for a surprise: our Rat is still very much at large, and upon this night, the mollies of London and all of their confederate devils will be shackled in Newgate.'

He lifted his stick and thrust it hard against the roof of the carriage.

'On driver, quickly! On!'

CHAPTER SIXTY-TWO

For all the thrill that was lost to Mother Clap's Molly House during the shadowy reign of the Rat, it had rebounded now, ten times over, for the hidden hall on Field Lane had never been so tightly packed with carefree rejoicing. Indeed, it was unclear whether the new surge of patrons were mollies at all – though many arrived wearing gowns and lady's wigs and professed to be mollies in spirit – for they seemed to enjoy the music, drink and scandal more than the mollying itself.

With each passing round of drinks, more and more revellers arrived to kiss Lotty's famous round cheek for trapping the treacherous Thomas Rat. Meanwhile, the traitor was yet to be dug out of his hole and lynched, as he so deserved to be, though nobody could yet think what a molly lynching might look like ... It mattered not, for being disliked and spoken of in suggestive terms felt like punishment enough, and besides, the city's population of pretty fellows was fit to bursting with all their frustrated pleasures, so they jettisoned all caution and thoughts of retribution, and instead revelled in the arousing knowledge that it was at last safe to be sinful.

Lotty had tried to tell them that Thomas was innocent. She had voiced her doubts to Clap about the safety of so many new faces all at once. She had rejected all accolades, all compliments and suggestive invites from her admirers, young and old, yet her change of heart seemed one revelation too many. It was an inconvenient development to those invested in the previous and far more reassuring conclusion that they were not only safe but vindicated: they had always suspected the new fellow with his pretty face and slow adaption to their rites – he had refused to be birthed it was said, and thought himself very pretty even though he was vile, and invented the name Verity True-tongue himself, the conceited sod – so it suited them nicely to trust in Thomas Rat's toxic reputation, regardless of the truth. Besides, it was a Sunday night, and introspection wasn't the mode; now it was time for fun and freedom.

Lotty watched from her post beside the entry door, discreetly checking men's necks and wrists for the Society mark, avoiding their grateful kisses and slaps on her bare back. She twisted her gown, feeling the seams stretch around her stomach and hips. *Thomas*, she thought, *I hope you never see what I've done.*

Naturally, Lavender was in full voice, holding court with younger mollies at a nearby table. 'I said from the start it was True. Why, if they'd listened to me, Lotty Lump would have trapped him sooner and saved all those lives, dumb bitch. Nobody listens to Lavender though, and then what happens? Jacky's dead, Martha's dead, Daisy's dead, Fump probably dead too, for all we know, and gawd only knows what else. Lotty should be strung up for accusing me and my Duchess, that's what I say.'

The Duchess plucked tobacco from her tin, the initials now camouflaged amidst a make-do pattern of swirls. 'They who betray us must be punished without sympathy,' she said, accepting a cup of wine from a handsome admirer. 'Yet we must always be kind.'

Lavender nodded so enthusiastically her wig fell down her face. 'From now on, any molly who acts differently and doesn't obey the culture is a Rat. We'll shun 'em, destroy their molly name, good riddance to 'em. Trust suspicion, that's what I say. And we must never disagree again, not on the slightest thing, long as we all agree to think it, and if someone doesn't think it ... well, make 'em think it, or they're a rat too.'

The Duchess nodded. 'That does sound wise, my dear. It was our generous forbearance that granted Thomas Rat the opportunity to betray us in the first place.'

'So it was. We were wrong to be kind. Oh but will you look?' Lavender gestured to the shrivelled wretch sitting between them like a poisoned weed. 'Vivian's plight has to be the cruellest of all Thomas Rat's crimes.'

Vivian Guzzle's pale eyes wandered around the balcony, still searching in hope she might spot dear Nelly Fump in one of her preposterous wigs. Disappointed, she raised herself from her stool, removed her gown in folds to the floor, then staggered to the exit.

Lotty followed her out. 'Time to go, is it?'

'Ay,' said the old man, jabbing his finger at the sky, 'time to go up there you mean. I no longer enjoy my life, dear. It's all too sad.' At that, he turned unsteadily on the gangway and took Lotty by the hand. 'I do not believe your young friend Thomas True was the Rat, and though my eyes are failing me, I can see you agree. My darling Lotty, life is so terribly short, shorter still for the likes of us. There are no bad deeds larger than love, no words so terrible they cannot be repaired.' He patted Lotty's chest. 'Young folks think companionship is about racing hearts and giddy words, but such things come and go. Tell Thomas you are sorry, my darling, before you are too late.' He tapped Lotty's cheek. 'Give him the second most precious gift in life. He will treasure it, I know he will.'

'And what's that?' said Lotty.

'A heartfelt apology.'

'And the first?'

'What you shall doubtless receive in return.' Mister Vivian's face opened up with a bright smile. 'Forgiveness, sweet man. Forgiveness.' The old man stepped back, taking the rail as his knees buckled.

Lotty jumped forwards to steady him. 'If Thomas ain't the Rat, then who is?'

Vivian gave a weary laugh. 'The Rat, the Rat, the Rat. There is always a rat.' With trembling knees and much shaking and nodding of his head, he toddled towards the dark passageway, his bent skeleton eaten up by the shadows.

Lotty stepped back inside the hall, thinking about what the old man had said, yet her thoughts were instantly shot to pieces by the thumping of the music, as the mollies chanted: 'Thomas Rat, Thomas Rat Thomas Rat!' Mother Clap strode onto the stage in a wig of tight red curls and a ruff the size of a cartwheel. She held out her arms and stamped her boot for silence. Three hundred bewigged heads stared up at her, holding their breath.

'Mollies, new and old!' she cried. 'For how many years have we been banished by the righteous? How many gods have hated us without saying so? How many friends were hanged to the cheering of good people? How many hands clamped in irons, faces slapped, skulls broken? Ay, ladies, don't gimme them looks, your mother sings a prickly rhyme, she knows it – but ain't this a ballad we've sung before? Don't fret, for the banished built Paradise. Ay, and the martyrs died so others can live. The men what swung watched others swing before them and never feared. Them hands in irons touched passion – and more besides – and them faces were proud before they got a slapping and were all the prouder for it afterwards. Skulls broke but never hearts, my darlings.' Her face grew grave, her hands reaching out. 'We welcomed a traitor into our little sanctuary.' She nodded as a hiss grew up from the crowd:

'Thomas True, Thomas Rat!'

The hiss grew louder, the hall drumming to the heels of so many fellows chanting his name with bulging eyes and spit from their lips. Clap paraded upstage, nodding. 'Danger is ever at our door,' she said, 'and I know I have the body of a weak and feeble woman. But I have the heart and stomach of a king, and a king of the mollies too!' The crowd threw their drinks above their heads and roared. Mother Clap tore her doublet away to reveal a breast plate of polished iron. 'And think foul scorn that the Society should dare invade my molly house, for I have the biggest and bravest warship of all Christendom at my disposal, and no creeping boy with pretty lips can withstand her thundering cannon balls! Lotty Lump, get up here in that gown, ye great woman-o-war, that we may applaud you!'

The crowd let out a thunderous cheer of approval, clapping their hands as Lotty was transported against her will to the stage amidst a downpour of splashing cups. Once on the stage, she felt those three hundred eyes mocking her distended stomach and hairy chest and looked at her huge feet as they chanted, 'Lotty Lump! Thomas Rat!'

'I should have told you, Clap,' she said, her voice lost amidst the din. 'It wasn't him. Thomas don't deserve this.'

She would tell them all, as soon as they stopped chanting. She would clear Thomas's name, then fetch him home from Highgate so they could apologise to him. She would go the very next morning; that was the honest thing to do. Mister Vivian was right: it is best to apologise, though forgiveness wasn't something Lotty deserved. She would stop calling herself the molly guard and never return to Clap's or any other molly house. It was time to leave London and start a new life on her own somewhere far away, where she couldn't hurt anybody ever again. She looked up, ready to make her confession, yet there was a commotion by the entry door, and the hall was split by the sound of marching boots and screaming.

Clap stepped forwards. 'What's this? What's happening?'

Lotty peered through the smoke-filled hall in horror as a wave of panic shot through the crowd. Constables were flooding in through the unguarded door as mollies clambered over each other in a heap to get out, tearing off their costumes while scratching at the walls as though escaping a fire. Lotty spotted Lavender and the Duchess amongst them, clinging to one another amidst the stampede. The rioting mass of mollies parted in front of the stage as three men cleaved through them, surrounded by a squadron of guards. Marshal Queed was at the vanguard, and behind him, two justices in black robes, false noses strapped about their heads like ravens' beaks.

'That's him,' shouted Queed. 'That's Gabriel Griffin the molly guard. Bring him down here at once and arrest him.'

Mother Clap stamped her boots and hollered back. 'Treacherous little bastard! Ain't I paid you enough these past years?'

Queed's face was purple, pointing his dagger at her. 'And that's Mother Clap. Arrest her too, the dark witch, and gag that mouth of hers.'

Clap kicked out as two guards reached across the stage for her ankles. 'Forty years I've run this place,' she said, 'and never a red coat crossed my threshold. Now, they think we'll go without a fight, do they?' She clutched a bottle and smashed it against the wall, swinging the jagged glass above her head and hollering so all her ladies could hear: 'Arm yourselves, mollies! Let's show 'em who the real men are!'

With that, she flung the bottle at an approaching constable, tearing a slice from his eye. The room shook to the sound of splintered wood and thundering boots as the remaining mollies quit their cowering and grabbed chair legs and broken jugs, flinging themselves in a frenzy at the invading army of constables with all the ferocity of savage Highlanders. The battle raged, men lying prostrate on the floor, bleeding from their heads, while others leapt into the private chapels to escape the onslaught. Some of the invaders snatched up gowns and pulled them on to disguise themselves as sodomites, then fled the scene squealing. Lotty fought as hard as she could, keeping herself far from Queed's clutches as she scythed through the oncoming mass of the marshal's men, flinging them into the air like discarded corn husks, yet still more swarmed through the entry door, slowly, inexorably overwhelming their stricken captives. Clap kicked an oncoming constable in the face and clambered back onto the stage.

'No use Lotty, it's over,' she cried. 'Get out while you can.'

'I ain't leaving,' said Lotty.

Clap took a knife from her boot and flung it between the eyes of an oncoming guard. 'Too late to save 'em now; Thomas Rat's done his work.'

'It wasn't him, I got it wrong.'

They edged back to the middle of the stage as constables climbed up on all sides. 'What does it matter now?' Clap took one last look at her molly house, the constables tearing out walls and smashing tables. 'No matter who it was, they've won. You go, or it'll be the noose.'

Lotty stood beside her, holding a plank of wood for a club. 'And you? Always together, ain't that the cry?'

'Ay,' she said as the constables charged, 'but not tonight.' She stamped her boot three times and Lotty dropped through the stage, catching a last glance of Mother Clap throwing herself back into the fray as the hall was torn to pieces, shafts of daylight streaming in through split walls, and beyond them, a long line of broken mollies being led down the gangway in chains.

CHAPTER SIXTY-THREE

Tyburn sat amidst scrubland and littered fields, a crossroads opposite a flat bank of grass where deserting soldiers were periodically shot. The crowd gathered in their thousands below the October sky, a thrust and jostle of men, women and children, all slipping about in the mud to claim the best view of the gallows. Footpads and cutpurses crawled through the mob, the air ringing to the cry of gin sellers. 'Gin-ginny! Gin-ginny!' they sang, hawking their bottles to the thirsty lips of their customers. Above them, the gallows loomed: a triangular set of wooden beams, eighteen feet high, surrounded by a gallery of raked pews towering sixty feet into the air like a humungous wooden collar. The choicest seats were already filling up with spectators, craning their necks and leaning out as a row of hearses drew up, each with a black coffin inscribed with the names of the condemned. Gabriel could read two of them.

George Lavender
Timothy Rettipence

'Hold fast,' thought Gabriel, pulling his hat low. He looked at the dangling ropes, anticipating the snapping noise they would make under the weight of the men. The burst of moisture from their stretched fibres. The creek as they twisted.

He felt a shuffling at his shoulder and turned to see Henry pushing to his side in a fur-lined coat and thrum cap, staring straight ahead. 'Where you been, Gabe?'

'Things to do.'

'That so?'

'Ay, that's so. What you doing here? You don't like hangings.'

'Wanted to make sure it wasn't you up there.'

Gabriel met his eye then turned his attention back to the gallows. An hour passed as the spectators thickened around them, a dark energy growing through the crowd as the carts were spotted in the distance. He could just make them out, a cloud of rocks and rotten vegetables following the slow-moving procession like flies.

'The last leg,' said Henry. 'Poor wretches.'

The carts inched along Oxford Street, the marshal's men on horseback clubbing their way through till, at last, they emerged onto the Tyburn flats, and the crowd buzzed with excitement.

'Come, Gabe,' said Henry, turning away, 'let's go.'

Gabriel caught sight of Mister Vivian standing alone amidst the press of people. They met eyes and nodded. 'You go. I have to stay.'

He felt some commotion behind him and groaned to see the Squinks barging through towards them.

'Move, foul wenches,' came Mistress Squink's unmistakable squeak, followed by her husband's voice.

'Ay, let us through. You can have a free candle if you buy four!'

Gabriel gritted his teeth, yet before he could escape, the man's head popped through a tight scrum.

'Why Mister Griffin and Mister Sylva, how lovely to see you. We thought you might have been captured with the murderers and the sodomites, ho ho!'

His wife jabbed him in the ribs with her elbow. 'To say such awful things to a pair of respectable fellows.' She looked Gabriel up and down with beady eyes. 'I must thank you both for proofing our little home against the windy weather. I have never been so dry. Still,' her eyes sharpened, 'business is not so brisk, is it husband?'

The man gave a sad nod. 'Not since Thomas and Abigail left.' He held up his basket, filled with lumpy candles shaped like carrots. 'I confess, I do not have a talent for moulding.'

'Pish!' said Mistress Squink, holding up her own assortment of strange shapes. 'These are of superior quality.' She fluttered her bald eyelids. 'Is this your first Tyburn, Mister Griffin? Surely not.'

'No,' said Gabriel. 'Not my first.'

'Mister Squink and I long for the thrill of our first execution; one can never quite recapture the pleasure of it. I don't know how many hangings and burnings we've been to now.' She hit her husband on the back of the head. 'How many executions have we been to now?'

'Fifty at least, my petal.'

'Yes, at least fifty,' she said, before rounding on him in a fury. 'Why, I should think it's closer to a hundred! We have attended so many, it is hard to keep a tally. Of course, today is a special Tyburn: a good number of sodomites, a little villain boy and a murderess.' Mistress Squink chopped the air. 'Diced her husband into little pieces with a cleaver like he was a chicken for the roasting.' She leaned around Gabriel to Henry. 'Just like a chicken, Mister Sylva! What was it I said earlier, husband?'

Mister Squink tittered so profusely he could barely speak. 'You said it'll be the murderess roasting today.'

Henry gave a hollow laugh as Gabriel turned away with a grunt. Mistress Squink stared at them both in expectation of some shared amusement, only to grow stale. 'I suppose not every man can appreciate a good jest, even on such a happy day. I shouldn't like to have such gloomy faces as my last sight from the gallows – what a punishment. Still, all the better for those filthy sodomites; may they dance for an hour.' She pulled her shawl around her neck and tugged down her cuffs, muttering to her husband about common courtesy at hangings these days. 'Why, it's no better than Bedlam, all those people pushing past us to see that funny little queen with her peruke made of straw.'

Henry leaned close to Gabriel's ear. 'Been worried about you. Bet sent me here, and she don't need the strain.' He cleared his throat, looking up at the gallows, black against the gathering clouds. 'Didn't know if I'd be saying farewell to you.'

'I ain't a murderer.'

'Didn't think you was.'

Gabriel looked at him from the corner of his eye and cleared his throat. 'You saw what Mister True wrote on the roof.'

'I did.' Henry raised his eyebrows, stifling a chuckle.

'You laughing at me, Henry Sylva?'

'No, Gabe. I don't understand and don't want to, it's just … You and me, we've been through a lot and it feels like I never knew you till I saw them words. It's like your special friend says, ain't it? Since we was tiddlers, Gabe and Henry, always together.'

Gabriel clamped his jaw shut and controlled his breathing as the drum began to beat and the condemned prisoners pulled up below the gallows, each searching for their name on the caskets. They were flanked on both sides by guards on horseback, and by the looks of them, they were ready to die.

The murderess was wild, spitting and snarling at the crowd. Her lover and conspirator followed behind, along with two deadly men from Tyrone and Cardiff. Each wore a noose about his neck, the Welshman cheerful, calling back to the crowd, giving as good as he got, while the rest were silent as they stared at the beams ranging above them. Their elbows were tied, that their hands were free to pray, yet most of them trembled too violently to make use of their fingers, and any prayers were lost to the baying of the mob. In the third cart, a boy was weeping in his father's lap, his pa stroking his hair. A poacher and his son, they had been caught with a single pheasant.

Gabriel felt Henry tense up beside him. 'Poor souls, they don't deserve this.'

'They don't.'

Just then, a huge black horse cantered into view beside the gallows, lunging into the crowd. Marshal Queed was mounted high, his spurs barely reaching the beast's flanks. He flitted his eyes over the crowd, resting them on Gabriel before moving on.

'That devil gives me the shivers,' said Henry. 'Reckon he looked at you.'

Mistress Squink nodded enthusiastically. 'Who couldn't quake in the presence of such power? What a reassurance it is to know that our fair city is in godly hands. Why, it is a mystery to me that the king doesn't give the marshal a thousand more men to protect us from such evil. Why, there's enough of it about and not only amongst the murderers, thieves and sodomites. I should begin with Bedlam.' She tapped Gabriel's arm. 'We went there this morning you know. It's a tradition of ours to view the lunatics in the morning, then enjoy a hanging in the afternoon.' She held her husband's arm with a girlish smile. 'We never sleep so well as we do after a hanging.'

'Christ's bones,' said Henry, covering his nose as the final cart hove into view to the continuing beat of the drum, its cargo smothered in human faeces. A group of wretched men in ripped gowns looked down. George Lavender and Mister Rettipence were amongst them, sitting side by side. Lavender was thinner than ever after her week in Newgate, the noose hanging heavy around her scrawny neck, her wrists bandaged and bloody. There were tracks down her powdered cheeks, dried and cracked, for she had grown too tired and too frightened to cry. A shout went up as a young girl scrabbled alongside him. She begged the guards to let her brother go, reaching up to touch his feet. George looked down at her for a moment then fainted and fell back against the others. Mister Rettipence was beside him, his plump cheeks unshaven, stammering and bewildered as though he had only just realised his fate. The poor man looked at the noose around his neck then stared in disbelief at the baying crowd. 'My wife?' he was saying. 'My children.'

First, the murderers were forced to stand at the rear of the carts, while their ropes were thrown over the beams above their heads. Beside them, a chimney of black smoke was already rising from a pile of faggots arranged at the feet of the murderess as the drum grew silent. The dry brushwood crackled and fizzed, embers flying around the woman's dress. The soldiers could not retrieve the rope in time to choke her without scalding their hands, and suddenly there was a puff of sparks as the flames drew up her writhing body, wrapping her screaming face in bright liquid as the sky sucked the blistering heat into a whirl of yellow ribbon.

'Candle keepsakes of the murderess,' cried Mister Squink, holding up his basket. 'Give her another burning in your own home!'

People rushed to part with their money, jostling and bickering, only to change their minds when they saw the warped and knobbly candles on offer.

'This ain't human,' said Henry as the drum struck up again. 'What sort of a world is this for my little girl to come into?' He gave a nod. 'Yesterday morning, Gabe. You're an uncle.' Gabriel had never seen him so anxious.

'You'll make a fine pa.'

'I'm already useless, Gabe. I need you around.' He nodded to the cart where the men stood, waiting for the drop. 'I can't watch this. I'm off. Just ... never let me see you up there, eh? Be too embarrassing when the rope snaps.' He squeezed Gabriel's arm and left, pushing past the Squinks with a curt nod.

Gabriel felt his chest pounding through his ribs as the condemned men stood above him, some crying, most of them shivering in the cold. Queed looked down from his horse, ready to give the nod, his scarlet doublet glinting amidst floating embers against the grey sky. The drum fell silent and the horses were geed away as the first two men slipped into thin air, the skin of their necks rumpled to their jaws as they flapped and buckled.

The condemned mollies watched in dumb horror as the dying wretches dangled beside them. It was the father and son's turn next, the boy searching for his pa's fingers as he waited for his smaller noose to be fixed to the pole. He did not find them, for there was hardly time for the drum to start beating when they fell, twisting and bouncing with startled faces until a kind onlooker jumped up and tugged their feet for clemency.

The crowd roared, baying for more hangings as the steady drumbeat returned. George Lavender was quivering, his jaw slack, eyes wild with panic. He cried out in terror as the cart was jolted by a startled horse, then looked down at the crowd and met his sister's eyes. He smiled, and Gabriel read his lips through the din. 'Pray for me,' he was saying. 'I want my ma.' And then he looked up at the beam as Mister Rettipence took his hand, their clasped fingers spattered with spit from the scandalised crowd.

'Together!' came a voice, and Gabriel turned to see Mother Clap standing on a barrel some way back in the crowd, her hands cupped to her mouth. She was dressed all in black, a snapped peacock plume sticking up from her tricorn hat. 'I say together!' she repeated, and she was hit by a stone, her legs pummelled with fists. Gabriel pushed his way through to her, beating people back.

'What the Hell are you doing?' he said, lifting her back to the ground.

'Solidarity,' said Clap. 'Shame.'

Gabriel wrapped his arm around her, warning people against a fight. 'Nothing for you to be ashamed of.'

'A week of whipping and oakum-picking in Bridewell. That's all I got, long as I go back to paying Queed his garnish. Not like them.'

The drum slowed as the condemned mollies were forced to stand at the edge of the cart.

'You're an ally, Clap,' said Gabriel. 'Nobody's ever done so much as you.'

The horses stirred as Clap gripped Gabriel's hand.

'Allies may shout the battle cry,' she said in a solemn voice, 'but they'll never shed the blood.'

Mister Vivian appeared between the press of the mob, his head nodding uncontrollably as he reached out his bone-white hands. 'Will you hold me up, my dears? I have seen this too often, but never without my companion to console me.'

The drum gave its last three beats and fell silent. The crowd waited for the marshal to nod. He did so and Gabriel, Clap and Vivian stood together, showing their friends that even though they were about to die frightened, cold, betrayed, they would not do so alone.

The cart slid away.

And they dropped.

Their ropes snapped.

They flapped and jerked.

Doubtless they screamed in their heads and thought of their childhoods and the people they loved. Some tried to reach for their necks with their shackled hands, others searched for each other with frantic eyes. They stretched their toes to the ground and gasped for breath through strangled throats, and never let anybody tell you that mollies are feeble, for every single one of them danced for more than fifteen minutes before their hearts gave up.

Don't look away, thought Gabriel, as soldiers surrounded the men to make sure their legs weren't pulled for mercy. *Don't look away*. Yet he could not help it, and in weakness, he turned his face and met the glinting eyes of Marshal Queed.

CHAPTER SIXTY-FOUR

Gabriel raced as fast as he could from Tyburn, trapped amidst the crush of so many people. Should he run into Hide Park? He looked back to see the marshal and his men trying to beat their way through on horseback. They would be upon him in a matter of seconds if he ran into the open. He ploughed east along Mount Street, tearing people out of the way, falling under carts in his desperation. Damn his size! He turned left then right and right again, taking any small alleyway until he found himself in a dead end, imprisoned on all sides by high, windowless walls. He turned to run back, only to see Queed riding into view.

The marshal turned his head and smiled. 'There you are, Mister Griffin,' he called along the narrow alleyway. 'Guards, I have him.'

Gabriel looked around, hoping in vain to see foot holes or a ladder. He pressed his back against the bricks and tensed his muscles.

The marshal steadied his horse, moving into the alleyway at a slow trot, flanked on both sides by his men, their swords drawn. 'It never ceases to amaze me,' he said, 'the way men run when they know it's too late. There isn't a place to hide in this city. I am everywhere. Now, you can either come quietly that I might ask you a few questions, or you can cause trouble and we'll cut your face open.'

Gabriel pushed himself from the wall. 'I'm a dead man either way. The Rat's still out there. It's over for you an' all.'

The marshal smiled. 'The justices have left London already. I carried out their raid with due diligence, and they have no evidence against me and no desire to find any. They head north again. Tireless disciples they are.' He tutted. 'I should never have expected you to catch the Rat. Mollies are weak in mind and morals. I thought it was better to let you find him, but now I know I should have done the job myself.' He pulled the reins and looked down at Gabriel. 'I'm told he fled to Highgate. Is that so?'

'Don't know where the traitor is, but it ain't Thomas True, so leave him be.'

Queed rolled his eyes. 'We have to blame somebody, so it might as well be him. When your molly friends see what I've done to you and your sweetheart, they'll never cross me again. My brazen bull has been silent for too long. I miss his music. I believe you'll fit, and so will Thomas True, when I find him. What a sweet thing it will be, the pair of you roasting together inside that belly. Won't it be cosy?' He moved closer as the guards dismounted.

Gabriel balled his fists and sprung forwards with a roar, smacking two men against the walls then punching a third in the jaw with a smart crack of bone. He spun around, connecting his fists with another guard's eye socket, the man reeling away as a fifth charged up with his staff, only to be swung into the air like a fish on a rod, crashing onto one of his comrades. A sharp blow connected with the back of Gabriel's head and he fell with a cry of agony.

'Caught the bear at last,' said Queed, staring down. 'Let's get him back to my yard. I won't wait for Mister True. I fancy my bull is hungry. Mister Griffin, you will make him sing most tunefully before sundown.'

Gabriel felt his legs and arms being lashed, yet just as he was being lifted from the ground, the sound of ringing bells drifted over from some hidden chapel and the men looked around the alleyway, wondering what sort of bells made such enchanting, malevolent music.

'Get along with it,' snapped the marshal. 'What are you waiting for?'

Gabriel smiled as a swarm of tiny bodies crawled over the edges of the walls, bleeding down in a bramble of glittering limbs. They covered the bricks, then sprang like spiders to the screams of the guards as Marshal Queed toppled from his horse. Gabriel wriggled as the Blackguard gripped him by the legs and arms and carried him away like a loaf of bread up the steep walls and over the roofs of London.

CHAPTER SIXTY-FIVE

Gabriel lay still, his feet against a miniature fireplace while his head was propped up on an armchair no larger than a footstool. By his side stood Glimmer Littlethorn, looking down at him with their glass pendant caught in tangles of black hair.

'Stupid doddlehead,' they said with a wrinkled nose. 'Dangerous donkey.'

'You saved me,' said Gabriel.

'We'll tip Grubble Griffin off a bridge like an old bottle if he doesn't do as he's told. We're owed.'

'Owed what?'

'Kind Thomas.'

'What about him?'

'We had a bargain: one good man for one bit of knowledge.'

'Ay, well your clue was about as useful as a glass hammer. Thomas had to flee. Wasn't safe.'

'Because of you.'

Gabriel stretched his arms against the ropes. 'Ay, because of me. I made a mistake. I'm sorry for it.'

'Save him then.'

'He's safe.'

Glimmer snorted. 'He ain't.'

Gabriel looked across the small room to the miniature window plastered with faces. 'You know where he is?'

'We do.'

'Who told you?'

'You did, in the alleyway.'

Gabriel nodded. 'You heard me tell Queed, course you did. Ay well, he's safer in Highgate than here.'

'No, he ain't.'

'Well, you save him then, like you did me.'

'The Blackguard don't leave London, dung for brains.'

Gabriel groaned as he looked beyond his feet to see a pair of pixies approaching him with cup-sized cauldrons of steaming fish stew. They stood beside his head and ladled it into his open mouth. He hadn't realised how hungry he was. When was the last time he'd eaten? Two days ago, maybe longer.

'Grubble Griffin needs the strength,' said Glimmer. 'To catch his Rat and save Kind Thomas.'

Gabriel complained, straining against his ropes. 'Can't, I've tried. Maybe it was Lavender or Rettipence, I don't know.'

'The Rat is still alive. They want Thomas killed.'

'You can't know that.'

Glimmer gave him the steady look of an unimpressed cat. 'We heard their plans as they made 'em, blubber bones.'

Exasperated, Gabriel sat up. 'Enough of your riddles. Tell me who it is.'

Glimmer shook their head. 'Blackguard never told a growner nothing. Can't trust none of you, except Kind Thomas.'

'Sounds like you have to trust me if you want him back. And I want to tell him I'm sorry.'

The Blackguard began chanting slowly and softly, the noise of their voices sweeping from the room into the street beyond, chiming from all around.

Glimmer listened as the decision was passed through the window, then poured the rest of the fish stew into Gabriel's mouth and slapped him about the face. 'We will help you remember, Grubble Griffin, that is all we can do. The Blackguard don't give secrets to nobody, so you'll have to remember your own.' The child pressed their sharp thumbs against his eyelids, pushing them open so he had to stare out as a fresh chanting grew up around him:

'You know who knows. They told you. You know who knows. They saw him. You know who knows. They said so.'

Gabriel looked at the little creatures. 'What are you saying?'

'You know who knows. They told you. You know who knows. They saw him. You know who knows. They said so.'

'I can't think.'

'You know who knows. They told you. You know who knows. They saw him. You know who knows. They said so.'

Gabriel grew angry at first, yet their soft chanting sent him into a strange waking sleep, his mind softening as thoughts and memories floated up through the gaps in his aching brain. 'Fump,' he said in a dreamy voice. 'Fump's the only one who saw the Rat with his own eyes. Tried to warn us.'

'Fump knows. They told you. Fump knows. They saw him. Fump knows. They said so.'

Gabriel murmured, lost in a crowd of swimming faces, 'Who saw him? Where?'

Warm hands pressed over his eyes as each of his muscles relaxed and he melted into the floor. His thoughts were outside of him now, no longer trapped, and he imagined them floating around the room like feathers. He was walking back to Tyburn, people surrounding him as though they were in a dream. There was Mister Vivian and Mother Clap. There was Queed and his guards. There were poor George Lavender and Timothy Rettipence high on the cart. There was the burning woman, and Henry too and ... and the Squinks. Gabriel turned to face them, watching their thin lips and long faces as they spoke. They had said something that had stuck in the pit of his mind amidst the horror.

'Fump knows. They told you. Fump knows. They saw him. Fump knows. They said so.'

He heard her speaking, Mistress Squink, in that haughty voice: 'It's no better than Bedlam,' she was saying, 'all those people pushing past us to see that funny little queen with his peruke made of straw.'

Gabriel sat up so fast he hit his head against the low ceiling. 'Bedlam,' he said. 'Fump is in Bedlam!'

CHAPTER SIXTY-SIX

Thomas was lost in his thoughts, staring down at the distant city. The view accounted for the greater share of his existence by far, yet London lived inside him as though he'd been there all his life. He knew its streets and alleyways like an old friend; now it was out of reach, distanced less by miles than by shame and scorn. He smiled. Down there was his old home on the bridge and Mother Clap's Molly House with her music and dancing, and the old peruke shop in Covent Garden, and Gabriel Griffin. He pushed back from the window and sat on his bed, clicking his tongue as he looked around the attic. He gave a long groan of boredom and pulled a chain from his pocket, opening it in his palm. He should never have taken it, yet somehow, he'd never managed to give it back. It was precious to him. A keepsake gifted by chance, the only lie he'd ever told. He pictured the chain snapping from Gabriel's neck as they'd plummeted through the black water under the bridge. He clicked it open and lifted the locket to the light from the window, staring at the blank, grey faces of a woman and child, their features washed away. 'All will be well,' he told himself. 'I will see him again, I know it.'

Life with his parents and Abigail at the rectory was even more uncomfortable than his childhood, and already he could feel himself shrinking. He was weaker there, as though the stocks on the green and all those painful memories were a disease eating away at his flesh. Abigail was sympathetic, in her own way, yet all she ever wanted to do was live in the past, remembering the games they'd once played together all those summers ago.

Thomas gave a longing sigh and hung the locket around his neck. He would travel back to London at the first opportunity, find Gabriel, who must surely know he was innocent by now, and give him back his keepsake. It was impossible for them to ever be friends again, he knew he wasn't wanted, but still, they needn't be enemies.

He crawled under his cool bedclothes and closed his eyes, picturing Gabriel's face, clear as a reflection in a pond. *I will*, he thought, holding a blanket to his body. *I will see you just one more time and that will have to be enough for me.*

CHAPTER SIXTY-SEVEN

Gabriel had often wondered what the asylum was like on the inside, yet he had never joined the throngs of visitors who visited the hospital to gawp at the Bedlamites. To him, it seemed cruel to treat such unhappy men and women like so many animals in a zoo.

They passed through heavy doors, the sound of rattling chains all around them, un-bodied voices ranting, hallooing, and gibbering.

'A fearsome place, this,' said Mother Clap.

'Indeed it is,' agreed Mister Vivian, hobbling past each inmate, inspecting the faces behind the bars. 'My darling Fump, are you here?'

No sooner had they passed into a central atrium than they were pushed apart by a large man in a straw hat playing invisible bagpipes, arguing with the wall over his inheritance. Following him was a hairless woman, laughing at her own hands, while hidden behind a low recess could be heard the voice of a child, crying out for his mother, only for a naked gentleman to pop up and cartwheel sideways like a Russian tumbler, all to the disgust of a long-toothed schoolmistress in a tattered shawl and necklace of rabbit paws, who beat him along with her cane.

'Hurry,' said Gabriel, 'there's little time.'

Edging sideways to a short doorway with a low arch, they sank deeper and deeper, the light growing thin as they made their way to the men's quarters, then peered into a lonely cell where a heavy chain ran across the stone floor to a brazier. The light of the fire shone on the moonish face of a boy, perhaps in his fifteenth year, his pale eyes keen beneath a tangled mop of mouse-brown hair. He wore a loose shirt backwards, the laces open at his sharp spine, and his legs were bare to his blackened toes. 'God's teeth,' muttered Gabriel, thinking the boy's feet must have been eaten by the worst gout in London. The boy regarded his audience with glassy eyes.

'Young man,' said Mister Vivian, 'do you know of a gentleman here named Fump?'

The boy shifted and scratched his armpits. 'Yes,' he said. 'Queen Fump of Bedlam resides in her palace, that way.' He pointed with his foot up the stone steps from the dungeon then, to Gabriel's horror tipped his other foot into the brazier where his toes popped open in the flames like burst sausages.

Mister Vivian whimpered at the sight. 'Oh my dear Fump, what sort of a man will you have become amidst such horrors?'

'This ain't no hospital,' said Clap, 'I'm going mad just looking at them poor souls.'

The three of them passed up a flight of stairs, the gloom opening to a long, whitewashed gallery, the high plaster walls lit up on one side by tall windows, while a set of heavy iron doors ran along the other. Some of the cells were standing open, each a cursed trinket box, spilling a different kind of mayhem onto the floor. There were manacled men singing for pennies, some grinning, others shielding their faces in shame. One portly fellow lay beneath a barred window, crying for the universities, while a second bit his own fingers off, complaining he could never again play the flute. At the next cell, a pair of lady visitors nodded approvingly as a young man painted Bible verses in excrement across the wall, while a witless prophet spoke eloquently about wisdom. There was a sea captain spurting such a torrent of breathless opinions he regularly fainted, and beside him a man who nodded along, his mouth covered by a mask fashioned from his own skin, lest a virus turn him mad. All the while there came strange noises from the locked cells, the clanking of chains, discordant songs, all perfectly insensible to their visitors.

At last, there was only one cell left, surrounded by a fascinated crowd of onlookers. Gabriel, Vivian and Clap pushed through; and there he was: Mister Fump, sitting high on a pile of stuffed mattresses, blinking as a cloud of pipe smoke settled around his lofty shoulders. He held a turnip in one hand, carved to look like an orb, while in the other he held a majestic broom handle. There were sheets of white material draped from each of the four corners of the cell, ruched at the centre of the ceiling in a linen rose. The regal patient wore a loose suit made entirely of ripped sheets trimmed with mouse fur, all stitched together most artfully with brown twine, while his peruke of ringlets and high curls had – just as the Squinks reported – been fashioned out of straw, the tufts and clufts styled with tallow wax. He had lost a great deal of weight, his once jolly face diminished to sagging cheeks, while his round belly had grown hollow as a rotten tree. Still, his eyes were no less twinkling, and when they rested on his visitors, they did so with the usual haughty poise.

'Good subjects,' he said, 'it has been too long.'

Vivian clung to the bars. 'My dearest Fump,' he said through grateful sobbing, 'how long have you been locked behind these bars, you daft bitch?'

'About six weeks, I should say,' came Fump's answer. 'My dear, you look hideous in that coat. Wait there.'

Duly, he clambered down from his makeshift throne, commanding his admirers to leave and – to Gabriel's surprise – unlocked the cell door and stepped out like a gentleman off for an afternoon stroll.

Mister Vivian sobbed, wrapping his arms around his dear love. 'I told you to be home in time for supper. Will you ever do as you are told? It's been over a month.' He pulled back to look at his companion. 'However have you survived all this time in such a wretched place? I would have gone mad.'

Fump looked back at his cell. 'On the contrary, I do believe I have grown quite sane, I keep saying sensible things. It's horrible.'

'Did you not tell them you were well, so you could come home?'

'Indeed, I did tell the physics about my various sensible thoughts, yet they informed me there is no surer mark of a madman.'

Gabriel wafted pipe smoke from his face. 'Who put you in here, Fump?'

The man clutched his face, a picture of tragedy. 'Alas, I cast myself as a lunatic after escaping the justices, thinking I would be safer here. I knew I was for the drop when I saw the Rat, so I wrote you a secret letter as quickly as I could, yet almost as I sent it, two muscly constables were invading my quarters, so I climbed from the window and fell into a bush then ran away disguised as a young and buxom laundry maid (a virgin from Halifax, not yet twenty), catching a midnight mail coach back to London. A pack of brutes then stripped me naked and took advantage of me on the roadside, mostly against my will. I was going to seek your help, dear things, yet I realised if I was caught, I would be dead in the ditch. Well, Lotty, much as I should like the attentions of your pulling pole, I decided it was better for all of us if I hid for a while somewhere nobody would find me. In the meantime, my darling Vivian would be safe in his ignorance and brave Lotty could catch the Rat.' He gave Gabriel a cautious glance. 'Did you read my little letter, perchance?'

Gabriel rolled his eyes. 'Ay. Could you not have told us who the Rat was without all this fuss?'

Fump stood back, clutching his chest as though he'd been shot through the heart with a bolt. 'But I did tell you! As soon as I arrived in London and before I lodged myself in Bedlam, I rushed to Tower Hill and confided in that honest cutpurse, Jack Huffins. I told him everything, and he promised to let you know precisely what I'd seen.' Fump gasped and fell back against his throne, a look of horror spread over his face. 'Did he not pass on my message? A pox on him, the freckly knave!'

Gabriel rubbed the back of his neck, remembering the poor man in the chapel room. 'He tried to. They cut his tongue out then fed him to the lions.'

'That seems a little much,' said Fump. 'Poor thing, he had a fine tongue.'

Clap crossed her arms. 'Cut the gassing. Who's the Rat?'

Fump laughed. 'Well it isn't the Duchess, or Lavender Long-legs, dear me, no.' He gripped Vivian's hand. 'One of our sweet friends? A ridiculous slur, they would be outraged to hear it.'

'They couldn't hear a thing,' said Vivian sadly. 'They were hanged at Tyburn this very morning.'

Fump covered his face. 'Don't say so. Oh, those poor ducks. I was sure I'd saved you all.'

'You can save the rest of us now,' said Gabriel. 'If you'll only say the bloody name.'

Fump gave an imperious sniff. 'Thomas True, where is he?'

Gabriel nodded, his insides turning cold. 'Then I was right. Thomas True is the Rat after all.'

'Oh shush, Lotty, did I say that? I merely ask where he is.'

'At his family home in Highgate.'

'Not in London? I am relieved to hear it.'

Gabriel pressed in. 'Why relieved? Spit it out or I swear to you I'll throw you out the window.'

Fump took a deep breath. 'I suppose I shall bless you all with my wisdom, though you might have worked it out for yourselves. The identity of the Rat is...'

Seconds later, Gabriel was charging through the hospital grounds, his mind reeling. He wished he could sprout wings and fly straight to Highgate, for he understood now that he had not banished Thomas to safety at all.

CHAPTER SIXTY-EIGHT

'Are you not happy to be home?' Abigail asked, watching Thomas as he folded his clothes.

'Never less so,' he replied curtly. 'You should not have told my parents I was going home to London. Why must you meddle?'

Abigail's look of concern flattened out to something bland. 'This is your home, Thomas, not London.' She sang a little song to herself, dancing to the window. 'You must miss your friends.'

'I do,' said Thomas with a happy sigh. 'But I shall be seeing them again soon.'

'I'm sure you will.'

Thomas saw her sad expression and softened. 'Forgive me, cousin, I know you only have my best interests at heart. How lucky I am. If I hadn't been able to confess all my secrets to you these past weeks, I should have gone mad. I have treasured our private conversations.'

Abigail searched his eyes. 'I am grateful for your honesty, Cousin Thomas; you did the right thing by telling me the truth about your mollying.' She pulled her cuffs down and clapped her hands. 'But you are safe here, far from sin.'

'I would rather be a sinner in London than an angel in Highgate.' Thomas closed the drawer, tracing his eyes over the papered walls and cracked ceiling. Every inch of the room told the history of his miserable childhood.

Abigail turned to the window, staring out to the green where the stocks stood empty. 'Rather be a sinner than stay with me?' A soft breeze blew through the open sash and caught her shawl, tugging it to the floor.

'Come now, Abigail,' said Thomas, fetching it up for her, 'I didn't mean it that way; you know how lonely I was living here as a boy. I discovered myself at Mother Clap's. Coming back here feels like stepping into my own grave.' He held out the scarf, and as she reached up to take it, he caught sight of a mark on her wrist. He gripped her hand, frowning.

'What is this? A bruise?'

Abigail pulled back, snatching her shawl. 'Get away, don't touch me.'

She darted to the door and ran to the landing as Thomas followed her.

'Where are you going?' he demanded as she went to her own sleeping quarters and attempted to slam the door. He was too quick for her, jamming his foot against the frame and forcing it open.

She fell back, her face livid with tears, and set about slamming shut the drawers of a chest that stood against the bed. Thomas narrowed his eyes, forcing himself to smile.

'Cousin, what is all this? What was that mark?' He stepped towards her. 'What are you hiding?'

'Step back,' snapped Abigail.

Thomas frowned. 'I won't step back. Show me what's in that drawer.'

'Never.'

There were men's voices below, and the sound of feet climbing the stairs. Abigail gave a triumphant smile. 'Now then,' she said. 'We shall see about you leaving.'

Thomas went to the landing and looked down. His mother and father were mounting the staircase three storeys below, followed by two men dressed in black robes and grey wigs. As they climbed, they looked up: their eyes searching, false noses strapped to their heads like ravens' beaks. He pushed away from the banister and marched back into Abigail's room to find her on the bed, looking up at him as innocent as a lamb.

She smiled. 'They will get you now,' she said. 'I tried to save you.'

Thomas stared at her. 'What have you done?'

She did not answer, yet when he stepped deeper into her room, she jumped up and covered the drawers, a wild look in her eyes. Thomas wrenched her away, pulling the drawers open to find papers covered with scribbled lists. He blinked in horror as he saw his own name, and Gabriel Griffin's too. Hundreds more in list after list of mollies. These were his friends from Mother Clap's and beyond.

The footsteps from the staircase grew louder, the sound of his father chanting prayers, the two men and his mother echoing him in harmony. Abigail stood from the bed, her hands outstretched, the mark of the Society drawn in blue ink on her wrist.

'Forgive me,' she said. 'I tried to save you.'

She toppled as Thomas pushed past her, a collection of translucent objects scattering from her skirt pockets across the floor. 'No!' she said, attempting to scoop them up as Thomas bent down. He picked a square lump from the boards, lifting it up to his nose and sniffed. 'Tallow,' he said, holding it back to see the cast of a lower lip. He looked down to see all sorts of noses, chins and ears strewn over the boards. Thomas had a vision of the Rat at Ned Skink's, his lip peeling away into his drink. The room turned deathly cold.

Abigail got up and took Thomas by the hands. 'Don't be angry with me, it was all done for the good, and I am here to protect you. We were married once as children, don't you remember? I think you must have forgotten. Your parents made us walk through the rectory garden as the blossoms fell from the apple trees, and there we stood in our little suits – I can picture it now, clear as a pretty painting. And we were betrothed, Thomas, you and me, below this very rectory with God as our witness.' She lost her voice then, pressing her hand to her breast. 'I know it's silly of me, but when a child becomes infatuated, they can never truly escape it. I know you are not my husband, Thomas, but I wish somebody could tell my heart; it simply won't listen.'

'We are cousins, Abigail.'

'And you a sodomite, Thomas.' She gave him a frosty glare. 'Which do you think is worse?'

Thomas went to the door and locked it as the chanting climbed the stairs. 'You are mad.'

'And you are sick.'

'Rat,' he whispered, shaking his head as he backed away. 'Rat.'

'My darling cousin, you were lost.'

'I was found. After so many years, I was found. Now I am lost again. I told you everything. I trusted you. My friends...'

'The justices have carried out their raids. Your friends will answer for their souls. They must repent.'

'And must I repent too?'

'I pray that you will. Every night, I pray.'

'They are innocent men.'

'They were sodomites.'

'They are lovers.'

'They are burning this very second for their sins. My father and mother watched them hang at Tyburn yesterday morning. They would like us to return, and make some more of our pretty candles. I have told them we are to marry, and they are delighted. Ours has always been such a close family, after all.'

Thomas clutched his head. 'This is all too much. You say my friends will burn for their sins but will you burn for yours?'

The door rattled.

Thomas threw himself against it. 'All this time, it was you.'

'I thought you were helping me deliberately at first, telling me their names and giving me such colourful details about their birthing rituals and sexual perversions, then I realised you were too foolish to understand the good work you were doing.'

'Too trusting.'

'The Lord our God thanks you for it, Thomas. You must only repent, and your soul will be cleansed.' She gripped his chest and threw her hands to the ceiling. 'Out, demon!' she cried. 'Out, Satan!'

A voice came through from the landing. It was Reverend True. 'Thomas, Abigail, stop playing now and come out, we have visitors.'

Thomas looked over his shoulder and set his heels against the floor. 'This is what you've done to me?'

Abigail snarled. 'You told me about your adventures and your pretty new friends, leaving me alone every night without a care. You didn't want to share anything with me, did you? Leave the spinster at home with her parents night after night while you cavort with those devils until dawn. You are just like my mother and father: inconsiderate, careless, selfish.'

Thomas gave a groan of realisation. 'Mister Fump saw you, didn't he? And then disappeared. Where is he now?'

'Locked away in Bedlam, and may he rot there. Mother and Father have been visiting him to make sure he doesn't escape, and when the time is right, they shall poison him.' She stepped to Thomas's side. 'Come back to live on the bridge.'

'I'd rather die.'

'I used to hate living there too, but as I grew older, Father let me travel alone to buy supplies. I met all sorts of fascinating sinners, from actors to minstrels, and that's when I learned my own talent for playing parts and making disguises. It meant I could go out alone at night and be free, just like you. I followed you everywhere you went. You were so careless...'

'My God. You tried to kill me at St Paul's!'

'That was petulant of me.' She melted the nose between her fingertips. 'I heard everything you were talking about with Mister Griffin. Don't you know what they're calling it? The Whispering Gallery. By God's design, the faintest voices travel around the dome, right to the other side.' Abigail's face flushed, tears pricking her eyes. 'You called me a pathetic spinster. I thought we were sweethearts, but you ignored me, just like everybody else. I lost my temper and wanted you dead. I exalted folly, yet the Lord inclined his head to me and heard my cry.'

'My own cousin, the Rat.'

'Rats feed on man's filth, Thomas. The more filth, the more rats. Call me what you like, I could only share what you and your molly friends told me. The two old hens in Covent Garden for a start. Oh yes, they were giving me secrets like custards long before you joined us on the bridge.'

'Fump and Vivian would never betray the mollies.'

'Not willingly, yet they betrayed you all the same. Little jests and japes, tiny nudges and winks; snatched gossip in the back of their shop when they pretended I wasn't listening. They would visit the bridge, you know, and flirt with my father for cheap candles. I would ask them where they were spending their evenings so late.' Abigail gave a prim smile. 'And they would answer, desperate to confide, keen to boast; mollies are all the same.'

'And you scuttled straight off to the Society.'

Abigail laughed, snatching at the door. 'I had no need to scuttle. Mother and Father are Society stewards; they organise the movement from our office above the shop. We captain the Society hounds from the Tower all the way up to the exchange. Lucky for you, or you'd have been clubbed to death on more than one occasion.' She flinched. 'Watching poor Daniel take his beating was awful, almost as bad as that young man Martin when they cut his throat.' She giggled, covering her mouth. 'I thought it was great fun employing your lover and molly guard to work at the shop. The pair of you really are pathetic. Still, he's long dead. I blew him up in the gunpowder stores at the cathedral.'

Thomas bit his tongue, relieved she was ignorant of the truth. 'That was you who set off the explosion?'

'I was only home for a second when you came running down the stairs. If you'd looked at me properly, you would have noticed I was already wearing my cloak. But then,' she gave him a sardonic smile, 'you never have noticed me, have you Thomas? I have only ever been a pair of ears to listen to your adventures, a pair of eyes to admire your pretty clothes. Just a plain, pointless woman, of no interest to a man like you.'

Thomas sank to the floor, sweeping the pieces of wax aside. 'I noticed everything about you, Abigail. I saw how talented you were, how clever how...' he lifted a wax cheekbone '...how inventive. You are right though, I was so busy with my own adventures, I didn't spend enough time with you.' He looked up, a tear rolling down his cheek. 'And for that, you have murdered my friends.'

Abigail scoffed. 'They murdered themselves. If they'd married and followed a righteous path, they'd never have been arrested. I said so to Jack Huffins just before we cut his tongue out.' She met Thomas's eye. 'Do you know what his last words were?' Thomas shook his head and she laughed. 'Nor do I. We didn't allow him any. He was a pitiful, crippled, cutpurse sodomite. It was a kindness to kill him.'

'You are evil.'

'I am pure, don't you see?' She kneeled beside Thomas, her hands clasped in prayer as the door rattled and the chanting beyond the room grew to a crescendo. 'You will understand, very soon, that we have saved you too.' She touched his cheek. 'Please, don't hate me, but I must open the door and let them in.'

She ran across the room before Thomas could stop her. He looked on as she turned the key and pulled the handle.

'I do hate you,' he said, knowing what was to come. 'Rat.'

She looked at him – her eyes turning to balls of white ice – then turned the key, the room swelling to the sound of God's righteous disciples. Thomas's father stepped inside first, solemnly carrying his wooden cross, duly followed by Mistress True, who covered her face with her handkerchief, weeping that he had always been a good boy. Behind her came the two elderly justices, who each took in the room – one with lascivious inspection, the other chanting with the merry smile of a missionary.

Thomas sat before them on the floor, surrounded by false features in wax, loose papers bursting from the open drawers above his head.

Abigail lifted her finger and pointed at him, her face boiling.

'Sodomite,' she hissed. 'Sodomite.'

CHAPTER SIXTY-NINE

The horse charged along the road, veering into hedgerows as Gabriel spurred her on, mounting the hill to Highgate. He had stolen the impressive mare from a tying post outside Bedlam, not caring whose it was, for there was no time to lose. Thomas was with Abigail Squink, and in terrible danger.

He smashed straight through a turnpike in a cloud of splinters, the animal beating the road, white foam at her shining flanks.

Soon, he was above London, fast approaching the southern reaches of Highgate, where the tumbledown cottages huddled more intimately together, the lane carpeted with yellow leaves. The town was teeming with people, its verges packed on both sides with hastily abandoned coaches and carriages. Whatever had caused such excitement, it seemed to have finished, for the farm labourers were returning to their work, while up ahead, a group of men were squabbling outside a drinking house, pushing and shoving to be first inside. Gabriel ignored the attention of three young boys who were sitting on a stile, scrutinising him with sticks at their feet, their pockets weighed down with rocks.

He rode to the gatehouse in the very centre of town and dismounted. Across the way, two kidney-shaped ponds were split by a road fringed with trees. Beyond them stood the stocks in the very middle of a triangular green, their footings raised upon a set of shallow steps. He walked towards them with a growing sense of unease as a pair of milkmaids passed him by. They were wiping sweat from their gleaming heads, chattering excitedly to one another.

'He's a pretty fellow for a sodomite, I should say,' said one.

'Ay, very pretty,' said the other, 'Shame, innit? What a waste.'

'Not too brave though. I should say he was weepin.'

'Weepin' like a girlie he was.'

Gabriel stepped into their path. 'Who are you talking about?'

'Oh look, Polly, if it ain't a bear!' said the older woman.

'So it is, Milly. What's he growlin' at us for?'

Both maids had powerful arms, covered in a foul paste of egg, filth and fur right up to their elbows. The stink was enough to make Gabriel heave.

'Who were you talking about?'

'Why, Mister True,' said the older of the two women. 'Did you miss the fun, sir?'

Gabriel pushed between them, marching across the green to a constable who was standing with his thumbs stuck proudly in the buttonholes of his coat. Behind him, the stocks were caked in blood, shoe prints in the filth, while the remains of dead animals, rotten vegetables and putrid eggs gathered in heaps and slapped up the central post, itself half buried in a pile of rocks, their ragged edges stained red.

'Thomas,' whispered Gabriel. 'Thomas, what have I done to you?'

'Too late, good fellow!' said the constable, brushing a sticky mess from his fingers with straw. 'You missed a fine pillorying, right enough.' He nodded to the stocks. 'It's usually the lowest kind of skip-jack in there. Thieves, highwaymen, whores, that sort of sinner, you know? Poachers, vagrants, and the like. Not this one though.' He tutted to himself. 'A nice young fellow, so I'm told, just back from London, poisoned by the city sods. You wouldn't get me there, not for all the wool in Wales. And to top it off' – he raised his eyebrow with a wink – 'he's only the damned rector's son.'

Gabriel did all he could to remain still. He had to hear it for himself, every detail, yet all the while as the constable spoke, he craned his neck in the hope he might see Thomas somewhere around the ponds, washing blood from his face. He squeezed his eyes shut and swallowed hard.

'Good constable, tell me what happened.'

'Well, don't mind if I do, sir. What are the stocks good for if it ain't to be shared abroad? It started off all peaceful like, my fellow constables forming a ring around the stocks for the protecting of the knave, and the women stepping inside ready to shy their eggs and whatnot. But people can't pillory if they don't know what they're pillorying, can they? By all accounts, this young man was well respected by the townsfolk in general, though there were rumours of course, but his being the rector's son, he was liked. So wasn't it a strange sight, seeing him standing there all lonely with his head and arms locked tight, looking around at so many befuddled faces. "Thank you," says he to the women, though his voice was strange, like his tongue was too large for his gob. Still, he goes on all polite: "Thank you for not hurting me," and then people look at each other wondering if the Messiah himself has come to Highgate, for he looked quite pretty and if there wasn't a ray of sunshine descended to his crown. Some minutes passed, and by that time people were getting bored and restless, going home or back into the fields. Well, as Jesu liked to say himself, let he who is without sin cast the first stone, and there ain't many round here who ain't done something sinful in their lives.'

'They spared him?' said Gabriel, hopefully. 'Then what's all this?' He gestured to the bloody rocks and dirt.

'Well, hold your horses there, sir,' said the constable, enjoying the telling of his story. 'All stayed peaceful and polite, till a young lady appears over there at yonder rectory window.' He pointed across the green, to where the white eaves of the building peeped above the trees, topped with a tilting tower of wooden slats, cut into crenulations like a makeshift castle. 'She leans right out and shouts as loud as the town crier, with her hands cupped to her lips: "Sodomite!" That's what she cries, her voice knocking the birds from the trees. "Punish the sodomite!"' she says. "Smite the sodomite! Death to the sodomite!"' The constable shook his head in wonder. 'Well, the silence was like nothing I ever heard, sir. It was like my very ears had been pulled off, for everyone was looking at Mister True in the pillory, and he was staring up at the window, while the townsfolk were edging closer to him like wolves. He saw them and begged them not to hurt him, his mouth still sounding stuffed. Well, my fellow constables and I had to tighten our arms now, because the rabble was getting lively. You can't keep the womenfolk round here from a good shying, you see, and sure enough they raised up their missiles and tells the bugger what he deserves in language my good uniform would blush to repeat. "No, no, please!" says the miserable man in that funny voice, and like any common braggard, he starts twisting and turning his head against the locks, banging his hands to get free and kickin' his feet as they approach, but the locks was tight. They always are.' The constable lifted his chin proudly, tapping a key which hung on a chain from his hip. 'Well, I should say the first stinky egg was not well aimed, hitting one of my fellow constables directly on his noddle, yet the ladyfolk are practised enough, this being a busy thoroughfare for scoundrels. Yes,' said the constable, seeming for a moment to be touched by the memory of what he was describing, 'he cried like a babe as the rocks started hitting him, daft lad, and it pure cheered my heart to hear him squeal. Just like a pig, he was. After another while, the muck got stuck up his nose and he fell silent. By then of course, his whole head was caked, so I had to shake my boots and come over to scrape it away so he could breathe. "Open yer mouth, or you'll choke," I says to the lad. "You can't breathe through your nostrils alone, not with all this mud flying about." Dumb sod, but he wouldn't so much as part his lips let alone unclench his teeth, no matter how hard I slapped him. Queer thing ain't it?' The constable tapped Gabriel's shoulder for his full attention. 'He found Christ in them stocks, you know, so don't tell me this ain't a good way to wash away a man's sins. As my good wife says, ye can't coddle a stain out of a boy's breeches.'

'Found God?' said Gabriel, confused.

'Ay,' said the constable with an excited hop. 'Had a vision at the very last, so he did.'

'Of what?'

'Not what, but *who*.' The constable looked in all directions from beneath his bushy eyebrows, tapping the side of his nose. 'His teeth were clamped shut, but I heard him whispering the very name, and even with his whole body shakin' like a winter leaf, I could reckon what it was.' He chuckled. 'The name of an angel, sir, I swear it. Here, I bet you can't guess which.'

'Gabriel.'

'Oh, well sir! A lucky guess indeed. That is the very name he was chantin'. The knave's eyes were fixed on the ground, blood pouring from his head, but I heard him speak it. "Gabriel," he was saying to himself, as though in prayer. "Gabriel."' The constable folded his arms, hopping on his heels. 'It went on for a full hour and twenty, the sheriff allowing a little longer since people was robbed of their reason to hate the man at the beginning. My, did they make up for it though!' He tapped his boot against the stocks. 'Here, sir,' he said with a troubled frown, 'do you think I told my story well enough? I should like to get the detail straight, or the wife won't be happy.'

Gabriel gritted his teeth, his fists clenched. 'Where is he now?'

'Oh,' said the constable, flapping his hand impatiently, 'he was fairly choked when we took him down, but free to crawl off wherever he liked, his punishment being served. Mind you, if the Reverend wasn't his pa, he'd be doing the Tyburn jig by now, so I took some pleasure to see him a few minutes later, over there by them ponds being dipped and dunked by the children as he tried to drink some water. A nice bath for a buggerantoe, I says to myself. In the end, the girl from the rectory came out to collect him and then I do recall she led him away like a stray dog towards the rectory, sweet angel she is.'

The constable gave a soft moan as his face was slammed into the upper beam of the stocks, crumpling his nose to the back of his head, and before anyone could sound a hue and cry, Gabriel was bowling away to the ponds.

CHAPTER SEVENTY

There were handprints in the mud beside the ponds, surrounded by knee prints and finger marks where Thomas had clawed at the wet banks. From there, his tracks led to the lane, where they were indeed joined by a woman's footprints, leading him towards the graveyard opposite. Gabriel followed them, and as he approached the rectory, he heard a shout from above. He looked up to the makeshift tower, where a man was waving a cross over the wooden ramparts.

'Thomas?' Gabriel shouted, straining his eyes in the dimming light as the clouds turned dark. 'Is that you?'

It might have been, until a second later, when a dying ribbon of light shone through, illuminating the man's face. He was the very picture of Thomas, only many years into the future, for his hair was white and his face wrinkled and wild.

'Away, Devil!' cried the man, shaking the cross above his head. 'Away, I command you! Leave this house of God, for by the power of Jesu and the commandment of His most righteous angels, thou shalt not enter.' With that, he flew into a vigorous rage, swinging his arms about his head, jabbing invisible bolts of lightning from his fingers.

Gabriel looked back to the green beyond the ponds, where the constable was surrounded by his fellow men. A second later, they looked up and spotted Gabriel, calling out for his surrender. Gabriel moved quickly along a high wall of flint pebbles that traced the perimeter of the gardens to an open gate. He saw Thomas's footprints leading inside and followed them into an overgrown graveyard, packed with ancient pits covered in moss and uncut weeds. Gabriel scanned the headstones.

'Thomas, are you here?' he called. 'Stand up so I can see you.'

Rain began to patter the gravestones as the rector's voice continued to ring down. Gabriel moved deeper, calling out Thomas's name, checking behind each of the stones, hoping to see his lover waiting to be rescued. What if Abigail Squink were there? He didn't like to think what he would do if he saw her.

'Thomas, can you hear me? Raise your hand so I can find you, we don't have long.'

He circled a crumbling tomb, its plaster grown through with saplings, then caught sight of a bloody handprint on its corner. There were spots of crimson on the heads of a dead cow parsley too, and Gabriel called out again, catching sight of townsfolk approaching the gate behind him.

'Thomas, don't hide, there ain't time.'

Fat raindrops were slapping down from the clouds now, and the sky was the colour of bruises. He shielded his face, searching the outer edges of the graveyard and suddenly, a flash of white appeared above a far wall as Abigail Squink ran towards the rectory.

'Were you helping him?' Gabriel shouted. 'Is he there?' Gabriel stumbled towards her, tripping in rabbit holes, but as he waded through the long grass, he caught sight of a tuft of blonde hair.

He stumbled to the corner of the wall where the stones were crumbling, and peered down, panting for breath.

'Found you,' he cried out in relief, seeing Thomas lying below, his face looking up. Yet while his eyes were raised, there was no Thomas in them, none at all, only the vacant stare of a corpse.

Part Six

CHAPTER SEVENTY-ONE

Perhaps Thomas did see Gabriel, if only for the last glimmer of his life. Perhaps he lifted his face in that final second as his companion appeared above the loose stones.

'No,' said Gabriel, scrabbling over the wall and falling to his knees. Thomas's face was covered in scratches, his nostrils still plugged with dirt, brown water pouring over his bloodied lips. His forehead was cleaved open, his chin split to the bone.

'Come now,' said Gabriel, crawling closer. He cradled his lover's head, rubbing mud from his cheek with a wet thumb. 'I am here.' He rocked him, feeling the warmth of his clothes, squeezing his dangling arms.

'Can you hear me? Speak if you can.' Gabriel pulled a stray curl of hair from Thomas's forehead. 'Needs cutting,' he said. 'I can cut it for you when we're home.' He waited for a reply, yet Thomas was staring at the sky, the rain hitting his eyeballs without a blink. Gabriel lost control and wept pitifully. 'Don't leave me. Please, Thomas, don't.'

A great hullabaloo rang across the gravestones as a rabble of men and women edged towards the wall, armed with old swords and pitchforks. Gabriel looked back to Thomas's face and caught a tiny flicker in his dimpled cheek.

'You're still there,' he cheered. 'Ay, you're a fighter, you're still there, I knew it.' He tapped Thomas's cheek and rubbed his arms to keep him warm. 'Heard you were brave in them stocks, Thomas, heard you did yourself proud.'

Still, the grey eyes stared back at him, one disappearing behind swollen eyelids, the other ringed with a scarlet corona.

Gabriel crumpled. 'What do I do?' He touched the young man's torn lips and tried to open his jaw, but it was clamped shut. 'Come now, Thomas,' he coughed. 'Talk to me, you always do, even when I ask you to be quiet. Don't hush now. You said my name in the pillory, when you were frightened, eh? When things were getting hard near the end. Did you think I wouldn't come to save you?' He took his friend's fingers and rubbed them. 'I'll tell you something first. Should have told you before. I was afraid to say so, but ... I do, Thomas. You showed me. I know what—'

He looked up to see the townsfolk and constables almost upon him. He shook the rain from his back as blood whistled in his ears, then rose to his full height, lifting Thomas over his shoulder. The sky was thundering now, thick clouds gathering above the town, while far away down the valley, London was swallowed by the approaching storm. With a groan that tore his heart, Gabriel turned to face the townsfolk and constables.

'Damn you!' he yelled, his voice volleying against the old rectory. 'Come and take this man from me now; I would see you try.' He caught sight of a woman staring out from the rectory window, Abigail Squink standing behind her in shadow. He gave them such a glare it made the distant glass squeak, then raised his head to the top of the tower and thundered: 'Your son is dying, Reverend True. Scream your prayers louder, he can't hear them now. If he is in Hell, then it is a better place than your Heaven could ever be and it is not my Heaven, do you hear that? It is not mine. And you – you were never his family.'

He raised his arms, sucking the storm into his lungs, then bellowed the rage of a lifetime. 'I have so much pain in me!' Clouds rolled to the head of the valley, barrelling and cracking. He gripped Thomas and strode across the graveyard, his coat torn back by the wind as his feet pounded fresh holes in the sodden earth. The sky cracked white as a bolt of lightning struck the wall, sending stones in every direction, and Gabriel fell. He reached out to Thomas, whose shining face lay beside him on the grass. His mouth was open now, his white teeth parted in a smile, and there upon the grass lay a silver locket, open between them.

'Dear Lord have mercy on us,' Gabriel said, taking his lover's cold hand, 'My Thomas, I have so much pain in me.'

CHAPTER SEVENTY-TWO

They filed from Newgate Prison, nothing to hear but the howling of voices, clanking of chains, and the slamming of iron doors. Gabriel stood blinking in the sunlight, his face sallow after a week in the cells, teeth chattering as his irons were struck from his wrists and ankles. The mourning bells rang from St Sepulchre as they drove through the open gates to where the impatient crowd boiled up around the wheels. The city guards led the way, cleaving through the mob with their swords and truncheons while men and women hurled stones, rotten eggs, filth, and insults at the infamous sodomite.

Slowly, the horses inched their way around Snow Hill, past the Fleet Ditch, then along Holborn, where Gabriel strained to catch a last glimpse of his old home. It was visible, if only for a second, then gone in a moment.

In all, the procession lasted three hours, so notorious was the giant molly bear of High Holborn that everyone wanted to catch sight of him. The cart turned onto Tyburn Road as the crowd exploded. 'Sinner!' they screamed. 'Foul buggerantoe bastard! Get a brogging in Hell! Burn on spits, nasty pig!'

Gabriel gripped his locket, rubbing the metal with his thumbs.

'The marshal won't need to hang us at this rate. The crowd'll rip us apart before we get to them gallows.'

Thomas could hardly turn his head, he was so bruised and broken after the pillory. They had endured their summary trial and inevitable sentence together, facing the Newgate gallery from the draped pit.

'I'll be glad when all this is over,' he said. 'Dying once was enough for me.'

Gabriel frowned at him. 'Not afraid?'

'How can I be? I'm with you.'

'Thought I'd lost you, Thomas.'

'Never.'

At long last, Tyburn Road opened out, the cart pressing into an immense crowd. They arrived at the gallows beneath a dry, silent sky, the towering beams looming over their heads.

The people were wild; even the spectators in the pews behind the gallows were shaking their fists and spitting like commoners. The huge viewing platform had been constructed especially for the grand event, three tiers higher than the previous one to rake in more profit from the public interest. Thomas's aunt and uncle were high up in the gods, looking hungrily towards the gallows. Beside them, the two justices glowered down at the condemned, muttering and nodding while rubbing their legs. And there was Cousin Abigail, staring straight ahead with blank eyes.

Gabriel searched across the rest of the faces while the cart was moved into position. The rector and his wife had not made the journey.

The drum began to beat as Thomas gripped Gabriel's hand.

'Is it happening now?'

'Ay.'

They stood and made their way to the back of the cart, balancing side by side. The ropes around their necks were thrown over the beams, ready for the drop. Gabriel looked for Marshal Queed, but there was no sign of him. The cart shook and Thomas whimpered as the horses grew agitated by a new sound, weaving its way between the beat of the drum: the plaintive tolling of bells, ringing soft and sweet in cascading rounds as though the city itself were weeping.

Gabriel squeezed Thomas's palm. 'Hush now, don't fret.' He smiled and nodded to old friends.

Mother Clap was in the crowd, her black tricorn hat at her breast. Mister Fump was there too, wearing a black coat and wig speared with peacock feathers. They mouthed the word, and Gabriel nodded.

Together.

He understood now why most condemned men decided not to shout out their truth at the moment of death. What if their punishment in Hell were made worse by their obstinacy? What if the guards made their deaths last longer? What if God were considering clemency if they had only repented? What if it weren't true, and they were not together at all?

A few yards behind Clap stood Henry, Bet's face buried in his shoulder. She was carrying a bundle strapped to her chest in a fur sling. Gabriel wished he could have seen the little girl's face, for he knew it had many smiles to look forward to. Henry met Gabriel's eye and nodded, raising his hands. Even in such a moment, they found a reason to smile, for Henry was holding a hammer and a saw. Ay, they had built much over the years, a true friendship not the least.

Gabriel felt Thomas trembling. 'Easy now,' he said. 'Not long to go. It'll be over soon enough.'

The high pews creaked as the paying spectators leaned out, sensing the drop at any moment. The guards had stepped solemnly to the front of the cart, holding the horse's reins, ready to gee the animal forward.

Thomas spoke quietly. 'Will you let go of my hand when it happens?'

'No.'

'Find me.'

'I will.'

They looked at each other, and though Thomas's face was swollen, Gabriel could still make out the freckles on his bruised cheekbones, his grey eyes peering out between pus and torn eyelashes, and somewhere beneath the welts and shining skin lay that dimpled smile. His injuries didn't matter, for though Thomas had once been the handsomest man Gabriel had ever seen, it was never his face that had given him joy, rather the sense that beyond anybody else alive, such a kind and gentle man had chosen him, of all men, to love.

The guards stood ready, waiting for the sign. Gabriel could sense the great wooden structure of the pews at his back, complaining under the weight of the crowd, and as he traced the roofs of the opposite buildings, he could make out what appeared to be a line of crawling pixies, scuttling across the eaves.

The crowd fell silent.

The drum slowed.

The city held its breath.

So these were the last seconds of their lives. In a matter of moments, they would be gone and people would carry on, very soon forgetting about them, deciding that the past was a very uncivilised place, and wasn't it better now? And perhaps those men deserved to die.

Gabriel and Thomas had been warned by the minister: *Do not anger the Lord your God in your final moments. Repent with your last breath and save your soul.* Yet, as the noose hung heavy on the nape of his neck and with Thomas shaking beside him, Gabriel decided once and for all that it was his last breath to own, so he took it deep and filled his lungs, then bellowed into the din with all his might:

'WE ARE MOLLIES. ALWAYS TOGETHER.'

His voice startled the crowd, silencing them as the words volleyed and sundered against the sides of the buildings, rolling across the rooftops to the distant dome of the cathedral where the statues lowered their heads. On the bridge, a candle shop split its moorings and tumbled into the river, while somewhere above the city in an abandoned chapel, a congregation of sleeping bodies shifted in their soil and turned in expectation of an old friend. In Clerkenwell, the terrorised citizens shut their windows to quell the sound of a screaming bull: *'Queed!'* it cried. *'Queeeed!'* A cot on Red Lyon Street jumped its pegs and fell in spindles to the open boards, while an empty bed sat emptier still, dusted with white plaster. Far up the valley, a makeshift tower caught fire, burning the rectory and its righteous disciples to shells, and in the uppermost corner of the graveyard, a crumbling wall shielded a burrow. There, a frightened little boy used to hide, yet now it was laid over with ash and loose stones, so that nobody could hurt him again.

Tyburn seemed to be mesmerised by its own outrage, until a voice rose up in the silence, muffled by the wind.

'Always together!' it said, the words hanging above the heads of the people as though written in a banner across the clouds. Mother Clap climbed onto a barrel, her fists raised. She shouted again: 'Always together!' and then a second familiar voice joined her chant. It was Mister Fump, standing on a raised bank, waving his hands in the air. 'Always together!' he called, as another voice joined them, and Gabriel looked down to see Henry standing with his shoulders back, daring the men around him to make him stop. Bet joined him, holding her baby close, and a little girl from Smithfield Market did the same and soon there was a chorus of voices calling out in one declaration of defiant pride, knowing it would win them nothing but violence. And yet declare it they did, for it was true and, no matter the Society, it would ever be thus: 'Always together!'

The drum stopped.

'Is it now?' said Thomas, his teeth chattering.

'Ay,' said Gabriel. 'It's now.'

And the world shot up.

CHAPTER SEVENTY-THREE

Gabriel's legs thrashed as he twisted and bounced, drowning as pain raked through his body. He kept hold of Thomas's hand for as long as he could until their fingers were wrestled apart by a violent shaking. He kicked his legs to let Thomas know he was still there, but the world was turning red and he couldn't find him. He went to cry out to comfort his companion, yet the sound of the crowd was deafening, and he could do nothing but choke as the weight of his flapping body wrenched the noose tighter around his windpipe. He felt a rush of bodies around his legs, grateful that people had taken pity on him, waiting for the force at his feet to break his neck. Perhaps death came quickly, for the red sky turned white and for the first time in his life, he felt light as a dandelion seed. It was as though he was flying, the immense pressure in his skull blowing out through his ears. A strange calm drew over him, and he found himself beside the abandoned chapel: two boys laughing and playing around the crumbling walls. He watched the larger of the two – round-faced and thick of limb – lean over and kiss the other boy on the lips. Gabriel stepped out to speak to them, yet the untouched grass turned to floorboards and the chapel stones were plastered walls and he found himself back in his old quarters on Red Lyon Street, though the light was brown, filled with hundreds of candles burning black flames. He blinked to see himself as a younger man standing beside the bed, holding the hand of a woman in labour. Gabriel stepped towards them. 'Emily,' he said, and suddenly the wall ripped at the edges and he was away again, flying above himself through alleyways to a hall filled with men who danced together hand in hand. There was Jack with his impish grin and bright-red curls, young Martin filled with fun, George Lavender with a raised eyebrow, and Mister Rettipence, pensive yet free. Gabriel stepped back, searching for the door with rose-coloured glass. He wanted to go back and comfort his wife, yet there was a hand upon his wrist. 'Come,' said a familiar voice, and Gabriel turned to see the wise and gentle face of Mister Vivian, who led him through a bright doorway to a woman with dark, flowing hair. She was cradling a baby in her arms.

'Emily,' said Gabriel, his voice coming as a choked rattle. 'And little Dot, is that you?' He reached out his arms to take them, yet the ghostly woman raised her hand to the locket hanging around his neck and gave a peaceful nod.

'Sweet husband,' she said, in a voice he hadn't heard in more than three years. 'We are well. You must let go.'

The child blinked and smiled, wrapping her hand around Gabriel's thumb and, with such pain in him, he gaped his mouth, lowered his head to the floor and howled as the room skidded sideways, the sky filling with toppling beams while people fell screaming towards his face and all was thunderous noise and flailing posts, bodies gutted and beheaded by swinging planks.

Gabriel lay still, crushed far below the earth in a coffin of wooden shards and bent nails. It was unbearably hot down there, and he couldn't breathe for the terrible weight upon his chest. His every nerve sang with pain, and there was the rumble of an approaching inferno. He managed to reach his neck and pulled the noose open.

Then I am in Hell, he thought.

He tried to move, shifting his boot, then pressed his hands against the wood and pushed with all his might, feeling something shift above his shoulder. He pushed again, harder this time, and saw a sliver of sky, stricken with racing shadows. Gabriel gritted his teeth and exploded upwards, shards of wood flying apart as he was born back into the world.

At first, he thought all of London must have been destroyed in a war, the ground covered in every direction with jagged struts and upturned carts, yet far away he could still make out the dome of St Paul's, intact beyond the ashen sky. He turned in a circle, searching for the gallows, yet they had disappeared; so too the towering pews behind them.

'Collapsed,' shouted a voice from a distant pile of bent planks. The figure clambered over the wood with a crazed laugh. 'Gabe, it collapsed right after the drop!'

'Henry?' said Gabriel. 'Are you in Hell too?'

Henry gave a wild laugh. 'Ay, Gabe, no doubting that. But you are alive, old friend, and you'll stay that way if you escape.'

Gabriel wiped dust from his eyes. 'I saw them. I saw Emily and Dot, they were happy.'

'Tell it to the monks,' said Henry. 'There ain't time for revelations. You have to go now, before the guards spot you.'

Gabriel saw the men charging around the piles of wood, searching for bodies. 'Tell me what happened,' he said. 'How am I saved?'

'Them galleries were overfilled,' said Henry. 'Whoever built 'em must have done a shoddy job. One clumsy joint and well...' Henry held up his hands '...the whole thing comes tumbling down.'

Gabriel wiped his mouth with the back of his sleeve. 'Only one joint?'

'Maybe a few.' Henry winked. 'The crowd were jumping and cheering when you dropped, then a strange sort of bell started a-chiming and the whole thing folded inwards like playing cards and came down in a heap. Some of them spectators hit the ground before they could stop their celebrating.' He shook his head in wonder. 'Strange sight they made. And the sound ... I should never like to hear it again. Now go. Reckon there might be a horse for you back at the abandoned chapel.' He reached out and took Gabriel's hand. 'P'raps I'll see you again my friend, one day. I'll tell the little one all about her uncle Gabe, and if you ever meet a young lady named Molly Sylva, you'll tell her to do as she's told?'

Gabriel looked at him in surprise.

'Bet's choice,' said Henry. 'Blurted it out when you shouted your last words.'

The men embraced with gruff words of encouragement, promising a reunion as soon as it was safe. They parted with a shake of the hand, and Gabriel made his unsteady way across the rubble, scanning the mess of timber, for legs and arms. At the far side where the pews had stood, a single section remained high above the scene of devastation: a bench balancing precariously, like a crow's nest some fifty feet tall. Gabriel shielded his eyes, following the lonely strut to the very tip, where he could just make out the swinging feet of five stranded souls. He stumbled back to get a better look at them, straining to make out their faces. There were two justices in black robes and false noses, clinging to one another for dear life as they hung above the drop, and beside them, the panic-stricken Squinks adorned with dangling candles as they argued, while to their front, seemingly insensible to her predicament sat Abigail, her hair blown across her face. The breeze snatched at her kerchief, pulling it tightly around her neck as a swarm of iridescent bodies rose up the pole from the ground, climbing quickly like ten thousand beetles up a tree, until they reached the top and engulfed the sitters in a cloud of scratching claws. The shrieks carried across London, yet Abigail was spared their mass, for she had chosen to plunge to the ground with her arms stretched wide, greeting the hard smack of death with a smile, and where she landed, a panel of wood cracked open.

'Help!' came a voice from below the rubble.

CHAPTER SEVENTY-FOUR

'There's one thing I don't understand,' said Thomas, riding on Gabriel's shoulders as they skirted the northern reaches of the city.

'Only one?'

'My riddle; the one Glimmer Littlethorn gave us.'

'Ay, what about it?'

'I kept thinking about it in the pillory.' Thomas recited it, line by line, his fingers tapping it out:

'You search for the Rat.
A man, mostly that,
With faces, not one, but a few.
They crawl foul and pretty
Across this cruel city
First truth, but treachery too.
A tragedy hidden
Banished and bidden
A molly, discovered and lost
With an envious eye,
He'll kill then he'll die
And together – the Rat is the cost.'

'Turns out nonsense can be right after all,' said Gabriel, carrying Thomas along a dusty track past the Foundling Hospital.

'How so? What does any of it have to do with my cousin Abigail being the Rat?'

Gabriel shrugged his aching shoulders. 'She wasn't though, was she? Not all of it anyways.'

'You're talking like the Blackguard now.'

'She was only ever part of the Rat, Thomas. Ay, she is responsible for what she's done, but the rest of it came from London. The Society, the Church, the king, the law and us too.'

'Us?'

'Ay, the mollies. Backs turned on each other when the trouble started.

False loyalties and secrets. Accusations, jealousy, fear making us foul. Truth and treachery, I know enough about that from my days pulling corpses from the ditch.'

'Then where are we banished and bidden to?'

'Mother Clap's, Sodomites' Walk, Newgate ... our own nightmares.' Gabriel squeezed Thomas's leg. 'To each other, and to the traps laid for us by the Society. To the stocks and Tyburn and Hell. And we are, ain't we, us mollies? Whether we're banished by everyone or nobody, we have a way of banishing ourselves.'

Thomas rested his cool hands on Gabriel's head. 'And together – the Rat is the cost.'

They neared the upper perimeter of the city and slowed down to make sure they were safe, then made their way to the head of Black Mary's Hole, where Henry had left old Peter tethered to the abandoned chapel. Gabriel hoisted Thomas to the cart. He took the reins and steadied himself for a long journey.

Soon, they were far above London, surrounded by open grassland, where the cattle swished their tails, and the birds chirruped and swooped beneath the autumn sky. Thomas rested his head on Gabriel's arm and chatted away about the adventures they would have together.

They avoided the main roads, passing through tollgates and villages, under tunnels of trees and across rickety bridges towards some unknown place where they could be forgotten. Gabriel geed Peter on all the while, grateful for Thomas's company, and grateful for his wife and daughter, who were not in Red Lyon Street and had never been apart. His tormented imagination had conjured them to be so, when they had been safe and together all along.

He thought about Emily's words to him: 'Sweet husband, let go.'

The words were final and wise. He guided Peter to stop beside a bridge spanning a shallow river and peered down into the clear water. Silver fish were darting between rocks and swaying reeds, the last of the day's light sparkling on the surface. He turned to face Thomas.

'Have to let you go too, eh?'

Thomas smiled and gave a slow nod.

'Didn't make it through that pillory after all?'

Thomas shook his head then reached out to touch Gabriel's cheek, and kissed him.

Gabriel drew the locket from his shirt and threw it into the water, where it chinked against a rock and sank to the bed. He sat high and alone on the cart and wiped a single tear from his eye. He was so very sad, yet somehow complete for the first time in his life. Not ashamed anymore, and no longer afraid.

He looked out across the fields as the sun cracked open and poured gold across the horizon.

'Ay,' he said to himself, speaking the words at last. 'I know what love is.'

AUTHOR'S NOTE

Unlike in Gabriel and Thomas's story, justices of the peace in the 1700s did not roam the darkest corners of the country carrying out summary executions of homosexual men, though it seems likely to this author that arbitrary lynchings may well have taken place. (I speculate of course, but what is a novel if it isn't the marriage of speculation and imagination?) Magistrates were landed gentry, overseeing cases of petty crime and limited to their own districts. They operated under 'summary jurisdiction' – hearings without juries – committing the guilty to punishments including fines, whippings, pillorying or committal to houses of correction. The most serious cases, or felonies, would have been heard by a jury at the Old Bailey in London. It is partly thanks to court papers from these grim cases that we know as much as we do about molly houses and molly culture.

On another note, the author is sorry to report that there was no recorded fire at the west entrance to St Paul's Cathedral, nor a gunpowder explosion for that matter, though gunpowder was used to demolish the pillars of the previous church, sending lumps of stone flying through neighbouring windows. The author invented both incidents, or rather his characters did, and he makes no apology for it. What folly it is to respond to fiction with fact; one might as well boil butter with ice or climb the stairs in search of the cellar. After all, if a novelist were to limit himself to the detail of historical record, he would run the serious risk of writing non-fiction.

That said, some facts did slip through the proverbial net. There were indeed scaffolders working on and around St Paul's Cathedral right through to the 1720s as final touches were added to the exterior and interior of the building, not least an upturned teacup of wooden beams and walkways, allowing the fresco to be painted inside the dome, much to Sir Christopher Wren's dismay.

Mother Clap's Molly House did, in fact, exist, though the details here have been skewed somewhat. The joyously vice-infested den was open a few years after the setting for *Thomas True* – between 1724 to 1726, until a raid shut it down. It was a coffee house and guest house, accessed up a flight of stairs beside an archway next to the Bunch o' Grapes tavern, with rooms for mollies wishing to 'marry' (have sexual intercourse), socialise and cavort.

Perhaps these men were rejecting gender-normative, patriarchal, colonialist, heteronormative, oppressive societal constructs ... Perhaps they were simply having fun. The author leaves such questions to greater minds and moves to the Old Bailey archives, which tell the sorry tale that inspired this novel.

One Sunday night in the frosted February of 1726, some forty 'notorious sodomites' were arrested in a raid – caught with their breeches unbuttoned, though none of the men were engaged in sodomy. It didn't matter. On Monday the 9th of May 1726, in spite of there being virtually no damning evidence and following witness statements defending the good character of the men in question, Gabriel Lawrence, a forty-three-year-old milkman, William Griffin, a furniture upholsterer of the same age, and Thomas Wright, a thirty-two-year-old wool-comber, were taken by cart to Tyburn and hanged by their necks until they were dead. A woman named Catherine Hayes was also executed on the same date, burned at the stake for the unconnected grisly murder of her husband. (She became the subject of Thackeray's novel, *Catherine*.)

These people perished to the cheering and baying of the mob. Mass executions were popular, with wealthy spectators paying to sit in raked stands erected by the landowner to offer the best view. On the same day the mollies were hanged, the stands collapsed under the weight of 150 spectators, killing six people. By the by, Gabriel Lawrence's body was duly cut down from the gallows and dissected at Surgeon's Hall, again to the delight of spectators.

Sodomy was considered one of the most heinous sins a man could commit in the 1700s, the 'receiver' having committed the greater transgression and therefore more liable to receive a death sentence than the 'giver'. Meanwhile, men caught in the act of petting or general romance were more likely to be pilloried or fined. Nonetheless, as we have seen, the sentencing of accused sodomites was arbitrary at best.

Pillorying, mind you, was hardly an attractive commutation. Mollies received special attention from the crowds, and it was common practice to pelt gay men with stones, bottles, dead animals and human faeces. Some victims died of their injuries or even suffocated if their airways weren't cleared in time with sticks dragged over their mouths and stuck up their nostrils. According to contemporary accounts, male assailants were often held behind a ring of constables, while the womenfolk were given free rein to mete out their brutal pelting.

In the eighteenth century, mollies, pretty fellows, he-whores and buggerantoes – as they were variously maligned – were often perceived as misogynists, hating women rather than being attracted to men, while society, including leading voices in the academic and philosophical fields, thought homosexual men a corrupting influence, liable to bewitch even the most righteous Christian with a sudden lust for sodomy.

Amidst such superstition and abject stupidity, the Society for the Reformation of Manners appeared and wasn't fully lanced until the 1750s. Ostensibly, its aims were the suppression of profanity, immorality and lewd activities in general. In reality, it was a self-appointed gang of hypocritical religious zealots, motivated as much by financial reward (bounties were paid for entrapping gay men) and moral grandstanding as by piety. The Crown endorsed the Society, which operated in tiers, the uppermost consisting of the gentry, lawyers, judges, MPs and the like, followed by a middle tier of professional tradesmen, with quasi-constables making up the lower tier, along with a network of informants and provocateurs marshalled by stewards who oversaw each parish. Some of these spies posed as mollies; others seem to have been active mollies themselves, turned traitor by bribes or under the threat of arrest. The raid on Mother Clap's Molly House seems to have taken place partly thanks to an embittered molly informer, Mark Partridge, who was angry at his lover for revealing his sexuality. He duly gave so much information to the constables, they let him off all charges and protected his identity in court.

Doubtless there are eminent scholars who would take issue with this story's interpretation of their fine research, but the author has done his best to bring such archaeological evidence to life for a modern reader, while telling a timeless tale of love and loss amidst great danger. The Society did not carry tattoos to mark their membership; scented candles were not – to the author's knowledge – invented on old London Bridge in 1715; men were not employed to 'pull' bodies from the Fleet Ditch (though someone must have done it); and Alsatia was not home to a miniature world inhabited by ethereal, wall-scuttling children (the reader is encouraged to dive down the Blackguard rabbit hole – it is both fascinating and heartbreaking). And though Thomas, Gabriel, and their various friends and foes, feel very real to the author indeed, and though they are most certainly formed by the ghosts of real men and women from the time, they are – alas – fictional.

That does not mean Thomas's story isn't true, mind you. Fiction is not a lie, it is the soul telling the truth, and the existence of this book is testament to the indefatigable endurance of the mollies of old London; their absolute determination to be remembered and the sacrifice they made for being who they were.

The author humbly begs you to keep the mollies alive by sharing their story.

You can find out more at www.ajwestauthor.com

—A.J.

ACKNOWLEDGMENTS

To Patricia Cornwell: I would not have been able to finish this book without you; I am forever in your debt. To my publisher, Karen Sullivan: without your determination and belief in original fiction this book would not exist.

My heartfelt thanks to David Headley, my agent and champion, who told me to write this story; and Emily Glenister my co-agent, who told me to breathe.

West Camel, your edits were brilliant; thank you for accommodating the eccentricities of a fickle perfectionist.

Nicholas Robinson, you are the patient power in my life; thank you for being my husband. Victoria Hyde, nobody knows better the agony I've been through writing this book – you have been my counsel and my guide. Will Hollinshead, you are my Henry. My mum and all my family, you inspire my writing.

To Dale Stephens, Clocktower Books, Hay-on-Wye, and Stanton Stephens, The Castle Bookshop, Ludlow – for listening into the wee hours and helping me escape London when I so desperately needed to; you are both true gentlemen. To Jon Appleton, for your keen and clever eye, likewise Dale Townshend, scourge of the Oxford comma. To Claire Ward, who helped to make this story beautiful. Amanda Stebbings and all at The London Library – you have given my imagination a home.

Andy Goff, my friend and illustrator of my two novels, you have such an incredible way of bringing my imagination to life on the page, thank you.

Thanks to all queer history academics for their ongoing research; I ask you to accept my quirky interpretation for what it is. To the Old Bailey – how fortunate we are to have your archive. Special mention to Dr James W.P. Campbell, author of *Building St Paul's* – I could not have constructed Gabriel the carpenter without this brilliant book. Maureen Waller, author: *1700, Scenes From a London Life*; Catharine Arnold, author: *Bedlam: London and its Mad*; Liza Picard, author: *Dr Johnson's London* – I highly recommend them all. Ned Ward's book *The London Spy* is also invaluable. Though Ned was a scurrytongue and hardly an ally, he has nonetheless helped the legend of the mollies live on, and his book remains my favourite time machine in all the world.

My thanks go to Rictor Norton, whose tireless archaeological work bringing molly culture back to life has given me the chance to go on my own journey of discovery. His book *Mother Clap's Molly House* and his eponymous website are a must-read for anyone seeking more information on the subject.

John Parker, CEO, the Arboricultural Association – anachronistic weeping willows have duly been removed. Helen Windsor, Tower Captain, St Clement Danes Church, Strand – the bell heard by Shakespeare and Gloriana herself still tolls! Susan North, curator of fashion, 1550–1800, at the Victoria and Albert Museum, I can undo a Georgian man's breeches thanks to you. Susan Trackman, the Highgate Literary and Scientific Institution – maps understood. Suzie Edge, for helping me bring history to a huge audience online and more importantly, listening to my nonsense. Mark Small, historian, for his sage advice. Simon Sladen, curator, V&A Museum, for his fabulous and fruity assistance with old English pantomime humour; same to panto impresario Jon Bradfield, the filthy bitches.

The authors I admire and treasure as friends will know who they are, and I hope they will understand that, at deadly risk of causing offence to those not mentioned, I will thank them personally and with true gratitude.

To my kind early readers and supporters, Vanessa Heron, chairman of the Oscar Wilde Society, Daniel Bassett, Graham Sillars, David Gillin, Robert J. Evans, Martyn Dore, Michael Lewis, Robert Hicks, Jamie Rich, Graham Porter, James Masson-Wood, Alan Maund, Edwina Louise Quatermass-Palmer: this will remain a list of people who supported me through a very tough time.

To those in the publishing industry who doubted this book and its author, you have kept me alert, inspired, furious and determined. I humbly beg you, have faith in me.

To the Irish mammy outside Halfway to Heaven in summer 2023 who said she loved her son no matter his sexuality because her mantra in life was 'Be together, always together', ours was a snatched conversation in the rain, but the uncomplicated humanity of your words gave me the battle cry I'd been searching for.

Last but not least, to the mollies of old London. Truly, I could never do enough to pay tribute to your bravery and defiance.

Always together.

—A.J. West